DEATH PLAYS POKER

A CLARE VENGEL UNDERCOVER NOVEL

DEATH PLAYS POKER

ROBIN SPANO

ECW PRESS

Published by ECW Press
2120 Queen Street East, Suite 200, Toronto, Ontario, Canada M4E 1E2
416-694-3348 / info@ecwpress.com

Library and Archives Canada Cataloguing in Publication

Spano, Robin
Death plays poker / Robin Spano.

ISBN 978-1-55022-987-5 (PBK); 978-1-55022-994-3 (BOUND)
ALSO ISSUED AS: 978-1-77090-086-8 (PDF); 978-1-77090-085-1 (EPUB)

I. Title.

PS8637.P35D425 2011   C813'.6   C2011-902867-0

Cover and text design: Cyanotype
Production and typesetting: Troy Cunningham
Printing: Friesens 1 2 3 4 5

The publication of *Death Plays Poker* has been generously supported by the Canada Council for the Arts which last year invested $20.1 million in writing and publishing throughout Canada, and by the Ontario Arts Council, an agency of the Government of Ontario. We also acknowledge the financial support of the Government of Canada through the Canada Book Fund for our publishing activities, and the contribution of the Government of Ontario through the Ontario Book Publishing Tax Credit. The marketing of this book was made possible with the support of the Ontario Media Development Corporation.

PRINTED AND BOUND IN CANADA

JANUARY / 2011

MONTREAL, CANADA

PROLOGUE

Willard Oppal, the spotlight is on you. Or is that a reading lamp? In a faux antique armchair, in an old world hotel room, you're flipping pages on your ebook reader as the wind howls wildly off the St. Lawrence River. You sip premium Scotch from the minibar. Why shouldn't you drink the good stuff? The government is footing the bill.

Josie Carter is dead. Jimmy Streets is dead. And here you are, the hero of the RCMP, sneaking in to save the day.

There's a knock on your door. You look through the peephole and smile, like a cat with a mouse he's not quite ready to kill. You're pretty sure this person is the Dealer. You've been working him, making him trust you. You gesture expansively to invite your new friend into the room.

It happens fast.

You're pouring a drink for your guest into a cheap hotel tumbler when you feel a rope caress your pale, flabby throat. You move to push the rope away and it tightens. You twist to fight and you can't. You're locked into the Poker Choker's expert grasp.

Zoom to the next morning: Canadian Classic Poker Tour, Casino de Montreal. The players have just been told about your death.

Elizabeth Ng smiles discreetly as a huge pot is raked her way. Later, in an interview, she'll say that your murder terrifies her, that she's thinking of leaving professional poker until the Choker is caught. At the moment, though, her hands are looking pretty damn steady.

Joe Mangan is wearing a curly red wig and a clown nose. As he tosses his cards into the muck, he thinks maybe at the break he should take off his costume and wear normal clothes out of respect. The thought passes quickly when he picks up his next hand and sees aces.

Mickey Mills mutters something approaching pro-fanity. He's careful -- doesn't want to get penal-ized by the ten-minute no-swearing rule. But he's not angry about your death. Some kid has just made a terrible play that cost Mickey half of his chip stack.

George Bigelow sits in the spectator stands, laptop running as he takes it all in. He taps a finger to his lips, wondering: what happens to a dead man's chips? Are they removed from play, or blinded off until there's nothing left? He'll need that information for his blog.

Fiona Gallagher flits around like a CNN announcer covering an earthquake. She's interviewing players, commenting on the scene, and unlike Joe, she has already changed into elegant mourning garb. She tilts her microphone toward T-Bone Jones for his reaction to your death.

"Oppal was a cop," T-Bone grunts. "How much do you miss a guy who rifles through your suitcase like he thinks he's fucking God? Don't put that in your stupid TV show, either."

And now there are three. Isn't that the magic number when you're identifying a serial killer? Except it's nearly two months later, and you'd think there would be cops crawling every corner of the scene.

They must be here. They must be hiding in plain sight.

FRIDAY / MARCH 18

NIAGARA FALLS

ONE

CLARE

Clare could beat aces. It was the flush she was worried about. She studied the old man across from her. "What do you have? Aces?"

"Nah, I don't got aces," the old man said, meaning, *Maybe I do, maybe I don't.*

Clare tried to find a clue on his face. Deep lines made his skin look more like leather than anything human. The eyes, of course, were blank.

"Raise." Clare shoved some chips in forcefully. What she meant was *Please fold.*

"Re-raise you all in." The man touched the rim of his cowboy hat. A real tell, or a fake one? And how was Clare supposed to single out a killer in a room full of professional bluffers? "Go home, kid," the old man said, meaning, *You're out of your league in this card room.*

But Clare wasn't going home. She wasn't going anywhere until she'd proven she could do this job. "Do I threaten you?" she asked.

The old man snorted and Clare thought she saw his nostrils flare. "Sure," he said. "Kids like you threaten my game every day.

You make it so profitable I get lazy and forget how to take on real competition."

Clare drummed her fingers on the black table felt. If she called the bet and lost, she'd be out of the game. She could already hear Sergeant Cloutier's scorn as he pulled her off the case and sent her home to dreary beat work chasing graffiti artists and bicycle thieves in Toronto.

But she couldn't keep folding either. This man had been bullying her — or bullying Tiffany James, Clare's fancy new cover character — all day. He couldn't have the best hand every time. And the nostril flare — that had to be involuntary, right?

"Call." Clare pushed the rest of her chips past the bet line. She could feel her hands trembling. The chip stack nearly toppled on its way into the pot.

The old man squinted at her. "You got something wrong with your brain? Unless you got a flush, Princess — which you shouldn't, the way you've been betting this hand — that was an easy fold."

"The bets have been made," the dealer said. "Mr. Jones, please show your cards."

The old man flipped his cards over, muttering, "Trip kings."

"Straight." Clare could hardly believe it. She'd just conquered T-Bone Jones in a battle of wits. She set to work organizing her new larger chip stack, and let out her breath with relief.

The old man peered at her. "That your daddy's cash you're burning?"

"No." Clare faked indignation as she examined the manicure she'd been given the previous morning. It felt funny on her hands — she was so used to chipped nails with motor grease riding the crescents. "Every penny I spend is from my own trust fund."

"Well, then." T-Bone's eyebrows lifted, and Clare wondered why he didn't lick his chops with greed. "Let me help separate you from it."

Clare's heart was still thumping, but she gave him the coolest grin she could muster. "You just tried to take my money; I took yours instead, remember?"

"I'm not talking about some piss-ass tournament chip stack." T-Bone's lips curled into a sneer. "I'm talking about putting your money where your mouth is. In a cash game tonight."

Shit. Clare had just told this guy she was loaded, but before she could say yes to a cash game, she would have to get the funds approved from her handler. "I don't think I'm ready for a side game. I want to get my legs in this tournament first."

T-Bone narrowed his eyes. "You got a big trust fund for gambling, but you won't bring a few grand to a side game?"

Yeah. The guy made a good point. "I'm not gambling." Clare tried to inject a haughty tone into her voice. "I've been reading tons of theory, and this poker tour is a solid investment. I think it's smarter than playing the stock market, given the state of the global economy."

"It's not an investment if you can't play the game."

"I learn fast." Clare met his eye, with maybe more Clare than Tiffany. "Tell you what: if I cash in this tournament I'll play in a side game in Vancouver."

"Just play with us," Joe Mangan said from down the table. Clare recognized him from TV, though his frosted tips and smooth skin were well hidden behind a white hockey mask. To complete the ensemble, Joe wore an L.A. Kings shirt with the number 99. "What's a few grand from your trust fund?"

Clare flicked her wrist dismissively, flashing a sparkly pink watch that cost what she made in a month. Good thing the RCMP was footing the bill for her wardrobe. "If I want to give money away, I know more worthy charities than you guys."

Joe raised his eyebrows and the mask shifted upward on his face. "Says the girl with the Piaget on her wrist. You're not giving the money away if you have a good time playing. You're buying entertainment."

"A 'good time' is a shopping trip to Paris." Clare wrinkled her nose and tried to look disdainful. "My time spent here is work."

She didn't want to alienate herself, but Clare could not afford to seem overly ingratiating. Willard Oppal had been made and killed before his handlers had even seen it coming. Clare had to play it cool, like she could take or leave the players' friendship.

"That's the right attitude, kid," said Mickey Mills, whom Clare also recognized from TV. Like Joe, Mickey had an average height and a stocky build. Unlike Joe, he was wearing dress pants and a pressed shirt. And Mickey was in his sixties — nearly double Joe's age. "Don't let these no-lifes talk you out of your money. You can dress 'em up and stick 'em on TV, but that don't change their basic nature. Everyone's a hustler here. You want to survive, you gotta learn to hustle back."

"And let me guess," Clare said, rolling her eyes, "you're just the man to teach me."

"Nah, I'm a hustler, too." Mickey tipped a small plastic peanut bag so five or six nuts fell into his hand. "But at least I say so up front."

TWO
ELIZABETH

Elizabeth Ng set her comb on the counter and appraised her reflection in the hotel bathroom mirror. She wished they were getting ready to go anywhere other than this stupid poker party.

"People like Tiffany James should not be allowed to play in these tournaments," Elizabeth said, loudly enough to be heard in the bedroom. "You know what hand she busted me out with?" She glanced out at Joe, whose attention was focused on the flat-screen TV. "Ten-seven suited."

"You'd play that, in position." Joe Mangan kicked off his sneakers and pulled his sockless feet onto the king-sized bed.

"But I'd play it for deception, or drawing odds." Elizabeth picked up a sparkly earring. "Not because I felt lucky that day. You know that your feet even *look* smelly."

"They do?" Joe seemed to like this. "What do smelly feet look like?"

"Gross. You can practically see the vapors rising from your shoes."

Joe grinned. "You played a good game, Liz. You can't control when luck runs the other way from you."

"Easy for you to say." Elizabeth put in the second earring and studied herself anew. She hadn't been looking her best lately — her skin seemed oilier, and her long black hair, normally totally manageable, was riddled with flyaways. "You coast into every final table like you were born to be there."

"I'm on a good streak." Joe paused to take a sip from the Coke can on the bedside table. "I'd love to win first place one of these days. But whatever; we can't have everything we want. So does Tiffany bug you because she can't play, or because she's another hottie on the scene when you've had that spot to yourself for the past few months?"

Elizabeth spun around and glared at Joe from the bathroom doorway. "Because Josie died?"

Joe shrugged and shoved a handful of Sun Chips into his mouth from the bag in his lap.

"That's a horrible thing to say. Josie and I had our differences, but we were friends, at the end of the day."

"You mean frenemies?" Joe turned the volume up on *Jersey Shore*.

"Are you Lindsay Lohan? I mean friends. I didn't like what she was into, but I liked who Josie was. She didn't deserve to die."

"What was Josie into?" Joe glanced at Elizabeth. "Drugs?"

"I guess she did a bit of blow, but no, that's not what I mean." Elizabeth went over to the bed and took a Sun Chip from Joe's pack. "I think — I don't know for sure — but she hinted that she was involved in some kind of cheating ring."

"Why would she cheat? And if she did, why would she tell you about it?"

"I haven't figured that out." Elizabeth wanted to peel off her blouse, wrap herself in the plush white robe, and forget about poker for one night. Instead, she returned to the bathroom to try to do something about her tired-looking face.

Joe turned the TV volume back down. "Did Josie tell you what kind of cheating?"

"She didn't *tell* me anything." Elizabeth picked up her powder foundation and scrutinized the label. It was supposed to be all natural, but maybe it had chemicals that were causing a reaction. "It was more of a 'Hey Liz, if you had the chance to know other people's hole cards, and you weren't technically doing anything illegal to find out . . .'"

"That's a theoretical question," Joe said. "Not an admission of guilt. It's like asking what you'd do if you found a magic lantern and a genie to grant you three wishes."

"It was the lift in Josie's voice. Like she was so clever to be hiding something." Elizabeth caked on another layer of powder.

The sound of chips crunching accompanied Joe's voice. "Aren't you finished getting ready yet? It's just a bunch of poker players. There won't even be cameras there."

Elizabeth took out her earrings. They were too flash for a night with a bunch of poker players. She came back into the main room where Joe was still sprawled in his jeans.

"You look great." Joe crumpled his chip pack and tossed it into the garbage bin. "I love you in that buttoned blouse. It makes you look so stern and secretary-like — all I can think about is ripping it off. We should get you a pair of glasses."

"You know those are biodegradable now?"

"Secretary glasses?"

Elizabeth rolled her eyes. "Sun Chip bags."

"You want me to find a compost heap in a casino hotel?"

Elizabeth shrugged. Joe didn't want children; what did he care about leaving the world how he found it? "Hey, do we have to go to this party?"

"*You* don't," Joe said. "But I want to win some money."

"You win money every day." Elizabeth gazed out the window at the giant waterfalls, lit up with pink, purple, and blue like they were some kind of carnival attraction instead of a natural wonder. "We don't have to stay in. What about a night on the town?"

"In Niagara Falls?" Joe arched his eyebrows. "Sure, baby. Let's go to a wax museum and the Olive Garden."

"Good point."

"Come on," Joe said, getting off the bed finally and grabbing Elizabeth's hands. "Maybe you'll even see your best friend Tiffany again."

"Ugh. Why did you have to mention her name?" Elizabeth shook Joe's hands off hers.

"I bet you'll like her if you give her a chance," Joe said. "She's bankrolled to stick around for the whole tour. You might as well be ready to pounce when her luck runs out."

"How do you know so much about Tiffany's bankroll?" Elizabeth had to find a way to rein in her jealousy. She either trusted Joe or she didn't; she couldn't stay in this place in between. She grabbed some clean socks from Joe's drawer and handed them to him.

"Thanks. I was at her table when T-Bone was giving her the gears. She held her own pretty good against him."

"Yay." Elizabeth could hold her own against T-Bone Jones or anyone.

"I saw her with one of Dan Harrington's books in the lobby when I was checking in. She's committed to learning."

"Yay again." The bitch could read. "If we're going, let's go. Wait — are you not even planning to wash your feet before you put new socks on?"

Joe laughed. "I guess that means you want me to." He stopped short of putting his right foot into the clean sock, stood up, and headed for the bathroom. "You know what's weird, though?" Joe said. "She smokes."

"So?" Could they get off the subject of Tiffany fucking James?

"Rich people don't usually smoke."

"Who says she's rich?" Elizabeth put the earrings back in. Maybe she *should* look flash tonight. "She might have backers."

"The way she plays?" Joe was shouting over the running water in the tub. "I said she was learning, I didn't say she was good."

THREE
CLARE

Sergeant Cloutier sawed a chunk off his rib-eye, looked at Clare, and lifted his fork to his mouth. Before taking the bite, he said, "You're still in the tournament after the first day. That's better than I thought you'd do."

"Believe me, it's luck." Clare took a sip of Corona and leaned back into the leather booth. The beer tasted watery and bitter, but orders from Amanda were premium only for Tiffany's precious tastebuds, and Clare had yet to find an import that came close to replicating Bud. "I thought I knew how to play poker — I've been reading every book there is and practicing online with my own money. I've already won enough for a killer new pair of motorcycle boots. But when you're thrown in with a bunch of seasoned professionals, the normal rules get tossed out the window. Those players are mean."

Cloutier chewed deliberately. His thick jowls reminded Clare of a hippopotamus. When he'd finished, he said, "I know. That's why I'm recommending you don't move on with the tour to Vancouver."

Clare sat up straight. "What?"

"You're not ready. This game is hard, and the players are harder. I know you like to think you're tough, but I can't send you on. You're new at this. You could get killed; I can't have that on my conscience."

"Will the RCMP even listen to you?" Clare knew Cloutier didn't think much of her job skills, but after the last case they'd broken together involving political murders on the University of Toronto campus, she didn't think he'd sabotage her. "You're just some handler from Toronto. *They* think I'm ready."

"The RCMP will hear my advice and make their own decision." Cloutier began to cut another piece of steak. "For now, you can tell me what you saw today. You learn anything about the players?"

"Mostly that they're assholes." Clare felt her jawbone tighten. She was not going to let Cloutier push her off this case. "But there's this one guy, Joe Mangan, who was decent to me."

"Mangan. A young guy, right?"

"Mid-thirties?" Clare was guessing. "He came third in the World Series of Poker main event last year. He's been on TV at a few other final tables."

"I know the kid. No bracelets, right?"

"Huh?" Clare sliced a morsel from her striploin. She could have cut it with a bread knife, it was so smooth. "No, I don't think he wears any jewelry."

Cloutier groaned. "First place finishes. I thought you said you knew this game. A bracelet's what they give you if you win a major tournament."

"Seems like a girly prize in a field full of men." Clare popped the steak into her mouth. She had to admit it was delicious, even if she thought it was a rip-off at forty-five dollars without any side dishes.

Cloutier grunted into his cloth napkin. "Nothing girly about the prize money."

Clare scowled. "Everything is always about money. I believe in capitalism, but I don't understand how people can be so fascinated by pursuing dollars for their own sake."

"Your time in that university paid off." Cloutier smirked.

"Oh, shut up," Clare said. "So listen, there's this guy T-Bone —"

"T-Bone Jones?" Cloutier stared.

Clare nodded.

"You met fucking T-Bone Jones? Were you playing at the same table?"

"If I get you his autograph, will you let me stay on the case?" Clare asked. "And he's one of the assholes. He's one of the meanest guys here."

"So he thinks you're a spoiled dumb, rich kid."

Clare frowned. "No, he doesn't. You said I didn't have to act dumb or spoiled."

"Looking like you do, you'd have to speak like fucking Einstein for anyone to give you credit for a brain."

Clare remembered why she never wore makeup in the first place. "That sucks."

"It doesn't suck. You want these players to underestimate you."

"For what? Five minutes, before you send me back to Toronto?"

"You gotta see this as more serious, Vengel," Cloutier said. "You forget what happened to Willard Oppal?"

Chills ran through Clare. "No."

"Good. Because this job was nearly yours in September. They gave it to Oppal instead because I said I didn't think you were ready then either."

"Thanks. It's great to have a handler who believes in me. I can see myself really going places with support like that behind me."

Cloutier set his glass down hard. Some beer splashed up, but none spilled out onto the table. "This isn't some dress-up game, Vengel. Your cop skills are hit and miss at best, and Willard Oppal showed us that when you miss too much you end up dead."

"You think it's Oppal's fault he died?" This struck Clare as impossibly cold.

Cloutier shrugged one broad shoulder. "It's his fault if he got made. It's his handler's fault for not pulling him sooner. The point is, you're here now because you're about the furthest thing from what people think a cop looks like."

"And because I figured out who killed the mayor."

"You got lucky on that one. But yeah, it looks good on your record."

Clare set her fork and knife down. "What about the other victims? You think it's Josie Carter's fault she's dead?"

"No one deserves to be murdered. But nor are they often completely innocent in their own demise. Josie was a party girl — she liked to snort coke and watch the sun rise with a new man each day. Not saying that's what got her killed, but when you live on the edge, you sometimes get sliced up real bad . . ."

"Harsh," Clare said. "And Jimmy Streets?"

"Old-time poker player. Came up through the ranks with T-Bone Jones. They were new kids together in Texas. The man was no saint."

"Wow," Clare said. "Anyway, I guess T-Bone does think I'm stupid. He invited me to play in a cash game tonight."

"You got invited to play in a cash game with T-Bone Jones?" Cloutier's hippo jaw hung open.

"Don't look so jealous," Clare said. "The idea terrifies me."

"Why? It's not your money."

"No," Clare said. "But this game is in the back room of a bar."

"And what? You're afraid you'll get killed for your winnings if you do well?"

"That's not it. I don't want to ask the RCMP for more money. I can't use the casino credits they've set up for me in an illegal side game."

"Are you stupid?" Cloutier tapped two thick fingers against his head. "You're not asking for a new car. You need money for the job, you can't be shy about it."

Clare picked up her beer bottle and set it down without taking a sip. She'd forgotten for a second that she was supposed to be drinking from the glass beside it. "I hate asking for things."

Cloutier gave her a look that felt like it was piercing into her brain. "Vengel, grow a pair."

"Good one," Clare said. *Bite me*, she thought.

"I'll run this by the finance wizards. For tonight — because I doubt I'll have their answer in time — consider yourself authorized to gamble. You got enough spending money left?"

"Yeah." Clare hadn't touched the ten thousand dollars the RCMP had deposited in Tiffany's name in a bank account.

"Good. Feel free to lose it."

Clare felt her eyes bug out from her face. "The whole thing?"

"I'll make sure your account is replenished tomorrow."

"But that's, like, the entire entry fee to each tournament. I can't blow that kind of cash in one night."

"We've been over this, Vengel. Ten grand is nothing to these guys. You gotta show them you can play on their terms, or they're not going to have any respect for you."

"Fucking materialists. If you don't have money you're not good enough."

"It's not materialism; it's gambling." Cloutier shook his head. "Shit, you really just don't know enough."

"I can learn," Clare said.

Cloutier took a deep breath. "I'm going to insist they pull you."

Clare slumped in her chair. "You always want to pull me. It's like your favorite thing to want. Have you ever thought maybe *that's* my whole problem? It's like driving with someone sitting beside you pointing out all your mistakes — you're going to screw up even more because you're self-conscious."

"You want a boss who doesn't care if you live or die?"

Clare wrinkled her nose. What *did* she want? "I want to dive into this role, play this spoiled rich kid, and find out who's been killing all the poker players."

"I want that for you, too." Cloutier frowned. "But the stakes are too high. There will be other cases as exciting as this one, but I think you should tackle them later, once you've wet your feet on smaller, safer cases."

"Come on. You know I won't be given smaller cases if I'm pulled from this. I've been waiting for a transfer to undercover for six months; no one's in a hurry to make that happen." Clare widened her eyes in case pleading would work.

"Vengel, kill the puppy-dog look. You're just proving my point. You're twenty-three. You don't know this job. You still think it's a game."

"I'm not working any more break and enters. If you pull me from this case, I quit. I'll go be a mechanic. And you should hope I never work on your car."

"That's not how to make me change my mind." Cloutier spoke more softly than usual.

"What will it take for me to convince you I can do this?"

"You need to understand that you could die."

Clare felt the same chills that she'd felt earlier when he'd mentioned Willard Oppal. "Okay," she said. "I get it."

"I don't like the idea of you going off to Vancouver."

"Why? Because Vancouver is such a dangerous city? Are the hippies going to attack me with their lava lamps?"

"But," Cloutier said. "I'll strike you a deal. If you can cash in this tournament, it will show me you're serious, that you can play on the same level as these guys."

"And if I can't magically find my way into the money?" Clare asked, because he was really talking long shot odds.

"Then I'm going with my gut and having you pulled."

"That's the stupidest thing I've ever heard," Clare said. "You can't strike gambling deals over someone's career."

"Vengel, does the whole cop hierarchy thing mean nothing to you? You're supposed to at least pretend to treat me with respect."

"Okay, that's one thing I like about you," she said. "You can take it if I challenge your authority."

"Yeah? Well, Amanda can't take being challenged so well."

"Who said I was challenging Amanda?" Clare shook her head when the waitress offered her another beer. If she did have another, it would not be that watery piss they called Corona. "And anyway, I'm on loan — I don't have rank with the RCMP, so I don't have to answer to their hierarchy."

"Amanda's going to be your handler in Vancouver. If you go."

Clare dropped her empty bottle to the table with a clunk. "No."

Clare had never met anyone more different from her in her life. To morph Clare into Tiffany, Amanda had spent nearly a full week with her. They went shopping in Yorkville, where snooty boutique employees exchanged smug glances because Clare didn't care about the distinction between two shades of blue. They ate sushi and other precious food that Clare was shocked cost so much more than a decent pub meal that would actually fill you up. They went to Civello on Yonge Street, where Clare was wrapped in seaweed by a smug woman named Serenity, and manicured by one of the shallowest bimbos she'd ever met. And Amanda seemed to enjoy every minute of this.

"I know it's hard to part with me." Cloutier smirked. "But Amanda's a pro. And she'll look the part — a fashionable friend you can go shopping with."

"I already went shopping with Amanda. I have enough nice clothes to last the rest of my life."

"Tiffany James might beg to differ. In fact, she wouldn't wear the same dress to two parties with the same people."

"How do you know?" Clare glared at her soon-to-be ex-handler.

"I've dated a high-maintenance woman or two in my time." Cloutier sucked in his cheeks and picked up his beer glass with his pinky sticking straight out. He looked more like a blowfish with a broken finger than anything posh, but Clare got the point.

"Are you calling me high-maintenance?"

"I'm saying you have it in you."

"So if you think I have it in me, why would you recommend I get pulled?"

"Because having it in you and using what you have are two completely different things." Cloutier pulled in his pinky and took a sip of beer.

"I did fine on my first case."

"You were posing as a student where the victims were

politicians. Here you're posing as a poker player where the victims are poker players. You don't get a second chance when your first fuck-up gets you dead."

FOUR
GEORGE

Mickey Mills fidgeted with his cigarette pack on the table. "I'm telling you, Georgie. You should take me up on my offer. There's thousands of people — maybe millions — who want to read my life story. You stick your name on this sucker and your writing career will soar through the roof."

George stared past Mickey and out of the diner to the main floor of the casino. Slot machines dominated the scene — waves of neon and flashing LEDs with bells and cheap carnival music to make you think it was a game, giving away your welfare check to sit there all day in an adult diaper. A large woman in spandex stood midway between two machines. She played them both with a dexterity George would have admired had it not been for the desperation in her posture — the quick, tense movements that told George she would mortgage her cat for another token to put in the machine.

George turned back to Mickey. "Unfortunately, Mick, most of those thousands are either poker players or your relatives, which means that even if I write the most brilliant biography in the history of time, they'll wait until the free copy hits the library."

"No, man. I got fans. You should check out the Internet. The World Wide Web. I got fan clubs all over the place."

"I'm sure that's true. You're a poker legend." George pushed his thick red glasses up on his nose. Seeing smudge marks, he pulled them off and wiped them with his shirt.

"So what are you pretending to hesitate for? You don't like my terms? They're negotiable." Mickey took out a cigarette and started rolling it between his stubby fingers. A busboy walked by and looked nervously at Mickey. "Don't worry," Mickey told the kid. "I'm not gonna light up."

George hadn't smoked for four years, but watching Mickey toy with his cigarette made him want one. And what *was* he pretending to hesitate for? George had only agreed to this meeting because Mickey had cornered him when he'd been having a heart-to-heart with Fiona, and the fastest way to get rid of Mickey had been to say yes. No way was George writing Mickey's biography. "I have a lot on the go at the moment. Maybe try one of the other writers."

"I want you."

"Why?" George hazarded the guess that Mickey had peddled this offer to the other writers on the scene and come up dry.

"People take you seriously." Mickey spoke earnestly, as if from a script. "If you write my biography, they're gonna take *me* seriously. You're not like the other poker writers. You're classy."

George had once heard someone say that if you used the word classy, it meant that you weren't. Not that the judgment would bother Mickey even if it were true.

"Why do you need strangers to take you seriously?" George asked. "You win piles of money at poker. Isn't that its own reward?"

"Maybe thirty years ago the cash was exciting." Mickey cast his glance down in dejected dismissal. "But that thrill is long gone. I still like beer more than Dom Perignon, and most of what's extra goes to my douchebag ex-wife."

"That must piss you off," George said.

Mickey shrugged. "I still got enough to send home, keep my parents in style. They won't move outta Southie, even though I keep sending brochures for these tropical fucking paradise old folks homes I wouldn't mind checking myself into for a rest. But I paid for their new furnace last year, and when my mom broke her hip, I arranged for a nurse around the clock. That feels good."

"So why a book?" George asked, pulling at a pill on his plaid flannel shirt sleeve and making it worse. "You just said it: the human rewards are way more exciting."

"Because look at me." Mickey grabbed a chunk of his graying black hair. "My parents don't got too many years left. I'm gonna need something else — something that ain't material — to make me feel like my life has some kind of purpose."

"Then you should think about doing something, not having something written. Volunteer in a youth home. Start a charity. What do you want to see done differently in the world?"

Mickey snorted. "I want to see a new book on the shelves. No offense, George, but stop trying to know me. I know what I want, and I want you to help me. Can you just say yes or no?"

"What about a ghost writer?" George tried to sound upbeat. He didn't hate Mickey; he just didn't want to write this damn biography. "You tell the story how you want it, and it's only your name on the cover."

"Maybe you haven't been listening to me. Which is sad, George. I thought writers were supposed to be good listeners. I want your name on the cover."

"I have too much on the go right now."

Mickey cast his glance around the diner like he was trying to find the secret angle, the one that would finally convince George. "Think of all the books we could sell if we do this together. You know how hot *Suicide Kings* is?"

Of course George knew. He tracked sales statistics for his poker strategy book obsessively. It wasn't exactly falling off the shelves, but it was holding its own, close to the top in its category.

"People are going to buy something right now just 'cause it's by you. Add my name into the mix and we got an instant best-seller."

"Thanks for the praise, Mick. I'm gonna take a pass."

George could only imagine what his family in Boston would say if he started writing biographies of poker players. He might as well get a tattoo saying *Charlatan* in big red letters on his forehead and wear it home for Christmas.

Mickey was scowling. "What does that mean, 'take a pass'? What a stupid expression. Just say, 'No, Mickey. Fuck you. I'm not writing your goddamn biography.'"

"I said exactly that." George took a sip of the tepid black coffee. "Minus the fuck you."

"This is nuts!" Mickey's coffee splashed over into its saucer as he slammed it down. "You guys should be banging down *my* door. Fucking snobs, all you writers."

"I'm sorry, man. I'm really busy," George said. "I have my blog, I'm guest hosting Fiona's show for the Vancouver leg, I'm pitching 2+2 Publishing about a sequel to *Suicide Kings*. Not to mention I'm playing in a tournament."

"You call that playing?" Mickey snorted. "More like blinding off until you fade away. You have to actually play a hand sometimes."

"I choose my spots carefully." George knew Mickey was right about his game. Although Mickey had busted out in the second round of the tournament, he had gone out with gusto, and had probably already made his entry fee back from the cash games he'd been playing all afternoon. George's poker game, though technically competent, was too peppered with fear to ever make him a star.

"Let's hope you choose your writing projects less selectively than your poker hands, or you'll be out of work until you're a hundred."

"Thanks for the offer, Mickey." George pulled out enough money for both coffees and set it in the middle of the table. "I'm sure you'll find the right fit for your project."

"Take your fucking money." Mickey grabbed the ten-dollar bill and thrust it into George's hand. "You think I'm such a degenerate gambler, I can't pay for a coffee when I invite someone out for one?"

"No. I didn't think that." George replaced the money in his wallet and stood up. "I'll see you around."

As George rode the elevator up to his room, he felt anticipation tingle in his veins. Tonight, he was continuing his real writing project — the one he hadn't told a soul about.

FIVE

CLARE

Clare was walking through the hotel lobby after dinner with Cloutier when she practically collided with Mickey Mills.

"Watch where the fuck you're going."

"Sorry." Clare looked up to see an unshaven face scowling at her. "I guess I was lost in thought."

"You're the kid who pissed off T-Bone." Mickey's hostility vanished as quickly as it had come. "Good for you."

"How did I piss off T-Bone?" Clare found that dramatic. "I called down one hand. He was bullying me all day."

"Well, you're under his skin," Mickey gestured with his hands, sliding two fingers under his other palm, "which is a piece of very good luck. You can use that if you're at the same table again."

"I can?" Clare wondered if this stocky little man was about to give her some tips. She hoped he would, but quickly. She wanted to go upstairs and phone Kevin, her boyfriend, at home. And change into some sweats — even if they had some designer logo on the ass. And fall asleep.

Mickey's dark eyes flitted around the lobby. He ticked his

pointer finger in her direction. "I can help you make T-Bone's temper work in your favor, but you gotta do something for me in return."

Naturally. "Thanks. I'll be all right."

"You mental?" Mickey furrowed his brow. "I said I'll help you take down T-Bone Jones. Most newbies would jump at that chance. Hell, most newbies wouldn't *get* that chance."

"I'm not most newbies." Clare studied the tips of her pointy pink boots. She wasn't used to wearing heels with jeans, but there was something cool about it. She liked feeling taller as Tiffany. "I don't like to owe people favors."

Mickey's eyes relaxed. "Is that all? You can do the favor up front. Then I'll owe you."

Clare thought about this. "What if your advice doesn't work?"

Mickey laughed. "Then I'll coach you for free. Hell, I'll do that regardless — I like the spirit in you. You following the tour to Vancouver?"

Clare wished she knew the answer to that. "Probably. I'll think about your offer." She started to walk toward the elevator and stopped. "Anyway, what's the favor you want from me?"

A grin spread across Mickey's face. "Promise you won't get creeped out?"

"No."

"I need a date for tonight."

"Creepy." But Clare stayed where she was.

"Don't take it the wrong way. You don't gotta have sex with me or nothing. I just need a date for this party."

"You don't have one yet?" Clare looked at her watch. "It's almost nine."

"It's not the kind of thing you normally bring a date to. It's just . . . okay, my ex-wife is hosting it."

"Your ex-wife lives in Niagara Falls?" Clare was surprised.

"Loni? No. She lives in L.A. She's hosting the party in the back room of a bar and grill."

"Why the back room?"

"It's a poker game. Nosebleed stakes. You know how much a casino robs you for, playing for that kind of money?"

"No." Clare assumed it must be a lot, or the RCMP wouldn't have such a liberal budget to ensure that poker stayed safe in the public eye.

"They rake as much as you can win, if you're playing half-decent players." Mickey shook his head with scorn. "I feel like I'm working for the government half the time, and the other half I'm earning for the goombas running the casinos."

"I still don't see why you need a date. If you're going to gamble all night, what's my job?"

"Your job is to cheer me on. Bring me drinks. I'll buy them — I don't want you to be out any cash for this — but a sweet girl on my arm will do wonders for my game."

"How?"

"My ex's new boyfriend is T-Bone Jones."

Clare laughed. It sounded a bit like a snort, so she quickly pitched her voice higher and turned it into a Tiffany-style titter. "I should have known your motivation for helping me beat T-Bone wasn't pure."

"No one's motivation ever is."

Mickey shifted his weight from one foot to the next like a kid who had to use the bathroom. "So not only will you beef up my self-esteem — which is more fragile than people think — but if you play it right, T-Bone's gonna frustrate himself into giving me all his money. Then he'll hate you even more, and it's gonna be that much easier for you to get him to lose his cool at the table."

Clare wasn't sure if Mickey's logic worked, but she had to take him up on his offer. Getting in with Mickey Mills might be just the way to show Cloutier she was the right person for this case.

"How will a fake date beef up your self-esteem?" Clare didn't want to seem too eager to accept the invitation.

"Because my ex-wife is a total fucking cunt — pardon my

language — and I would love to see the look on Loni's face when I walk in with the hottest new broad on the scene."

Clare wasn't used to being thought of as hot — not by so many people in one day. She knew she shouldn't like the feeling too much — it was only her cover character inspiring the attention — still . . . "Two conditions," she said.

Mickey's eyes widened.

"No PDAS."

"What the fuck's a PDA?"

"No cuddling, no hand-holding. Nothing."

"Fine, I wasn't gonna be all over you. You just have to come up to me the odd time, maybe rub my shoulders —"

"I'm not rubbing your shoulders."

"You don't gotta be so cold about it." Mickey brushed his arms and shivered as if it was forty below.

Clare put a hand on her hip. "Condition two: if anyone asks, we're there as friends."

"Ah, come on. Why can't we say we're on a date?"

"Because you're thirty years older than me, and if I meet someone I *do* want to date, it won't be worth any poker lessons if I have to turn down real romance."

"Fine," Mickey said, glancing down as if she'd hurt his feelings. "We'll say we're friends. But only if we're asked directly."

"Deal. So why is your ex such a . . ." Clare wasn't prudish, but Tiffany wouldn't repeat Mickey's epithet. ". . . bitch?"

"You mean besides the million bucks she convinced the judge to award her in our divorce, which I'm still fucking paying in installments?" Mickey scowled at the lobby carpet. "I'm not worth a million bucks. Don't know why she should be."

"Maybe the judge went by income instead of net worth," Clare said.

"Fucking hell. You on her side already?"

"Would I have to change clothes for the party?" By her own standards, Clare was dressed up already, but she had a whole new wardrobe in her hotel room, courtesy of the RCMP.

"Up to you," Mickey said. He was in dress pants and a pressed shirt, which seemed to be his everyday attire. "You'd be sexier than Loni if you wore a paper sack."

"I have this blue D&G dress I've been dying for an excuse to wear." Clare might as well do this wholeheartedly. She had to show Cloutier she was serious. "I'll meet you back in the lobby in ten minutes."

SIX

NOAH

Noah Walker frowned as he glanced around the bar. The room was filled with loud, ugly white trash, and he was supposed to make these people think he was their new fucking best friend. Good thing he liked challenges.

It was an odd room, with cheap wood paneling and swanky new lighting, like it couldn't decide if it wanted to be rustic or modern. Maybe ownership had changed recently. Maybe ownership just didn't give a shit.

The two poker tables were already full and the rest of the room was filling fast. Great White North — yeah, right. More than half the people there were American, like Noah. Hoping to cash in on what they thought was weak play, given the Canadians' reputation for reticence and politeness. Please. The Canadians were a savvy crowd. They might smile and act polite, but they knew how to hold onto their money.

Noah had crashed the party. It hadn't been hard to find, with all those players yammering about seeing each other later in the back room at MacCauley's. Wink wink, bring money for gambling. Like the cops cared about busting up their stupid side games. And like that should be the players' biggest fear, with a killer basically picking them off, one by one, with some rope around their throats as they lay sleeping in their hotel rooms.

Noah willed a smile onto his face. You didn't get anywhere good being negative. He only needed to think of his mother to remember that. She'd spent most of his childhood brooding around in depression, nursing her moods like she was a martyr to so much affliction.

Joe Mangan set his Coke on the bar rail beside Noah.

"Hey," Noah said, seizing the chance to talk to one of the few people there who didn't look like he'd just rolled in from a long shift in the scrapyard. Joe, though he had a small scar on his otherwise baby-smooth face that indicated he'd likely fare just fine in the scrapyard, at least took the time to gel up his hair and wear decent shoes. Most of the other clowns wore discount store jeans and old sneakers.

"Hey back," Joe said. "Doesn't look like this is your scene."

Noah shrugged. "Why not? I like to win money."

"Against this crowd?" Joe's eyebrows lifted. "How good are you?"

"Good enough." Noah knew he wasn't as good as Joe and the other pros, but he had cash to throw around. His instructions were to infiltrate this scene, and he could afford to lose a bit up front, because soon he was only going to win. "You know how to get on the waiting list?"

"Yeah," Joe said. "You give your name to Loni."

Noah glanced toward the bar where Joe was indicating. "Big blond with the rack?"

Joe nodded. "Looks good from a distance, huh? You can only tell her age when you get up close."

"How old is she?" Noah's mom would be off in a rant about women like Loni — fake breasts, probably fake lips, too — making women who didn't artificially enhance their appearance feel inferior. His father would defend a woman's right to plastic surgery. His mother would get insecure, and the conversation — if there had been a conversation — would degenerate.

Joe shrugged. "Late forties? Why, you want to hit that?"

Noah struggled to keep the slice of pizza he'd just eaten in his stomach. "No."

"Don't knock the powers of a woman with experience. Never had her myself, but I've heard good things."

Noah studied Joe, whose eyes seemed to be on both poker tables at once. The tables were half a level below them on the other side of the rail, like a boxing ring for everyone to gawk at. Did Joe know that his game — his careful hand-reading, his assessment of odds, his strategic bullying — was being compromised by a ring of cheaters?

But hang on — here came someone interesting. Noah's gaze shifted toward the entrance to the private room, where a young woman was walking in with Mickey Mills. All right, so she was wearing a bright blue dress that was a bit fashioned-up for this crowd — Noah didn't have time for high-maintenance bullshit. But this girl had intelligent eyes which, unlike the rest of the players he'd met, looked like they could see beyond her own selfish interests.

"You know that girl?" he asked Joe.

Joe stopped watching the game and followed Noah's gaze. "The brunette with Mickey? Why? You like her?"

Noah shrugged.

"That's Tiffany. She's the bane of my girlfriend's existence."

Noah felt a corner of his mouth lift in amusement. "Why do they hate each other?"

"It's one-sided," Joe said. "Liz hates Tiffany. She donked out and cost Liz her tournament."

"What's Tiffany doing with Mickey Mills?" Noah asked. "Are they dating? He looks like he's twice her age and then some."

"More likely he's coaching her." Joe turned his gaze back toward the poker tables. "She's hot. I can see why you like her."

"She's not that good-looking." Noah set down his beer and leaned into the bar rail. The rail wobbled a bit, so Noah stopped leaning — he didn't think the players at the poker tables on the other side would like him to come crashing into their game. "But when you compare her to the rest of the women here, she stands out by a mile. You know what her story is?"

"She's a trust fund kid," Joe said. "She's read a few poker books and she thinks this poker tour is a better investment than the stock market."

Noah laughed. "She any good?"

"At poker? No. But she's smart. I saw a couple of moves that would make Sklansky proud. Too bad her eyes give her game away. Still, with Mickey coaching her — and maybe a pair of dark glasses — she might pick it up in time to do okay in Vancouver."

"Is she going to Vancouver?" Noah was surprised to feel his hopes rise.

"I think so."

Noah took a smoke from his pack. The nice thing about an illegal side game was the bar bent the idiotic bylaws about smoking. The nice thing about hanging with white trash was that most of them smoked. "You don't think she'll cash in Niagara?"

"Not a chance," Joe said. "She might get a few more flukes, but the odds are she'll give her chips away as quickly as she got them. I'd lay, like, six to one she doesn't cash."

Noah smirked. "Is everything an odds game to you?"

"Pretty much."

"What would you give my chances of getting Tiffany out on a date?"

"Depends if I ask her first." Joe tilted his head to one side as if he was contemplating it.

"You just said you have a girlfriend."

"Yeah?"

"Tiffany's not going to date a guy who's taken."

"How do you know? I thought you'd never met her." Joe slurped at his nearly empty Coke can.

"I can see it in her eyes," Noah said. "She has integrity."

"You're a funny guy. All right, I'll give her to you," Joe said.

"You don't have to give me anything. How about a prop bet?"

Noah felt pretty clever for thinking of this. If he could get a long-term bet going with Joe — especially a secret one, that no one could know about — it would be an indefinite in.

"What?" Joe shook his head, as if trying to understand what Noah had proposed. "No way. My girlfriend would have a fit if she found out I made a bet about dating someone else."

Noah felt his phone buzz in his pocket. It was probably Bert, wanting to arrange the next day's meeting. "I was thinking more than a date. And you're the one who basically told me you're willing to cheat on your girlfriend . . ."

Joe's eyes widened. "You want a prop bet on who gets Tiffany into bed?"

"Yeah," Noah said. It was a long shot, but if this worked, it was his easy ticket into the in crowd. He wished he could send tips back to his thirteen-year-old self, which was the last time he could remember giving two shits about the in crowd.

Joe wrinkled his forehead in the same way Noah had seen him do when he was pretending to think about a big hand on TV. "You'd have an advantage from the get-go. With Lizzie around, it will be a challenge finding time to nail Tiffany."

"Fair enough," Noah said. "But you're famous. I'm not. So you'll get her attention faster."

"I guess that's a wash." Joe glanced around the room. He smiled and waved when he made eye contact with Elizabeth, safely out of earshot.

"Are you willing to call my being handsome a wash with your charm?"

Joe laughed. "Yeah, that's fair. Although I do have a cult following on the gay scene."

"Seriously?"

"Someone started a Facebook page called 'I Want to Blow Joe Mangan.' Sixteen hundred fans; twelve hundred are men."

Noah wasn't surprised. "Might be the frosted tips."

"You think?" Joe patted his short, spiky hair. "What's the bet for? Five grand? Ten?"

Noah shrugged. "I could go higher. Make it twenty."

"Twenty, huh?" Joe pursed his lips and nodded. "You're on. What's your name, anyway?"

"Nate Wilkes," Noah said, shaking hands on the bet.

SEVEN

ELIZABETH

Fiona Gallagher twirled a strand of red hair around her index finger as she scanned the party — presumably for someone more important to talk to. "I like the new girl. Too bad we can't keep her."

"Tiffany? Why can't we keep her?" Elizabeth asked. She'd like to be talking to someone other than Fiona and Loni, too, but she wasn't rude enough to show it. "Joe thinks she's here for a while."

Loni Mills tapped her cigarette holder over the black plastic ashtray. Elizabeth wanted to tell her that the cigarette holder made her look old, not glamorous. "She's a real polite thing," Loni said. "Comes up to me, 'Excuse me, Miss, can you please tell me how the waiting list for the poker game works?'"

Elizabeth snorted. "I'd love to see Tiffany play at these stakes. She'll drain that trust fund in no time."

"I can't play poker," Loni said. "Doesn't stop me from sticking like glue to this scene."

Fiona tossed her glance down the bar so Loni could follow it. "And look — Tiffany seems to be coming onto this scene just like you did. Notice how she's hanging all over your ex-husband, bringing him beers like some dog who's just learned how to fetch."

"Hey, I never fetched anything for Mickey." Loni pushed her chest out and glanced down as if saying, *With a rack like this, it was Mickey who did all the fetching.* But Loni's smile faded. Her gaze remained on Tiffany and Mickey.

Fiona sipped her white wine. "What do you think she wants from him?"

Elizabeth had had enough of Fiona. But she had nowhere else to go except home to bed. "I seriously doubt Tiffany James — How old is she? Twelve? — wants anything from Mickey Mills except to learn how to play poker."

"I like her dress," Fiona said. "It looks like new Dolce and Gabbana. You think it's real?"

"Who cares?" Elizabeth thought Tiffany looked like a bridesmaid at a legion hall wedding. All she needed was a stick of bubble gum to complete the image.

"I hate that about tournament poker," Fiona said. "None of the women look like women." She paused and corrected herself, badly. "Um, present company excepted." Fiona laughed slightly. "But you know what I mean. Most go around in old jeans and men's T-shirts. It sucks for the ratings."

Because it was all about Fiona being a superstar. She was a backwater poker anchor and she walked around like she was hosting the Oscars.

Loni took a long sip of beer and said, "Why not ask Poker Stars and Full Tilt to vamp up their women's clothes. Might not be Versace, but least the sponsored girls will look sexier on TV."

"Good plan." Fiona pulled a pen from her purse and made a note. "Thanks, 'Miss.'"

Elizabeth groaned. "Oh my god. Please can we not all talk like Tiffany?" And really, when Elizabeth thought about it, was "Miss" a word a little aristocrat would use? It sounded more like trailer trash to her ear.

"Loosen up, Lizzie." Fiona reached over and undid the top button on Elizabeth's blouse. She appraised it, and undid one more. "Much better. Now you'd never even guess about that pickle in your ass."

Elizabeth looked down and did one of the buttons back up. She met Joe's eye — he was standing with some dark-haired guy she didn't recognize — and he gave her a thumbs-up.

"See," Fiona said. "Joe likes it better undone."

Elizabeth winced. She didn't know why she was at this party when she was in no mood to gamble. She'd never understood the point of socializing for its own sake. There were so many valid reasons to interact, like work or family obligations; to arbitrarily invent one seemed bizarre.

"At least you're actually with Joe," Fiona said. "Poor old George looks at me like I'm only being single for now, and I'll eventually find my way home to him."

"You're both lucky," Loni said, her eyes still fixed firmly on Tiffany. "Mickey looks at me like I'm the devil."

"You did kind of take him for more than he's worth," Fiona said with a grin.

"I had a good lawyer." Loni patted her big blond hair into place.

"Also, Fiona, you still sleep with George," Elizabeth said. "So maybe that's a factor in his so-called self-delusion."

Fiona looked at Elizabeth sharply. "How do you know about that?"

"What's the big secret? You're both single; you're allowed."

"No, it's just — I didn't know anyone cared who I slept with."

"What else do we have to do, honey?" Loni stubbed out her cigarette and set the holder on the bar beside the ashtray. "We're with each other day and night; we're going to know each other's business."

"True," Fiona said. "Like earlier tonight — maybe I shouldn't say anything, but it's better you know, Elizabeth, rather than everyone talking behind your back —"

Loni sputtered on a mouthful of beer. "Fiona, some things are better not said. There's a reason people protect their friends from the truth."

"Tell me." Elizabeth glared at them both.

Fiona shrugged. "Don't shoot me because I'm the messenger, but I overheard Joe and that guy he's talking to . . . I'm pretty sure they made a bet."

Elizabeth glanced at Joe with the dark-haired stranger. "A bet about what?"

"Don't get mad," Fiona said. "I might be wrong about what I heard."

"Fiona, cut the dramatic build-up and say what you have to say."

"I think they have a bet about which one of them can get Tiffany into bed first."

Elizabeth felt poison creep into her veins. Fiona liked to stir shit up, but why would she invent this?

"Tiffany might think she's here to stay." Fiona sipped her white wine. "But I think the three of us can convince her she's better off back in the real world."

EIGHT
CLARE

Clare looked around and felt like laughing. She was standing at a bar with a stocky middle-aged gambler, wearing an electric blue dress that was almost certainly over-the-top even given her cover role, trying to find a killer in a haystack. If this was law enforcement, Clare wondered how anyone slept at night.

Of course Cloutier was right: Clare wasn't qualified to be there. But she didn't know what else she'd do for a career. She could take cars apart in her sleep, and she enjoyed it, but she didn't get any thrill from the idea of spending her life as an auto mechanic. Undercover work made Clare feel alive. It used all her skills and senses. Her cover costume — in tonight's case, the cocktail dress — was her superhero cloak. Wearing it, Clare wasn't the angry kid from the trailer park, but a confident woman who could save the world from bad guys.

"You want another beer?" Mickey pointed to her empty bottle.

"Sure," Clare said. "This round's on me."

"Keep your money." She had picked up her purse, but he waved her off. "It don't look right if people see you buying me drinks."

"On the contrary." Clare unfastened her glittery clutch. "It looks like I actually want to spend time with you."

A grin spread across Mickey's round face, making him look like a happy old monkey. "You sure you don't want to date for real?"

"Positive." Clare ordered a Bud for Mickey and a Heineken for herself.

"You ever change your mind, kid, I'm not half as bad as they say."

"Tell you what." Clare handed Mickey the Budweiser, wishing she could keep it and pass off the Heineken. "If all the men my age die or get herpes, I won't totally discount the possibility."

"You make an old man blush."

From behind Clare, a female voice said, "You're really splashing onto the scene, huh?"

"Hi, Elizabeth," Mickey said. "Have you met Tiffany?"

"We met this morning. She donked me out of the tournament." Elizabeth's gaze moved up and down Clare, making her feel like she probably did look ridiculous.

"Rough luck," Mickey said.

"At least I played my cards right. Anyway, congratulations . . . Tiffany. You're sure making an impression your first day."

"What do you mean?" Clare toyed with her beer label. That was one habit no cover role could cure her of.

"I mean all the guys have noticed you. Which is a real feat, considering most of them are only fascinated with their bank accounts and the cards in their hands."

"I'm sure you don't have trouble getting men to notice you." Clare smiled benignly.

"I never said I did." Elizabeth frowned. "I have a boyfriend, anyway. He's over there in the striped shirt."

"His mother pick that out for him?" Clare said, then wished she hadn't.

"The shirt? I did."

"Oh. It's nice."

"You don't have to like the shirt," Elizabeth said, "but you don't have to patronize me either. I'm not a dumb little debutante like the rest of your friends."

"What?" Clare didn't think there was such a thing as a debutante in this day and age. Maybe in the Deep South, but not in Canada.

Mickey snorted. "Elizabeth, where do you come from that you think speaking like that is okay? You think the kid doesn't have feelings? Sorry you lost today — but fucking get over it."

Elizabeth's eyebrows lifted. "Etiquette lessons from Mickey Mills? What's next, poker lessons from Tiffany?" Elizabeth walked a few steps away, then pivoted on her two-inch heel and returned to the bar. "Listen, I want to apologize. I'm tense tonight. I don't like losing. But it's not your fault."

"No?" Mickey glowered at Liz. "So why the Jekyll and Hyde act?"

Elizabeth clenched her teeth so hard that Clare could see her cheeks tighten. "Tiffany played well today. I came back to say good job, congratulations, maybe we can be friends."

"Um. Thanks." Clare tried to keep the skepticism from her voice. "I know I didn't play well. I hope to soon, but I'm still learning the game. Today I got lucky."

"Whatever happened," Elizabeth said, "I'm sorry I was a bad sport."

"Yeah, *that* isn't like you." This from Mickey.

"Remind me never to apologize to *you*." Elizabeth scowled as Mickey made a retreat in the direction of the men's room. "Listen, whatever he's told you about me, I swear I'm harmless."

"I'm sure that's not true either," Clare said. "I've seen you on TV. You're ruthless."

"Thanks." Elizabeth smiled, this time from her eyes. "Are you on the waiting list for tonight's game?"

"Yeah." Clare felt her breathing constrict as she said it. It didn't matter whose money was on the line; she was nervous as hell to play in a cash game with these people.

Elizabeth said, "I could help you. T-Bone's steaming. You can use that."

"Maybe some other time." Why was everyone so concerned with helping her? At least Mickey had been up front about what he wanted from Clare — or from Tiffany, because the real Clare on his arm might not be such a trophy — in return.

"Mickey already offered to help you."

"Um."

"You don't have to answer, if it's supposed to be some secret."

"It's not a secret." Clare glanced in the direction of the washroom, where Mickey was chatting with someone. "I don't know what it is. I'm feeling a bit overwhelmed."

"By the poker scene?"

Clare nodded.

"Not the same world you read about in *Harrington on Hold'em*?"

"Right," Clare said genuinely. She wasn't sure if she was reacting right now as Clare or as Tiffany. "This is nothing like I pictured it would be."

"It gets easier." Was Elizabeth being kind?

"It does?"

"Yeah," Elizabeth said. "You learn who your friends aren't."

NINE
GEORGE

George cupped his hands around his mug as he watched his MacBook boot up. The hotel was quiet — most people were out at the gambling party. He had the evening to himself to work on his secret project.

He took a sip of the coffee he'd made from the so-called espresso machine in the room. It was as bland as any motel room percolator's, but at least someone was trying to make a change in the right direction. He reread his first scene, about Willard Oppal's death, and he began to type the next scene.

```
June 2010


Halifax, Nova Scotia


Flash back to the beginning. The poker scene is
normal -- not a hotbed of murder; just a bunch
of selfish people trying to make a living off of
other people's mistakes. Peter Pan would be proud:
every night's a party, every day's a photo op. The
real world is as far away as Mars.
```

Josie Carter.

You're alone in your hotel room. You've had a good
day at the tables and you've poured yourself a
drink. You have a date tonight, but you're not
going to make it.

You don't know this, though, so you slide into a
cocktail dress, some slinky thing that shows off
your 26-year-old curves, and you bring your drink
into the bathroom to apply your makeup.

The TV's on -- an *Entourage* rerun. You like the
raunchy humor, the *au courant* cultural refer-
ences. It makes you feel hip, in the game.

You light a smoke. You know this shit is killing
you -- but wait -- smoke away, Josie. You're one of
the few people who can enjoy the privilege with
impunity.

If George ever learned his date of death, he would start
smoking again immediately. He had quit smoking often, each
time deciding that a long life was worth more than the delicious
pleasure, the romantic satisfaction, the perfect vile taste of cigarettes.

You exhale into the mirror. You smile as you catch
your own eye. You wonder if this is how the TV
cameras see you, while you crack jokes with your
opponents at the tables, while you slowly amass
all our chips.

There's a knock on the door. You don't want to
answer. You're enjoying your alone time. As much

as you love the spotlight, you're an introvert at
heart.

George had no idea if Josie was an introvert or an extrovert or
a pervert. But this was his book, and he could dream away. He'd
change the names at the end — he'd make it look like fiction. He
could even change the victims' genders — Josie could become Jose.

"Just a minute," you call.

You toss a brush through your hair and look
through the peephole. It's someone you recognize,
so you open the door.

Should George identify the someone? Give the killer a name?
Not for now.

"Do you want to come in?" You say this reluctantly;
you hope the caller doesn't take you up on the
invitation.

George hesitated. Should he at least give the killer a gender?
It was better, he thought, to give readers something they could
sink their teeth into. And a male killer — at least to George — felt
more menacing than a female.
He dried the sweat from his palms on his rumpled dress shirt
and kept typing.

Your friend comes in. He accepts the drink you
offer; he makes himself comfortable on your bed.

"I'm about to leave for dinner," you say. "Mind if I
keep getting ready?"

"Nah," he says. "Just came to hang."

```
"Fine." You're irritated. "You like Entourage?"

"You kidding? It's my favorite show. Is this the
one where Vince is banging the vegan?"

"Yeah," you say. Less irritated for the common
ground.

You top up your own drink.
```

George got up for more coffee. It took three cups of this shit to give him the same kick as a real cup of caffeine. He should have grabbed a large from Starbucks — sorry, a *Venti* — on the way up to his room.

Maybe one day George would take the plunge and buy the writing space he craved, in New York or New England. Old, and real, and his. Or maybe he'd pack his things into storage and move to Paris for a year, like the old-school alcoholic writers had done.

One thing he knew: his writing space would have a decent coffee maker. He would grind his beans fresh for every cup. He might even learn how to roast them.

He gave his attention back to Josie.

```
You're lifting your blush brush to your cheek
when you catch your friend's eye in the mirror.
He's followed you into the bathroom.

"What's with you tonight?" you say. "You need some
extra attention or something?"

"Nice job." You think he means the makeup. You
wonder if he's flirting. You don't think so; he's
one of your buddies. But -- what the fuck is going
on?
```

Before you notice, he's slipped a rope around your
throat. For a second you think it's some crazy
kind of foreplay, but when he doesn't draw the
rope away, you become alarmed.

You struggle with your friend. Why is he trying
to kill you? Has he taken drugs that make him
paranoid? You try to get your fingers between the
rope and your skin for long enough to reason with
him.

He says in a clear, unimpaired voice, "I told you
not to stray from the plan."

And you know. You pull frantically at the rope.
You want to tell him you're sorry. You'll get back
with the plan -- you won't breathe a word. You'll
be the perfect little poker cheater from this day
forward.

You try to scream.

Too late.

You're dead.

George rolled his eyes at his own melodrama. Of course he
wasn't going to submit this to any publishers in second person.
But he would edit later, when he swapped out the real names for
fictional ones. It felt good to be writing this freely. Normally he
criticized himself so much as he wrote that he probably averaged
four words an hour.

You're Victim Number One. The police think you
were killed in a crime of passion. They interview

your friends, interrogate your exes, and arrest
the middling poker player you've just begun to
date. When there's no evidence, they release him.
They let the leads dry up until your case becomes
one unsolved of many.

George closed the document and double-clicked its icon, making sure his password worked. Yup. Sealed up nice and tight. He didn't want the world to see these words until they were very, very ready.

TEN
CLARE

"I hate it here," Clare moaned into her Android phone with the stupid pink case. The party was over, she'd lost three thousand dollars at the poker table, and she was nowhere closer to knowing who the killer was. "I wish like hell that I could tell you where I am."

"I wish you could, too." Kevin's voice was strong, and Clare wanted to be wrapped up by his body. "I could fly out and see you on the weekend."

"You could drive," Clare said. "I haven't even left the province yet. And by the looks of things, I'm not going to."

"Are you allowed to tell me that?"

"I don't care." Clare stared at her primly made bed. She should have requested a room with no flowers on the bedspread.

"You should care. I thought you loved your job."

"I love it when everything's going right." If Clare ever found the perfect man, it would be someone who didn't feel compelled to give her advice about her own job. "Anyway, you couldn't visit, because my character is supposed to be single." And then to drive home the point: "In case I have to get close to someone for the assignment."

"So I shouldn't consider it cheating." Kevin was good-natured, which wasn't the response Clare had been aiming for.

"Exactly. But you have to stay faithful, because you're still the same Kevin Findlay. With a girlfriend named Clare."

"Girlfriend?" Kevin said. "I don't know what you're talking about. My girlfriend doesn't exist. She vaporized yesterday."

"That's not how it works." But Clare smiled despite herself.

"No? You'd better tell me how it works, then."

"Pretend I'm an actor. The real me and the real you have to stay faithful to each other. But if I'm in a movie — or in this case, a cover assignment — my character might have to interact romantically with another character in the movie."

"Or the cover assignment."

"Right."

"For artistic reasons."

"Yeah," Clare said. "Or for espionage."

"What a life you lead."

"It's pretty awesome."

"So what if I'm off on an electrical job, and — for argument's sake — a super-hot housewife wants to blow me and double my pay. Does that count as sleeping around in the name of a job? Or would that be cheating?"

"I think that's prostitution," Clare said. "Which would be a relationship-ender on a couple of levels."

"Fair enough." The sound of Kevin cracking a can of beer came through the phone. "Okay, so let's say she — it's the same hot housewife — calls me over because her outlet can't handle her plug-in vibrator, and it keeps shorting out or blowing a fuse. Is it cheating if I watch her use the vibrator until I can figure out the problem?"

"No," Clare said. "In that exact situation, you can watch the hot housewife masturbate with no negative impact upon our relationship. You can even help her out, if the situation demands it."

"Great. Well, thanks for that clarity."

"No problem." Clare was starting to feel both more and less homesick. "So we're good then? You and Clare, that is?"

"Yes." Kevin grumbled. "And Anastasia DeWitt, or whatever name you're operating under, is free to mess around with whomever she likes."

"Thanks." This was the best of both worlds, right?

Then why, when Clare tossed her clothes on the floor and crawled under that floral-print bedspread, did she feel like she was alone in both worlds?

SATURDAY / MARCH 19

ELEVEN
NOAH

Noah woke up ten minutes before his alarm was set to ring. It was a gray morning, which was fine with him. He was feeling kind of dim anyway.

He wasn't sure how he was going to handle Bert. He'd lost a pile of money the night before and he didn't have anything to show for it. Sure, there was the bet with Joe — but was that really for the job, or did Noah just want a piece of Tiffany and need the added push to ask her out? Fuck, he had to stop overthinking things. He should have stayed at NYU and done something normal for a career.

Noah made a coffee and waited for the knock on his door. Halfway through the cup, it came. He rose to let Bert in.

"Nice room." Bert bent down as if to remove his shoes but seemed to have a change of heart and left them on. Like the casino hotel carpet wasn't good enough for his designer socks. "Shame about the slob who's staying here."

"Sorry," Noah said. "Didn't realize cleanliness was part of the code."

"I should make a handbook." Bert took an armchair by the window and set two Tim Hortons cups on the table beside him. "So what have you learned?"

Noah coughed into his hands and steadied his nerves. "I have leads. I'm not ready to discuss them."

Bert shook his head. "Always the same with you people."

"We people? Because my mother's Jewish?"

"Yeah, I'm suddenly a racist prick, you schmuck. I mean, you people under thirty. Think you're so hot, you can run the whole show."

"I don't think I'm so hot." If he had, then a lifetime of being told otherwise by his father would have permanently cured him. "I don't want to waste your time unless I know my leads might go somewhere."

Bert sighed. "So don't waste my time telling me you have them. Are you going to sit down, or do you plan to keep pacing the whole time we're talking?"

Noah rolled his eyes as he took the other armchair. "If I tell you nothing, you'll think I'm pissing away your resources. I lost twelve grand last night, incidentally."

"Incidentally?" Bert's mouth opened, and stayed that way. "Did you lose it down a drain, or at a card table?"

"A card table. Obviously." Noah knew he was being rude. It was his natural reaction when he felt like a cornered fuck-up. Maybe one day that would change, but for now he just had to go with it. "I'm making headway with some of the name players."

"Like who?"

"Joe Mangan." Noah looked at his jeans and noticed a small red stain from the previous night's pizza. He flicked at it with his finger, but the sauce was embedded pretty deeply. "I have a prop bet with him. We both want to nail the same girl."

"Who's the girl?"

"Tiffany James. She just joined the tour. She's a trust fund princess, but she looks like she'd be fun in bed."

"Is she involved in the hole card mess?"

"I don't know," Noah said. "But I wouldn't mind getting messy with her."

"This isn't about you getting laid, Walker. It's about the family-friendly game of poker being compromised without our consent."

"Without our consent," Noah muttered. Of course the problem wasn't the game being compromised; it was that Bert and Co. weren't in on it.

"Tell me about Joe Mangan," Bert said. "He must be filthy rich from all his tournament successes."

"And celebrity endorsements. He's in beer commercials, car commercials; I wouldn't be surprised to see him in condom commercials. Nice guy until you get him talking."

Bert chuckled. "They're all nice when they want to take your money."

"Yeah. Joe's the guy who took most of mine last night."

"Never mind," Bert said. "It's going to be worth it in the end."

"You mean I'm going to make more cheating than I can lose playing?"

"Careful what you say." Bert looked around the room pointedly.

"I checked a million times. The room's not bugged."

Bert squinted, like he might see something Noah had missed.

"My god, you're like an old-time mobster."

"I like that comparison." Bert grinned. "You shouldn't knock those guys. They had style."

"Whatever. They all killed each other in the end."

"Make sure you don't get blindsided by the girl's body," Bert said, serious again. "I don't want you distracted from your mission."

"My mission. You make it sound like I'm going to Mars."

Noah blinked hard. "You have to be prepared to exploit this girl, if the situation calls for it."

"I know."

"You have to be prepared to see her as your enemy."

Noah stared at the rim of his coffee. "I know."

TWELVE
ELIZABETH

Elizabeth stood by the thick stone wall and gazed at the cloud of mist obliterating the bottom quarter of the falls. She could barely hear her thoughts over the thundering water gushing down in freefall for 170 feet, but she liked it that way. Her thoughts had been so dark recently; they could use some obscuring. She had no idea what might inspire someone to plummet over in a barrel, but she admired the courage of those who had tried.

Her peace was interrupted by a chirpy voice saying, "Morning."

Elizabeth reluctantly turned to see Tiffany James carrying a giant take-out coffee that made her small frame look even more miniature. Tiffany clearly hadn't showered yet, but even with messy hair and no make-up, the kid managed to look adorable.

"Morning back." Elizabeth was going to be nice to this girl if it killed her.

"Are you looking forward to Vancouver?" Tiffany joined Elizabeth at the wall and peered over the edge.

Elizabeth wondered how much force it would take to toss Tiffany in. "No."

"Have you ever been there?"

"Vancouver? Once or twice. I grew up there."

"Oh." Tiffany nodded knowingly, like she might have the first clue about Elizabeth's life. "And your family's still there?"

"They live in Richmond," Elizabeth said. "The same suburb as the River Rock Casino."

"That's convenient. Are you staying with them for the Vancouver leg of the tournament?"

"No," Elizabeth said sharply. The last time she'd played at the River Rock, she and Joe had slept in her old bedroom for almost a week. Before their visit was over, Elizabeth had been ready to scream at pretty much everyone. "Joe chartered a boat. We're keeping it moored at the casino."

"In winter?" Tiffany shivered dramatically in her short white ski jacket.

"It's nearly spring. Vancouver's mild. Not like Ontario, where the people and the temperature are cold and bitter." Elizabeth was pretty sure Tiffany was from Ontario. She had Entitled Little Toronto Bitch written all over her.

Tiffany shrugged. "I hope you don't get seasick."

Elizabeth hadn't thought about that. They'd be moored in the river, but the Fraser was tidal and the water could get rough.

"So why do you hate your family?"

"I never said I hated them." Elizabeth wished she hadn't opened her mouth. She wanted Tiffany to go away so she could go back to being miserable alone.

"You didn't?" Tiffany looked surprised. "Oh. Sorry. I guess I just thought . . . do you get along with them well, then?"

"I get along with them fine." Which was true, because Elizabeth very rarely saw them.

"Are they hard on you about your career choice?"

Elizabeth furrowed her brow. She was tempted to say something snide about not appreciating the invasive analysis, but luckily, Tiffany kept right on talking.

"My parents wanted me to go to university, plod along miserably and learn useless things about literature and history," Tiffany said. "So I get it."

"Thanks," Elizabeth forced herself to say. "So what does your dad do?"

"He's in the import business."

"Is he?" Elizabeth's interest became genuine. "Mine, too. What does your dad import?"

"Furniture mostly."

"Same here." Elizabeth was surprised by the coincidence. "What's your dad's company called? I probably know it."

"Um." Tiffany bit her lip. "I'd rather not say."

"Why not?" This was getting good.

"It's — well — the point of all this is for me to go off on my own. Make my way in the world as an individual, not as someone's daughter."

Elizabeth snorted. "With a trust fund?"

"Oh." Tiffany lowered her glance. "I guess I'm not that hardcore."

Elizabeth wrinkled one corner of her mouth as she tried to make sense of this puzzle. Tiffany was lying about something. Maybe she'd call her brother, have him root through their father's contacts and see what they could find.

"Does he own his own business?" Elizabeth watched Tiffany's face as she asked this. A yes meant that he would be easy enough to find — his last name would be James, like Tiffany. A no would make things trickier — if he worked for someone else's company, Tiffany's dad could be anyone.

"Yeah," Tiffany said. "But can we not talk about my family either? I'm like you — I'm here to get away from them."

Maybe the secret was that innocent. But Elizabeth doubted it.

"You're doing well so far." Elizabeth forced cheer into her voice. "You're still in the game after the first day. That's better than I did in my first major tournament."

"Yeah?" Tiffany looked at Elizabeth and her eyes lit up like a kid's. "I'm doing better than you in this tournament, too."

Elizabeth smiled, because the alternative was punching Tiffany in the mouth. "Good for you."

THIRTEEN
CLARE

"Tell me about yourself," Joe Mangan said to Clare. "What's your favorite food?"

Clare looked quickly at her pocket nines and stayed quiet. It was hard not to laugh at Joe: in place of the previous day's hockey gear, he was now wearing a giant fruit basket on his head. She wanted to ask him why the costumes. Were they a publicity stunt, so he maximized his camera time? Or did he think they disarmed his competitors and drew their attention away from the game?

But these cards were important. Clare had to focus hard and make it past the bubble — that turning point between losing her entry fee and getting paid out a portion of the prize pool — or stupid Cloutier would pull her from the case. She had to hang on tight, playing only the best hands possible, until five or six more players were eliminated.

"You like Italian?" Joe said. "You look like you can handle spice."

Clare said nothing.

"Maybe Mexican? I'd say let's go for Indian, but curry's not my thing. I feel like my clothes smell for three days afterwards."

There was a nine on the board, plus an ace and a king, and Clare put in a bet for half the pot.

"Come on, honey. I want to know who I'm playing with." Joe's voice lifted playfully. "This game doesn't have to be so cold."

Clare thought she could beat whatever Joe held. He liked his hand; he didn't want to fold. Clare had him on either two pair or a flush draw. If she played this right, maybe she could double through him. If she played it wrong, he'd fold and leave her with a tiny pot.

She smiled benignly. "Ask me anything you like when I'm not in a hand. If you want to know more about me, we can grab a coffee after the game."

"Ah," he said. "Confidence. I fold."

Why had she opened her mouth? Clare mucked her trips and accepted the small pot when it was pushed her way.

"Not gonna show me what you won with?"

"Not a chance." Clare was disgusted with herself for giving her hand away.

"You played well last night," Joe said. "A couple times at MacCauley's, you made plays that I wasn't sure were genius or dumb luck."

"Please. You guys ate me for breakfast." Clare wanted to believe she was making good plays — she'd been studying the game intensely — but she knew when she was outclassed by a million.

Joe tossed some chips into the center and covered his hole cards with a protector chip. "Did someone say breakfast?" He pulled a banana from his hat and tossed it to Clare. "You should play in our Vancouver side game, too."

"Are you suffering so badly for weak competition?" Clare opened the banana and took a bite. It tasted good, considering it had been in someone's hat. She looked at her cards and saw aces. Her heart started thumping. She hoped Joe couldn't hear it across the table.

"Partly," Joe said. "But if you want to make a living at poker, you're going to have to get good at cash games. Tournaments have too much luck involved. That banana looks great in your mouth, by the way."

"Glad you like it." Clare toyed with her stack, wondering if sex was Joe's weakness. More likely not — he was probably trying to throw her off her game. Joe had raised, so Clare decided to play cautiously and re-raise with her aces.

Joe pulled a plum from his hat and started chomping. "All business, huh? That's cool. I figured you must be smarter than you look. Though what I can't seem to make sense of is why you're here, and not off touring the art galleries of Europe while you sort out who you want to be when you grow up."

"I don't like art. And people who study it are pretentious."

"Ah," Joe said, calling Clare's raise and closing the pre-flop betting. "A *truly* smart rich kid. I can see why T-Bone's pissed at you."

Clare rolled her eyes. "Has the almighty cowboy never lost a hand before? Or am I supposed to cower in his presence?"

The flop came king-ten-three. Two hearts were on the board. It wasn't great for her aces — the drawing possibilities to straights and flushes were dangerous. She probably still had the best hand at the moment, though.

"Not cower, exactly . . ." Joe looked at the flop, frowned, and checked. "Maybe stand back in worship."

"I read T-Bone's book. It wasn't exactly worthy of worship."

"Yeah?" Joe said. "Good book?"

"It sucked. I didn't learn a thing about how to play poker." Clare was pretty sure she was supposed to bet here; she just wasn't sure how much. She went with half the pot.

"You should tell T-Bone that," Joe said, calling quickly. "Maybe it will make him like you more."

"I don't care if T-Bone likes me."

"No kidding." Joe took a sip of Coke as they watched the turn come down: the ace of hearts. It gave Clare trips, which was nice, but it also put a flush and a straight possibility on the board

— both of which would beat Clare's hand. "Have you read my book?" Joe asked.

Clare shook her head. "Is it any good?"

"Probably not. It was ghost-written and I haven't even read the final published version. So you mean it about that coffee? Or would you rather go for a beer? I think beer's more personable." Joe stared at the community cards, wrinkling his mouth. "I'm thinking I should go all in."

Clare said nothing. She hoped he didn't go all in. This close to the bubble, with her career riding in the balance, she'd have to believe him and fold.

"Nah," Joe said. "Check. So — beer?"

"I'll take a rain check," Clare said, checking quickly.

"Perfect," Joe said. "It rains a lot in Vancouver, so I'll consider that a date."

"Consider it what you like." Clare grinned, though she'd been trying not to. The real Clare would love to have Joe as a one-nighter — he was a sleazeball, but he was seriously fun to flirt with — but with his girlfriend treating her with that suspicious mix of warmth and derision, there was no way screwing Joe could be a smart move. "And hey, maybe bring Elizabeth, so she doesn't get the wrong idea."

"Why? Do you have a wrong idea?"

The river card came. The ten of spades, giving Clare the full house she'd been hoping for. In a perfect world, Joe had the flush or the straight that had scared her on the turn, because now Clare could beat it, and he'd still be willing to commit a good portion of his stack.

"You're inviting me in front of all these people." Clare cast her glance around the poker table. A skinny kid in a backwards base-ball cap smirked when she caught his glance, and a disheveled academic type at the end of the table nodded at Clare with a glint in his eye. The table was clearly interested in their conversation.

"Hmm." Joe tilted his head to one side. He glanced at Clare's remaining chips and bet about half the pot. "I don't think these people will talk. I think we should go out one-on-one."

"I'll think about it." Clare pushed her chips all in. She bit her lip, clasped her hands, trying to look nervous so he'd call. "As in, I'll contemplate how socially suicidal I'm feeling."

"How is going out with me social suicide?" Joe leaned back in his chair and folded his arms across his chest, studying Clare, eyeing the cards on the table. "Most people would think a date with me was the opposite."

"I like Elizabeth," Clare said.

"Why? Lizzie hates you."

"But she pretends she doesn't, and that fascinates me."

"Ah, come on. One date. You might even want to have sex with me at the end."

Clare smiled, this time on purpose. "I'd rather fuck your girl-friend."

"Cool," Joe said. "I'll try to arrange that. By the way, I call. I'm sorry to knock you out of the game like this. I hope we can still be friends."

"What do you mean?" Clare flipped her cards and showed Joe her full house. She felt her heart sink when Joe's confidence didn't waver. "Don't tell me you have a royal flush."

"I don't have a royal flush." Joe flipped over two tens. "But my quads still beat you."

FOURTEEN
NOAH

Noah lifted a few of his chips and let them slide through his fingers back to their place in the stack. He was relieved to see Tiffany walk away from her table, defeated. Not that he wanted her to lose. But if she busted out before the bubble, she probably wasn't cheating.

So who was?

Noah looked at the players at his table. Most had their ears free. One woman was listening to an iPod Shuffle, but unless it was a cleverly disguised receiver, Noah was pretty sure she wouldn't be able to pick up the cheating info stream on it. A middle-aged accountant type was wearing a hands-free earpiece for a cell phone — which was dumb, because if your phone rang when you were playing, it was a ten-minute penalty. But an earpiece was too obvious for a high-level cheater — the guy probably just thought it looked cool. What aroused Noah's suspicion most were the thick red glasses on George Bigelow. Any earring or eyeglass arm could be set up to receive a Bluetooth signal.

Noah said to George, who was sitting to his right, "You're that guy who wrote *Suicide Kings*."

George nodded, his gaze still on the cards. "Crap title, right?

My publisher thought it was catchier than my working title, *Ace Magnets*."

"I agree with your publisher." Noah grinned in what he hoped was a gushing fan way. "The book was great. It helped my game a lot."

"I wouldn't call it a masterpiece."

Noah liked George on first impression. He was quirky, kind of hip in a retro-geek way, and he could self-deprecate like the best of them.

"I disagree," Noah said. "Your writing's cool and clever. You ever think of writing something else? You know, not about poker."

George smiled broadly. "I'm working on a novel now."

"What's it about?"

"Oh," George said. "A writer never talks about his current work."

Totally not true. Noah's mother had a million writer friends, most of whom had verbal diarrhea when it came to their current work. But Noah respected George's right to silence. And he was just as happy not to hear a long-winded saga.

Noah switched topics. "You're dating Fiona Gallagher, right?"

George shook his head. "We broke up a few months ago."

Shit. The guy looked really sad about it. "Sorry, man. Is it hard to be on the same scene? You must see her every day."

George shrugged. "We're adults."

Noah went in for the kill. "So where's Fiona while the tournament is playing? Does she sit in her booth and watch the hidden cameras?"

"Her techie does that. A kid called Oliver. She hates his guts, actually. Don't know why she doesn't fire the guy. Fiona stays out front and does exit interviews as people bust out of the game."

Noah nodded. His questioning line may have sounded clumsy, but he had the answer he'd been after: Oliver the techie had the hole card signal live. Was he the only person who did?

Noah folded his queen-ten. In late position, the hand was playable, but he wanted to play safe. Even if a timid game was unlikely to net him first place, it would keep him in the game longer. And until he found this signal, he was going to learn more at the table than away from it.

FIFTEEN
CLARE

Clare scowled at her reflection in the casino bathroom mirror. She'd busted out in thirty-eighth place: two off the bubble. If she'd been smart and played conservatively — if she hadn't been suckered into going all in with her aces — she would have finished in the money. And followed the tour to Vancouver. Now she was going home to boredom.

She hadn't even played the hand badly and that's what was so fucking unfair. Poker was luck at least half the time. So because of rotten luck, Clare's career was basically over. Fucking Cloutier. Clare could do this job if he wasn't always standing in her way telling her she couldn't.

She had one night left in the hotel. Cloutier the giant asshole had said she could check out the next morning — probably because it was too late to cancel the room without a penalty. So Clare had one night to find a critical piece of information from someone on this scene — something, anything, that would render Clare invaluable to the case, so that pulling her would be to the case's detriment.

She tugged her cosmetic bag from her fuschia leather purse. As she unscrewed the cap on her mineral foundation, a tall redhead strode into the washroom and set her purse on the sink two over from Clare's.

"Fiona, right?" Clare said.

The woman turned, gave a small smile, and nodded.

"I love your exit interviews," Clare said. "How do you come up with those hilarious questions on the spot like that?"

Fiona squirted soap onto her hands and lathered them intensely. "I pretend we're at a party that the audience is getting an exclusive glimpse of. Everyone likes to feel like they're in on the action. Are you playing in the tournament?"

"I was," Clare said. "Until Joe Mangan took all my chips an hour ago."

"Yeah, Joe can be a bitch." Fiona dried her hands on a paper towel and pulled a small round brush from her purse.

"It's cool," Clare said. "It's my first tournament. I can't expect to win right away."

"Right on." Fiona nodded. "The Zen approach."

Clare wasn't sure what was Zen about being realistic. Maybe Fiona had just smoked a joint and thought everything was Zen. She didn't smell like she had, though — she smelled like expensive perfume.

"How did you get into poker broadcasting?" Clare dabbed liquid blush along her cheekbones with the sponge, like her new handler Amanda had shown her. "Did you go to journalism school?"

"Ha ha. No. I started podcasting one summer with my friend at home in Denver. It was the summer between undergrad and law school — or what would have been the summer between them, if I'd ended up going to law school. The podcast was supposed to be this big joke. We nicknamed the players on TV — not their serious poker names, like Devil Fish or Kid Poker — we called them stuff like Fat MoFo and Skinny Crack Ho. T-Bone Jones was the Creaking Cowboy."

"Creaking?"

"Because he's so old he has to oil his bones."

Clare grinned, smudging her blush a bit. She wiped the excess away with her index finger — hopefully that's what you were supposed to do. "Why did you lose those names?"

"Sold out to go corporate. I kind of hate myself for it, but the money's way better, so what else would I do? The only name that stuck was Joe's. We called him Pretty Boy, 'cause he's, you know, kind of homosexual-looking, and now the industry's adopted it, so I'm allowed to use that on my broadcast."

"Awesome."

"Yeah, the whole thing's kind of awesome. I still can't believe I basically get to party for a living. How about you? Why are you here?"

Clare drew in her breath. "I'm testing a theory. I've been reading up on poker, and I think if I play in ten tournaments in one year, I can net a higher profit than if I'd invested a hundred thousand in the stock market."

"You have a hundred grand to toss into a theory?" Fiona lifted her eyebrows.

"And then some." Clare nodded. "But a hundred grand is what I convinced my dad was a reasonable amount to invest. It's my money, technically, but since he's spent his life earning the money to give me the trust fund in the first place, I wouldn't have taken the risk if he didn't green-light it. It wouldn't seem fair."

Fiona dropped her brush back into her purse and fished out a colored lip gloss. "How the hell did you get him to green-light a poker tour?"

Clare gave Fiona a lopsided grin. "My brother has lost nearly half a million of his fund in the dumbest investments you could imagine. He thinks he's god's gift to the club district — well, he basically is, but as a financial donor, not as an ingenious entrepreneur. I guess my dad figured he could allow me the same room to explore. And he liked that I made him a presentation with graphs and flow charts. Shows him I'm taking it seriously, looking at this as a business plan."

"That's, like, seriously cool," Fiona said. "To convince a cold hard businessman that his sweet little daughter should go make her way on the poker scene. Kudos, man."

"I'll take the kudos when I win. So far I'm down ten grand with nothing to show for it."

"We should party," Fiona said. "What are you doing tonight?"

Clare put away her makeup. "Taking poker lessons from Mickey Mills."

"Mickey's old. He'll be in bed by eleven. We should hook up after that for drinks."

"Yeah, sounds fun." As Clare gave Fiona her false name and the text details for Tiffany's phone, it occurred to her that this exchange had been far too easy. Clare knew her own motive — to embed herself in the poker culture deeply enough that she'd be a clear asset to the case. But Fiona had been the one who'd suggested drinks. Why?

SIXTEEN
GEORGE

George was thrilled with his twenty-sixth place finish. He'd played his cards more boldly than usual, and the aggression had paid off. He was pumped to dive into his so-called fiction.

He had almost reached the elevator when Mickey approached him. "Have you reconsidered my offer?"

"Was I supposed to?" George pressed the Up button.

"'Course you were. You gotta come to your senses. We can make millions together."

George smirked. "Biographies of poker players don't even make hundreds."

"Because the ones on the market are crap. Have you ever stopped to think that maybe the first top-notch poker biography has yet to be written? By you and about me?"

"No," George said. "That's not something I stopped my life to think about."

"Well maybe you should, instead of prancing around telling everyone you want to write fiction."

"I don't prance." Where was the elevator?

"You don't make anyone feel like you want to be here. Nobody likes a snob, George."

"Do you get most things you want by insulting the person you want them from?" George asked, and realized that yes, Mickey probably did.

"It's how I got Loni." Mickey smiled almost fondly. "Found her in a bar one night, asked her if she was as easy as she looked."

George groaned. "You probably lost her by insulting her, too." But what did George know? The longest he'd kept a girlfriend had been Fiona Gallagher for two years, and he still wasn't over her.

"*Au contraire*," said Mickey, in an accent that was anything but French. "I lost Loni by being too permissive."

"She was your wife, not your dog. They get to do what they like nowadays."

The elevator arrived. George got on.

"Yeah, well. They shouldn't." Mickey followed George into the elevator. "You know what my favorite T-shirt says? 'If I wanted your opinion, I'd take my dick out of your mouth.'"

George snorted. "How are you still alive?"

"You mean, how am I not the Poker Choker's latest victim?"

"What I meant was why has no one beaten you to death for your mouth? But in light of recent events, I guess my remark was off-color."

"Where'd you learn to talk so formal?" Mickey adopted a mock-nasal accent that George hoped he didn't have: "'In light of recent events,' blah blah blah."

"Fucking hell. Sorry I tried to apologize."

"That was an apology? Asking how come I'm not dead? And *I'm* the one people consider uncouth . . ."

The elevator bounced to a stop at George's floor. George stepped out, held the door open, and used his arm to block Mickey from following him. "Was there something you wanted?"

"I told you." Mickey furrowed his brow. "I want to know if you've come to your senses."

"I have," George said. "Next time you invite me for coffee, I plan to say no."

"Would it help if I had information about some players who may or may not be cheating?"

Of course it would help. But George couldn't jump on that too quickly. "Information the rest of us don't have?" George asked. "Names, details, a method maybe. Or is this the same speculation we've all heard too many times to count?"

"This is brand new. Thing is, I don't know for absolute certain that what I saw is what I saw."

"Of course you don't." George's arm was getting tired.

"You going to let me off this elevator?" Mickey moved closer and George could smell peanuts on his breath. "At least hear what I have to say."

"Why should I?" George was anxious to get back to his writing before his good mood got spoiled. But he also wanted Mickey's information.

"Stop blocking the door and I'll tell you. I have beans to spill. Information that might help with your oh-so-secret pet project."

How did Mickey know about his writing project?

"Don't give me that look. I read faces for a living. I can see your ears perk up when anyone talks about hole card cameras, cheating, and your precious friend Fiona. You're like a dog who hears the word 'food.' What else would you be working on?"

George glared at Mickey. "What does Fiona have to do with this?"

"Let me come in for a coffee."

George unbarred Mickey's exit route. "I can't guarantee you'll like the coffee."

"I can't guarantee you'll like what you hear." Mickey scrambled after George down the hallway. "But if you do, can we talk about my book?"

Motherfucker. George used his key card to open the door. "Of course we can."

SEVENTEEN
NOAH

The sports bar was noisy with happy hour drinkers. Noah had to speak more loudly than he was comfortable with, but Bert was comfortable, so that was the main thing.

"Twenty players left and I'm still in the game."

"So you can play poker," Bert said, shrugging his shoulders.

Noah leaned forward and rested his elbows on the table. "I know how the scam is going down."

Bert twirled a finger, meaning, *Get to the fucking point.*

"You know Fiona Gallagher? The slutty redhead who anchors the tournament on TV?"

Bert arched his eyebrows — were they getting some gray in them? — which Noah took as an invitation to continue.

"Fiona has a techie — this British kid, Oliver Doakes. He sits in a booth and he can see the players' hole cards while the hands are being played. I think Oliver is sending hole card info to select players through a wireless broadcast — or encrypted podcast — or some other electronic way, during the game."

"How would that work?" Bert leaned in too, so his elbows almost touched Noah's.

Noah inched back a bit. "The cheating players would pick up the signal on a wireless device, say a phone or a pocket computer. Maybe an iPod Touch. They'd have a code to access the broadcast, so not just any random clown could find it. They'd transmit the signal to an earpiece — probably via Bluetooth, but it could be as simple as iPhone earbuds — and they'd know what everyone else at their table was holding."

Bert drummed his fingers on the wood laminate table. "I don't see why iPods are even legal in these games. Is this just a Canadian thing?"

Noah smiled patiently. "No. Walkmans and iPods are legal in games around the world. They minimize distraction from guys like Joe Mangan, who make a project of turning their opponents' minds away from cards."

"Yeah, well, they scream cheating opportunity to me, and I barely play the game, so you don't get any brownie points for ingenuity. And what do you suggest we do with your theory? I don't get what's new about it. We already knew people were cheating. We already figured it had something to do with the hole card cameras. We already knew who had access to that — maybe not by name, but yay, the kid's called Oliver. Not like we can walk up to Oliver and tell him to give us what he knows."

"No?" Noah said. "I thought that was exactly our style. We tie him down, we search his room, we scare him into saying what he knows. Maybe hold a gun to his head if he refuses to cooperate. Then we go home heroes."

Bert leaned back and folded his arms across his chest. "Walker, what are you doing here?"

Noah met Bert's eye, surprised.

"You act like you're thirteen, like this is all beneath you. I'm starting to feel like I'm in this game alone."

"What the fuck?" Noah said. "You're not even *in* the game. I'm winning money, and I think I've just figured out how I can win even more. If either of us is useless here, it's you."

Bert sipped his Scotch. Who drank neat Scotch at a sports

bar? "I know this isn't brain surgery, like your family had preciously hoped for you, but you're going to find this job much easier when you can accept yourself for doing it."

Noah was tempted to ask if he looked like he wanted a shrink or a life coach. But he opted away from sarcasm and said, "You want to hear the rest?"

"Sure." Bert nodded slowly. "Especially if you have a plan to (a) identify the cheaters, and (b) get the signal so you can listen in."

"Yup. Both. I'll break into Oliver's and Fiona's hotel rooms. I think between them, I should find the info I need — ideally the encryption code, but if not that, then something — to figure out where to go next. Once I'm cheating, it's easy to spot the other cheaters. They're the guys who make decisions that seem a bit too savvy."

Bert took a long, slow sip of whiskey. He looked like he thought he was at a speakeasy, except booze had been legal for all of his fifty-six years. "And if Fiona and Oliver aren't dumb enough to leave incriminating evidence lying around?"

Noah sighed. "Then I break into players' rooms."

"Looking for . . ."

"Earpieces?" Noah shrugged. "Trouble is, I don't think the earpieces will be obvious. It's a bit 1980s spy game, but an eyeglass arm or an earring — or even a tiny stick-on tab — could do the job easily. And I doubt I'll find encryption codes, because those would probably be on the smartphones or pocket computers, which would be on the players at all times. But like I said, I think Fiona's and Oliver's rooms will yield something."

"Sounds like a plan," Bert said. "Think you can get into either room tonight?"

"I think I should wait until Vancouver."

Bert shook his head. "We don't have that much time."

"What?" Noah was confused. Bert was normally allergic to haste; it felt strange that he would recommend it all of a sudden. "Since when was speed an issue? I'm making money for you.

Even if I'm the next guy eliminated from the tournament, I've already made back everything I lost last night *and* enough to pay Joe if I lose the bet about Tiffany."

"This isn't about job sustainability. I got orders from above to get in and get out. With three murders already, Canadian cops should be all over this thing, whether or not they know about the cheating. Fact that they're not means the scene is probably infested with undercovers."

"But . . ." Noah cast his eyes down onto his beer bottle to keep himself from laughing as he pictured undercover cops scuttling around a poker room like cockroaches.

"You're not here to make money for the cause and come home. The money's a perk, but you know what we're after."

Noah nodded. "The method."

EIGHTEEN
CLARE

"Sorry I'm late, kid." Mickey slipped his stocky body past Clare, who had been waiting outside his hotel room for nearly fifteen minutes. "George Bigelow is writing a book about me. Our conversation dragged on longer than it should have."

"That's exciting." Clare followed Mickey into the room, feeling both defeated and determined. She didn't need poker lessons if she wasn't moving on to the Vancouver game. But maybe she'd learn something else from Mickey — something murder-related — that would force Cloutier to keep her on the job.

Mickey took off his jacket and hung it carefully in the closet. "Let's hope the book's exciting, or it won't sell. And now I'm gonna turn you into a little poker genius. You want some peanuts?" He grabbed a large jar from the dresser and handed it to Clare. "I got three more of these in my suitcase, so eat up."

Despite the image of jars of peanuts hanging out in a suitcase full of dirty clothes, Clare poured some nuts into her hand. She didn't really give a shit if Tiffany would or wouldn't eat them. Tiffany might not exist by morning.

"I'm going to set up the cards like a full table of poker." Mickey cleared the phone and other items from the desk. There wasn't much to clear — the room was immaculate. Clare could picture Mickey's sweaters folded perfectly in drawers, pressed pants hung carefully behind closed closet doors. "Only you're going to be all the players. You want a Coke or something? Help yourself to the minibar."

Clare took a Coke from the fridge.

"And hand me a Bud. But Rule Number One: never fucking drink while you're gambling."

"Weren't you doing both last night?"

"When you're winning thirty grand a night you can allow yourself the privilege. But hell, I probably would have made fifty if I'd been sober."

Mickey dealt nine pairs of cards face-down onto the small desk. He placed a dealer button on top of one pair and big and little blind buttons on two others. He gave each set of cards a little chip stack. "Pick up the first hand after the blinds."

Clare looked at an ace and a jack, and showed Mickey.

"What do you do?" Mickey asked.

"Raise."

"In first position? I thought you'd read some poker books."

Clare was having trouble caring. "What would you do? Call?"

"Fold it faster than a housewife in a laundry race. The hand may look pretty, but it's more likely to get you in trouble by being second best. You're out of position and you don't want no part of it. Fold."

Clare mucked the cards.

"Pick up the second hand."

She showed Mickey a pair of threes. She didn't think too hard before saying, "Fold."

"You kidding? In an unraised pot with healthy stack sizes?" Mickey clicked his teeth, like this was going to be harder than he'd thought.

"But threes are so low," Clare said. "The book I just finished said not to play low pairs in early position. Someone's bound to flop a higher pair if they're not already starting with one. The odds of flopping a set are seven point five to one."

"At least you know some math."

"I think I'd rather be psychic." Clare threw her hands in the air in her best spoiled princess style. "Can't I just figure out a way to know what other people have?"

Mickey's brow furrowed. "You shouldn't joke about that."

Clare set down the threes. This might actually be something. She tried to keep her voice playful as she said, "Why so sensitive?"

Mickey shook his head. "Forget about it."

Clare met his eye with what she hoped was a cajoling grin. "Come on. I touched a nerve. What was it?"

"You should stop fucking smiling, too. There are people playing like they're psychic, and not because they've been gifted with any ESP."

"Um . . . ?" Clare felt her eyes bug. Cloutier was going to love this. "You mean they're cheating?"

Mickey snorted. "Yeah, kid. That's what I mean."

"Call me thick," Clare said slowly, as if it was just occurring to her that the whole world might not be honest. "But if everyone knows people are cheating, why is anyone playing in the tournament?"

"Because 'everyone' doesn't know. And those of us netting profits are still netting profits, so there's money to be made. Just not as much."

Mickey lit a cigarette. Clare fished her pack from her purse and followed suit.

"Is it only the Canadian Classic?" Clare asked. "Or are they cheating in other tournaments, too?"

"Shit, I've already said too much. Listen, kid, people are dying on this scene. Have you heard about that?"

Clare wasn't sure how to answer that. The deaths had been publicized, but not widely. "I heard about a woman in Halifax," she said. "Have there been more?"

Mickey nodded. "Two more. I think it's safe to say it's a serial killer."

"So why is anyone still here? Is poker so alluring that it's worth risking your life to lose your money to a cheater?"

Mickey snorted. "When you put it that way, you mind helping me pack my bag?" But he didn't pull his suitcase open. "There's a few reasons people stick around. For the common guy off the street — take you, for example — you didn't know none of this was going on, or you wouldn't have signed up. Am I right?"

Clare nodded.

"So you got the innocents. Then you got the predators — the few of us who know our win rate is gonna stay high no matter if a couple extra guys are suddenly poker geniuses and they're in the money with us because they're cheating."

Clare nodded again.

"And the middling pros — they play okay, they net profit long-term, but they'll never be world class — they get the hell off the scene and go south to the American games. So with the middle knocked out, you got two classes of players — the champs who you know to play cautious against, and the weekenders who can't play worth shit, they're just here because their wife bought them an entry for their fiftieth birthday, or whatever. Playing suddenly gets way easier, it's like taking lollipops from babies. Yeah, I busted out of the Niagara game early, but that's poker — luck is always gonna be a factor. Overall, since the cheating started, I'm making more than before. And *not* from cheating."

"That sounds so cold." Clare shivered for real.

"Life is cold," Mickey said. "This game gets coated in Disneyland colors — every Friday night poker player thinks they're the next success story waiting to break out from the pack — but the reality is most people, if they play the game long enough, are gonna lose their shirt first and their house last."

Clare wondered if Willard Oppal, before he died, had stumbled onto the cheating scam as well. She should ask Cloutier if he'd said something to any of his handlers.

"So," Clare said, feeling like she was jumping into an icy swimming pool with no bottom, "is the cheating related to the murders?"

"That's the million-dollar question. That's what I'd like to know."

For the first time, Clare wondered if Cloutier might be doing her a favor by pulling her from the case. But the thought was fleeting — she wanted to stay.

"And another thing, kid: you need to get yourself some shades."

"Sunglasses?"

Mickey nodded. "You got these great eyes. Everyone loves to look at 'em. But we can read your emotion loud and clear. And when you got a great hand, we know right off we can fold."

NINETEEN
GEORGE

George's fingers trembled on the keys of his computer. If Mickey had been telling the truth about Fiona, the whole game had just changed.

But he'd get to that soon enough. First, he had one more death to write.

September 2010

Calgary, Alberta

Jimmy Streets.

You're alone in your hotel room. It's midnight and you've had a few. The lights are on. You're watching *Bound* on cable and jerking off.

Your performance at the tables today was stellar as always. You're a seventy-year-old card-playing machine, and you've been on the scene since it was dangerous.

But you don't care about poker now. You're about to get off, and Jennifer Tilly is the image in your head.

There's a knock at your door. You try to ignore it -- you're so close to coming, Jen can practically taste it. But the knock becomes insistent.

"Who the fuck is there?" you shout.

"It's me." A familiar voice. A man's. You have to answer.

"Gimme a minute!" you yell.

You wish you could go back to Jennifer -- a particular shame, since you'll never get to see her again.

You pull up your jeans. You open the door for your killer.

The cops write you off quicker than Josie. Like doctors write off lung cancer patients with little emotion, you're seen as a victim of the world you chose to play in. And you're old -- the public doesn't weep for a man in his seventies. No connection is drawn between your death and Josie's. Why would it be?

George frowned at his page. Maybe the line about age was harsh. Jimmy was dead, but there were other people in their seventies who might not like to feel disposable. Could George afford to offend an entire demographic of potential book buyers in one go? He highlighted the line; his finger hovered above the Delete key. In the end he left it in; this first draft was supposed to be edit-free.

And anyway, George didn't give a shit about Jimmy Streets or any of the Poker Choker's victims. He'd care again, but for now he had a more pressing mystery to worry about:

```
Fiona Gallagher. With your perfect blow-dried
hair and your stunning little smiles that make
everyone around you feel like they're not good
enough to eat the fucking dirt you tread on. How
are you involved?
```

TWENTY
CLARE

Fiona fingered the stem of her martini glass as her gaze wandered somewhere Clare couldn't follow. "This scene didn't use to be so antisocial. Until July . . ." Fiona sighed. "Until July, there'd be a bunch of us hanging out in bars like this on any given night. Now everyone keeps to themselves. Couples couple off, gamblers stay at the tables . . ."

Clare picked up her cosmo and took a slow sip. It was pretty good — stronger than it looked. It didn't taste pink. "What happened in July?"

"My best friend died. Josie."

"I'm so sorry." Total cliché, but what else could Clare say? *Did you kill her?* wouldn't sound right. "Are people still really sad?"

"They're too selfish to be sad. Josie's long forgotten. Two more have died since her."

"Mickey told me." Clare chose her words carefully. "He said there's a serial killer. I'm kind of thinking I should pack it in — maybe invest my trust fund in something more normal, like university."

"Yeah." Fiona's voice was almost wistful. "If my career wasn't here, I would have packed up long ago."

"But this afternoon, you seemed so thrilled to be here."

Fiona smiled sadly. "This afternoon I was working. I was still miked up in the bathroom — and even if I hadn't been, I was in smile-for-the-camera mode."

"Oh." Clare wanted a cigarette, but the bar was non-smoking and Fiona didn't smoke.

"So why the Canadian Classic?" Fiona asked. "I would have thought with a trust fund like yours, you'd want to try the European tour. North American casinos are so grubby. I take three showers a day and I still feel gross."

"I figured I'd start close to home," Clare said. "But maybe that was dumb. Why isn't this serial killer in the press? You'd think that would be huge headlines."

Fiona shook her head slightly, like she had no idea what the outside world might care about. "Josie's death made headlines in a couple Maritime papers."

"But when the others died . . ." Clare wasn't sure if she was smart to urge the conversation in this direction. She knew why the story had never taken off — the RCMP had never publicly acknowledged that this was a serial killer, and no journalist had made it their mission to find out. She didn't want Fiona — a minor public figure with access to TV publicity — to run with the story herself.

"No one cared about the second guy. Sorry — I'm sure that sounds horrible if you never knew him, but Jimmy Streets was a snake. And the third guy, Willard Oppal — we're pretty sure he was a cop."

Clare tried to keep her eyes steady when they wanted to bug out from her face. She'd known Willard Oppal must have been made to get murdered, but she never dreamed his cover had been blown so wide open that it was cocktail conversation. *That* was something Cloutier might be interested to know.

Clare tried to reason like Tiffany would. "But if he'd been a cop, and he'd been murdered, other cops would have pounced on the scene. Everyone knows you can't kill a cop and get away with it."

Fiona swiveled her bar stool to face Clare. "Do you know how much tax money casinos generate? I was thinking of doing a piece on the murders, but this tournament is my livelihood. I don't want people scared away until I have something better lined up. Take you for example." Fiona's eyes ran the length of Clare's body, from her new chin-length haircut down to her surprisingly comfortable black heels. "You would never have come onto this scene if you thought there was a serial killer running rampant."

"True."

"Word is that half a dozen of the new players on the scene are undercovers. Obviously not you, though." Fiona laughed. "That would be a seriously deep cover."

Clare grinned. For the first time, she thought Amanda might have an ounce of intelligence for the way she'd crafted Tiffany's character. "What about the people who do know? How come they're not all parachuting the hell out of here?"

"It's too surreal." Fiona took a long, slow sip of her cosmo. "Plus — this is the strange part, at least to me — the pattern isn't like most other serial killings. Josie was murdered in July, Jimmy was September, and Willard was January. You get what I'm saying? If there's any trend, it's toward slowing down, not speeding up. You know anything about serial killers?"

Clare shook her head.

"I do," Fiona said. "My plan was to go into criminal law, and I minored in psych in my undergrad. Serial killers — the kind who kill because they're compelled to, biologically — kill more frequently as they go along. It's like a drug they develop a tolerance for — they need a stronger hit more often to keep themselves satisfied. This could be an exception — something about the second murder might have scared him for a while. But more likely it means people are getting killed for a reason. You'll only be a victim if you get in the Choker's way."

"How do I stay out of his way?" Clare asked.

Fiona shrugged. "Play by the rules."

Which of course was not an option for Clare.

She tried one more line of questioning. It was maybe too bold, but she needed answers fast if she didn't want to get sent home in the morning. "Is it true that some players are cheating?"

Fiona uncrossed and crossed her legs on her barstool. "How would I know? I'm not a poker player."

"Fair enough." Clare plunged along. "Hey, I've always wanted to know something, when I've watched poker on TV. When the game is on, can you or the other commentators see the hole cards live, or do you have to wait for tapes? It sounds so real, the way you commentate — it sounds like the tension is live — but then it seems like it would be too risky for security if the cards were being shown to someone as it happened."

Fiona smiled thinly. "You're right. I can't see them."

"Can anyone?"

"I don't think so. Maybe a techie, to make sure the feed is working. But they wouldn't be sitting there watching."

"Makes sense. It must be such a rush, to be on the inside of the game like you are."

"Not really." Fiona's shoulders had tensed and her eyes had become more focused. Clare wasn't sure when the shift had occurred, but she'd been more relaxed when they'd been talking about murder. "If I had the choice to make over again, I would have gone to law school."

"Really? Because you know, murders aside — I don't mean to be a suck-up — but you seem like a natural on camera."

"Maybe I'm good at it, but this job is like living at summer camp. Repetitive recreation with no substance."

Clare had never gone to summer camp, and had never known the luxury of too much down time.

"I probably use more brainpower asleep when I'm dreaming than I need in my day job. I'm not complaining — it's my own choices that got me here — but Sudokus aren't cutting it anymore. I need to get back to the land of the living, if only so my brain synapses have a direction to fire in."

And Clare needed to get back to her task at hand. "So who are these techies?"

Fiona looked at Clare hard. "Don't even go there. As long as hole card cameras have been around, there have been people trying to beat them. No one has succeeded."

"OMG," Clare said, nearly gagging on the wording she'd chosen for Tiffany. "I'm sorry if you thought — that's totally not what I meant."

"Good." Fiona arched her eyebrows. "Because there are easier ways to make money. Like rocket science."

"I have a trust fund." Clare pulled her snottiest look from her repertoire. "I don't need to cheat. I'm just interested in the mechanics of how the game is run. In case I ever open a casino."

Fiona's laugh sounded to Clare like the smoothest witch's cackle in the world. "Just how big is your trust fund?"

SUNDAY / MARCH 20

TWENTY-ONE
ELIZABETH

"Did I tell you recently how amazing you are?" Elizabeth reached past Joe to get the soap. She loved showering with him. The way he lathered himself up and liked to slip and slide against her made her feel like they were two seals playing in the river. It also turned her on.

"No," Joe said. "But go ahead."

"You're my hero. I love the way you took Tiffany out two spots before the bubble. Poor little bitch must be steaming." Elizabeth turned the water temperature down and stood aside to let Joe get wet.

Joe tilted his head back. The water splashed his hair into a mat against his head. "I beat her just for you."

"You could say that more convincingly."

"Sorry," Joe said. "I'm nervous about the game today."

"You are?" This was new.

"Weird, huh? I keep having all these final table finishes, but I can never get first place. I'm sure it's my own fault, but I'm starting to feel like I'm cursed."

"It's not your fault." Elizabeth took his hand.

"Of course it is. Once, twice — even five times, I could put it down to luck. But this is happening too often — these are players I can beat, in side games. I get to the final table and then *bang* — suddenly I can't play for shit anymore." Joe squeezed Elizabeth's hand and released it. He ran his hands over his wet hair, smoothing it back. "It's probably my ego. I'm probably getting too cocky and forgetting to play good poker."

Elizabeth's mind was churning as she began to soap up her arms. "I don't think it's your ego."

Joe cranked the water back up to Elizabeth's hotter preference and slipped past her to give her a turn under the stream. "It must be something in my mind. Maybe I'm giving a win too much importance and killing my game because of pressure."

"I don't think it's that either. Joe, there are bad people at work here. Someone's cheating. Someone's killing people. I think it's those people — or that person — who's preventing you from winning first place."

"Whatever. I'm still winning money."

Elizabeth tried to see behind Joe's smile. "Why does money matter so much to you? It's not like you were spoiled by too much of it growing up. You got through okay."

"Money is freedom," Joe said, fixing his eyes on the shower curtain. "Growing up, I was always someone's burden. You have no idea how powerless it feels to have to let people treat you like crap just to get food and a place to sleep."

Elizabeth swallowed hard. "I can imagine."

"No, Lizzie, you can't. You can hate your family all you like, but you can't imagine not having them."

They were quiet for a minute, hot water falling on Elizabeth's shoulders as she wondered what she could say to make Joe okay. "I know you don't like watching yourself play," she said finally, "but I think we should watch the footage when Fiona does her preview after the game. Especially the final table."

Joe frowned.

"Maybe you're making mistakes," Elizabeth said. "So worst

case, we can analyze that and catch it. But maybe you're not. We should watch for players who play like they know too much."

"What, catch the cheaters?" Joe looked amused as he picked up the tiny bottle of hotel shampoo.

"Here, use mine. The hotel shampoo is crap."

"Why is it crap?" Joe took the larger bottle from Elizabeth.

"It's full of parabens and other chemicals."

Joe smirked. "Good thing I have you."

"Don't forget it. Yes, catch the cheaters. What can it hurt to try?" Elizabeth moved to switch places again.

Joe stood in the water. He looked either vacant or deep in thought — Elizabeth couldn't decide which.

"You planning to let me rinse this conditioner out?" she asked eventually.

"Sorry." Joe moved aside. "I'm trying to remember all my recent final tables. T-Bone's been at more than his fair share."

"T-Bone was winning before the cheating started, so why would he jeopardize a lucrative career? Just pay attention going forward. We'll figure this out together."

TWENTY-TWO
CLARE

"They call him the Poker Choker." Clare looked out the passenger window onto Lake Ontario.

"Cute." Cloutier's eyes stayed on the highway in front of him.

Clare reached forward to press in the car lighter.

"People close to horror need to lighten things up to make sense of them," Cloutier said in response to her silence.

"I don't need to lighten things up. I can handle reality fine."

"Yeah?" Cloutier changed lanes to pass an Indian family in a sedan. Clare tried to figure out how there could be enough seat belts for all the passengers. "What's your sarcasm all about, then?"

"My sarcasm reflects the way I see the world," Clare said. "I don't take myself too seriously."

"You've just proven my point."

"Which point? The point about me not being qualified to follow the tournament to Vancouver?"

"I meant the smaller point — about lightening up reality. I don't need to justify my decision about your job."

Clare continued to stare out the window. "I think some of the players might be cheating. Have you heard anything about that from the RCMP?"

Sergeant Cloutier shook his head. "Wouldn't surprise me, though. Poker's not known for the honest people who are drawn to the game. You got names?"

"I think that's why Willard Oppal died."

"Come on, Vengel. Stop clutching at straws."

"I'm serious. About Oppal. Send me wherever you want — undercover yoga, for all I care — but I think he got made as a cop when he was sniffing around this cheating scam."

"Hm." Cloutier moved his jaw to one side. It made him look French. "Where are you getting this impression?"

Clare opened her pack and took out two cigarettes. "Mickey Mills and Fiona Gallagher."

"Yeah?" Cloutier accepted the cigarette and the light.

"I could fly out to Vancouver and —"

"Can you be quiet for five seconds? I'm thinking."

"About my job?"

"And the rest."

Clare frowned at her glittery pink manicure and wondered why she'd been drawn to a job that forced her to be so duplicitous.

After three or four minutes, Cloutier rolled the window down a crack and said, "Tell me more about the cheating."

"Mickey says he thinks some players are tuning into the hole card camera feed. So they can basically play like they're psychic."

"And why did Mickey tell you this?"

"Because he's coaching me. *Was* coaching me."

"Shit, Vengel." Cloutier smacked his fist into the vinyl dash, accidentally flicking ash forward.

"What?" Clare had no idea what she'd said wrong.

"You want to keep your job, you might want to open with that. Getting coached by Mickey Mills is a legitimate in. Better than any of this speculation about Oppal and hole card scams."

Clare felt stupid for not seeing that before.

Cloutier brushed the ash from the dashboard. It smudged a bit, but he didn't seem bothered. It was the government's car.

Clare didn't say anything for a couple of minutes. Then, "So can I stay?"

Cloutier did that thing with his mouth again, moving his lower jaw so it wasn't aligned with his top one. "I know you think you can do this. But even the fact that you didn't put your best argument forward — you're stumbling. Maybe you'll stumble onto something great, like you did with your first case. But to survive in this field you need to act aware. Knowing, not guessing, is what gets the job done well. It's also what keeps you alive."

"That's not entirely true." Clare tried to keep her voice level and respectful. "Too much confidence can close your mind. I want to be a damn good undercover cop one day, and I know I still have lots to learn. But I think my open mind is a good thing on a case as complicated as this. The only way I'll get killed is if I get made, and Amanda did a great job creating Tiffany as someone who *won't* get made anytime soon."

Cloutier glanced at her briefly and turned his eyes back to the road.

"I want to figure out a way into this cheating ring," Clare said. "What do you think?"

"You want to cheat at cards?" Cloutier shook his head from side to side, like a bobble-head toy. "I think you'd have to be fucking mental."

"And I want to take a closer look at Loni Mills."

Cloutier ashed his cigarette, this time out the window and on purpose. "Why?"

"Because she's everyone's ho. I'd put money on her playing a supporting role."

"You'd put money on it, would you? Because now you're a professional gambler."

Clare rolled her eyes. "You want to hear my theory?"

"Why not? We have half an hour before we're in Toronto, your job's still up in the air, and there's not much on the radio."

"I'm trying to figure out why I thought I'd miss you."

"Because you're an excellent judge of character."

"True," Clare said. "But for some reason I like you anyway. I don't think Loni's the instigator, but my guess is she's been brought in by whoever is."

"Hold on." Cloutier put his hand in the air like a stop sign. Clare was impressed that he could do this and not look like a choreographer. "Brought into the murders, or the cheating?"

"Cheating," Clare said. "Because the way Mickey thinks the scam is working, it needs at least two people to operate. My guess is the killer is only one person."

Cloutier nodded.

"Loni's on the sidelines, Loni knows the winning players . . . and according to Mickey —"

"Who might be lying."

"Sure. Might be. But according to him, the scam needs someone who isn't playing to coordinate it. And who better than the woman who walks around the Players Only zones like she was born there? Security doesn't blink if she crosses the little red rope."

"You always ramble when you talk, or did that actually make sense in your mind?"

"It makes sense in yours, too. Stop pretending you're obtuse."

They drove in silence for the next several minutes. They turned north on Highway 427 and east onto the 401. Clare was trying to figure out Loni's connection, and presumably Cloutier was off in his own thoughts as well. She'd barely noticed they'd come into the city when Cloutier pulled to a stop on Dundas West in front of the antique store she lived above.

"So are you letting me go on?" Clare chewed at her lower lip.

"Yeah, kid. I think I am."

"Will the RCMP be fine with that?" Clare couldn't stop her mouth from widening across her face.

"Should be. I haven't said anything to them about pulling you yet."

"Because you thought I'd come through?"

"Because I thought you deserved the chance."

"What do I do now?"

"Lay low for today. Grab a cab to the airport in the morning. A Town Car, in case anyone sees you arrive."

TWENTY-THREE
ELIZABETH

Elizabeth picked at some fluff from the seam of the leather couch. She squeezed Joe's hand. Neither of them wanted to be at this viewing, but she thought it was important, and Joe, for once, had listened.

They were gathered in the players' lounge — the one where the players really hung out, not the fake VIP room where players put in appearances so fans would think they were partying with the stars. Everyone's attention was glued to the giant flat-screen.

Normally Elizabeth couldn't be bothered to watch tournament footage. There was always a better way to spend the last night in a new city than sitting around rehashing every play through the lens of Fiona Gallagher's narcissism. Even the Criminals Hall of Fame wax museum would be more entertaining. But tonight, Elizabeth was convinced that she and Joe could learn something.

"Okay, guys, you know this is rough still." Fiona said. "Feel free to give commentary — what you like, what you don't think we should air. I don't get final say, but the producers listen to my feedback."

"I think you should wear a lower cut dress," T-Bone said from his armchair.

"Yeah," Joe said. "Maybe you could get them to CGI the neckline. And you know, fill it in with Loni's rack."

Elizabeth punched Joe's arm lightly.

"Come on, guys. This is serious." Fiona pretended to pout. "I really value your input. Okay, play it, Oliver."

Oliver, Fiona's goateed teenage assistant, pressed a button and the show came to life.

Elizabeth swirled the ice around her iced tea and focused on the TV.

Onscreen, Fiona brushed a flyaway hair from her face and gave the camera her best serious journalist smile. "We have eight players left. T-Bone Jones has the big stack, but the way this game's been playing, anyone could still be crowned the champion."

Elizabeth cringed at the rhetoric but knew the fans gobbled it up. They wanted to be spoon-fed so they wouldn't have to think too hard.

Back onscreen, Fiona was saying, "Nate Wilkes has a pair of sevens in first position. He's new on the scene, but he's a savvy New Yorker — these old pros can't push him around. He's cute, too — the shaggy dark hair and deep brown eyes make him look intense and brooding. I wouldn't mind seeing more of him. He wisely limps."

Loni Mills, Fiona's guest host for the Niagara game, chimed in with her own opinion: "Now, honey, I agree that this newcomer's a looker — and he looks about your age; you should find out if he has a lady friend back in New York — but why is limping wise? I don't claim to be no professional, but I always thought the rule was when you're first in a pot, you raise."

"A rule a lot of players swear by, Loni. And it's not without merit. But the unique thing about small and middle pairs is you can only afford to commit about 5% of your stack preflop, which means you can call a raise profitably, but it's a mistake to call a reraise. So you limp, and hope to catch a set."

"Ah, math." Loni waved a heavily braceleted hand in dismissal. "I knew there was a reason I couldn't stand this game."

Fiona grinned and looked straight into the camera. "Pretty Boy Mangan looks down in third position and sees ace-queen. He makes a standard raise, with one limper, to four big blinds."

Elizabeth hated Joe's nickname. "Pretty Boy" made him sound gay, when in fact he was flamboyantly heterosexual.

Back onscreen: "Action folds around to T-Bone, who calls on the button with king-ten suited. A loose play for an amateur, but T-Bone's no rookie. He's counting on a combination of position and skill to guide him after the flop."

"He's got some skilled positions, all right," said Loni.

Elizabeth could picture Fiona coaching Loni about coyly playing up her relationship with T-Bone. When Elizabeth had guest hosted in Halifax, her instructions had been to talk about Joe in a "lovingly competitive" way. Fans loved to think they were seeing inside the lives of their stars.

"Tell me, Loni," Fiona said, on camera, "in your private life, what would you say is T-Bone's greatest skill?"

Loni batted her eyelashes — definitely rehearsed. "I thought you said this was prime time, dear."

Fiona laughed indulgently. "Nate Wilkes calls the raise."

The odds shot up on the screen.

"These three players are as even as you can get before the flop. And here it is: the flop comes queen-jack-seven rainbow.

"First to act is Nate, who has soared into the lead with trip sevens. He makes a rookie move and checks — you never want to slow-play trips against multiple opponents. But maybe he's counting on a bet: both Joe and T-Bone are known to be aggressive."

"Well, I wouldn't know about Joe," Loni said. This woman was made for TV. "But are you saying three of a kind isn't a strong enough hand to trap with? Hell, when I get trips, I'm coy as a cucumber."

Elizabeth cringed at the mixed simile. Viewers would forgive it.

Fiona grinned. "Luckily for Nate Wilkes, Joe Mangan loves this flop — poor guy doesn't realize he's only 3% to win. He bets out three-quarters of the pot."

"Motherfucker," Joe muttered from his seat beside Elizabeth. "Why are we watching this shit?"

Elizabeth put a finger to her lips.

Back on Fiona's show: "T-Bone makes the call, and here's where Nate should make his move. He's a 70% favorite on this hand, but he doesn't want to give away any free cards. There's only one good move: he should go all in."

"That's my favorite move when T-Bone makes it."

"Prime time, Loni. Prime time."

"Right. Sorry about that."

Fiona smiled. "Instead Nate goes for a minimum raise. He's hoping to lure in someone like Joe, whose odds are too low to even call that. And it works. Joe makes the call easily. But so does T-Bone, who has exactly the hand Nate should fear.

"The turn is the deuce of spades. Now Nate makes his all-in move. But it's too late. The pot is huge, and while Joe correctly tosses his top pair, top kicker, T-Bone calls in a flash. He has a straight draw, a flush draw, and easy odds to call it.

"The cards are turned over. Nate's grin takes over his face, because even though he's messed this hand up royally, he's more than a 70% favorite to double through T-Bone. But luck plays its role, too, because the river is the eight of spades, and T-Bone's flush beats Nate's trips."

"That's my baby." Loni clapped her hands. "Go, T-Bone, go."

"Our eighth place finisher, Nate Wilkes. Played a great game, but ultimately wasn't ready to take on the pros. We'll be interviewing him after this break."

Back in the screening room, the real-life Fiona told her techie, "Okay, you can cut it here, Oliver. We'll get feedback on this first segment before moving on."

Fiona's sullen little helper pressed a switch and paused the feed. Oliver was one of those kids — maybe nineteen or twenty — who dressed in baggy clothes and had ten thousand piercings that made it impossible to know what his real face looked like.

"You're doing great!" Fiona said to Loni, who off-camera was perched on the thick arm of T-Bone's chair. "Full of life, the right amount of innuendo; fans will devour you."

"I'm having fun," Loni said.

"Hey, I'm not officially allowed to ask you this, because it's the network's decision who to hire . . . but it's a pain in the ass to constantly search for a guest host — more than half the time I end up with some player who falls flat on camera. No offence to anyone in this room."

No? Then why was Fiona staring straight at Elizabeth?

"If I could convince the network to make your spot permanent, would you be interested?"

"Me? Working for a living?" Loni patted her big blond hair. "I'd love to."

Elizabeth felt Joe's hand touch hers.

"You saw that, right?" Joe said quietly enough so only Elizabeth could hear.

Elizabeth pursed her mouth. "Saw what?"

"That hand. The way Nate played it."

"Like a novice?"

"No." Joe shook his head almost imperceptibly. "Like a guy who knew what everyone else held."

TWENTY-FOUR
CLARE

"Vancouver, huh? That's exciting." Roberta stood up from her crouched position beside a motorcycle. She shook her head so hard that some dark red hair came loose from its ponytail. "Stupid bike isn't making any sense."

Clare bent down to peer at the motorcycle. She didn't know what she was looking for, but the first step was to get acquainted with the machine. Clare didn't work here anymore, but she loved hanging out in Roberta's shop. From the sweet smell of gasoline to the double-wide workbench with tools scattered logically across it, it was like being at home — back when home was a place Clare had liked to spend time.

"Have you ever been out West?" Clare asked.

"Waaay back when." Roberta's eyes glassed over.

"Before Lance was born?" Clare figured she was making progress — it wasn't painful to say Lance's name anymore.

"Before I'd even met his father," Roberta said.

Clare nodded at the motorcycle. "Mind if I take a crack at this?"

"Be my guest."

Clare undid the screws that were holding the headlight onto

the Virago. It was an old bike, from the late eighties, and Clare found the lines on it beautiful. Not quite as nice as her Triumph, of course. But it had character. Too bad for its owner that it didn't want to start.

"What's Vancouver like?" Clare took the headlight from its casing and set it, together with its screws, onto a corner of the workbench.

"Depends who you are."

Clare picked up a flashlight and looked at the wires inside the plastic casing. "Do you want to answer that any more cryptically?"

Roberta smiled. "I was seventeen. I smoked pot and hung out on the nude beach. Since I don't think that's what you'll be doing, I doubt I can describe the city as you'll experience it."

"You did what?" Clare had trouble picturing Roberta as anyone other than the single mother she'd been since Clare was twelve. "You've always seemed so serious and hard-working."

"You've only known me when I've had responsibilities."

"Fair enough," Clare said. "So did you like smoking pot naked?"

"For a while. It got boring quick. Too many days strung into the next. The fantasy dries up and you realize your life has nothing in it."

"So you came back East."

"Came home, got pregnant, and that was that."

The wires behind the headlight all looked fine. Clare reattached the cover. "You've checked the fuses, right?"

"Yup. But feel free to check again. So what are you afraid of, kid? You love adventures, and here you are shaking like a leaf at the thought of getting on a plane."

Clare frowned. "I seem afraid?"

"So maybe you're not shaking literally. But I've known you since you were twelve."

Clare opened the auxiliary fuse panel. Roberta was right: the fuses looked good. She moved down to the main fuse by the battery. "The wire covers are frayed near the main fuse."

"I saw that. The wires themselves are fine."

"Oh." Clare disconnected and reconnected the fuse. She turned the Virago's key and the light went on. "I got the headlight on."

"Try starting it."

Clare pressed the starter, but nothing. A second later the headlight went out again. "Damn. I can see why this bike's got you crazy."

"You still haven't answered my question."

Clare shrugged. "My handler keeps telling me how dangerous this all is — the poker world, the murderer — but that doesn't scare me."

"Of course not." Roberta snorted. "You're twenty-three. You're not smart enough to know what danger is yet."

"I think I'm afraid I might suck at the job. My handler nearly pulled me because he thinks I don't know enough. What if solving the politicians' murders was a fluke, like he says it was, and I'm actually a terrible cop?"

"Then you'll find that out," Roberta said. "Wouldn't you rather find out by doing what you love, instead of chasing after burglars on that beat you hated so much?"

"I guess," Clare said. "But at least on the beat my screw-ups were relatively private. Now I feel like every mistake I make will get magnified. There are so many people watching what I'm doing."

Roberta tilted her head. "Why are you still thinking about yourself?"

"Oh my god. Am I supposed to be a Buddhist? Because I'm not superhuman, or forty."

"I'm not asking you to be either." Roberta sat at her workbench. "I'm trying to help you turn a key, to live your life easier."

"Maybe you could let me turn my own keys." Clare didn't mean to be unkind, but there was something intrusive about someone wanting to see inside your brain.

"Fair enough," Roberta said. "So what do you think about that Virago?"

Clare stared at the battery, which seemed to have all its fluid levels in order. "I think it's confusing us on purpose."

TWENTY-FIVE
ELIZABETH

Where the hell was Joe? It was almost ten p.m. and Elizabeth couldn't find him anywhere. He was neither answering nor returning calls, and he hadn't so much as texted her since they'd watched the final table footage. He'd Tweeted an hour ago — some nothing line about how the beer was stronger in Canada. Since Joe didn't drink beer, Elizabeth was pretty sure it was the lead-in to some new promotional deal he'd signed.

She'd checked the players' lounge and the high stakes poker room, but although people in both places had seen Joe, they all thought he'd left a lot earlier. Tiffany James had gone back to Toronto. Allegedly. Or was Joe in her room with his clothes off?

Elizabeth grabbed the phone from its cradle and pressed a button.

"Front desk," the bored female voice answered.

"I'd like to connect to Tiffany James' room."

"James . . ." The sound of typing came through the line. "I have a Tiffany James who checked out this afternoon."

"Thanks."

Then who *was* he with? Elizabeth almost never drank, but at the moment she was tempted to raid the minibar of all its booze. Instead, she picked up the phone again.

"Front desk."

"I'd like to connect to Fiona Gallagher's room."

"One moment, please."

How many times could a phone ring? Of course Joe was there. Why wouldn't Fiona pick up, otherwise? After twelve or thirteen rings — or maybe twenty — Elizabeth slammed down the phone. She quickly picked it up once more.

"Front desk."

"Sorry to keep bugging you. Can you tell me the room number for Fiona Gallagher so I can just dial her directly?"

"Six-o-three," the bored voice told her.

"Thanks."

Elizabeth threw on the clothes she'd been wearing before she'd changed into the plush hotel bathrobe, and she headed for the elevator. She patted her pocket to make sure she had her phone. She was going to catch her man.

TWENTY-SIX
CLARE

"How did you swing a night off?" Kevin was caressing Clare's inner thigh in the tangle of sheets on his bed.

"It was a mistake," Clare said, "caused by my handler assuming I was too stupid not to die on the job. Are you complaining?"

Kevin's mouth pursed, making him look like a middle-aged woman. "Is your assignment dangerous?"

Clare traced her smooth new nails down his back and watched him smile in response. "Not if no one finds out I'm a cop."

But despite his smile, Kevin's eyes didn't relax. "Has your cover character slept with anyone?"

"My cover character is disgusted with her options."

"I'm glad to hear it."

"Want to go for a walk?" Clare asked.

"You kidding? I want to stay in bed with you."

"Cool." Clare slid down the bed, gripped his outer thighs, and licked lightly around the base of his cock. He felt warm and manly; she wanted to stay there forever. "I probably shouldn't be seen outside anyway. Not in this neighborhood."

"Mmm. Your cover character too good for the Junction?"

"Not too good. Maybe too snooty. Anyway, the Junction's trendy now. My character's just . . ." Clare didn't want to think about Tiffany.

Kevin stroked her head, messing up her new hair. "I thought you looked more put-together than normal. It suits you."

"No it doesn't." Clare took his hand off her head and moved away a few inches. "Take that back."

"You want me to take back a compliment?" He laughed and reached for her head again. "What's wrong with you?"

"You're not complimenting me." She moved back up the bed so she faced him. "You're complimenting my stylist. Who, incidentally, thinks I have *no* personal style, and who I'm stuck with as a handler for the rest of the case."

"You have a handler who's also a stylist? I thought the RCMP was sparing no expense."

"Believe me, it baffles me, too." Cloutier was frustrating enough to work with, but Clare had no idea how she was going to get through the whole case with Amanda as her only source of counsel. "If I tell her I can't get my mind around some clue, she'll probably recommend a seaweed wrap followed by an afternoon of shoe shopping to clear my head."

"Doesn't sound so bad. Some days I wouldn't mind packing in my tools and listening to nature music while my pores are gently exfoliated."

"Very funny. How's your electrical world?"

"Good," Kevin said. "I'm thinking of striking out on my own. My dad's retiring soon, so his clients would come my way eventually. But I'm ready to work for myself."

"No more Findlay and Son? How's your dad taking that?"

"We'll still be affiliated; I'll just go with an edgier name — maybe Findlay Wires & Things. I want to appeal to the younger crowd. You know how many people our age —" Kevin grinned; he was six years older than Clare, which sometimes felt like a completely different generation. "Okay, *my* age, and a bit older — are buying houses?"

"Um, no. I don't have those statistics."

"A lot. And most of them are yuppies. They don't know the first thing about electrics, but they want to feel like a savvy consumer."

"So you're going to prey on that?"

Kevin laughed. "I'd prefer to see it as catering to that. I'm planning to create a YouTube channel to teach people how to fix their own basic problems, like fuse replacement, for free."

"Aren't basic problems the meat of your business?"

"Yeah," Kevin said, "but I feel guilty taking someone's eighty bucks for something they could do in five minutes."

"That's kind of genius," Clare said. "If someone helped me change a fuse online, I'd trust him not to rip me off on a complicated job. Not that I'd need help changing a fuse."

"No. You're not a stupid yuppie." Kevin moved his hand tentatively back toward Clare. He traced a finger along the side of her neck. "But this way, my dirty housewife could change her own light bulb, and she'd only call me in when her vibrator gets busted."

"Not really, right?" Clare was suddenly insecure. "You're not going to, like, go searching them out or anything, are you? As part of your new business plan?"

"Clare."

"What?"

Kevin frowned. "You have no idea how much I like you, do you?"

Clare shook her head, hoping he'd tell her.

"Maybe one day it will be clear." He held her hand. "But for now, if I take back the compliment about your new look, will you go back to what you were doing before?"

"I'll think about it."

"All right." Kevin took a sip of water from the glass on the bedside table. "You're ugly with makeup. You look so much better when you don't brush your hair. And I prefer your baggy jeans with the real rips from real life than those designer things that hug your ass so perfectly."

"I'm not sure that counts." Did men not get it? All those time-consuming fashion things only masked a woman's true appearance. Or did men want to be fooled into dating someone who was only attractive on the outside?

Kevin sighed. "Clare, you're gorgeous to me no matter what you wear. I'm sorry I even looked at your external vestments. In my perfect world, you'd be naked all the time anyway."

"All right. That counts." She slid back down the bed and picked up where she'd left off.

TWENTY-SEVEN
GEORGE

George highlighted the paragraph he'd just written and hit Delete. In the last half hour his brain had begun to go mushy. He was sick of hotel coffee, but if he wanted to get any more work done he would need another infusion of caffeine.

He threw jeans on over his boxers, grabbed a sweater from his suitcase — still unpacked from his arrival three days before — and left his room. He hoped the Starbucks in the lobby was still open, even though they were a deregulated franchise and charged rip-off prices.

Elizabeth was in the hall, banging like a madwoman on a door a few rooms down from his.

"Are you all right?" George touched her shoulder and she spun around quickly.

"I'm fine," Elizabeth said. "But Joe won't be if I find him inside this room."

George looked at the number plate beside the door. "That's Fiona's room."

"Sorry if it hits home."

"Why do you think they're together?" George stared at the door.

"Because Tiffany James has gone home to ride her pony in Toronto, and who else is there to fuck?"

George thought about it. Female poker players were not renowned for femininity. If Joe was cheating, Fiona was a good bet. Of course, Joe could have picked up anyone in town — or taken his pick from the groupies — but George decided not to speculate out loud.

"I phoned Fiona's cell," Elizabeth said, holding up her own phone for emphasis. "It's ringing inside this room."

"Have you tried calling Joe?"

"His phone goes straight to voice mail."

George frowned. This couldn't go anywhere good. "Come for coffee with me," he said.

"And give up trying to find Joe?" Elizabeth's dark eyes narrowed.

"He'll turn up. There's probably a simple explanation."

"Sure there is: Fiona."

"Fiona," George said, wondering how much of their conversation was being overheard on the other side of the door, "is anything but simple."

Elizabeth rolled her eyes at the door. "Fine. I could use a coffee." She followed George to the elevator.

"Anyway, Joe's not her type," George said as they were walking.

"No? What's Fiona's type? Angst-ridden writer geeks who only sometimes remember to shave?"

George felt his face. She was right: he had two days' worth of stubble.

"Fiona likes intellectuals."

Elizabeth smirked. "Tell that to the biker she was fucking in Montreal."

"What biker in Montreal?"

"You didn't know."

George tried to shrug but ended up making some jerky shoulder motion. "It's none of my business. We're not together anymore."

"But you want to be." Elizabeth stabbed the Down button.

"I don't know. We're only friends now, technically. But sometimes she lets me think she wants more, and it's driving me insane." George wasn't sure why he was speaking so candidly to Elizabeth.

The elevator arrived. Elizabeth went in first.

"So many women are like that," Elizabeth said, shaking her head. "Fiona doesn't want you. She wants you to want her."

"She's doing a good job," George said with a sad grin. "She asked me to be her co-anchor in Vancouver — I've been on the schedule for over six months. Then, like three hours ago, she sends me a Facebook message saying she wants to use Loni Mills instead, for her permanent co-anchor going forward."

"She wrote that on your wall? That's kind of harsh."

"It was a private message. But she has my phone number. She knows what room I'm in."

"Maybe it's a good thing," Elizabeth said. "The less you see Fiona, the sooner you'll forget her."

"Unlikely, unless one of us leaves the scene. But it's not as bad as all that. I'm dating."

"Who?"

"I talk to women online."

"Internet dating?" Elizabeth tossed him a skeptical glance. "Can you have sex online, too?"

"Some people think so. There are USB attachments you can buy — his and hers — I guess they vibrate based on what the person at the other end is doing."

"Gross," Elizabeth scrunched up her face. "I wouldn't go anywhere near someone's computer if I knew they did that. You don't, right?"

"Right." George had contemplated buying the attachments, briefly, but the thought left him hollow. "I met one of my online dates in person. She lives in Pittsburgh. I arranged a stopover during the holidays."

"Did you run screaming when you saw her real face?"

"No. We had a lonely night of motel sex and I cried as soon as I was alone." George was shocked how easily the words had fallen out of his mouth. They were true; he'd just never told anyone.

Elizabeth touched his arm as they navigated through the casino crowd toward the coffee bar. "You'll fall in love again. You totally have chick appeal."

"I do?" George nudged his glasses up on his face.

"Sure. The whole geek-with-an-edge thing is getting hotter every minute. Look at Mac Guy. He's sleeping with Drew Barrymore. Or maybe that's *was*. I can never keep her men straight."

"I have a Mac," George said brightly.

"Then you're set. Which is more than I can say for myself, trapped with a man who screws around with other women when he's staying in a hotel with me."

George was happy to see that the lobby Starbucks was still open. "Why do you stay with a guy who cheats on you?"

Elizabeth stopped walking and faced George. "He's cheating? For sure? Do you know something I don't?"

"No." George felt a slow, confused smile spread across his face. "Are we having the same conversation? You just told me Joe was sleeping around."

"I don't *know* he is. I suspect it. What you said sounded like knowledge."

"Sorry." George shook his head. He had his suspicions like anyone else, but nothing concrete.

"At least it's Fiona and not Tiffany James."

"What do you have against Tiffany?" George had seen the young woman who was already creating her own buzz. She was cute, but she didn't seem to have much substance. Maybe that was the appeal.

"I feel like if Joe cheats with Tiffany he might not come back."

"That's nuts," George said. Was that even a comforting thing to tell someone?

Elizabeth shrugged. "I know he wants her — he can't stop talking about her. That's why I'm working from the other end."

"What other end?" George was both baffled and impressed by the complexity women could assign to human dynamics.

"Tiffany's end. I'm working on being her friend. I can't stop Joe from wanting her. But I can stop her from feeling morally okay about fucking him."

"Crafty. Good luck with that."

"Yeah, it's hard considering I hate everything about her."

They arrived at the coffee bar and ordered their drinks. George paid the extortionary price and waited while Elizabeth fixed her tea. He watched the casino. Ten years before, when he'd first joined the poker scene, he'd found the lights and the bells of the slot machines magical. They'd been an invitation; a giant welcoming hallway into a world he had wanted to be a part of. Now they were sad. It wasn't just the people playing them; it was the machines themselves. They made George think of a has-been seaside town in England. The lights and the bells were still working, but the crowds had moved on to other things.

When Elizabeth's tea was sugared and milked to her liking, they went outside and strolled toward the center of town.

"Have you ever felt like you had poison in your veins?" Elizabeth asked out of the blue. "Crawling through them, taking you over and making you feel kind of evil?"

George tried to imagine what she meant.

"It's been happening to me a lot lately. It's happening now."

"What does it feel like?" The dark roast tasted good, but it was still too hot; George burned his tongue trying to drink too quickly.

"Like poison." Elizabeth let out a sigh. "Aren't you listening?"

"Sorry." George suppressed a smile. "I don't know what that feels like."

"Sometimes it starts with a weird feeling in my head. Not

strong like a headache, but physical pressure, like something's trying to push my skull outward from within."

"Are you dehydrated?"

"It's weirder than that. Sometimes it starts in my mouth, with this metallic taste. And other times it starts in my arms — like right now — they feel all trembly and weak, and I know the poison is coming. Soon the feeling takes control of my head and starts living in me."

They turned down the main drag and passed Screamers House of Horrors. "You sure you haven't been spending too much time in there?" George said, pointing.

"Oh, ha ha. Seriously — I haven't told anyone this yet. I feel it in my neck and shoulders, too."

"Sounds like tension."

"If it was tension, I would call it tension. This is like poison, which is why I call it that."

"And you're feeling it right now?" George asked.

"Wow. You're good."

"I take it there's an emotional component as well."

"Sorry." Elizabeth stopped walking. "I'm not trying to be rotten, but yes, the emotional part comes next. The world becomes dark and pointless, I'm positive people hate me, and worse than that: I'm sure they're right to. So then — as you've just witnessed — I start saying mean things — almost like, if people are going to hate me anyway, I might as well give them reason to."

"That's weird, Liz." George wondered if there was a polite way to suggest a sanity test, if such a thing existed.

"And then not too long later — maybe an hour, or two at the most — it'll clear up again, and I'll be my regular self."

"Charming and peaceful," George said with a straight face.

"Oh my god. Make fun of me all you want. But this is real, and it's starting to freak me out."

"I can see why. Does something usually trigger it? Like thinking Joe's out cheating on you?"

"Sometimes. But sometimes it comes on its own, when I'm feeling great."

George's mind went to the darkest place it could. "Have you thought about going for a CT scan?"

"You think I should?"

"What can it hurt? At the very least, a scan can rule out all the scary options."

"Yeah," Elizabeth said. "Or it can confirm them."

MONDAY / MARCH 21

VANCOUVER

TWENTY-EIGHT
CLARE

Clare stood outside the airport smoking. Vancouver air felt thick. Even through cigarette and car exhaust fumes, it smelled fresh and healthy — like back home in Muskoka, but denser, like the air was pressing down on her skin. It was three p.m. but it seemed later, probably because it was six o'clock back in Toronto.

She missed Kevin. She was glad she'd seen him — though it might have been nicer if the night off hadn't been a direct result of Cloutier doubting her skills. Clare wondered if she'd ever feel like a real cop. She couldn't imagine being married to the job like so many of her colleagues. They said stuff like "It's in my blood," or "This is who I am." They talked about "civilians" like they were another species of human.

Clare tossed her smoke to the curb and rolled her suitcase to the taxi line.

Her hotel was downtown, which annoyed her. She wanted to be where the action was, in the casino hotel with the other players. How was she supposed to get up close and personal with the poker crowd if she was fronting as some posh bitch who thought she was too good for their gritty underworld?

Clare got out of the cab in Yaletown. She wrinkled her nose as she looked around. All the buildings were the same: tall, glass, aiming at upscale but managing to look cheap because of their completely unoriginal design. From one of these buildings, Amanda emerged, immaculate in a tailored green pantsuit. For a supposedly intelligent woman, Amanda poured a lot of her creative energy into looking good. When this assignment was over, Clare planned to wear her oldest jeans and her rattiest T-shirt for a week without washing. Amanda probably felt like the job was forcing her to dress down.

"Clare!" Amanda's smile was bright.

"Hey." Clare's was less so.

"Your hotel's just up the street."

Amanda took the suitcase, leaving Clare with her laptop shoulder bag. Clare had planned to rest the shoulder bag on top of the suitcase and roll it. But she lugged her computer along silently. In her ignorant way, Amanda was probably trying to be helpful.

The air still smelled fresh in the middle of the city — that made a change from Toronto. When they came to a stoplight, Clare looked down the cross street and saw water.

"That's False Creek," Amanda said. "Nice, huh? You're going to love it here."

How could she possibly know that?

They arrived at a modern-looking building. A doorman let them into a trendy lobby. Clare supposed it was meant to be artistic, but she felt like the hotel had been designed to intimidate her. Or maybe it was the staff who were designed that way.

She got her room card from the front desk and she and Amanda rode up in the elevator.

"Thanks for coming with me." Clare slid her card into the door and let them both into her new room. It was small, but that was fine. There was a desk with an Internet connection and a window from which she could see False Creek, a million moored boats, and several more of those glass condo buildings.

Amanda set the suitcase against a wall. She frowned, pushed

blond hair from her face, like she wasn't sure what to do next. "Should I leave you alone? You must be exhausted."

"Thanks." Clare hadn't slept much, but she wasn't tired.

"Do you have plans for the evening?"

"Um. Yeah. I mean, nothing official." Clare wanted to get her bearings on her own, maybe grab a coffee and walk around the neighborhood for an hour, then get to work. "I thought I'd head out to the casino, see if some of the players are around."

"Good idea," Amanda said. Her tiny nose and ears made her look twelve years old. No wonder she had to dress for success, wearing three-inch heels even in daytime. People would probably be more inclined to give her candy than respect otherwise.

"Is the River Rock Casino far from here?" Clare asked.

"Maybe a twenty-minute cab ride."

"Does Tiffany take cabs? I thought maybe she'd rent an Aston Martin for her stay in Vancouver."

Amanda laughed. "She takes cabs. It's also twenty minutes by SkyTrain, so count yourself lucky."

Clare fingered her clingy pink shirt. The cotton and silk blend felt great against her skin, and it made her breasts look at least one size larger. She just didn't like the divide it represented — like she was supposed to feel superior somehow for wearing a more expensive shirt. "Why am I staying downtown? Is that to be close to you, or is the casino hotel too grubby for Tiffany?"

"You're staying downtown for protection."

Clare was surprised. "Mine?"

Amanda nodded. "At the casino, there's too much action. Too many of the suspects are moving around legitimately. Here, we can monitor who's coming and going. If someone from the poker scene goes into your hotel, it's a red flag."

"This is Canada, not some international spy game."

"So we want the criminals to believe."

Clare rolled her eyes. "Am I being followed?"

"Not so far. I'll let my boss know where you're going today. The guys at the casino can look out for you."

"The guys?"

"RCMP has extra security on this. Plainclothes — they should blend in as background players."

Clare didn't know why this rubbed her wrong. Of course she wanted the killer found, and maybe it was a job for more than one person. But having other undercovers there made her feel like the RCMP didn't trust her to do good work. "Are these other guys playing in the tournament?"

Amanda shook her head. "You're the only one in the game."

That, at least, was something.

"This is your first case, right?" Amanda sat down in the armchair, which the room didn't quite have the space for.

"Second," Clare said.

"But it's your first with the RCMP." Why was Amanda asking if she already knew the answer?

"Yes."

"Okay. I'm not being rotten, but working with us is different than working with a small-town police force."

"I worked in Toronto." Clare wished there was a balcony where she could smoke. "I figured out who killed the mayor."

"Okay." What was Amanda smiling about? "I thought there must be a good reason we took on someone so young."

We. Like hiring Clare had been partly Amanda's decision.

"But there's a difference to how the RCMP runs a case. We're set up for undercover operations in a way the police departments aren't. We don't throw you into the field and say 'Go.' We have teams, working together to cover each other's backs."

Clare didn't like to hear the Toronto Police maligned. She'd only been with them for not quite a year, but they were still technically her employer. She hoped her displeasure was apparent from the scowl on her face.

"There's nothing sinister here, Clare. We trust your instincts, which is why you have this job. But a hotel room isn't a safe place right now. Anyone from the RCMP who's watching you is only watching over you."

"Fine," Clare said. "And by the way, I need a pair of sunglasses."

"You can buy sunglasses. Just keep the receipt."

"Okay. It's just . . . I don't want to buy the wrong thing. They have to be heavily tinted so you can't see my eyes. And they should be, you know, blingy. Something Tiffany would wear."

Amanda grinned. "You're starting to like your new wardrobe."

"No, I still hate it."

"Don't worry," Amanda said. "Your secret's safe with me."

TWENTY-NINE
GEORGE

"Were you fucking Joe Mangan last night?" George knew there was probably a more tactful way to phrase the question. He didn't care. The sun was setting on their first day in Vancouver. The new leg of the tournament would begin the next morning, and Loni would be Fiona's co-anchor, not George.

"No." Fiona gave him a small smile as she looked up from her veal marsala. It was early for dinner. Six p.m. But it was three hours later in the time zone they'd just come from, and they both wanted to crash early. "Were you?"

George watched her chew. Her lips stayed together and her eyes were thoughtful, as if she wanted to fully experience the flavors of the meat and the sauce and their pairing. He hadn't seen this sensual side of her for a while. She normally kept it hidden behind makeup and microphones.

"Why did we break up again?" he asked.

Fiona swallowed. "Because you took issue with me screwing other people."

"I still do."

The light from the candle brought out gold highlights in Fiona's red hair.

"But that's not going to work for you, is it?" George asked.

"No."

"Are you seeing anyone now?"

"No one special. But listen, George, let's not do this."

"I know. I promised I wouldn't ask about your sex life. I'm sorry."

"It's not that." Fiona set her fork down and gestured around the half-full room. They were the only two without gray hair. "It's this. What are we doing at a romantic Italian restaurant in a quaint Canadian fishing village?"

"You don't want to stay friends?" George reached for the bottle. It was good wine — a Sangiovese from the middle of the list. George had contemplated Amarone, but as he was pretty sure he wasn't getting laid the ninety bucks didn't seem worth it.

"This is what lovers do," Fiona said.

George frowned. "I like that we have history. It makes the mood that much more potent."

"That's because you're a writer." Fiona laughed sharply. "You think that if you torture your soul enough, your true brilliance will emerge."

George topped up Fiona's wine and his own. "I'm working on a fiction project."

"You are?" Fiona's eyes crinkled as she smiled this time. She was getting tiny crow's feet in the corners. George thought they made her look wise. "George, that's great. Can you talk about it, or is it all top secret intelligence until you're finished?"

"I'll say that it's a murder mystery. Not the great American novel, but it's a start, right?"

"It's more than a start," Fiona said. "You're doing what you love."

George thought about saying that he'd rather be doing *who* he loved, but they'd just left that topic. "What about you? Isn't it about time you got back on track and went to law school?"

"Yeah, that. I'm not going."

"Never?"

Fiona shook her head. "I've deferred acceptance too many times. I'd have to reapply, and I'm not sure how forgiving Harvard would be about my lack of commitment when there are hundreds of qualified applicants dying to go there."

"So you're giving up? Tossing it in? Who cares about other law schools — if Harvard won't have you, what's the point?" George wasn't sure why he was being aggressive.

"I wanted to go into law so I could change the world. But that's not what would happen. I'd be stuck in an office while my life passed by outside."

"It's passing you by now."

"I know," Fiona said. "But this way I have fun while it's passing."

George studied Fiona's face. She wasn't even thirty and she looked tired, like she'd lived an entire lifetime. He said, "What would you do if you could be catapulted into whatever career you chose? No school required, no cut to your salary. You wake up tomorrow and you're doing it."

Fiona didn't say anything for a moment. "I'd be a kindergarten teacher."

George pictured Fiona dashing around a roomful of five-year-olds, smiling at their finger paintings, helping them sound out words in picture books.

"Kids that age haven't lost sight of what matters," she said. "I could help make them strong, make them want to make a difference."

"They'll have forgotten it all by the time they're angry teenagers."

"So maybe I'd be a high school teacher. Arrange fun volunteering assignments, show kids how they can keep the world good going forward — and learn to like themselves in the process."

"Come on, Fiona. You're more than a teacher."

"What does that mean: 'more than'? Why are you such a snob?"

George ignored the second question and answered the first. "You love the spotlight. You want to live in it, not help other people find it."

Fiona grabbed her wine glass with both hands and traced her index finger forcefully along the stem. "You have no idea what I want. And why do you care so much?" She took a long sip.

"Because you're not happy."

"I'm not your problem."

George shook his head. "Have you never been in love? It doesn't work like that."

"Oh my god. Please don't be morose."

"How should I be, then?" George should shut up, but he'd had one glass of wine too many for that. "I sit here with you, and everything would be perfect if you didn't want to sleep with other people, date them, maybe even marry one of them. If I was designing a torture chamber for myself, I'd put your image on the wall."

"Why do you do this?" Fiona's eyes grew watery. "We're having a lovely time, and as soon as you realize it doesn't mean we're getting back together, you go in for the attack."

"Why do *I* do this?" George pushed his plate to the side of the table. There was food left, but he was finished eating. "You're the one who comes to my hotel room, all innocent and lonely, wanting to cuddle all night. When you reach for my cock — so casual, like you could take it or leave it, which is probably exactly how you feel — it's like all my emotions get thrown into some flaming caustic substance. I can't tell you to stop, because it's all I want to feel, but when it's over, the elation deflates into a pathetic puddle at the base of my stomach. It's worse than coming down from ecstasy. I'm depressed for days."

"George, you have to stop this." Fiona folded her cloth napkin and set it on the table. "I think we should go back to the hotel."

George stood up. He gave the waiter his credit card and asked him to call them a cab.

"One of us needs to leave this scene," he said. "It's ridiculous, what we're doing to each other."

Fiona shrugged. "I don't have anywhere to go. Do you?"

"I'm looking."

THIRTY
CLARE

"Mickey! What's wrong?" Clare had just gotten out of her second taxi of the day and was walking toward the casino entrance where Mickey was flicking a lighter at his cigarette as if he couldn't connect them fast enough. The evening had grown overcast, which was fine with her. Compared with the mirrored blandness of downtown, this ugly industrial neighborhood made Clare feel instantly at home.

"I'm livid is what's wrong." Mickey tossed the cigarette he'd just lit to the pavement. "I can't even smoke, I'm so angry."

"Why?" Clare lit a cigarette of her own and had no trouble smoking it. It felt like this whole city took pains to be smug about nicotine.

"No comment." Mickey stalked a few steps away, pivoted, and walked back toward Clare. "You're better off not knowing."

Clare leaned against a trash bin, trying not to show interest. She realized that Tiffany would never lean against a trash bin, and straightened up. "I guess you're in no mood to give me round two of those lessons."

"I don't know what I'm in the mood for." Mickey fumbled in his pocket. "What did I throw my smoke away for? Now I gotta light another one." He lit a new cigarette and moved closer to Clare so he could lean on the bin she'd abandoned. "You staying at the casino?"

Clare shook her head. "Downtown."

"Smart kid. I'm staying here, and I just blew twenty-four grand as something to do between lunch and dinner."

"No shit?" Did Tiffany swear? She did now. "No wonder you're so angry."

"Huh? No, the money doesn't upset me. It's the other way around: it's because I was pissed off I lost it. Rule Number One: never gamble when you're negative. Angry, sad, nervous. Doesn't fucking matter how the cards fall. You're gonna lose."

"I thought Rule Number One was 'Don't drink when you're gambling.'"

"So this is Rule Fucking Two, then. You gotta be so concerned about particulars?" Mickey squinted at her, inhaling.

Clare shrugged. "I guess not."

"Good. Anyway, this is why it's a stroke of fucking genius that you're under T-Bone's skin. You can knock him off his game just by talking shit to him."

Clare frowned. "That sounds like a lousy way to win."

"You'll never be a better card player than he is. You gotta find your edge where you can catch it. Don't think there's anyone here — including me — who wouldn't push your buttons if they knew how to find them."

"That's so cold. How can you justify making your living that way?"

"So cold my ass. Don't give me that judgment crap." Mickey stared at the sidewalk. "Maybe you got your education in fancier schools than the rest of us, but you want to join this game, you're no better or worse than any of us."

"I don't think anyone's better than anyone else. Still . . . can't I try to win by playing the cards well?"

"Sure," Mickey said. "Play how you want; it's your entry fee. But you'll never know cards better than T-Bone as long as he's still breathing on his own, and you're leaving money on the table if you don't at least consider what I'm saying."

"Leaving money on the table?"

"Not winning everything you could."

Clare tossed her cigarette into the road but made no move to leave. She felt like her head was swimming in poker. "So what has you so angry?"

"Forget about it." Mickey tossed his own smoke away — this time because it was finished. "Rule Number Three: there are some things you're safer not knowing."

THIRTY-ONE
ELIZABETH

"This boat is gorgeous." Elizabeth looked at Joe, lounging on the deck in the rising moonlight. "You sure we can afford it?"

"Nice, huh? Don't worry about the money; this one's mine."

Elizabeth took a can of chickpeas from her cloth shopping bag and reached up to place it in a cupboard. She felt disoriented. She'd spent the afternoon shopping at what used to be her local grocery store, and she'd been terrified that she'd run into someone she knew. At the same time, she felt let down that she hadn't. "Fine: can *you* afford this?"

"It's only for a week. Should I be saving my money until I'm too old to enjoy it?"

Elizabeth shrugged. "I like to live sustainably. You'd have to guarantee a final table finish to make this leg break even."

"Don't tell me you're turning into a hippie." Joe groaned. "Last week it was shade-grown coffee. This week it's sustainability. What's next week? Living off the land?"

"We could buy fishing rods," Elizabeth said with a smile.

"Yeah. The two fish we'll catch this week will make up for all the fuel we'll need to find them. I bet it's not even fish season. Come sit down. You want a drink?"

Elizabeth shook her head.

She was glad she'd run into George the night before, glad he'd been able to talk her away from beating down Fiona's door and either finding Joe or not. George was nice — the kind of guy she wished she was attracted to, but wasn't. Joe was nice too — too bad he was nice to so many people.

"You want to go for a ride?" Joe asked.

"It's risky at night, with all the logs in the river."

Joe rattled the ice in the bottom of his empty drink. "Where's your sense of adventure? We have a searchlight and you can be my lookout."

"Fine," Elizabeth said. "As long as we can sail north."

"There's no sail. It's power." He looked at her fondly, like he found women's lack of common sense both expected and endearing. "What's north?"

"Vancouver. Gibson's. Indian Arm."

"Ah," Joe said. "You mean not Richmond."

Elizabeth shrugged. "There are some great spots to drop anchor, or tie up and go in for dinner later. South is just . . . I don't know . . . boring. There's Steveston and Ladner, then you're pretty much at the U.S. border."

"How far from the States are we?"

"Maybe half an hour by car. Probably two or three hours by boat. Why? Are you homesick already?"

Joe snorted. "Homesick for what? Anyway, why the aversion to seeing your family for one polite meal?"

"Have you ever had a family?" Elizabeth wanted to pull the words back as soon as she'd said them.

"Ouch. You know I haven't."

"Sorry." Elizabeth reached across from her chair and touched his hand. "You know I didn't mean . . ."

"Don't worry about it." Joe flashed the grin the cameras loved so much.

"You don't need to keep that smile on for me. You can be angry if you want to."

"You sound like Father Leo." Joe pulled his hand away and got up to fix himself a new drink.

"Are you Catholic?" Elizabeth had never heard Joe talk about religion.

"How would I know? I doubt I was baptized."

"Who's Father Leo?"

"He's a priest I met in Battle Creek."

Elizabeth smiled. "I would never have guessed you'd had a friendship with a religious leader."

"Religious leader? I said he was a priest. If you're religious, you're a follower. Unless you're Buddha or Jesus or someone with something original to say."

Elizabeth rolled her eyes. "How old were you when you knew him?"

"Young — maybe eight. The house I was living in was one of the worst — not for physical abuse, but the head games were unreal. I used to run away and hide in the church."

"And the priest found you there?"

"I found him. I asked if I could work for room and board. He said no, but we started having conversations."

Joe found the key for the boat and pushed it toward the ignition. His hand was shaking; he had to try a few times before the key slipped into its slot. Elizabeth untied the ropes that held the boat to the dock. She wasn't sure she'd ever seen Joe's hand shake.

"That sounds like something out of Charles Dickens."

"I guess." Joe started the engine. "The guy actually helped me a lot. He showed me how to get my foster parents to treat me with respect, taught me how to react like an adult when the assholes bought their real kid a Nintendo for Christmas and gave me an ugly T-shirt that was way too big for me, but it came free in a case of beer."

"That's horrible." Elizabeth's family was looking all right in comparison.

"Whatever. It wasn't the worst thing they did."

Joe eased the boat out of the dock. It had thrusters, which supposedly made it easier to maneuver, but Elizabeth was still impressed with his dexterity. "Which way's north?"

"We have to get into the strait first." Elizabeth pointed Joe left.

Joe's face was still locked in that irritating perma-grin. "This is fun. I haven't driven a boat since that time in Monaco. Remember what we did when we dropped anchor?"

"Yeah." The poison was coming. Elizabeth smiled through it. "We should find somewhere secluded and maybe do that again."

"You okay? You look weird."

"I'm fine," Elizabeth said. "Why wouldn't I be?"

THIRTY-TWO
NOAH

Noah watched Tiffany smoking outside the casino. She looked peaceful, leaning against a streetlamp in the moonlight. It could be a scene from a musical, complete with grubby passers-by and the four-story parking garage behind her.

He wasn't sure why he was nervous to approach her. Noah could afford the twenty grand if he lost his bet with Joe. Bert might grumble, but as long as Noah handed him cash at the end of all this, he could justify blowing some in the name of the cause.

He glanced again at Tiffany. Why would some spoiled twenty-three-year-old stress him out like this? It made no sense, so Noah made his approach.

"You're well connected, aren't you?" he said from a few feet away.

"What do you mean?" Tiffany blew smoke into the space between them.

It had been a crappy pick-up line. But since he couldn't think of a smooth way to save it, Noah went with the charming buffoon theme. "I saw you out here with Mickey Mills earlier. I wanted to come over and say hi, but I was intimidated."

"By me or by Mickey?"

The real Noah would walk away at that point and come back when he was more in control, if ever. But as Nate, he felt emboldened to be honest. "I guess I just think you're really hot."

Tiffany snorted. "Is that supposed to be pathetically endearing?"

"Come on. You think I'm hot, too." Shit. That wasn't what he'd meant to say. Noah cringed internally as he waited for her reaction.

"Oh really?" Tiffany's eyebrows arched. She seemed more amused than pissed off, which was good.

"Yeah," Noah said. "And you would love to come for a drink with me."

"No thanks."

"What?" Noah was surprised how casually she'd turned him down.

"I said no thanks. I hate arrogant men. Which is a shame, because you're cute. Very cute, actually; I love short hair when it's shaggy."

Noah grinned. "You're right. I was arrogant. I'm nervous. I really like you. Would you like to have a drink with me?"

"No thanks."

"So how did Mickey get you to go to bed with him?" Ouch. He'd taken it too far. Noah wanted to kick himself.

"I'm not sleeping with Mickey."

"Of course you're not. You're too good for us poker players." Maybe he should walk away and let Joe win the stupid bet. Noah seemed to be messing this up anew with each word he spoke.

Tiffany wrinkled her face. "I'm not too good for anyone. But I'm not going to randomly screw old men . . . or arrogant ones."

"Okay," Noah said. "I get it. My opening line was crap and my recovery has been even worse. But I like you — I like what I see, and I even like the superior bitch in you."

Tiffany rolled her eyes.

"Can I ask you out one more time?"

"No." But now a grin tugged at her face. "Well, maybe you can give it a shot. I'll probably say no, but I'm interested in what your third approach might be."

"Hi, I'm Nate. I'm a bit of a babbling idiot when I see a girl I like, but underneath I'm kind — a bit insecure even — and I respect women as full decision-making people. And I'm not an arrogant asshole, despite the reasonable conclusion you could draw from our conversation up to this point. Would you like to come for a drink with me?"

Tiffany kept leaning on the streetlamp like it was the most comfortable position in the world. She ashed her cigarette. "No thanks."

"Why not? I thought that last one was pretty good."

"It was all about you."

"Do you not drink?" Noah's insides screamed, *Walk away!* But his feet weren't moving anywhere. "Maybe you'd like to go for coffee."

"I drink plenty. If I said I didn't want to have sex, would you think I was a lesbian?"

"Joe Mangan thinks you're a lesbian. He said you want to fuck his girlfriend."

"His fantasy. Not mine." Tiffany tossed her smoke to the ground and started walking toward the cab line.

Noah followed her. "Listen, one more time for real. I think you're really cool, I think you have an original take on life, and I'd love to keep this conversation going over a drink."

Tiffany stopped walking. "That was pretty good."

For fuck's sake, finally. Noah waited for her to say more; he was afraid to speak in case he wrecked it again.

"Okay," she said. "Let's have a drink."

THIRTY-THREE
CLARE

The night was freezing cold, but Clare had a deliciously soft fur-lined leather jacket, and she was still in love with how fresh the air smelled in Vancouver. They were on the patio of the Elephant & Castle at the Delta hotel, by the river. In this city you couldn't even smoke on patios, but the waitress was turning a blind eye. The fact that Nate smoked was a point in his favor. But why was Clare giving him points? She had Kevin at home. This was business.

"So . . . New York," Clare said. "What's it like there?"

"That's a massive question." Nate drained his beer and motioned to the waitress for two more. "Have you ever been?"

"No." Clare hadn't, but why wouldn't Tiffany have been to Manhattan at some point in her privileged life? She took a stab: "Too dirty and dangerous."

"Please. New York was rough in the eighties, but it's been cleaned up since. Anyway, what's wrong with dirty and dangerous?" Nate grinned wickedly.

How had Clare even contemplated accepting a date with Joe Mangan when the Marlboro Man himself had sent his younger, hotter incarnation to her side? Still, she was Tiffany: she had to play hard to get. "Is that how you see yourself? I'd pegged you for tortured and misunderstood."

"Why did you agree to drinks with me again?"

"Beats a lonely hotel room." Clare shrugged. "I had no idea how boring this poker tour was going to be."

"I'm sorry you find us so dull." Nate yawned, stretched, and pretended to consult his watch as he leaned back in his chair. "You have a boyfriend back home? Or do you scare them all off with that sweet disposition?"

"They scare me off," Clare said. "With their sheltered stupidity."

"So a dirty dangerous New Yorker might be just your type."

"Might be." Clare felt her cover character all but slip away. "You want to do a shot of Jack?"

"Rich girls don't do Jack."

"Because you've met every single rich girl."

"I've met enough."

"So don't do a shot with me; pigeonhole me, instead." Clare looked up at the waitress, who was back with their second round. "We'll have two shots. One Jack, one . . . what should I have, Nate? What do rich girls drink?"

Nate was still leaning back in his exaggerated bored pose. "Do you have a shot called Sarcastic Prima Donna?"

The waitress shook her head. "What's in that?"

"Don't worry. We'll have two Jack Daniel's."

"So let me guess," Clare said when the waitress had gone back inside. "Your father's a writer — no, an artist — and your mom supports him by waiting on tables."

"You could not be farther from the truth."

"So what's the truth?"

Nate took a sip of beer. Clare wasn't sure if he was buying time, but his eyes were wandering everywhere. "My father's a doctor. My mom does nothing."

"You're such a chauvinist. You mean your mom looks after the house and meals, and you consider that nothing."

"I mean she does nothing." Nate's brow lowered and his eyes met Clare's hard. "She has a cleaner come in once a week and the rest of the time the apartment's a pigsty. If she cooks, it's take-out from Zabar's, but more often they go out or order Chinese. She has one hobby: watching daytime talk shows."

"I'm sorry." Clare meant it.

"Yeah, just be careful who you pigeonhole."

THIRTY-FOUR
GEORGE

George highlighted three paragraphs and pressed Delete as hard as he could. His index finger hurt for a couple of seconds, but whatever. His crap writing wasn't what was tugging at his conscience.

He'd been a jerk at dinner. He wished there was a pill that could erase the foolish way he felt. Not some drug that made him stupid for an hour, but something that would boost him permanently, give him confidence he didn't have.

He'd always been his own worst enemy. He couldn't go to a party or any social gathering without later hating himself for saying something he was sure made him look like a ridiculous asshole. But tonight he was right to be down on himself. He and Fiona were supposed to have moved on — it was supposed to be a friendship without strings. George should be mature enough to maintain that. It wasn't like he was some lovesick fool in his twenties, which was how he was acting.

He closed his computer file. Wine and negative emotion, despite the folklore, went nowhere toward producing good writing. They might help words flow, but the words would invariably be sloppy, and they would need to be ripped up later.

There was a knock on the door and George jumped. He managed a smile — his first in several hours — when he remembered that life wasn't quite so dark outside his murderous pages. Yeah, people were dying. But not every knock on a hotel room door was a death knell.

He put his eye to the peephole and opened the door immediately.

It was Fiona. Shaking. "My room was broken into."

"Just now?" He ushered her inside.

"Of course just now. If it had happened before, I would have mentioned it at dinner." She slumped into the armchair by the window.

"Was anything taken?"

"Yeah."

"Anything important?"

Fiona nodded. George waited for her to speak. It took several seconds. "Some notes. I've been receiving them since Halifax. Since . . ."

George knew what she was telling him. It's what Mickey had told him already.

"I — can I have a glass of water?"

George went to the bathroom, keeping his eye on Fiona until the wall obscured her. He came back with two waters and sat in the other chair.

"I've been . . . God, I can't even say it."

"It's okay," George said. "Whatever it is, I've probably done worse."

"No, you probably haven't. I've been helping people cheat. The hole cards. During the tournaments."

"Jesus, Fiona." George felt too heavy to even reach for his glass of water. He wasn't sure he wanted the answer, but he needed to ask: "Who's been paying you?"

Fiona shook her head. "I don't know, and I don't want to know. I want it to be over. I'd even go to the police if I didn't think it would get me killed."

"You've been getting paid anonymously?"

"It's all in the notes. I got the first one in Halifax, a couple of days before the tournament started. They come under my door with instructions. I wouldn't have even considered cheating if it hadn't been — but the person must know me pretty well, because the first note said, *Do you want to save your mother's house?*"

Fiona's weakness. George knew it; who else did?

"You can't protect her from everything, Fiona. A lot of people lose their houses — especially in the past few years. She could move to an apartment. You could have helped her with that, with the money you make legitimately."

Fiona rolled her eyes. "Yes, George. That's what I should have done. But it isn't, okay? My mom worked her ass off to get us all through school. And the bank — it was one of those mortgages where the fine print should be criminal. So I thought I could be Robin Hood. Steal from the hollow selfish poker world and give the money to someone more deserving."

"You've been contributing to that household since your dad left. How old were you? Ten?"

"Eleven. And a paper route and other odd jobs don't count. All I did was buy my own clothes and pay for the odd school trip. My mother was the one working nights to keep the heat on."

And breaking down periodically, and not working for months on end while Fiona got her sister's and brother's lunches packed. But this wasn't the time for George to point that out. "I'm guessing the house is now safe from the collectors."

"She's paid off the whole mortgage with the money I've sent her. Now all this cash I'm getting from the scam is just . . . paper. And there's no way out."

"There's always a way out," George said, not sure if he believed himself. "Could you leave a note for the guy who's leaving you notes, asking him for options?"

"He calls himself the Dealer," Fiona said. "It's like this is a game to him, so he can show everyone how clever he is."

"Or how in charge he is. Do you think he's also rigging the deal somehow?"

Fiona shook her head. "That would be way too complicated."

George wasn't sure she was right. Still, he asked, "What would be his motivation to cheat?"

Fiona looked at George like he'd asked if a flush beat a pair. "Pretty sure it's the money."

George frowned.

"Money drives everything, George. We can't all be artists like you and find richness in the life of our soul. For some of us, the material world is all we have."

"You can find a way back from this, Fiona." George wondered if that was true. She was already breaking down. If she made her weakness too apparent, this Dealer wouldn't be able to trust her for much longer. Fiona smiled sadly. "I'm not so sure."

"I'll help you. Maybe you should crash with me until this whole thing is resolved."

"You mean I should sleep here?" Her eyes grew wide. George loved when she looked vulnerable. "You're not still mad at me from dinner?"

"At *you*? No. Come on. I'll go with you to your room. We'll get your stuff."

TUESDAY / MARCH 22

THIRTY-FIVE
CLARE

The sun hit Clare's eyes, waking her up and telling her she had a headache.

At least she hadn't slept with Nate. Clare might have, but she'd kept enough of her senses to remember that Tiffany was not such an indiscriminate slut.

Her phone was ringing. Had it been ringing for a while? She had vague memories of the phone ringing in one of her dreams. She checked call display: Amanda.

"What?" Clare's voice was hoarser than she'd thought it would be.

"Clare. You okay?"

"Why wouldn't I be?"

"I'm at the Elbow Room. We were supposed to meet for breakfast."

Clare looked at the clock beside her bed. "Shit. Sorry. You want me to meet you there now?"

"No time. Your tournament starts in less than an hour. Are you just waking up?"

"Yeah. I thought I set my alarm, but I must have messed it up." Did that sound believable in anyone's world?

"Were you up late? When I didn't see you this morning, I called in. Reports have you leaving the casino around ten."

Well, kudos to whoever was spying on her. "Reports are right. And then I had drinks with one of the suspects."

"How many drinks?"

"Your people didn't follow me to the bar? I was sure I saw a goon sitting inside."

"How many?"

"Just one. He was sitting at a table inside where he could see the door to the patio, pretending to read a newspaper."

"A goon is a thug, Clare. These men are officers. If you weren't here on loan, they would almost all be senior to you. And how many drinks, was my question."

"Two or three." Which was half true if shots didn't count.

"Okay. Well, don't worry about breakfast. We can catch up tomorrow. Good luck today."

Clare was off the hook this easily? Cloutier would have been screaming for her badge.

"Oh, and Clare?"

"Yeah?"

"I'll leave your sunglasses with the concierge at your hotel. Pick them up on your way out. They're blingy."

"Awesome." Had Clare really just said "awesome" about a pair of sunglasses? "Sorry I messed up your morning."

Clare showered quickly, smoked half a cigarette on the curb while she waited for a cab, and slid into her tournament seat with four and a half minutes to spare.

"Forget to blow-dry your hair today?" T-Bone sneered at Clare on his way past her table.

Clare looked up. "I didn't want to stand out in this crowd by appearing too well groomed." She made a note to spend some quality time with a comb and a mirror during the break.

"Touché." T-Bone fingered the gray ponytail poking out from his black cowboy hat. "Good luck with the cards, kid. Don't want you busting out before I can humiliate you at my table."

"Ditto," Clare said. "Which means, good luck with the cards, T-Bone. Make sure you accumulate lots of chips so I can take them all at once."

Elizabeth, from her seat at Clare's table, said, "You two should get a room."

Clare made a gagging motion.

T-Bone said, "You think I want to see her bony ass naked?"

"You think I want to smell what's under that cowboy hat?"

Elizabeth eyed Clare as T-Bone sauntered away. "You have a lot of confidence for someone who can't play this game. Is Mickey still coaching you?"

Clare nodded.

"You're lucky. For all his annoying personality traits, Mickey plays a seriously good game."

"He's a professional poker player," Clare said. "Don't you all play a good game?"

Elizabeth nodded slowly. "But some people — like Joe and T-Bone — rely on people-reading and gut-related factors for their edge. Others — like me — suck at people-reading, so we grind away using numbers and odds."

"Which one is Mickey?"

"He's both. He acts like he's such a crazy man, shooting from the hip. Makes everyone think he's a gut player. Well, his gut is good — it's on a par with Joe's and T-Bone's. But he's got science down better than I do. He's probably the only player on the scene that scares me."

Clare wondered why Elizabeth was still pretending to be nice to her. She should use this in while she had it. "Is Loni Mills bipolar?"

"What?" Elizabeth looked at Clare oddly. "I don't think so. Why?"

"When I met her she was super nice. Chatty, talked to me about the waiting list at that Niagara Falls game. Now I think she hates me."

"She does," Elizabeth said. "But don't worry. It's not personal.

Loni hates anyone who steals Mickey's attention away from remembering her."

"I don't get it."

"You don't have to. But you can trust Loni. Who she says she is is exactly who she is. If she has something against you — as I guess you can tell — she'll show it or she'll say it to your face."

This seemed like a strange thing for Elizabeth to say. Clare was tempted to come right out and ask why Elizabeth was pretending to like Tiffany. Instead, she said, "What about Fiona?"

Elizabeth frowned as she pushed her long black hair behind her ears. She had an expression like she was swatting away a mosquito. "What about her?"

"Can I trust Fiona? She's been friendly. And I like her."

"Up to you," Elizabeth said. "My rule with Fiona is I trust her as long as she's in my line of sight."

Clare found that answer unhelpful. "What's her angle, though?"

"Her angle is herself. If you make Fiona look good, she'll want you around. If she senses competition, not so much."

"Competition for men?" Clare wondered if Fiona was interested in Nate.

Elizabeth shook her head. "Competition for the spotlight."

THIRTY-SIX
NOAH

Noah toyed absently with his chip stack, letting the heavy clay disks slip through his fingers and clack against each other as they fell back into their pile. It was soothing, like running his toes through pebbles at the beach and listening to them shift. Not that he ran his feet through pebbles a lot in Manhattan.

He stared at the black table felt with the red maple leaf — the Canadian Classic logo — in the center. The scratchy British voice came through his earbud: "T-sixteen. P-six, seven-deuce clubs."

Noah peeled back the corners of his cards to see the seven and two of clubs. Perfect: he'd just learned that he was at Table Sixteen in Position Six.

He watched Fiona standing at the entrance to the poker room floor. Two cameras were on her and her hands were gesturing passionately.

The bug he'd left in Fiona's room hadn't told him much. She hadn't even been in the room for five minutes the previous night. There was a little shocked scream when she realized her suitcase had been broken into. Noah wondered if he should have made it less obvious — taken one note from the middle instead of the whole stack. But whatever. It was done. Then about half an hour later, two voices had been speaking. Fiona and a guy who sounded like George Bigelow. Noah's interpretation from the clips he'd managed to hear was that they'd come by to grab some things, and Fiona had spent the night in the other man's — George's? — room. She sounded afraid. Scared of the cops or scared of the killer, Noah couldn't tell.

It could screw up his plan if Fiona stayed in this other man's room permanently. He would have to bug that room, too. His first step was to find out if the man was George. His second — hmm — well, one thing at a time.

THIRTY-SEVEN
GEORGE

George watched the dealer set up the new hand. He was like a magician, dropping cards so quickly you barely saw his fingers until they'd moved on. He was impressed with himself — George could see that in the smirk he gave no one in particular as he set down the deck after dealing. But he was invisible. No one — not even George, normally — watched him work.

Was it strange that a person who clearly wanted to feel empowered — the Dealer of Fiona's notes — would choose such a background title for his name? Or was that part of the thrill — pulling the strings, dealing the cards, changing the outcome for everyone here while remaining effectively invisible?

A pudgy man across the poker table from George waved into the stands. George followed his gaze to see a woman waving back — equally pudgy, her eyes wide and her smile wider, clearly thrilled for her husband, who had probably won his seat to this tournament in a $5 satellite online. The couple didn't care if he won — their suburban mortgage would be under control and their kids wouldn't be in expensive schools. This trip was an adventure; maybe the wildest thing they'd ever done. The pudgy man looked at his hole cards, tried three or four different faces on before folding.

Watching this couple reminded George of what had drawn him to poker ten years earlier as a fresh grad school dropout. This scene was alive. It was the opposite of academia, with its meaningless theoretical conversations about events that had already happened or books that had already been written.

The skinny man who was next to play scowled and muttered and tossed his hand in the muck. "You're giving me nothing," he said in the direction of the dealer. "Can't you just reach into that pile of cards and give me something I can work with? I'm gonna get blinded away before I ever get to play a hand." His fingers were yellow; George guessed that he needed a cigarette.

George couldn't stay here much longer. He had money saved. He could buy a modest writing space. Maybe not the spacious New England log cabin of his dreams, with its gourmet kitchen and picture windows overlooking an isolated lake, but something, somewhere, that would work.

"Hey, George, you know about the game tonight, right?" Joe Mangan said from behind a pair of oversized pink sunglasses. He had a blond wig with ponytails and he was wearing a pink plaid shirt; George wondered if he was supposed to be Paris Hilton from *The Simple Life*.

The rest of the table perked their ears to this conversation — George could see it; their bodies even shifted slightly toward Joe. Like when the cool kids would sit by their lockers talking about weekend plans before class began, everyone was interested when Joe Mangan talked about his social life. Maybe that's what George liked about poker — for the first time, he was on the inside of the cool crowd. The dumb thing was, when you were in it, you didn't notice. The only bonus was that you no longer suffered the angst of being an outsider.

"Elizabeth invited me," George said. "I'm not sure if I'll make it."

"We're leaving the dock at eight. If you're coming, get there a bit early and text me when you get to the gate. I told Liz I'd take her for an early dinner. She gets all annoyed if our life becomes all about poker."

"I don't blame her," George said. "She's an amazing woman; she shouldn't be wasting her whole self on this game."

Joe, as Paris Hilton, shrugged. "I could play the game forever and not get bored."

"You gotta have more in your life," Mickey said, from down the table. "It's no good playing games all day and night without some bigger purpose. You want to learn about one-track obsession, you should see *Black Swan*. Swap poker in for the ballet, it's like your Ghost of Christmas Future."

"What's your bigger purpose?" Joe ignored the reference to a movie he was clearly never going to see. "A bigger jar of peanuts?"

"No way," Mickey said. "George is writing a book about me."

George's heart sank. He had promised Mickey this biography. But in his image of himself in his writing cabin in the woods, he wasn't writing poker books. It was fiction only — or this weird blend of fact and fiction he'd been working on lately.

"You're lucky," Joe said. "With George writing it, your book will be good. Mine's a load of crap. It sells well, but my writers were a team of hacks and I'm pretty sure it shows."

"You didn't write your own book?" George had no idea why he was surprised. He mucked his ten-nine offsuit.

"Who has time for that?" Joe said. "I mean, you do, obviously. You're a writer. I don't mean it's a waste of time. But it's not what I'm good at."

"What are you good at?" Mickey asked Joe.

"Playing games," Joe said, making a giant overbet before the flop. "And reading people."

"Yeah?" Mickey grinned. "Read this: all in."

"I read that I should fold." Joe flipped over two eights and tossed his hand in the muck.

"Good read." Mickey showed a jack and a five. "If you'd called that, I would have been out of the game."

George shook his head. "You guys are both cowboys. I'm sitting here trying to play textbook poker, wondering why I can't win a hand. And this is why. The so-called heroes are making moves even a novice would know to avoid."

"Except when we make the move, it's for a reason." Mickey seemed to be glaring at Joe. "Right, Pretty Boy?"

Joe laughed. "No one calls me that in real life, Crazy Mouse. And sure, I guess we always have a reason."

George had forgotten Fiona's old name for Mickey. He hadn't known her when she'd done her podcast, but he'd listened to each episode, sometimes more than once.

George caught sight of Fiona, flitting around like the extrovert she wasn't. He was glad to have her staying in his room again, even if it was fear that brought her there. It was how things should be. George wondered if she'd come with him to his writing cabin. Maybe if she was scared enough . . .

THIRTY-EIGHT
CLARE

"Doing anything on your break?" Nate came up behind Clare, his voice low and scratchy and sounding like it wanted a cigarette.

"Ah." She twirled around to give him a smile. "The arrogant New Yorker."

"The slutty Canadian," Nate fired back, but made a hurt face.

Clare rolled her eyes. "I'm grabbing a coffee. Come if you want."

Some dark hair flopped into Nate's eyes. He didn't brush it away. "Don't sound so excited to spend time with me."

Clare wanted to brush the hair away for him, but held back. "How are you doing in the tournament?"

"Crap," Nate said. "I'm playing okay, but the cards are killing me."

"It's probably karma."

"Thanks. How's your day working out?"

"Great." Clare started toward the coffee bar and was glad when Nate followed. "I'm playing so-so. But the cards are running my way. I've been saved twice by a brilliant river."

"I guess that's karma, too," Nate said.

"What else could it be?" Clare batted her mascara-laden eye-lashes. It felt strangely fun.

"Dumb luck," Nate said. "Have you run into T-Bone?"

"He stopped to insult my hair on his way past my table."

Nate looked at Clare appraisingly. "I assumed the messy look was an avant-garde fashion trend."

"You have too much faith in me." Clare grinned. "It's actually because some asshole kept me out drinking last night. I overslept and had no time to shower."

"Ew. Do you smell?" Nate waved a hand in front of his nose.

"It's amazing what perfume can do."

Nate laughed. "Anyway, I think it's hilarious how mad you've got T-Bone. You ready to take him on?"

"With verbal jabs, happily. But at cards?" Clare shook her head. "I'd rather wait until tomorrow. Are you ridiculously hungover?"

"Not ridiculously."

"You're lucky," Clare said. "My body is screaming at me to stop poisoning it."

They arrived at the end of the coffee line and stood together to wait.

Nate put a hand on Clare's shoulder. "What else does your body say?"

"It says that I should stay away from you." Actually, Clare's body wanted to stay close to Nate; it was her other instincts telling her to stay away.

"Do I tempt you away from your chastity vows?"

"Please." Clare attempted a haughty head-toss inspired by Blair Waldorf from *Gossip Girl*. As part of her Tiffany training, Amanda had made her sit and watch endless boring TV shows about rich kids. "I'm not chaste. I'm selective."

The line moved slightly. Mickey walked by them with a hot drink in his hand.

"Gotta love this game, huh?" he said in Clare and Nate's general direction.

"You look chipper," Clare said to Mickey. "What happened to that misery from yesterday?"

"Huh?" Mickey looked blank. "Oh. That was yesterday." He moved on to wherever he was going, his black suit jacket weaving through the crowd.

Nate watched him leave and said, "Has Mickey's coaching helped you much?"

Clare nodded. "The guy's a genius."

"What has he taught you?"

"I'm not going to tell you. What if we're up against each other in the tournament and I've spilled the secret move I want to use to take you down?"

"You're brutal." Nate pushed Clare lightly, reminding her to move forward in the line.

"It's a brutal game," Clare said.

"That one of your lessons from Mickey?"

"It actually is." Clare leaned in close. She liked Nate's after-shave: not musky, but manly. Probably Axe. "You know people are dying on this scene, right?"

"I've heard that." Nate frowned. "But I didn't join the tour until Niagara. No one died there, right?"

"Right. Or here. Yet."

They arrived at the cash register and they both ordered black coffee. Nate paid and Clare thanked him.

"No problem," Nate said, as they made their way back toward the poker room. "Maybe now you'll put out."

Clare laughed. "You're closer than you know. I like beer, but I can live without it. But cut off my coffee supply, and I'll happily whore myself out until my chemical balance is restored."

"Good to know. You were so insistent on splitting the bill last night, I was afraid I couldn't buy you at any price."

"Splitting? I wanted to pay the whole thing." Amanda had advised Clare to take every opportunity to grab the cheque, to create the impression that a hundred bucks was small change to her.

"I know," Nate said. "But if I'd let you pay, *I* would have felt compelled to put out. There's nothing less sexy than being a kept man."

"There's lots that's less sexy. Like men who cheat on their wives."

"You don't think cheating's hot, in a clandestine kind of way?" Nate lowered his voice even deeper to say this.

"I'd rather a man told me he liked to fuck sheep."

"Really?" Nate's eyebrows arched.

"I'd walk away regardless, but animals are a preference. Cheating's immoral."

"No kidding," Nate said. "Because I find moralistic people a turn-off. I'm going to make an exception for you, though."

"Appreciate it," Clare said, realizing that maybe fucking sheep had its own morality questions — like, for the sheep. "Hey, I heard a rumor that those murders might be connected to some cheating ring. Have you heard that, too?"

Nate's brow lowered. He took Clare's arm — carefully, so as not to spill the coffees — and led her to a wall where no one could overhear.

"Wow," Clare said. "Why the serious face?"

"You should be careful what you say out loud around here."

"Why?" Clare smiled blandly, trying her best to look innocent.

"I don't know where you come from or how sheltered your world was growing up. My suspicion is that a lot of your innocence is a fucking act. But you must understand that the killer could be anyone on this scene. You can't go around speculating out loud what these deaths do and don't relate to. If the wrong person overhears you, they could think you know something and you could become the next victim."

"Okay," Clare said. "I've never been around this world, around criminals, really. Well, my father had a friend who went to jail for fraud. But he wasn't a close friend — more of an acquaintance —"

"Shut up." Nate leaned in and kissed her, and Clare was glad she was leaning into the wall, because the feeling nearly melted her. She hoped her Juicy Couture perfume really did mask that she hadn't showered.

Was it cheating if Clare wanted Tiffany to fuck this guy?

THIRTY-NINE
ELIZABETH

lizabeth watched Nate kiss Tiffany, up against the wall like they were in some romance movie. What a little fucking drama queen.

At least it looked like Nate had won the prop bet. Which was good, because Elizabeth didn't know how long she could pretend to be buddy-buddy with Tiffany without vomiting on her own words.

She sipped her green tea. There were ten minutes left on the break and Elizabeth was alone at the poker table.

She saw Joe near the coffee bar. Joe caught Elizabeth looking and waved. He had that stupid grin on his face, the one he plastered on in the morning and left on all day in case the cameras caught him in one of their candid shots. At least he'd taken off his Paris Hilton wig during the break. Still, the poison started a dull throb through Elizabeth's body.

Shit. She did a double take, but it was true. Her brother Peter was standing there talking to Joe. He was animated, grinning — Peter looked like he thought Joe was the greatest guy on Earth.

The polite thing would be to go talk to them. Elizabeth used to care a lot about what the polite thing was, but that was one value the poker world had cured her of. Her veins wanted to explode, and now her head was beginning to go. She didn't trust herself to get up; she was afraid she'd say something horrible to Peter.

Oh, who was she kidding? Of course Elizabeth was getting up, walking over to the men, smiling broadly as she gave her brother a hug.

"Liz!" Peter squeezed Elizabeth like she was a teddy bear he'd found buried at the bottom of a moving box after several years in storage. It actually felt kind of good. "Great to see you. Did I miss the email where you said you'd be in town?"

Elizabeth gave a small laugh. "It's not you I'm avoiding."

"Good," Peter said. "Because I came to watch you play."

Joe wandered off, which Elizabeth appreciated. She looked her brother in the eye. "Please don't watch me play. You know it throws my game off."

"I watch all your games on TV. What's the difference?"

"I've already played them by the time you're watching."

Peter nodded at the indoor bleachers. "The spectators don't bother you?"

"They're just background noise; I don't see them as real people."

"How about a deal?" Peter said. "I won't watch you play if you come out for dim sum on the weekend."

"Who's going to be there?"

"Mom and Dad and me."

Her veins started pulsing, like the poison wanted out. "Do they know you're inviting me?"

Peter shook his head.

"I want to see you, Peter. It's just — Mom and Dad — and when everyone's together — I can't help feeling like I'm a teenager again. Only when I was a teenager I never disappointed them."

"You should hear them brag about you behind your back."

"So they can save face in front of their friends." Elizabeth wrung her hands together. Maybe she *should* go for dinner, if only to buy some time until the next obligatory visit. "They make sure to let me know how they really feel."

"How do they really feel?" Peter shifted his black vinyl brief-case from one hand to the other.

"Like I let them down when I stopped working for Dad and I've been letting them down ever since."

Peter didn't say anything.

"What's wrong?" Elizabeth worried that something she'd said might have offended him.

"I miss you."

Elizabeth bit her lower lip. "I miss you, too."

"So come for dim sum. It's one meal. It's painless."

"It won't be painless for me. How about we get together, you and me? You don't have to tell them I'm in town."

Peter's eyes moved around the casino. The warning bell sounded. Most players were already in their seats. "You can't not talk to them forever."

"I'm not *not* talking to them. I'm just, you know, not talking to them."

"I'm sure that's different somehow," Peter said.

"You don't know what it's like. They've never put the same pressure on you."

"Why do you think I became an accountant?" Peter gestured toward his briefcase.

"Because you love to be bored."

"Wrong. So I wouldn't have to deal with constant disapproval. I'm not strong like you are."

Elizabeth wondered why people seemed to think she was strong. "If I was strong, I'd go to dim sum and the shit they spewed would be in one ear and out the other."

"So make a shield."

"What?" Elizabeth pictured herself in the back of someone's metal shop, soldering and hammering until she'd built herself a medieval-looking shield.

"Build a little imaginary shield that you can put up to deflect their insults. Say *ping* in your head every time you use it. The insults will bounce right back to them."

"I don't want to ping insults back at Mom and Dad," Elizabeth said. "They're not like this on purpose."

"So ping the insults into the atmosphere." Peter held up his hand and used a finger from the other hand to demonstrate the insult reflecting off in the direction of the sky. "Or imagine the insults dissolving as soon as they've bounced off the shield."

"My brother the video game freak."

"Come on, Liz. Visualization works."

Elizabeth frowned. "I'll give it a try."

"So you'll come to dim sum." Peter's face lit up.

"Let me work on my shield first."

"Fine." Peter shrugged. "While you're working on that, I'll just take a seat in the spectator area."

"Peter!"

"Doesn't have to be dim sum. Dinner can work. Dad loves this place at Westminster and Three Road. Their soft-shell crab is dangerously good."

"I hate deep-fried food."

"You won't hate this."

"I have to get back to my table. The game's going to start in — shit, like five seconds."

"Okay. I'll be cheering you on." Peter gave Elizabeth a little wave and started walking toward the spectator stands.

"Please?" Elizabeth pleaded with her eyes. "I really don't want you watching me."

Peter stopped walking, but he didn't reverse his direction.

"Okay," Liz said. "Dinner. Or dim sum. This weekend."

"Deal."

"Oh, and Peter? Do you have time to do me a favor?"

"I love it when someone asks me that question before they tell me the favor."

"Can you dig around Dad's office for me? I need to find out everything I can about a furniture importer whose last name is James."

FORTY

GEORGE

"You think this is a bit cloak-and-dagger, Mickey?" George shrugged off his leather jacket and hooked it onto the back of his chair. "The bar downtown . . . the separate cabs . . ."

Mickey squinted as he glanced around the busy room. "You think I'm funny. But anyone overhears this, I'm toast, you're toast, we can both kiss all our dreams goodbye."

"All right, I get it," George said. "I say anything, we're both dead."

Mickey shook his head. "Joke all you fucking want to. There's already three people who ain't breathing too well anymore."

A waiter in black arrived at their table. He wore a little black apron from which he pulled a notepad and pen. Mickey ordered a bottle of Bud. George had the waiter list the microbrews on tap before selecting a local pale ale.

When the waiter had left, George leaned into the table and said, "You're willing to risk both of our lives just so I write your biography?"

Mickey nodded. "A deal's a deal. I'll share information about this hole card scam as I find it; you make this book as good as it can be."

"How can one book be worth so much to you?"

Mickey's face pulled a pained, almost pleading expression. "It just is."

The drinks arrived. The waiter set down two cocktail napkins and the beers, frowning the whole time. He gave an exaggerated wrist swirl before turning and prancing away.

"What, we're not gay enough for him?" Mickey said when the waiter had left.

George shrugged. "I don't think it's a gay or straight thing. I think he draws his self-worth from making himself feel superior to his customers."

"Why should he care who's superior? Anyway, it's you he hates. 'What kind of fucking microbrew?' Who asks that shit?"

George rolled his eyes. "I like beer that has flavor. And I understand why the waiter's sensitive. It takes brains to do his job well, but there's zero prestige associated."

"Who cares about prestige?" Mickey asked. "Is he living for himself or other people?"

"Who's your biography for, if not for other people?"

Mickey muttered something into his beer bottle.

"Pardon?" George said.

"I said it's for my fucking father."

George looked at Mickey for a moment and said, "Families are fucked. We can leave them, go out on our own and never talk to them, but we can't escape their criticism."

Mickey looked at George oddly. "Why you gotta philosophize about everything today? My old man don't criticize me. He's prouder than punch that I made it so far. Watches me on TV with his buddies all the time."

"So I don't get it."

"Obviously. I mean, I'm sorry about your family and all. They sound like pompous windbags, so I guess it's not your fault you're like you are. But at some point, George, you gotta claim your life."

George fingered the stubby base of his glass. It wasn't the smoothest beer he'd ever tasted, but it had body, and he liked that. "This isn't about me."

"Sure it is. You don't want to write my biography because you think it's not prestigious. You're as bad as that fucking gay waiter."

"You think he's judging you for preferring big blonds with silicon implants?" Yet another problem George had with the poker scene; it insulated the rednecks from ever having to change their bigoted ways.

Mickey snorted. "Don't make this about me being a queer-o-phobe. I had friends who used to beat queers up; I never joined them."

"Nice friends."

"Nicer than your fucking friends," Mickey said. "Making you feel like less than a man if you don't get all the perfect credentials from Snob School."

"Can we dispense with the abusive preamble and cut to the reason you called me here?"

"Yeah, all right." Mickey glanced around again. "So I'm talking to Loni after I bust out of the tourney in Niagara — it's her favorite time to talk, when she thinks I'm down — and she tells me she's thinking of playing in the Vancouver game."

"I was at Loni's table today," George said. "She's doing well in the game. I'm surprised."

"You should be fucking surprised. Not to malign her intelligence, because Loni is one of the most skilled manipulators I know. But neither math nor cards are her forte."

George hoped this wasn't the whole reason Mickey had wanted to meet. Sure, with cheaters in the game, it was natural to suspect everything unusual. But — "A monkey could win one of these tournaments if the cards chose to fall that way. Is this why we're here incognito?"

"We're not incognito. We're not wearing disguises."

"Sorry," George said. "Wrong word, but you get my meaning."

"As a writer, you should choose your words more carefully. Maybe I shouldn't have picked you to write my biography."

"Would you come off it, Mickey, and tell me what there is to tell."

"Fine. Anyway, Loni had had some drinks — it was the middle of the afternoon, but life with T-Bone drives her to the bottle at all hours — and she starts saying shit like what if there was a way for her to know everyone's hole cards."

"Really," George said. "Just out in the open. The most skilled manipulator suddenly forgets how to keep a secret."

"Shit," Mickey said. "You think she's playing me?"

"Either that or you're playing me."

"Why would I play you? I want to get to the bottom of this scam as much as you do. I would have bailed on this Canadian Classic bullshit tournament if I didn't think I could help fix it."

George wasn't sure what Mickey meant by "fix." "How many players do you think are cheating?"

Mickey shrugged. "There's two or three I'd lay money on. I don't want to say any names until I'm more sure."

"You'd lay money on them, but you can't say their names out loud?"

"To lay cash I need odds. To accuse someone of cheating, I need close to a hundred percent."

George half-smiled. "How did you get these names?"

"Other than Loni — who I'm going to call as a sure thing — I watch them play poker."

"And if they play a hand they should have folded, they go on your radar?" George asked.

"No. If their eyes say they can see my fucking hole cards, they go on my radar."

"How do their eyes say that?" George wondered what his own eyes were saying.

"Same way they say if they're bluffing or holding the nuts. I could always see behind people's eyes, since I was a kid watching my uncles play."

"What about the guys who wear sunglasses?"

"Well, they're the smart ones, aren't they? But there's other ways you can tell. How they handle their chips, are their hands shaking or even, are their shoulders tight or relaxed —"

George cut in, "So why would Loni bait you? What did her eyes et cetera say?"

"You know what interferes with my reading skills?" Mickey slammed back the rest of his beer. He held the bottle up and pointed at it to show the snotty waiter he was ready for a new one. "Loni. Because even though I know she's an opportunistic bitch who would throw me to the curb without glancing back to see if I was bleeding, she's still my ex-fucking-wife, and I still go crazy when we're in the same room together. She's the only thing on this whole scene that makes my radar go kaboom."

George wrinkled his forehead. "What Loni told you — whatever it means — does that put T-Bone on the radar as a cheater?"

Mickey nodded. "But what I don't got figured out — and maybe our two brains can work on this together — is why T-Bone would cheat."

"Yeah," George said. "I'm not sure either. He's been a winning player for over fifty years."

"I'm not saying the man isn't scum. If he was down and out he'd pimp his grandmother for a ticket to a tournament."

"But T-Bone's not down and out, is he?"

Mickey shrugged. "He hasn't been doing so hot. Since the game exploded into the public eye and the rest of us have been cashing in on these newcomers who like to take chances, T-Bone's game has been slipping downhill. He hasn't been able to make the right adjustments to the newer, looser play."

"Has he been losing money, though? Or just earning a bit less? Cheating seems drastic even for someone you call scum."

"Put it this way," Mickey said. "He wouldn't have a moral opposition. I've known the guy a long time. When you were off getting Ivy League educated, I was down in Texas playing cards with the real sharps. You can take notes about that if you like. The Texas years are going to be a great section in my book."

"Your South Boston friends won't be upset that you abandoned the neighborhood because you didn't think it had enough action?"

"I'm not dumb enough to think my Southie friends will read the book."

"Right. It's for your father."

"He loves books. Collects them. He says everything important that ever happened can be found in a book."

"He doesn't place a lot of importance on real life."

"He means big things. The things that change history. If I could come home one Christmas and give him a book, all wrapped up, with my picture on it, I'd think I really made it in this world."

FORTY-ONE
CLARE

Clare ran her finger along the rim of the aluminum bench. She frowned at a pigeon, who dutifully flew away.

"I'm not sure I made the right decision on that exclusivity clause." Through the cell phone, Kevin's voice was heavy.

"You don't want to be exclusive with me anymore?" Clare felt her phone shake in her hand.

"Of course I do. But I want to be exclusive with all of your many personalities."

Clare watched a tugboat churn solidly through the river, a massive train of logs gliding behind it. She much preferred this working river by the casino over the yuppies and their yachts near her hotel.

"I'm too late," Kevin said.

She nodded, though of course he couldn't see. He wasn't technically too late — nothing physical had happened with Nate except that kiss a few hours earlier.

"It's not really up to you." Clare tried to speak gently, so it didn't sound like she was dictating terms. "It's my job to be single — to be open to dating, if necessary."

"Are you falling for someone?" Kevin's voice rose in pitch, making him sound about twelve. If nothing else, it succeeded in making Clare feel less attracted to him for the moment.

"Of course I'm not falling for a guy who might be a killer." Clare wasn't sure why she wanted Kevin to know there was someone here. It was a horrible breach of security — she shouldn't be talking about the case at all. She tried to tell herself it was in the name of relationship transparency.

"What?" Kevin's voice deepened again, became angry. "Why would you take such a stupid risk?"

"It's my job."

"It's your job to catch the killer, not fuck him and then let him shoot you."

"How do you know I'm not aroused by that kind of thing?"

Kevin snorted. "No one is turned on by being shot."

Clare lit a cigarette. She decided not to correct Kevin by telling him the killer was a strangler. "How have you been the past couple of days?"

"Worried about you."

"Don't worry about me. I'm too safe for comfort. A million security guys are spying on my every move, and my hotel is nowhere near the danger zone."

"There's a danger zone? That doesn't help me, Clare."

"Whatever. You know I can't be more specific." She should have been a lot less specific. Clare hoped her call wasn't being monitored. "How's business? Have you started with the YouTube videos?"

"Yep. So far I've made 'Troubleshooting Fuses' and 'Maybe Your tv is Not Really Broken.' I haven't gone live with them. I want to do a big launch all at once, with, like six or eight videos to help solve common problems."

Clare smiled. "Do you care if I tell Roberta, and put the same idea in her head? A mechanic isn't competition, right?"

"Yeah, of course, tell Roberta. I'm not competitive anyway, even if she was another electrician."

That was true. But Clare wasn't hot for Kevin's non-competitive side. "How's my Triumph?"

"Sitting quietly in my garage. It's been lousy weather — rainy and windy. Besides, I wouldn't feel right riding your bike without you holding on behind me."

Kevin was the first man Clare had ever allowed to drive her motorcycle. Though she would never say so out loud, she preferred to be a passenger when she was with him.

"My Triumph likes you," she told him. "You'd be fine on it alone."

"Thanks." Kevin sounded surprised. "I think that's the nicest thing you've ever told me."

FORTY-TWO
NOAH

Noah watched the strange, goateed kid lug two bags half his size through the lobby. He was muttering as he walked, swearing when one of the bags knocked against his leg. If Noah's logic was right, this kid was the voice behind the hole card transmission.

"Those bags look heavy." Noah reached the elevator at the same time as the kid.

"Not heavy. Just full of bloody hard edges that aren't forgiving when they smash against my skin." The coarse British voice sounded exactly like the one that had been helping Noah cheat all afternoon. "If I showed the authorities my bruises, my boss would be thrown in jail."

"Your boss is that hot redhead, right?"

"Fiona," Oliver said. "She's not hot when you work for her."

"Dragon lady?"

"Perfectionist is a bloody understatement. I'm not even allowed to leave the wires set up overnight." He patted his giant load. "In case anyone's poking around trying to sort out our dirty electrical secrets."

It occurred to Noah that Oliver might be innocent in the hole card scam. He might not be aware that his voice was being broadcast to players live at the tables while he read out their opponents' cards so matter-of-factly.

Noah smiled. "Is there such thing as a dirty electrical secret?"

"You'd be surprised."

The elevator came and Noah said, "Here, give me one of those. I'll carry it up to your room."

"I can't let you do that. I'd feel like half a man." Oliver's build wasn't much smaller than average, but he didn't look like the kind of guy who worked out.

"You are half a man. Maybe not size-wise, but what are you? Sixteen?"

"Nineteen." Oliver thrust his chin out for a second before handing one of the bags over. Noah wanted to reach over with a razor and relieve him of the stupid triangle of hair on his chin. Goatees always reminded Noah of pussy, and he found men who wore them repulsively effeminate.

They rode up twelve floors. Noah pressed Record on his iPhone and tried to steer the conversation so Oliver was doing most of the talking. When Oliver opened the door to his room, Noah handed him his bag and glanced inside to memorize the layout for later.

"You have plans for tonight?" Noah tried to sound casual asking.

Oliver glanced at him quickly. "Why?"

"No reason." Noah laughed. Man, this kid was skittish. "Just thought you might want to grab a beer."

WEDNESDAY / MARCH 23

FORTY-THREE
GEORGE

Fiona stood in front of the camera. She scrutinized George, asked him to shift positions several times before declaring him good to go for his exit interview.

"So George," Fiona said, in the perky voice she had crafted with the help of her publicist, "can you tell us how this game played out for you?"

George smiled from the corner of his mouth. "It played out as well as it could. I'm just not very good at poker."

"Oh, come on." Fiona's laugh probably sounded natural to viewers at home. "Your book has helped thousands of readers improve their game. You clearly know something about how the game is played."

"I know something about romance, too." George glared pointedly. "Doesn't mean I always win."

"Whoa, it's early in the morning for a jab like that." Grin for the cameras. "Can anyone hook me up with a stronger coffee? Some of you may know that George and I used to date. It was fairly hot and heavy, so naturally he's not over me."

Though Fiona had spent the previous two nights in his bed, George couldn't resist saying, "No. But I'm sure someone else is."

"Sorry." Fiona touched George's shoulder and pressed on her earpiece. She looked at the camera, her perky voice replaced with the serious tone of a news anchor. "I'm afraid we have some breaking news. Loni Mills, ex-wife of Mickey Mills and T-Bone Jones's girlfriend, has been found dead in her hotel room."

George stifled his first reaction, which was to laugh: Fiona was talking as if they were live, but this wouldn't be broadcast until later, at which point Loni's death would not be breaking news.

Then he remembered what dead meant. The permanence overwhelmed him, and George felt incredibly heavy.

He watched Fiona speak, but he couldn't hear her words anymore. He needed to get to his writing while this death was still fresh. George left Fiona and went upstairs to work.

FORTY-FOUR
CLARE

Clare looked dumbly at her cards and mucked them. The news that Loni Mills was dead sounded chilling on the loudspeaker. Clare had been sent into this game to stop the killer and instead she'd been living it up, more worried about how she could have sex with Nate and not be cheating on Kevin than about making the Canadian gambling scene safe again.

The local cops weren't there yet, but they would be soon enough. Even though the RCMP was effectively the police force in Vancouver, Clare's cover was supposed to be deep enough that the local forces didn't know who she was. She hoped Tiffany James stood up under their questioning.

And why was the tournament still running? Shouldn't someone have called a break?

And then someone did call a break, right as twenty uniformed cops poured through the doors. In another mood, Clare might laugh at the overkill SWAT team effect, but she was too consumed with feeling like a failure.

When she stood up, she was relieved to see Nate, who had come over from his table to see her.

"You okay?"

"Fine," she said. "You?"

"Not fine." Nate stuck his hands in his pockets and took them out a couple of seconds later. "You want to grab a smoke? The cops are making us stay for questioning, but they're letting small groups out for smoke breaks."

"Do you know how long the tournament is breaking for?"

"All day."

"Cool." Because Clare was not up for pretending to care about poker.

"You want to go somewhere once they let us out of here? Stanley Park? Grab a coffee and go for a walk?"

"It's pissing rain." Clare instantly regretted her word choice. *Pouring* would have been more like Tiffany.

"I'll buy you an umbrella."

The offer was tempting, but Amanda had already sent her a text — news clearly traveled fast when RCMP officers were every-where. She wanted to meet Clare for lunch.

"Maybe we can hook up later?" Clare said. "This whole thing's kind of weird. I don't know how I'll feel after questioning, but I think I'll just want to hang at my hotel for a bit. Maybe listen to some music. Be alone."

"That's cool." Nate's eyes moved down to his sneakers and stayed there. "Text me when you're feeling better?"

"Yeah." Clare grabbed her jacket and started walking toward the door. Nate hung back, so she turned around and said to him, "Aren't you coming for a smoke?"

"Oh, right." Nate was clearly distracted by something. Clare wished she knew what.

"Buy me an umbrella in the meantime," she said as they walked toward the doors. "Then I'll have to go out with you."

FORTY-FIVE
ELIZABETH

Elizabeth stared at Fiona. She didn't try to pull her mouth shut; she left her jaw hanging to show Fiona how appalling her request had been.

"Seriously?" Elizabeth said finally. "You're conducting interviews about players' reactions to Loni's death?"

"Sure," Fiona said. "Does that offend you?"

Elizabeth didn't know how to begin answering that. "How could you even want to spend today that way?"

"I know this is hard." Obviously the camera was on, because Fiona was eying it flirtatiously. She flicked a wavy strand of red hair from her face. "But I think it's important."

"Fiona, you're not some important TV journalist who's been asked to cover an international tragedy." The poison was firing inside Elizabeth, shredding her brain; she didn't care what she said. "You have a shallow show about a shallow game, and you should stick to that."

"Wow." Fiona smiled broadly, like *Let's humor this crazy bitch.* "Were you and Loni close? Her death seems to have sparked a strong reaction."

Elizabeth thought she might punch Fiona. She had never

been in a fist-fight, but she was up for seeing how one felt. "You know Loni and I weren't close. You and I have been working and living in the same hotels and casinos for the past three years. You weren't close with Loni either, as much as you like to think you're everyone's best friend."

"We all have our unique reactions to grief," Fiona said, entirely to the camera. "It's what makes times like this so interesting."

Elizabeth smiled, broad and phony. She urged her arms to stay by her sides, where they would do no harm. "Yes, Fiona. Times like this are fascinating. Grief, like old age and senility, allows us to say what we like. And what I'd like to say is: why were you fucking my boyfriend's brains out in the Fallsview Casino on Sunday?"

Fiona faltered, which Elizabeth considered a good start. "I did hear banging outside my door." Fiona faced the cameras. "But since there's a killer on the loose — four people now have been found dead inside their hotel rooms — I didn't think it would be prudent to open the door when I was alone at night."

"Because I look like a killer, don't I?" Elizabeth kept her face calm. Maybe instead of punching Fiona, she should strangle her with her microphone cord. "They have those inventions on doors now called peepholes. When I'm alone at night — like when my boyfriend is off fucking some red-headed skank — I use the peephole to see if I'd be wise to open the door."

"Which brings us to another interesting point," Fiona said. "What *does* a killer look like? Is it a big, strong man with a menacing look and a rope in his hand? Or could it be a slender, quiet woman with a piece of rope hidden in her purse? We don't know, do we? And we won't know, until the Poker Choker has been caught."

"Jesus fucking Christ, Fiona." Elizabeth knew she should walk away. "Because I don't smile and nod and give you the exit interview you want, you paint me as some kind of killer?"

"Oh," Fiona said with a small laugh. "I guess that did sound a bit like you. It wasn't meant to. I was only illustrating contrasts.

I think it's important for the poker community that we open our minds and solve this case together."

"You're not a community detective. And you're no fucking martyr. You saved your mother's house from foreclosure. Big deal. Joe donated three hundred grand to help orphans in Michigan last year. He doesn't go around telling the public he's helping the world. He does it."

Fiona started shaking. Elizabeth wasn't sure what she'd said, but she'd hit home.

She peered into Fiona's eyes to gauge specific reactions. "What got you, Fiona? The orphans? Your mom's house? That's it. Your mom's house. Now why — since it's supposedly a nice thing you did for her — why would that reminder be unpleasant for you?"

Fiona signaled to her cameraman to stop taping. "Elizabeth, you have to stop this."

"Me?" Elizabeth smiled. "Whatever do you mean?"

FORTY-SIX
NOAH

Noah couldn't sit still. He paced the length of his hotel room while Bert looked on in annoyance. "I'm meeting Tiffany this afternoon, hopefully."

"You want me to find out her life history before then?" Bert tapped his Mephisto dress shoes against the cheap hotel carpet. "You don't ask for much."

"I don't need answers right away. But I want to know who she is."

"You don't believe her story?"

"A rich kid from Toronto?" Noah shook his head. "Maybe. But there are holes in her supposed education. When we got drunk the other night — well, when she got drunk; I can handle more liquor than she can — she spoke more freely. Unless Canadian private schools are dramatically different from the one I went to in New York, I'm going to go out on a limb and say she never went to one."

"Are they supposed to have different accents?" Bert asked. "This isn't England."

"She resents people with money." Noah stopped pacing and sat on his bed, facing Bert, who was in Noah's desk chair. "She seems to hate them because they've never had to work for what they have. Doesn't add up if she's a trust fund kid."

"People are complicated." Bert took a long sip from his coffee. "We don't always like ourselves, or what we come from."

"And the other thing — when we were ordering beer, I said I'd have a Bud, and she got all precious, saying she doesn't drink domestic beer. I mean, okay, you don't drink domestic. So order what you do drink. You only make a point about something if you're lying about it."

Bert nodded. "Let's say she's lying. It could still be innocent. Sometimes people put on airs. They want to paint themselves as someone they wish they were, or wish people saw them as."

Noah frowned. He wasn't saying this right, maybe because he didn't understand it himself. "The thing is, lying about her background doesn't fit with the rest of her character, which is totally not phony. If she *is* lying, I think she has a solid reason."

"What reason?"

"That's what I fucking wish I knew."

"Okay," Bert said. "You think Tiffany's cheating at poker?"

Noah didn't want to ask that question. She hadn't cashed in the Niagara game, but a careful cheater would throw a tournament here or there to deflect suspicion. "If she's telling the truth about her identity, no. But if she isn't, then yeah, maybe."

Bert frowned. "Are you emotionally invested in this?"

Noah got up and walked to the window. He looked across the river at Vancouver. He imagined Tiffany at her hotel, lying on her bed listening to songs on her little pink phone while she tried to process Loni's murder in her cute little head.

"Look, Walker. You can't indulge real feelings here. Acknowledge that you're into her. Then make yourself into a character who doesn't feel the same way."

Noah wrinkled his forehead. "I'm already in character. I'm Nate Wilkes. I can't change my identity in the middle of an assignment."

"You need to rewrite Nate Wilkes as someone who hasn't

fallen for this broad. Doesn't matter what the real you feels — as long as you know it, you can master it. You can't let a suspect manipulate you."

Noah pulled a memory stick from his pocket. "Here's that voice clip. The kid's name is Oliver Doakes. I'm pretty sure it's him on that other clip I gave you, the one that tells the hole cards during the game."

"Good work." Bert took the memory stick from Noah. "Here's hoping that's a match."

"Even if it's a match, it doesn't tell me who's behind Oliver pulling the strings. Maybe his boss, Fiona. Maybe a player."

"What kind of kid is he?"

"British," Noah said. "Disillusioned. Thinks the world should belong to him. Probably as annoying as me, ten years ago. We had a drink last night. I didn't learn much, but it's an in, right?"

"It's a start. You're going to have to become friends with this Oliver. Follow him. See who he's talking to."

"Yeah." Noah groaned. He didn't love Oliver's company, but they couldn't all be Tiffanys. At least if he had to bring Oliver down, he wouldn't feel as much anguish.

FORTY-SEVEN
CLARE

Clare studied the menu. There were a lot of salads, some frilly-looking pasta dishes — nothing normal, like spaghetti and meatballs — and a bunch of so-called sandwiches with pompous ingredients like carpaccio and focaccia. The place was perfect for Amanda.

"What are you having?" Clare asked.

"Insalata Caprese." What was that in normal language? "And a glass of Pinot Grigio. Unless you want to share a half-liter."

"Don't they have, like, burgers on the menu?"

Amanda laughed. "You want to get out of here and find somewhere that does?"

"No." Clare realized she was being high-maintenance. "Just tell me what the closest thing is to a club sandwich."

Amanda scanned the menu. "Maybe the *pollo pancetta panini.* Although it should say *panino,* since it's only one sandwich."

"Groovy." Because Clare had missed her Italian lesson for the week and was shaky on her plurals. "And thanks for the wine offer, but Tiffany drinks beer."

"Good." Amanda nodded. "Most new operatives stick too close to what they think would be expected from their cover character. But it makes them come across as one-dimensional. Real people are complex, full of inconsistencies."

"What are your inconsistencies?" Clare looked at her new handler, who seemed flawless right down to her bone marrow.

Amanda tilted her head to one side. "I'm addicted to Japanese animation, which most people who know me find surprising."

Clare found this revelation weak, but didn't say so. "Have you ever been in the field as an undercover?"

"No."

The waitress came and took their order.

"Have you ever wanted to go undercover?" Clare asked when the waitress had left.

"Yes and no. The idea of working the field scares me more than it excites me."

"So you let someone else take the risks." Clare hadn't meant to say that out loud, but whatever. "Did you call me here to talk about Loni?"

"Among other things. How are you holding up?"

"Fine." Clare wasn't about to share her insecurities with someone with such perfectly white teeth.

"You sure?"

"If I can't handle murder, I'm in the wrong job, right?"

"You're human," Amanda said. "You can't turn that off. You wouldn't want to, actually."

"I'll be fine."

Amanda lifted her eyebrows. "So fill me in on Loni. Had you met her? Where did she fit in the scene?"

"She fit everywhere. She used to be married to Mickey Mills — thus the last name — and she hated me because I'm taking lessons from him. When she died she was dating T-Bone Jones."

"Who also hates you."

Clare rolled her eyes. "I'm sure he's over that."

Amanda frowned.

"Why the disapproving look?"

"I think you're too young for this case."

Not again. "Because some old guy in a cowboy hat doesn't want me to be his best friend? I've been over all this with Cloutier already. I'm here — I'm embedded in the scene — you might as well find a way to use me."

The waitress arrived with their drinks. Clare picked up her bottle of Stella Artois. She knew Amanda wanted her to use the glass that had come with it.

Amanda touched the stem of her wine glass. "I think you're too young to understand how serious the situation is. I think you like the mental challenge, and you see your job as an adventure. But I don't think you quite get what death is."

Clare sipped beer from the bottle. "That's right, Amanda. I think all these dead poker players are hanging out on the sidelines, ready to pop back to life the instant I announce who the killer is. It's a fun game — too bad you're too scared to play it."

"Then prove me wrong." Amanda spoke quietly. "I'm on your side. I want you to do well."

"Because it's good for your career."

"Because it gets a killer off the streets. Never forget that's your first goal."

"I never have."

"Okay," Amanda said. "So Loni was dating T-Bone, used to be married to Mickey. Do you know any of the fine print?"

"Only from Mickey's side. I guess their divorce settlement left Loni richer than Mickey."

"Was Mickey paying alimony? Or was it a one-time cash payment?"

"Still paying, I think." Clare tried to meet Amanda's eyes, but Amanda was looking at the table.

"Have you seen them interact?"

"Loni and Mickey? Once."

"What was the dynamic?"

"Tense, a bunch of not-so-hidden digs. They both seemed to get a charge out of it."

"Fine line between love and hate, right?" Amanda said, smiling slightly. "Do you have plans for tonight?"

"I was invited to a game on a boat. It's hosted by Joe Mangan, which means it's co-hosted by Elizabeth Ng."

"Who also hates you."

"Elizabeth doesn't hate me." Clare should be more careful what she told Amanda in the future. "We're friends now. It's Fiona I'm worried about."

"Fiona. Fill me in."

"The anchor lady. She's only ever been nice to me, but I get this sense — she says things — almost like she's trying to scare me off the scene."

"Why would she want you off the scene?"

Clare traced her finger down the bottle. She decided to be nice and pour the rest into the glass. "Elizabeth thinks Fiona has spotlight issues. As in, no one better take hers."

"And Josie Carter — the first victim — she got a lot of attention, right?"

"I guess," Clare said. "And Loni was Fiona's co-anchor for both Niagara Falls and Vancouver. Maybe Loni was getting too much attention for Fiona's liking. But victims two and three were old men — not exactly prime choices if the murder motive is narcissism."

"This is complicated," Amanda said. "I want to know more about Fiona, but I don't want you to spend time with her alone."

"How about alone in a bar?" Clare said. "She doesn't know where I'm staying — the murder locations have at least been consistently hotel rooms."

"Will she be on the boat tonight?"

"I doubt it. She doesn't play poker."

"Who will be there?"

Clare ticked people off on her fingers. "T-Bone normally would, but I'm not so sure now that his girlfriend's just been murdered. Mickey was supposed to play, but again — Loni was his ex-wife. Joe, Elizabeth, Nate . . . they'll probably still show up. I think two or three others."

"Tell me more about Nate."

Clare felt herself smile. "He's from New York. He thinks he's bad-ass, but he's soft — he's just hiding from something."

"Hiding? You mean, like on the run?"

Clare hadn't thought of that. "I don't think it's so concrete. I meant hiding from himself. From his emotions. You know how guys are."

Their food arrived. Clare dug right in, but Amanda sat looking at hers for a half a minute before picking up her fork.

"Why is Tiffany having a relationship with Nate?"

"Because he's hot."

"Really? Because that's a bad reason."

Clare set down the French fry she'd been about to eat. She wasn't in a rush for it anyway — it was stringy and precious, like the restaurant. "What's a good reason?"

"Investigative. Do you think he's the killer? Does he have information that could lead you to the killer? Can dating him bring you closer to the suspects?"

Clare shook her head. "I don't know about any of that. I'm immersing myself in the scene, staying in character as best as I can considering this Tiffany person has nothing in common with me. That's what Cloutier said my role is."

"He's right." Amanda let the implicit dig slide. "That's good basic advice to give a complete novice, which you were on your last case, and even the beginning of this one. But it's time to start thinking more analytically."

"The thought I'd like to leave you with is this: for every door you open — like being allowed into Nate's world — you might close a door. Maybe you *are* better off cultivating a relationship with Joe Mangan — girlfriend or not. Maybe there's someone else on the scene — a techie, or a dealer — who would give you access to something different. Nate's a poker player, a novice like you. Hotness alone isn't enough."

"I see your point." Clare picked up her sandwich, which was nothing like a club, but actually tasted pretty good.

FORTY-EIGHT
NOAH

Noah sat at the corner table in the downtown café, his plain black baseball cap pulled down over his eyes. The rest of his face was buried in *Crime and Punishment*. He was in an ironic mood.

Two tables away, Fiona sat sipping a latte. She was reading too — *Shopoholic and Baby*. Every now and then she'd giggle. Noah was tempted to ask to trade books.

A woman came into the café. She shook out her plain green umbrella, catching Fiona with a few drops of spray.

Fiona flicked hair from her face.

"Are you Fiona?" the umbrella lady said.

Fiona looked up from her book. She smiled at the lady. "Yeah. Do you watch a lot of poker?"

The woman shook her head. "This is for you."

Fiona took the plain white envelope the woman handed her. "Have we met?"

"No. A man on the street asked me to give this to you."

Fiona's eyebrows lifted. "What did he look like?"

"He was wearing a hat." The woman shrugged.

"A cowboy hat? A baseball cap?"

"I had my umbrella up. I don't even think I saw his face."

Perfect. Noah smiled behind his boring book.

"Thanks," said Fiona.

The woman aimed her umbrella at the door and went back out into the rain. Fiona tugged the paper from the envelope and unfolded it.

Noah knew what the message said, because he'd written it:

```
Stop the broadcast.
```

Fiona set the note down, picked it up, and looked at it again. She seemed to smile. Was it possible she wasn't cheating because she wanted to, but for some other reason? Maybe at this point, she was scared not to. Noah thought about the money that had been with the notes he'd taken from her suitcase. He'd left the cash in place — no need to take what wasn't his until he won it fair and square by cheating. He wondered if she was saving up for something — maybe she wanted to hit the road and get the hell away from the scene.

Fiona slipped the note into her purse and stood up. She was definitely smiling.

Pity her good mood wouldn't last.

FORTY-NINE
ELIZABETH

Elizabeth stood on the wooden deck of *Last Tango*. Rain pattered on the blue canvas above her head. "What are you saying, Joe? Of course we're canceling tonight's game."

"Because Loni died?" Joe said. "You're sweet to care, but we have to go on with our lives."

Elizabeth frowned to see a scuff mark on one of her shoes. "Do you not care at all?"

"Who was Loni to us? I can see T-Bone being gutted. Maybe Mickey. That should give us an edge at the table."

"Did you really just say that?" Elizabeth squinted at Joe, wondering what she was missing. First Fiona had tried to capitalize on the death; now Joe's business-as-usual reaction. Was Elizabeth the crazy one?

"I'll take a more bleeding heart position in public, if you're worried. Like on Twitter, I said, 'Grieving loss of 1 of poker world's strongest female characters @Loni_Licious.' But be honest with yourself: will you miss Loni in your everyday life? The interesting question to me is: do Mickey and T-Bone show up tonight?"

"That's the interesting question? Not how are they handling it emotionally?"

Joe opened the compact fridge and grabbed a Coke. "When did you become everyone's den mother?"

"I have a social conscience. That doesn't make me a den mother."

Joe cracked his Coke and took a long sip. "You're trying to feel an emotion you don't because you think it's appropriate. I'm willing to wear my sad face for the world because they expect it. But why should I pretend at home?"

Elizabeth wondered if Joe had a point, or if he was spinning rhetoric like usual. "Are you even curious who killed her?"

"That's a different question," Joe said. "I'm dying to know — hopefully not literally — who the Choker is. That's why we *should* have the game tonight."

Elizabeth laughed despite her confusion. "You think we can smoke out the killer at a poker game?" When Joe didn't respond for a few seconds, she asked, "Is Tiffany coming?"

"I hope so," Joe said. "I invited Nate, mostly because I don't trust him as far as I can throw him and I want to find out what he's about. Where Tiffany goes these past couple days, Nate is never far behind."

Elizabeth was tempted to offer Joe her condolences about losing that prop bet. "You're not suspicious of Tiffany?"

"Sure I am," Joe said. "She shows up on the scene loud and clear after Oppal got done? You know Willard Oppal was a cop, right?"

Of course Elizabeth had known, but she found it a funny connection to draw between Oppal and Tiffany. "Tiffany can't do anything *unless* it's loud and clear. She could dress in all black Poker Stars gear and pull a hood over her face and she'd still stick out here. Just like T-Bone could cut his hair and lose the hat and he'd still get funny looks at any country club. If you're looking for a cop, look at Nate."

But Elizabeth's mind had started churning. Her brother hadn't found anything yet — no one called James who owned any furniture importing business in Canada, at least not large-scale

enough to fund Tiffany's long-shot attempt at becoming a professional gambler. Peter was checking into the U.S. and U.K. mar-
kets next.

"I don't think Tiffany's a cop," Elizabeth said. "The FBI might
get creative like that with a cover, but the RCMP is too boring."

"Yeah, good point," Joe said.

"But maybe her arrival right after Oppal's death is uncoinci-
dental for a different reason. Maybe the cheating ring is running
a relay team — switching up the players so no one notices any
one player's win rate spiking."

Joe cocked his head. "You know, you're actually starting to
make sense. You think Tiffany threw the first game so it won't
look suspicious if she starts winning now?"

Elizabeth shrugged. "I don't know. It's a theory. Nate, though
— he could easily be a cop."

Joe shook his head. "Nate doesn't have cop character. I think
he's here to learn — and cheat — but he says mob to me. As in,
gambling for the cause, to take the intelligence back home."

"He's not Italian."

"He has dark hair. Maybe Wilkes is really Wilconi. Do we have
any normal snacks? I don't feel like anything organic just now."

Elizabeth felt her hands begin to tremble. She should take
George's advice and get a CT scan. Her family doctor was a few
blocks away; she could probably get an emergency referral and
a scan within a day. But if there was something wrong with her
— something fatal — she wasn't sure she was ready to find out.

"There should be some Sun Chips," she said.

Joe must have seen her fear, because he took her hand. "Don't
be scared. I'm sorry I was callous. I'm freaked out by Loni's
murder, too — it's just my dumb reaction."

Elizabeth gazed out the plastic window at the rain-drenched
dock. She thought of Josie and all the others who had died over
the past few months. "I'm scared because I'm sane."

FIFTY
NOAH

Noah stood in line at Starbucks in English Bay. He thought about ordering a black coffee to give Tiffany when she arrived. Women liked it when you noticed what they liked. But maybe she wanted something different today, a cappuccino, or a tea to go with the rain. He pulled out his phone to send a text.

> In line @ Starbucks. What coffee u like?

The message from Tiffany came back fast.

> Giant & black. Stupid cab dropped me on other side of street. Waiting 4 light 2 change.

Noah looked out the window. Though she could only have been standing in the rain for a few seconds, Tiffany's dark hair was already matted against her face. He watched her cross the street and push through the double glass doors with an exasperated sigh.

"Your poor jacket." Noah left the line to greet her at the door. He put an arm around her. "You want to stay inside and dry off?"

"No, I love being out in the rain. And leather is nature's original raincoat — but thanks for caring about my clothes."

Noah rolled his eyes. "Here's the umbrella you ordered."

He had taken his time choosing the umbrella — black with silver piping — and he was pleased when Tiffany clapped her hands and said, "It's the same color as my motorcycle."

"You have a motorcycle?" If she did, Noah was about to fall unapologetically in love.

"No," Tiffany said quickly. "But there's this bike I have my eye on. I'm trying to work up the courage to buy it."

Great. He was falling for someone who wanted to live her life but was afraid to. But maybe that wasn't a bad thing — it would make it easier to leave when he would inevitably have to. "How old are you?"

"Twenty-three." Tiffany smiled. "You're thinking I should start living my life sometime soon?"

Or yesterday. "The poker tour was a good start."

"It was." Tiffany nodded slowly. "But I only signed up once my father agreed it was smart."

Signed up. Like the ten-thousand-dollar entry fee didn't matter at all. Noah wondered how much of that was an act. "So is it advice he gives you? Or decrees?"

Tiffany laughed. It was a cute laugh, an open one. "He words it like decrees. But I suppose I could consider it friendly advice."

"You still live with your parents." A statement, not a question.

"That obvious?"

"Yup." Noah hoped Bert would confirm her identity soon. He could deal with Tiffany being a liar; he just wanted to know who she was.

"Let me guess," Tiffany said. "You moved out when you were twelve, and you've been living on the mean streets ever since."

"Eighteen." Noah smirked. "But I'm a bit older than you. I've been on my own for ten years."

"Oh so world-weary."

They left the café armed with giant coffees.

"I like your umbrella, too." Tiffany nodded at Noah's choice for himself. "That color blue suits you. Very moody."

They crossed the street and walked into the park.

"Are you feeling better?" Noah asked. "Or are you still weirded out from this morning?"

"I guess both. I don't really know what I'm doing here. I'll probably leave after this leg of the tour."

Noah took Tiffany's hand and squeezed it. "Have you ever had sex in the rain?"

"You mean outside in the rain? With water falling all over you?"

Noah nodded. He wanted to win this prop bet here and now, so no matter what Bert uncovered he could collect the twenty grand from Joe. Or maybe it wasn't the twenty grand.

"No," Tiffany said. "Have you?"

Noah shook his head. "Don't you think it would be amazing? You'd feel so at one with the elements."

A smile crept onto Tiffany's face. "I'm not having sex with you. This is our first date."

"We had drinks the other night. And coffee yesterday. I'd call this date three. The sex date."

Tiffany laughed. "So you wouldn't think less of me for putting out."

"Are you kidding? I'd think highly of the first woman who had sex with me in the rain. I'd remember you for the rest of my life." Noah looked out onto the water, where only the large commercial boats were braving the rain.

"But if I wait to sleep with you in a hotel room," Tiffany said, "you'll forget about me by the time you get back to New York?"

"You never know."

"As romantic as you make it sound, all I can picture is slipping around in the mud, getting disgustingly dirty."

"That sounds unpleasant to you?" Noah tilted his umbrella

back, slipped under Tiffany's, and kissed her. Her lips were sweet — which was odd, for a smoker. It was hard to pull away, but he wanted to leave her wanting more.

Tiffany pulled her cigarette pack from her pocket and held it open in front of Noah.

"Thanks." He liked the gesture. Some women would take a smoke if you offered them one, but when they got out their own pack they were only thinking of themselves.

"I get turned on by conversation," she said. "Not so much by being badgered with direct propositions. In case you're wondering how to turn your fantasy into reality."

"Thanks for the tip." Noah pulled his Zippo from his pocket, lit Tiffany's smoke, then his own. "What topics turn you on?"

"Anything that gets my brain going."

"Like astrophysics?" Noah asked, while thunder sounded in the distance.

"That could work," Tiffany said. "Do you know about astrophysics?"

"No. Can I invent stuff?"

"It's better if you at least sound intelligent." Tiffany stopped walking and pointed to the rocks beside the path. "I think I just saw a fish jump."

Noah smirked. "If you're looking for a marine wildlife expert, I am definitely not your man."

Tiffany started walking again. "So why don't you tell me who you are. I feel like you know my whole family, including Buffy the dog. And I know nothing about yours."

Damn right. Because he didn't plan to tell her.

"Or maybe you have a secret passion?" Tiffany said. "Art? Chemistry?"

Noah laughed. "Art or chemistry?"

"I was pulling things at random."

"I got that. I love photography."

"Do you have a darkroom?"

"I only use digital. I guess my passion doesn't run too deep.

Do you have a secret passion? Other than getting ravaged in the rain, which *will* happen, by the way."

Tiffany's eyebrows lifted quickly, and Noah knew he could make his move anytime.

FIFTY-ONE
CLARE

"Yeah, I have a secret passion." Clare was very close to grabbing Nate and following the next path off the beaten track to seclusion. But Tiffany would play it cool, and besides, it was fun to be seduced. "But you'll think it's dumb. It's common."

"You want to be a princess."

"An actress. Same thing, right?" Clare had never wanted to be an actress in her life. The only acting she ever did was on the job, and that was more like lying, which she hated. But she figured someone like Tiffany would have dreams of being onstage.

"Did you do any acting in school?"

Clare nodded. "I was in every school play since kindergarten."

"Were you the little prima donna who was always given the lead?"

"I was a little prima donna. But I didn't usually get the lead." Clare definitely saw a fish jump, just past the rocks near the shore, but she didn't bother mentioning it this time. Nate clearly didn't care about the majestically beautiful scenery all around them.

"Did you stomp your foot and scream if you got a role you didn't like?"

"No." Clare might not like Tiffany, but that was no reason to make her unlikeable to the rest of the world. "I knew I wasn't a good actress. I just like it."

"You like pretending to be someone else." Clare thought she heard accusation in Nate's voice.

"Does that upset you?"

"No." Nate flicked his cigarette into the water. "As long as you don't act in real life. My last girlfriend had, like, seventeen personalities. She was phonier than Joe Mangan's smile."

"But let me guess. She gave blow jobs like a pro and that made it all okay."

Nate grinned. "Fine. Guilty."

"Men," Clare said. "You practically wag your tongues and beg women to deceive you. Then when you find out they're phony you think it's their fault." Nate had pretty much defined the reason Clare hated dressing up and wearing makeup. Life without illusions made a hell of a lot more sense to her.

"You're defending my ex-girlfriend?"

"No." Clare met his eye under the rim of the umbrellas. "Can we talk about what's really going on, though?"

"You mean the undercurrent of lust that we feel for each other?"

Clare gave him a small smile. "I mean the murders. The poker scene. I'm scared I made a bad decision coming here."

Nate took her hand. The umbrellas crashed into each other a bit, but it felt good. "We'll stick together. I'll make sure no one hurts you."

"How?" Clare trusted him and she didn't; her instincts weren't working. "Do you know who the killer is?"

Nate shook his head.

"Then how could you possibly make sure no one hurts me?"

FIFTY-TWO
GEORGE

"I'm taking you for dinner." Fiona bounded into George's room and started stripping off her work clothes.

"You are?" George was happy to shut down his computer. He'd been working all afternoon and aside from Loni's death scene, he hadn't gotten much done.

"Yup." She pulled a green cocktail dress from his closet. Almost all of her things were in George's room now. "We're celebrating."

"What's the occasion?" George found his lone pair of dress pants at the bottom of his suitcase. He held them up to assess whether they were too wrinkled to wear.

"The cheating is finished. I'm free and clear."

George set his pants on the bed. He was about to throw his arms around her but he stopped himself.

"What was that?" Fiona laughed. "Do you want to hug me or not?"

George sat down. "Not."

"Come on, George. Tonight we celebrate. Tomorrow we can go back to our miserable ambiguous relationship." She grabbed his hand and pulled him to his feet. She pulled him close and kissed him, open-mouthed and full of feeling.

He kissed her back. What else could he do? He kissed her and he slid his hand under her thong and he followed his impulse, like he always did. When they were finished — about fifteen minutes later — he said, "Wow. What just happened?"

"It was you and me," Fiona said. "Come on. I'm starved. I made a reservation downtown."

"The cheating's really over? No more hole card scam?"

"It really is." Fiona's eyes were wide.

George wondered if she was trying to convince him, or if she was successfully fooling herself.

FIFTY-THREE
ELIZABETH

"Hey, Elizabeth, grab me a beer."

Elizabeth did not budge from the sofa.

"You want me to get up and get it myself?" T-Bone looked baffled, like a woman had never told him no before.

"I didn't know you had beer on the boat," Elizabeth said. "Which case is yours? The Kokanee I picked up this afternoon, or the Grolsch Tiffany and Nate brought with them?"

"Didn't know it was BYO."

"It isn't, because we're not sixteen anymore," Joe said. "Lizzie, grab T-Bone a beer. Please?"

Elizabeth shrugged, got up, and went over to the fridge. If Joe had taken the night off from poker, she doubted the guys would treat him like their waitress.

"Grab me a drink, too, hon." This from Joe.

Elizabeth plucked a Grolsch swing-top from the fridge and glared at the back of Joe's head. Who called people "hon" unless they wanted to be diminutive? She mixed him a vodka seven. He didn't normally drink when he played poker, but tonight he'd relaxed his customary standards.

"Here you go, *muffin*." She set both drinks in front of Joe with a loud plonk. The beer was closed, but a couple of drops of Joe's drink spilled over onto the table.

"The fuck's her problem?" T-Bone said as his bottle got passed his way.

"You guys are treating her like shit." Thank you, Tiffany. "Especially you, Joe. T-Bone's an ass; he can't help that. You could be nicer if you wanted."

T-Bone grunted and said to Tiffany, "Not too grateful, are you? For a novice to be invited to a game like this is a one in a million opportunity."

Tiffany seemed to contemplate that. "I guess I could ask you the same question, T-Bone."

"The fuck does that mean?"

Tiffany took a quick sip of beer. "It means you don't seem so grateful either. For a fairly ugly, foul-tempered old man to be welcomed into the company of two sexy, intelligent women — my guess is that's also about one in a million."

Elizabeth snorted iced tea through her nose. For the first time since she'd met the kid, she hoped Tiffany wouldn't be the Choker's next victim.

T-Bone threw a sneer to Elizabeth. "What are you laughing at? I never agreed the pair of you were sexy or intelligent."

"Lay off them." Mickey folded his hand so forcefully that his cards nearly flipped over. "We're sorry for your loss. Hell, Loni's more my loss than yours. But you can't take it out on us. We're not your friends."

Elizabeth watched T-Bone's face as Mickey said this. If the old cowboy had ever felt an emotion in his life, she doubted if so much as an eye flicker had given it away.

"That's harsh, too, Mick." Joe pushed some chips into the center of the table. His costume tonight was minimal — a pair of geek glasses and a pocket protector with a fake pen stain. "Of course we're each other's friends. More like family. We're all we have."

Hearing Joe say that made Elizabeth feel more alone than ever. Had she traded her own family in for this? She grabbed the boat key from Joe's shirt pocket. "I'm going to start motoring back."

"In the dark?" Joe said. "You don't even like driving the boat."

"I feel like it tonight." Elizabeth wanted to fight with the waves, keep her eye out for logs, and feel like she was doing something physical and real. And she wanted everyone off the boat.

FIFTY-FOUR
CLARE

Clare envied Elizabeth. She wanted a job where she could be herself, too — natural, bitchy if she felt like it, open about where she came from. Playing Tiffany, she felt like a traitor to the trailer park, like her real past was some dirty secret she had to hide. Clare missed home, suddenly. She wanted to take a walk by Lake Couchiching and sit under a tree, maybe study a car or motorcycle manual, and not be playing poker on a boat.

She looked across the table at Nate like she could eat him. She couldn't help it. Clare had seriously wanted to take him up on his offer that afternoon, to have sex in the woods, in the mud and the rain. The slipping and sliding sounded awesome. But it would have been gratuitous — not what Tiffany would have done, just a perk for Clare. And the last thing she wanted to do was betray Kevin.

Thinking of Kevin made her smile — literally; so instead of folding her king-ten offsuit, she raised with it in middle position, in case observant opponents thought her involuntary grin meant she had aces. Kevin was the first guy in a long time who made Clare feel like she could be herself, with no apology or explanation. With Nate, Clare could tell, the dynamic would be far more complicated.

T-Bone, in the big blind, called. So did Joe, who had limped in under the gun. The flop came ace-six-four. T-Bone checked. So did Joe. Clare could bet, repping a high ace, or even pocket aces. But Mickey had told her to let the flop go, in last position with nothing, and bet the turn if it was checked to her again.

A ten came down. T-Bone checked. Joe bet two-thirds of the pot. Clare thought about it for a moment — she had second pair, but Joe was playing a multi-way pot, and his bet might actually mean something. She folded. T-Bone folded. Joe grinned, scooped the modest pot, and turned over two queens. Clare thanked Mickey silently for not letting herself fall into Joe's trap.

"What? No all-in raise?" T-Bone lifted his eyebrows at Clare. "That's your signature move, ain't it?"

"No," Clare said. "It ain't."

"Oh. Society Lady is making fun of my grammar."

"Would you prefer I make fun of your hat?"

"You should stop talking," T-Bone said, "if you know what's fucking good for you."

"Are you threatening me with something?" Clare smiled sweetly. "Because there are witnesses here."

T-Bone snorted. "Great. A member of Generation Wuss. Don't stand up and fight; hide behind witnesses and regulations."

Clare wasn't quite sure what he meant. Was she supposed to fight the guy with her fists? She doubted that, so she stayed with her weapon of choice: "Which is why my nose isn't ugly from being broken in so many places."

T-Bone touched his nose.

"And it's why, unlike some present company, I'll save myself the humiliation of being raped in jail."

"You know fuck-all about my prison time."

Mickey smirked at Clare across the table. He'd given her the line about jail to use on T-Bone, and apparently it had worked.

T-Bone looked like one of those angry cartoon people with a red face and steam coming out of his ears — minus the actual steam, of course.

"Sorry." Clare feigned an apologetic tone. "I guess I don't."

"Hey Joe?" Elizabeth said from the captain's seat. "Does the engine sound funny to you?"

Joe got up and went to the back of the boat. He poked his head over the edge. "Looks funny, too. We're dragging a big log."

"Should I turn the engine off?"

"I think so."

Elizabeth cut the motor and walked around the poker game to look over the back edge with Joe. Clare nearly got up to help them, but stopped herself in time. Tiffany's first impulse would not be to take a look at the engine.

Joe looked at the other players sheepishly. "Anyone know anything about engines?"

"Sorry, man." Nate shook his head.

"Can't help you," T-Bone said.

Fuck, that wasn't hot. Clare had expected as much from T-Bone, but she'd hoped Nate would prove to be more of a man.

Mickey stood up and moved to the stern. He looked over the edge. "Maybe take the log out of the motor."

Joe leaned over and tugged at something. "It's lodged right in there."

Mickey tried, too. No luck.

"Should we call that towing number?" Elizabeth said. "Or should we drive slowly and try to get back to the dock?"

Clare tried not to scowl. It didn't take a genius to realize that if the log had been caught by the motor, it could be uncaught. Maybe something was broken, but they could probably get back to the dock with some creative maneuvering. For a bunch of so-called clever people, they all seemed to lack common sense.

Finally, Nate got up. "I know nothing about boats, but let me see what I can do." He leaned over, stuck his hands over the side, and in half a minute or so, said, "That's the bulk of the log unstuck. There are a couple of twigs I can't reach from here. I don't know if it did any damage to the engine."

Right. And the way to find that out would be to lift the engine cover and look inside. But at least Nate had redeemed some of his earlier helplessness.

"I'll drive back to the dock," Elizabeth said. "You guys keep playing cards. I'll go slowly."

Everyone except Clare seemed to think this was a great idea. But since Clare wasn't on this boat — just some prissy thing called Tiffany — she didn't get a say in anything mechanical.

After a few minutes, Elizabeth said, "I don't think we're moving."

She was right. The land was in the same place. They might have even drifted back a few feet.

Joe laughed. "Let's call it in."

FIFTY-FIVE
NOAH

Noah's phone was vibrating in his pocket. He ignored it; it was most likely Bert, and he couldn't speak freely on the boat. But the vibrating persisted, and Joe said, "You going to answer that, man?"

Noah shook his head, gave Joe a knowing glance.

"Ah," Joe said. "You can use a stateroom if you want privacy."

"How long do you figure we'll be out here?" Noah asked. He and Joe were standing apart from the crowd, leaning on the port side rail while the main crowd was still seated at the poker table, but sound was funny on water; he didn't want Tiffany to overhear.

Joe shrugged. "The guy at the towing company says he'll be here sometime in the next hour or two. Then we have to get back to the dock. Another couple hours." He nodded at Noah's pocket where the phone was buzzing again. "That your girlfriend?"

"I think so."

"Will she be pissed if you don't call her back?"

Noah smirked. "Probably."

"Seriously, man. You're welcome to use a stateroom. Or is it you don't want Tiffany to get curious?"

"Kind of."

"I'll keep her busy. You win that bet yet?"

Noah shook his head. "I bet you'll keep her busy."

Joe grinned. "You can trust me."

"I don't trust you at all," Noah said. "But yeah, I'll borrow a stateroom."

Noah followed Joe down the short staircase to a room that looked like it wasn't being used. There was a single bed, which Noah sat on, and a small, dirty porthole through which he could only see black.

Under the bed was a suitcase. It looked like a Louis Vuitton knockoff. Or maybe it was real.

Noah phoned Bert.

"I can't really talk," Noah said.

"Can you meet me in your lobby bar?"

"Nope. I'm on a boat and we've just broken down."

"Who else is on the boat? Just you and the girl?"

"And a bunch of poker players. You going to tell me what you found?"

"Not on the phone."

"But you have something." Noah could feel the blood racing faster in his veins. And at the same time, he felt heavy. He wasn't sure he wanted to know.

"Yes. I have something. I'll fill you in when I see you."

Noah clicked his phone off and swore under his breath. He got up to leave the room and remembered the suitcase under the bed. He should have a quick look inside.

FIFTY-SIX
ELIZABETH

The night was getting cold. They had the canvas tarp closed over the deck and the heaters going full blast, but Elizabeth wanted a warmer sweater. She went downstairs to the main stateroom and remembered she'd stowed her suitcase in a different room. Space was tight on boats. It was annoying.

In the hallway outside the door to the room where she'd left her bag, she paused. The door was closed. It sounded like someone was inside. There were no voices, but maybe someone — Nate and Tiffany? — had taken it up on themselves to borrow a room to get it on while they waited to be rescued. Elizabeth had no idea why the idea bothered her — it was only a rental boat; it wasn't like she even had to change the sheets.

Should she give the interlopers privacy? Screw it — she was going in.

Elizabeth pushed open the door and saw Nate. His hand was on the door from the other side — presumably on his way out.

"Hi, Elizabeth."

"Is Tiffany in there with you?"

"No. No one is. Joe gave me the room to make a phone call. I was just leaving."

"Great. See you." Elizabeth went in, grabbed a sweater, and was about to shove her suitcase back under the bed when she noticed the front zipper not fully done up. She was meticulous about closing things — traveling around all the time, she was conscious of not leaving things behind.

Who had been in the case? Was it Nate? That seemed unlikely — why would he risk being caught rifling through her things with so many people on board?

It had obviously been Joe. But why would Joe snoop through her things? Elizabeth opened the zipper and felt through the front section. She pulled out the folder where she kept her travel documents. Everything seemed intact: her passport, boarding passes from their last trip, printouts of the emails with the confirmation details of their upcoming flight to Winnipeg, along with hotel and rental car details. She would probably have to change the dates — because the Canadian Classic had been stopped for a day due to Loni's death, it would probably run into overtime. But she could deal with that later. Nothing was missing, but why had Joe — or Nate — been through her bag?

She shoved the suitcase back under the bed and arrived upstairs just as the rescue boat pulled up beside *Last Tango*.

FIFTY-SEVEN
GEORGE

George tossed off the coarse comforter. Half of it fell on the floor and the other half lay crumpled on the lower end of the bed. He couldn't tell if it was hot in the room or if Fiona's sleeping body was heating him up.

George picked up the blanket and placed it gently back over Fiona. As quietly as he could, he slipped on some clothes, grabbed his laptop, and snuck out of the room.

He rode the elevator down to the lobby. No idea where he planned to go. He just needed to write, and he couldn't do it with Fiona in the room.

The casino noises were more jarring than usual. It felt like every slot machine, every inconsiderate person who pushed past George on the way to somewhere, was there to test his temper. When one man shoved him in an innocent, if inconsiderate, effort to move past him, George shoved back, harder.

The man turned around, scowled briefly at George, and kept moving. Not the reaction George had been going for, but maybe better than a fist-fight.

It was almost midnight — not really late, but he and Fiona had crashed into bed around eleven and Fiona had fallen right to sleep.

George found the door and pushed outside. It was cold out — he could feel that on his face — but he was boiling hot inside. He sat on a bench by the boats and opened his computer. He didn't even zip up his fleece.

He had to start piecing things together.

Note One: *Do you want to save your mother's house?*

You stare at the note. Of course you want to save your mother's house.

George had met Fiona's mother once. She was a spandex-wearing chain-smoker. But Fiona saw her as a martyr; a hero just for waking up each day.

Even once you get her house paid off, she'll find things she'd like, things she can't afford on her own. And you're willing to throw your life away to give hers more material comfort.

So you pocket the cash and say yes, you'd like to save her house.

Note Two: *We need to tap into the hole card audio feed live. It's one wire; one encryption code. Can you do this alone, or do we need to involve your techie?*

Ah, Oliver. The little scoundrel you loathe. Can't fire him now, though. And since you know nothing about the wires that make your job function, you have to say yes, you need to involve your techie.

Note Three: *Give your techie this encryption code.*

And more notes, more details that give you the
mechanics of the scam. It doesn't occur to you
that now you're redundant. The Dealer could go
straight to Oliver and save a bundle on your
middle management fee. He'd only have to tell
you the scam was off, and you'd be none the wiser.
You'd probably be next on his hit list, because
why have extra people knowing what he's up to?

George slammed his computer closed without shutting it down. Fiona was a sitting target. He ran through the casino, pushing all the people who didn't immediately get out of his way. He raced up the stairs instead of waiting for the elevator.

When he arrived in his room, he saw that Fiona was still in bed. He ran to her. He checked her pulse. Still alive. Still breathing.

"George?" She woke up and smiled at him.

"Fiona," he said, still shaking her. "We need to get out of here."

She pushed hair from her face. "What do you mean?"

"Your life is in danger."

"What are you talking about? The scam is over, remember? It's a get out of jail free card."

"This isn't Monopoly. It's a game of fucking . . ." He searched his head. "Clue."

"Clue?" She gave him an amused glance. "That's the most gruesome game you could come up with? Colonel Mustard with a rope in the hotel room?"

"Let's grab a rental car and head to the States. We're not far from the border."

"Why do we need to cross the border?"

George wasn't sure. "The killer has only operated in Canada so far. They might not cross a border to follow us."

"Can we talk about this in the morning?" Fiona rolled over and tucked her hands under her pillow.

George spent the rest of the night awake, watching the door.

FIFTY-EIGHT
CLARE

Clare lit a cigarette as she got out of the cab at her hotel. Thank god that boat ride had ended. Clare had begun to feel like she'd be marooned out on the strait all night, before that rescue guy had come on board and done what she could have done in five seconds if she hadn't been masquerading as a manicured bimbo.

She walked toward False Creek. It was almost one a.m. but the neighborhood was buzzing; she felt as safe as she would in broad daylight. Besides, her goons were probably following her — nothing kept you safe like being spied on.

She pulled out her stupid pink phone and called Roberta.

"Clare." Roberta's voice was groggy.

"How's the shop? Do you miss my nimble fingers?"

"More than you know," Roberta said. "This Virago is not getting any healthier. I fix one thing and two more get broken. But, uh, it's nearly four in the morning. Is there something on your mind?"

Clare smacked her head. "Oops. Sorry. I calculated the time change in reverse; I thought it was ten p.m. there."

Roberta laughed. "All right. I didn't like the dream I was having anyway."

"No, go back to sleep."

"Why? I'm up now. This is me, padding into my kitchen and pressing Go on the coffee machine. Maybe in the middle of the night that damn bike will help me solve its problems."

Clare smiled. She missed getting her hands grimy with engine grease. "Have you pulled apart the electrical system?"

"Yup, but everything looks like it's in order. Which is lucky for the owner. You know electrics are my weak spot."

"Mine, too. They're so fiddly. Is the owner getting antsy?"

"She started out antsy. She's a spoiled little housewife who doesn't understand why everything doesn't go her way."

Clare smiled. "I know the type."

"How could you possibly know that type?"

"From my break and enter days," Clare said. "You answer the call, you're taking their statement, and they suddenly interrupt themselves to ask why you're not already out catching the thief and getting back their diamond tennis bracelet."

"You must miss that job."

"It reminds me to be grateful for my current one."

"So can you talk now?" Roberta asked. "You alone?"

"I'm walking down a crowded street. But I'll chance it." The danger was more in being heard by whoever was following her — Clare would lose her job in ten seconds if anyone overheard her talking about the case with an outsider. But she needed the outlet. "I'm going crazy for someone to be real with."

"I hear you."

"No you don't." Clare laughed. "You're yourself no matter who's around, and you don't give a damn who thinks badly of you."

"I wasn't so confident when I was in my twenties."

"So you say." Clare still had trouble picturing Roberta as a younger, less wholly formed person.

"What's bugging you, kid?"

"I'm —" Clare took a drag of her smoke. She didn't know where to begin. "I'm falling for a guy who isn't Kevin."

"Falling for him? What's it been, three days?"

"A week if you count Niagara Falls. But it's fine, because when the case is over I'm leaving him — not like I could tell him who I am, if I happen to get lucky and find out he isn't the killer."

"Do you think he might be?"

Clare hesitated. She was moving into classified territory even mentioning Nate. She'd have to keep the details vague. "There's something off about him. I don't always believe things he says."

"Well, he is a man."

"I just — I think he's lying about who he is. Not, like, his name or anything. But — I don't know, maybe it is just a guy thing. I'm lucky with Kevin — he wears his heart on his sleeve, and not in some creepy emo-boy way. God, I wish he was here."

"You wish he was there because you miss him, or because then you wouldn't be falling for this other guy?"

"I don't know. Both. I'm also bummed because . . ." Clare had been about to tell Roberta about Loni, but even without giving her name, that would be pushing confidentiality too far. "The case is more complicated than it originally seemed."

Roberta clucked sympathetically. "I hear you on complicated. That's the same way I feel about this Virago. You getting pressure from above?"

Clare shook her head, then realized Roberta couldn't see her, and said, "Not as bad as on my last case. But no one's my friend. They're all cold and professional. At least Cloutier was emotional about hating my guts."

"You know you don't make sense, right?"

Clare smiled despite herself. "I guess."

"Your dad's not doing well, Clare."

"This is news?" Just the mention of her father conjured up the image of him sitting around the trailer in his sweats, playing Solitaire on the fold-out table with the oxygen beside him, going outside only when he thought he could sneak a cigarette without Clare's mother noticing.

"It could be any day now."

"So I heard six months ago. He could also live two more years."

"You know he won't."

"Have you checked the carburetor?" Clare didn't want to picture her mother walking over with a tray of tea, setting a plate of cookies beside her father that he'd make a huge display of not having the appetite for because all he wanted was sympathy for a condition he'd brought on himself. "A spoiled housewife might not know she's supposed to drain the gas over the winter."

"The carb was gunked up and needed rebuilding. Which I've done, but the bike still won't start."

"What about the main fuse? I know you think it's fine, but the wire casing was frayed. Changing it might be worth a shot."

"Hmm," Roberta said. "Yeah, I'll look into that."

They were both quiet for a moment. Clare said, "Anyway, what would I say to them? Should I lie and say I'll be sad when my dad dies, when really I think death will end his pain and make him happier? Should I agree with the whole fucking trailer park that my mother's a martyr for quitting her job and living on welfare to take care of my dad, when she hated cleaning motel rooms anyway, and all she does is drink vodka all night and turn a blind eye to the cigarettes we all know my dad is still smoking?"

"You're still smoking," Roberta said.

"I'm not fucking dying of emphysema. I hate going home because I don't know the right way to be. Sympathetic feels false, and anything else feels cruel."

"Tell them that," Roberta said.

"I'd be telling deaf ears. Anyway, I'm going to bed. I want to be well rested for the game tomorrow."

"You sound committed."

"I know it's only make-believe, but I really like winning."

THURSDAY / MARCH 24

FIFTY-NINE
GEORGE

George rubbed his eyes and rolled over. He thought he was dreaming when he saw Fiona in bed beside him, moving her legs like she always did in the last couple hours of sleep. She reminded George of a dog dreaming — they always looked like they were running.

Had he panicked for nothing, wanting to run away with her? In the morning, with the sun beginning to rise, it didn't feel as urgent to get Fiona away from the Canadian Classic. But when he recalled his logic from the night before, he worried again. Fiona knew a lot, and now she was redundant — until and unless the scam started running once more. He'd talk to her when she was awake.

He got up and threw on his jeans. Showering could wait. As he left the casino, Elizabeth fell into step with him.

"Starbucks?" she said.

George nodded. "What are you doing out? Don't you have a coffee maker on your boat?"

"Yup. It's actually a fairly fancy one with a built-in grinder. But it doesn't work without coffee beans."

"I'm jealous."

"Of an espresso maker? Hey, can I ask you a bizarre question?"

"No, I'm not sleeping with Joe."

"That wasn't my question." Elizabeth hit his arm. "It's about the poison in my head. I think it's neurochemical."

"Have you been spending too much time online?" George said. "Internet self-diagnosis can be dangerous."

"Which is why I want to talk to you. You have a history of depression, right?"

George stopped walking. "Who told you that? Fiona?"

"Never mind who told me. Do you think that's what I have?"

"No," George said.

"Why not?"

"You're up early taking a walk. Depressed people stay in bed and wish they could take a walk."

"Man. That must suck." Elizabeth buttoned up the collar of her long leather coat. "But you're up early. Are you over your depression?"

George smiled. "It comes and goes. But even when it comes, there are ways to fight it."

"You can fight it? It must be different, then, because when these chemicals take hold, there is nothing I can do to stop hating myself." Elizabeth pulled matching red leather gloves from her pocket and put them on. "It's freezing this morning. I thought it was supposed to be spring."

"I don't find it cold. Does mental illness run in your family?"

"Very funny."

"I wasn't joking," George said. "Well, maybe half. What about hormones? Is it possible you're pregnant?"

"No. Well, maybe. But pregnancy is supposed to feel good, and glowy, and stuff."

George shook his head. "When Fiona was pregnant, her emotions did all kinds of crazy things. She never called it poison, but it wasn't good and glowy. Actually, it was more like hell and fury."

"Fiona was pregnant?"

"Last year."

"Sorry, George. I guess it ended badly."

George shrugged. "Her decision, right? How was the poker game last night? Sorry I didn't make it."

"It was stupid," Elizabeth said. "Joe won piles of money he doesn't need, I broke the boat but someone fixed it in four seconds for four hundred dollars, and everyone hates each other."

"Sounds like another day in the wonderful world of poker."

"Right? I'm getting sick of this crap. After this leg I want to pack it in, maybe go back to school and do something normal."

"You do?" George was surprised that it wasn't just him who wanted out.

"Yeah. Some job where you won't get strangled in your sleep would be nice. Hey, here's Starbucks," Elizabeth said brightly. "Now the world can be a friendly place again."

"You sound like a commercial."

"Ha. I don't even like Starbucks — they pretend to be all environmental and fair trade, then you ask them for organic shade-grown coffee and they have, like, one kind on the shelf and it's not the one they're ever serving that day. But my brain is so fried I'd be as excited if we were coming up on Krispy Kreme."

"That's pretty fried."

"Yeah." Elizabeth pulled open the door. "That makes me feel like a donut. Something else I normally can't stand the sight of. Weird, huh?"

George shrugged. "Not weird if you're pregnant."

"Or if I have a brain tumor."

George stood with Elizabeth at the back of the line. "Have you gone for a scan?"

"When?" She held her palms in the air. "When would I have had time for a brain scan?"

"Sorry," George said.

"I'm terrified." Her voice went quiet. "Something's wrong — I know that much. I'm not sure I'm ready to find out what."

SIXTY
CLARE

"Why are you talking about the case with Roberta McGraw?" Amanda walked quickly, looking straight ahead. The sun had barely risen, but Clare guessed that Amanda was one of those annoying people who woke up at the crack of dawn and stayed perky until her six o'clock cocktail.

Clare struggled to keep up with Amanda's longer legs. Without shoes, Amanda was probably around the same five-foot-four as Clare, but since Clare was in sneakers and sweats for this early morning walk, and Amanda was already dressed for business in three-inch pumps, Clare felt like a pre-teen shrimp in comparison. "Did you tap my cell phone?"

"I was clear that you were being monitored, so don't even pretend to be surprised."

"But tapping my phone? Am I a suspect?" Clare pulled out her cigarettes, a difficult feat at this pace.

"Don't be ridiculous. We listen to your phone because we want transcripts of your conversations *with* suspects. Why were you talking to an outsider about the case?"

"Roberta helps me think. I was careful not to give her details, or even people's first names."

"You told her what time zone you're in."

"Big deal," Clare said. "She's not going to alert saboteurs to come looking for me all through the Pacific Standard zone."

Amanda's mouth twitched like she was suppressing a smile. "When you're undercover, you don't have the luxury of confiding in friends and family. That's what you have a handler for. What have you told your boyfriend?"

"You don't already know that, too?" Clare racked her brain trying to remember what she'd told Kevin. She'd hinted about Nate, but again, without revealing details. She didn't think it was anything that would get her in serious trouble.

"They're going over old recordings now."

"So am I fired?"

"I don't know."

"Who's it up to?" Clare hoped the decision didn't rest with Amanda. She was having no luck finding a handler who had any confidence in her.

"The final call is the superintendent's."

"Great. He didn't even want me on the case to start with." Clare stopped walking to light her smoke. "Come to think of it, I don't think there's anyone who wanted me for this case. Why am I here again?"

"Don't be defeatist." Amanda stopped a few paces ahead to wait for Clare.

"Why not? I'm being spied on by the people who are supposedly on my side. I have nothing but the right intentions, and that's not good enough. Give me a reason *not* to feel defeated."

"Because you're the one who screwed up. No one did this to you. Did you think it was okay to breach confidentiality?"

"I guess not technically." Clare exhaled and began to walk again, setting the pace more slowly this time. Amanda could fucking slow down if she wanted to talk. "I haven't told Kevin anything. I did mention that I was dating for the case. But that was just so I wouldn't be cheating on him." The words sounded really stupid to Clare when she said them out loud. "Is that a big deal?"

"We'll see once we have the transcripts, I guess. What day was this phone call?"

"You hate me, don't you?" Why had Clare said that out loud? Now Amanda would think she was a needy, pathetic loser.

Amanda looked surprised. "I don't hate you."

"Well, you don't like me."

"I'm not paid to like or dislike you. Nothing's personal about this."

It would be, when Amanda heard what Clare had said about her to Roberta. If she hadn't already heard.

"It's personal to you, though," Amanda said. "I can see that."

Was there something wrong with taking her job to heart? Did most people walk through life separating their emotions from their careers? Maybe it was optimal, but it hardly seemed human.

"Should I be colder?" Clare asked.

"I'm not sure. You have talent for this job; you let your whole self get involved and the suspects trust you fast. But you seem to have an equal talent for making giant mistakes."

"Meaning . . ."

"Your strength is your downfall. You think you're a character in the drama; you forget to keep a layer of separation."

"So what should I do differently?" Clare asked. She meant it. "I want to be great at this job."

Amanda put a finger to her chin. "Keep me in the loop more. Keep me posted on your emotions."

That wasn't going to work. "I don't know you well enough. That's why I called Roberta; I can trust her with those things."

"I understand it's not ideal." Did Amanda actually look hurt? "But you're undercover. If you need to confide in someone, that someone has to be me."

"I'll remember that. If I'm not pulled from the case."

"I'll get an answer on that by tomorrow," Amanda said. "Until then, carry on as if you're staying."

"What's your guess? Do you think I'll be pulled?"

"I'm not paid to guess."

"No," Clare said. "Of course you're not."

SIXTY-ONE
NOAH

Noah sat in the lobby with the newspaper. Peering past the edge of the paper, he watched Oliver swirl through the revolving doors and board the shuttle bus for the casino. When the bus pulled away, Noah strode quickly to the elevator and rode up to Oliver's floor.

He got into the room with little difficulty. Noah wasn't sure what he was looking for, but when he found the suitcase with the inside zipper — the same so-called hidden compartment where he'd found all Fiona's notes — he thought it might be a good place to start.

Noah slipped in his hand and felt paper. He pulled out a wad of American hundreds. He reached his other hand in and pulled out another wad. Noah eyed the door — dumb reflex, because what was he going to do if someone came in? — and he counted the bills. There was just over ten thousand dollars. It was a lot given Oliver's low-level job, but a trifling amount for someone involved in such a huge scam.

Noah left the cash where he'd found it and continued searching for notes. There were none in the compartment with the cash — at least the kid was smarter than his boss. But after what Noah considered an exhaustive search — drawers, suitcase compartments — he found no notes. Conclusion: either Fiona was the link between the Dealer and the scam and Oliver was being paid peanuts for doing the bulk of the work, *or* Oliver was smarter than his boss, and was disposing of the notes as soon as he'd internalized them.

Did Oliver know enough to resent his meager wage? Or was he happy with a wad of cash to flip a wire and look innocent? Bert had confirmed that Oliver's was the voice of the scam. Noah was pretty sure he'd also just confirmed Oliver as a willing — or at the very least, aware — participant. Was it as simple a cast as that? Mystery Man as the Dealer and Poker Choker, Fiona the overpaid go-between, Oliver the underpaid lackey?

Noah shook his head. That wasn't quite it. It was close, but he couldn't light the final cigar.

And he still didn't know what line he should take with "Tiffany."

SIXTY-TWO
ELIZABETH

Elizabeth searched the poker room for George. She didn't know why the guy was suddenly her confidant, but talking to him felt safe, like he'd never use anything she said against her. There weren't too many people like that in the gambling world — hell, there weren't too many in the world in general. George was the only person she wanted to tell what she'd just learned in the bathroom — or *head*, if she wanted to use boating terms — of *Last Tango*.

She found George about to sit down in the spectator stands. She tugged at his arm and led him away to where no one could hear them.

"What's up?" George seemed amused.

"I'm pregnant."

"You are?" George didn't have to look so pleased with himself. "Congratulations."

Ah. He thought it was a good thing.

"I'm not keeping it," Elizabeth said.

"Why not?"

She looked at him hard. "Because it's Joe's."

"I thought you were in love with Joe."

"It isn't mutual."

At least George had the grace to look sad now. "How does he feel about the baby?"

Elizabeth scowled. "Would you not call it a baby? It's a bunch of cells, and that's all it's ever going to be."

"Sorry," George said. "What was Joe's reaction when you told him?"

Elizabeth didn't say anything.

"You can't not tell him."

The poison was firing violent chemicals through her — at least now she knew what they probably meant. The tables were starting to fill up with players.

"You're just going to kill his baby." George's eyes dropped, like she was so horrible he couldn't even look at her.

Elizabeth didn't say anything.

"Give him a chance."

"Joe doesn't want kids. He's not — George, he's not normal that way. I can see it in the way he refuses to recycle, the way he laughs at me for caring what the world will look like in fifty or a hundred years. He's not interested in anything except living *his* life, then feeding some maggots underground."

"Just because Joe doesn't recycle doesn't mean he wants you to have an abortion."

"I want the abortion. If this pregnancy was a good thing, my body wouldn't be reacting this way." Elizabeth tapped her foot impatiently on the carpet. "It's — I think the poison is because it's Joe's. Is that horrible? I think his genes are so desperate to not reproduce that they're making me feel miserable so I terminate the pregnancy."

"Have you been studying witchcraft? I don't think genetics work that way."

"Our bodies know things." Elizabeth shook her head. "The game's starting soon. I should get to my seat."

"Tell him, Elizabeth. It's strange what can make a man want to settle down."

Elizabeth had been down that thought path on the short walk from the boat to the casino. "Maybe a baby would keep him entertained for a while. Maybe he'd even stay faithful for a month, though I doubt it. That's not the life I want."

"So you're going to break up with him?"

She looked at George sharply. "I didn't say that."

"But you just said . . ."

"I said I'm not going to tell him about the baby. I mean fetus. I still want to date Joe, for all the reasons I'm already with him."

"What possible reasons could you have, if you feel this way about your future?"

"Addiction." Elizabeth had never put it in these terms, but it was true. "I'm drawn to Joe, magnetically, and I'm not going to leave him until I figure out how to break that."

SIXTY-THREE
CLARE

Clare looked at Elizabeth across the poker table. Elizabeth was frowning, as usual, and playing her cards like the game was so fucking serious. Clare understood that there was a lot of money at stake; she just didn't understand how money alone could motivate someone to get out of bed each day.

Clare wrinkled her mouth at her cards, but in fact they were two tens, and quite playable. She put her sunglasses on and tossed some chips casually toward the center.

Elizabeth said, "I can see you like your hand."

Clare had no idea how the other players could all read her so easily.

"Raise." Elizabeth put some chips in the middle and stuck a circular gold protector over her hole cards.

Clare shrugged and called the raise. Trying for casual and most likely failing miserably.

"Seriously, Tiffany. You're not fooling anyone."

"What do you mean?" Clare asked, wondering if Elizabeth's old hostility was back.

"Forget about it," Elizabeth said.

The flop came ace-ten-seven, three different suits. Ideal for Clare's hand — her trip tens were beating everything but pocket aces.

"Are you mad at me for something?" Clare asked Elizabeth.

The first two players checked, and Elizabeth bet three-quarters of the pot. "No. But we need to have a talk."

"So talk." Clare called the bet and hoped she looked casual about her killer hand.

"Trust me: you don't want me saying this in front of eight strangers."

Clare had no idea what could be so top secret, but she'd take Elizabeth's word for it. "You want to get some lunch at the break?"

"Why not?" Elizabeth said. "I've been having a lousy day anyway."

The other two players folded and Clare was heads-up against Elizabeth. The turn card was a king. There were some remote chances Elizabeth was ahead, but if so it was dumb luck. Basically, Clare wanted as much money involved on this card as possible, and she didn't want Elizabeth to know why.

Elizabeth bet, making it another half-pot to Clare.

Clare gave a look that she hoped resembled worry. She looked at her stack. Looked at the dealer. "If I go all in, does she have me covered?"

The dealer did a quick chip count. "Yes."

"Okay," Clare said. Then she did something dangerous. "Call."

The river was a three, which suited Clare's plan perfectly. No draws could have come in, and unless Elizabeth had already had her beaten on the turn, Clare's display of weakness could now net her a very large pot.

"Check," Elizabeth said.

Clare waited a beat. "All in."

"Fold," Elizabeth said. "Disappointed, huh, Tiffany?"

Clare nodded, collecting the chips the dealer was raking her way. "How did you know I was ahead?"

"I'll tell you at lunch."

SIXTY-FOUR
NOAH

Noah listened to his earphone: dead silence, like he'd instructed. The black table felt looked darker than it had before, like something creepy lived inside it and was waiting for the right moment to reach its evil claw out and drag Noah into its underworld. He had to cut back on the gruesome late night TV.

He saw Tiffany and Elizabeth one table over. "Tiffany" looked frantic. She was clearly not a poker veteran; she was crap at hiding her emotions. But what was she frantic about? Did she miss having the other players' hole cards fed into her ear?

Elizabeth looked angry. She didn't normally smile, but today she was even more intense. Was she wondering why the signal had stopped?

Joe was at Noah's table, but he seemed as relaxed as he always did. Today he was wearing a pirate hat and saying "Arrrr" before making every play.

A few tables over, Noah saw T-Bone stand up, throw his cards down, and storm away from the table. Busted out? More likely he'd lost a hand to a bad beat, since he soon turned around and sat back down with a plonk. In any case, he was perfectly in character.

Where was Mickey? Yup: grinning. Cracking some joke, or laughing at someone else's. Noah couldn't hear the words from three tables away, but his face was the same as always.

Did it not matter that they'd lost someone close to them? Or were they just that damn good at putting game faces on?

Fiona was chatting with the two guys in the booth who ran commentary for a competing show. She tossed her head back and laughed at something one of them said. She looked perkier than usual. Was she so happy that the scam was off that she forgot she should be grieving about Loni?

And George, in the spectator stands, looked confused. Annoyed because he'd busted out early? Or was George listening in to the channel, wondering where the hell Oliver's voice was?

But none of what Noah saw was evidence. When the bell sounded for lunch, he wondered if he'd learned anything at all by stopping the cheating ring.

He'd either have to play closer attention, or raise the stakes a notch.

SIXTY-FIVE
ELIZABETH

"So how did you know I wanted a call for my trips?" Tiffany leaned into the restaurant table. Her wrists were too small for her bangly bracelets. She made Elizabeth think of an eight-year-old playing dress-up in her mother's closet.

"You're an opposite player," Elizabeth said. "When you like your hand, you act nonchalant. When you're bluffing, you're bold and pushy. It's fairly formulaic — I'm surprised Mickey hasn't tried to coach that out of you."

"So the sunglasses don't help?" Tiffany fingered the sparkly studs on the magenta frames that sat beside her coffee cup.

"Really?" Elizabeth laughed. "Your sunglasses are your biggest tell of all."

"What do you mean? They're supposed to be anti-reflective."

"I can't see your cards in them."

"You see my eyes through them?" Tiffany said. "Do my expressions give me away?"

Elizabeth decided to throw the girl a favor. Despite the donk beat in Niagara, she wasn't afraid of Tiffany winning this game. "You only put the glasses on when you have a hand you like."

Tiffany grinned. At least she could laugh at herself. "Should I keep them on all the time?"

"That would make sense." Elizabeth sipped her iced tea, which she found way too sweet. She liked the places in the southern States that let you add your own sugar. "So why are you pretending to be someone you're not?"

Tiffany's eyebrows lifted. "What?"

"I used to work for my father. He's a furniture importer, like your dad. Except I've never heard of your dad, and neither has he."

Tiffany's hands seemed to spontaneously start fiddling with each other. "You don't know my dad's name."

"I'm assuming his last name is James."

Tiffany swallowed. "Yeah."

Elizabeth leaned as far as she could across the table. It wasn't to avoid being heard; it was to intimidate Tiffany, to throw her even more off kilter. "You don't have to tell me your real name. But I want to know why you're lying."

"I'm . . . not . . . lying."

"Really? Explain this, then." Elizabeth pulled her BlackBerry from her purse and began reading, presumably a text message. "'Hey, Lizzie, no James in Canada — as you already know. Checked England — nothing. Only possibility left U.S. — but don't think so. Maybe it's another name? Message back if you want me to check something else.'"

"Who's that?" Tiffany asked.

"My brother."

"Why would you — what's the point of finding out my dad's company name?"

"Tiffany. Stop lying."

Tiffany flinched. She briefly separated her hands, maybe to try to make her nervousness less obvious, but in seconds they were back together like magnets, her bracelets clanking. "The business is in my mom's name. For tax reasons."

"What's your mother's name?" Elizabeth held her finger poised over her phone's keypad.

"I'm not going to tell you. You're deranged. My dad keeps that private, and now I can see why."

Elizabeth felt the poison pushing in. She wanted to fight it back, because as soon as it took over she couldn't trust her instincts anymore. She was pretty sure Tiffany was lying. But what if she wasn't? Now Elizabeth just looked like an idiot.

She tried one more push. "Your dad runs the company, though. So you say."

"Yeah."

"So it's his name my dad would know. And he doesn't."

But even Tiffany could see that there was doubt, and the balance had shifted in her favor. She bridged her hands in midair. "Why don't I call my dad and ask him if he's heard of any Ngs?"

The waitress set the food down. Tiffany's hamburger looked more appetizing than Elizabeth's oriental chicken salad.

"Why don't you tell me the real way you came into your money," Elizabeth said.

Tiffany had the nerve to look amused. "Um. How do you think I really got my money?"

Elizabeth glanced at Tiffany's steaming, chunky fries.

"Have one." Tiffany turned her plate so the fries were facing Elizabeth.

Elizabeth took a fry. "I think you're being funded by someone with an agenda."

Tiffany frowned. Elizabeth knew she'd hit on something.

Fiona sauntered up to their table carrying a slim leather briefcase. "Mind if I join you guys?"

Elizabeth did mind, but she'd finished with Tiffany for now, so she smiled instead. "Grab a chair."

"Man," Fiona said. "It's lethal in that room. Everyone hates each other normally, but since Loni's death, they're showing it." She glanced at Elizabeth as if she'd just remembered their recent argument on camera. She leaned in and asked in an affected voice, "Shit. No hard feelings, right?"

"No, of course not." Elizabeth felt her mouth curl into a very tight smile.

The waitress came by and Fiona ordered a Cobb salad.

"I'm surprised you guys are talking," Fiona said. "With that prop bet and all, I thought you'd be fuming, Lizzie."

"Prop bet?" Tiffany squeaked, like a parrot.

"Joe and Nate?" Fiona stared. "No one told you?"

Tiffany shook her perky little head.

"Wow, I suck. Sorry," Fiona said, not looking sorry at all, "but someone should tell you. Joe and Nate have a bet for twenty grand to see which one of them can sleep with you first. And rumor has it, appearances aside, that no one's won yet."

Tiffany tried to act disgusted, but Elizabeth could see she was flattered. "Are you kidding?"

Fiona shook her head. "Has Nate already won?"

"Nope."

"You haven't slept with Nate?" Elizabeth said. "Or is that another one of your lies?"

Tiffany faced Elizabeth and said calmly, "I've known Nate four days. Should I have slept with him?"

Elizabeth shrugged. "I thought you had loose morals."

"Where does morality come in? I'll sleep with him when I want to, not because someone else thinks I should or shouldn't."

"You sound like Joe. He doesn't believe in morality either."

"Maybe Joe could win the bet." Tiffany eyed Elizabeth defiantly. "I've known him four days, too."

"Maybe no one will win," Elizabeth countered. "Maybe you'll turn around and leave this scene as loudly as you came."

"Jesus," Fiona said. "What the hell did I just walk into?"

SIXTY-SIX
GEORGE

George watched Fiona leave the casino floor with Joe. She tossed her head back and giggled as if Joe was the mutant offspring of Chris Rock and Ricky Gervais. Looking at her, no one would know she should be terrified for her life.

"You ready?" Mickey said to George, patting the leather briefcase in his hand. "I got a lot of material for you. My mom's so proud I'm having a book written about me. She mailed me hospital records from when I was a kid."

"That should be helpful." George lifted his eyebrows.

"I don't expect you to write about my tonsils. But you gotta know where I come from. There's nothing irrelevant about backstory."

George followed Mickey as he headed for the exit. "Have you been taking writing classes?"

"I don't need a class to teach me what's obvious. I learned that bit about backstory online. For a while I thought I might have to write this book myself." Mickey pulled out a small bag of peanuts and held it out to George.

George shook his head at the nuts. "Separate cabs again?"

"Nah, we can travel together. I realized that was overkill. People know we're working on the book together — it don't look so weird if we spend time together."

They got into a cab and Mickey said to the driver, "Someone told me White Rock's nice. You know a place we can grab a beer? Nothing with loud music. We need to talk business."

The driver gave a lopsided nod and started the car.

On the long drive through ugly suburbs, George wondered if Mickey was being paranoid or sensible by not wanting to talk about the scam in a hotel room, or even in the taxi. By the time the cab left them on the beach front in White Rock, he'd concluded that when a killer was in play, paranoid and sensible were probably one and the same.

"It's good here," Mickey said, once they were seated with drinks by a large window overlooking the Georgia Strait. "Downtown, the waiters act like they should actually be driving a Bentley, but today they have to act lowly and serve you."

George preferred downtown, maybe for its more active pulse, but he saw Mickey's point. This bar they were in might be washed-out and run-down, but no one's pretensions would survive long. "So what's the news?"

"The news is this note I found." Mickey pulled a crumpled sheet from his pocket. "Maybe I should try to keep this in nicer shape in case it turns into evidence. But have a look."

George took the paper.

```
3rd Floor Ice Machine, half-price due to glitch
today. Same time.
```

George passed back the page. "What the hell does that mean?"

"That's what I'd like to know." Mickey tapped a finger to his head. "I was walking behind T-Bone, thinking how nice it would feel to yank the guy's ponytail so hard he screamed like a girl, when this fell out of his pocket."

George felt his eyes bug. "You think he received it, or he was planning to give it to someone?"

"That's one of the questions," Mickey said. "I think he killed Loni."

"Because you hate his guts?"

Mickey crinkled his face up, presumably thinking. "Maybe."

"Do you think he killed the others, too?"

"I don't care about the others, to be frank. Everything changes when your ex-wife is found dead."

George understood that. The scam and the murders had become stupidly real now that he knew Fiona was involved. "Do you still care about the book we're writing?"

"Of course I care about our book. It's been my dream since I was a kid. I just mean that the others — Josie, Jimmy, that clown Oppal —" Mickey ticked names off on his fingers. "— they're like characters in a play. I feel for their families and all that. But Loni makes it real."

"So what are we doing sitting here?" George said. "Shouldn't we be staking out the third-floor ice machine?"

"You want to?" Mickey's eyes shot open.

George shrugged. "Screw the sidelines. We're sitting ducks until this killer is caught."

SIXTY-SEVEN
CLARE

Clare pushed past Nate's attempt at a hug. "Was I a prop bet?" His room had a nice view of the river, but she wasn't about to say anything positive.

"Originally." Nate seemed awfully calm for a man admitting he was an amoral loser. "How did you find out?"

"When you say, 'originally,'" Clare said, sticking a hand on her hip and not having to pretend too hard to look angry, "does that mean you called the bet off when you realized we had a real connection?"

Nate frowned.

"No, I didn't think so. Does it mean you're not going to take the money if you win?"

Nate brushed his shaggy brown hair from his face.

"Not that you'll win," Clare said, "so I guess you can say anything you like if it will convince you that you're a decent guy." Clare couldn't believe this guy had made her doubt her relationship with Kevin, all for a big money prop bet. She was tempted to go find Joe and make him win right then. Before leaving the scene, because Elizabeth had pretty much told her she'd been made. Fuck, her career was in a bad state.

"I mean," Nate said, speaking slowly, "originally I'd had some drinks, I wanted to impress Joe, you looked amazing, so I made a bet."

"Why would you want to impress Joe? He's a womanizing douchebag." Clare wasn't going to let Nate's excuses soften her.

"You're right." Nate cracked a grin. "But he's been my poker hero for two years. Meeting him in real life was pretty cool."

"Is that why you wanted do me in Stanley Park?" Clare's blood was hot. She wanted to take off her jacket, but it would give the wrong impression, like she was staying.

"No," Nate said. "I wanted to have sex with you because you turn me on. But I understand if it will take some time for you to trust me again."

"Time?" Clare fished a cigarette from her pack. She didn't offer one to Nate. "More like we'll both have to die and I'll come back as someone who doesn't remember what you did to me for the sake of twenty grand. Anyway, fuck that. As soon as this game is over, I'm going home."

"Coffee?" Nate took the empty pot from the machine and went into the bathroom. For some reason, the sound of water hitting the glass pot infuriated Clare further.

She stared out the window at the mountains. She heard Nate return and pour water into the coffee machine. She turned around. "Why would I stay and drink coffee with you? Do you have a bet with Joe Mangan about who can be the first to serve me coffee?"

"Ouch. Come on, Clarissa."

"Who's Clarissa?" What had just happened? This was way worse than Elizabeth's suspicions.

"Shit." Nate looked away. "I meant Tiffany."

"Why did you call me Clarissa?"

"It was obviously a mistake."

Clare felt paralyzed in place. Her career was clearly over; she just had to make it out of the room alive. "Okay," she said.

"Okay?" Nate said.

Clare nodded. She couldn't move her legs.

"Jesus," Nate said under his breath.

"I thought you were Jewish." Really? That was all she could say? "What's the point of a Jewish person taking Jesus's name in vain? You don't even think he was anything special."

"My ex-girlfriend's name is Clarissa," Nate said. "Our break-up was a lot like this one."

"Fine," Clare said. "I'm, um, going to go now." Right. Just as soon as she could move.

"You don't have to leave. The coffee's almost ready. Stay and have one cup."

One poisoned cup, probably. "No, thanks." Clare studied Nate, who was pretending to watch the coffee percolate. How would he have discovered her identity?

Maybe he was another cop. Amanda had said none of the other RCMP undercovers were playing in the tournament, but maybe that's what she was supposed to say. Maybe Amanda didn't even know about Nate. But then why would Nate know Clare's identity? And if he *was* a cop who knew she was a cop, why would he waste his time coming on to Clare instead of getting to know the other suspects? Nope — not a cop.

But since she couldn't will her legs to move yet, Clare said, "If you tell me why you called me Clarissa, I'll consider helping you win that bet with Joe."

Nate peeled his eyes away from the coffee and glanced at her. "I don't care about the bet with Joe."

"You don't care about twenty grand? Well, I wonder why that could be, Nate. Is Nate your real name?"

Nate made a feeble attempt at laughter. "Have you gone a bit crazy? I'm sorry I called you my ex-girlfriend's name. I'm sorry I made a stupid bet with a poker player I was trying to impress. But I like you, for real. And yes, my name is Nate."

There was no saving this. Clare had to leave. As much as the idea drove her insane, she had to tell Amanda her cover was blown from two different sides. Unless . . . "I'm leaving." She was playing with fire.

"What do you mean?" Nate's eyes narrowed.

"I'm going home. Screw the chips I still have in the game. What's money when I could get killed if I stay?"

Nate's mouth fell open. "Is it because I said . . ." He looked like he wanted to finish the sentence.

Clare stared at him, compelling him to continue. When he didn't, she said, "Of course it is."

He bit his lip. "Do I need to say it out loud?"

"Yes."

"I know you're an undercover."

Clare felt the blood drain from her face. She sank into the closest chair. She knew she still had to lie for as long as she could. "Are you kidding?" she asked.

Nate shook his head.

Clare tried to laugh. "Undercover what?"

"You want to do this?" Nate said. "We could just come out in the open here, make things a lot easier." He set a coffee beside Clare. Yeah, right. She wasn't drinking it.

"Really," Clare said. "Do you think I'm a cop? A hooker? I'm totally confused."

"It's fine," Nate said. "My handlers told me."

Clare inhaled deeply. "Are you RCMP?"

Nate shook his head. "FBI. My name is Noah, by the way. It's good to meet you."

Clare rolled her eyes. And exhaled.

"You can't tell anyone," Noah said.

"Duh."

"I mean no one."

"My job and my ass is just as important as yours."

"So, um, did you mean it about the prop bet?" Noah's eyebrows arched.

"I did . . ." Clare spoke slowly, realizing she couldn't justify sleeping with Noah for pleasure. "But I don't think I can help you win that bet after all."

"It sounded too good to be true. What's the catch?"

"I have a boyfriend. The deal is I can sleep around as Tiffany — if it's, you know, relevant to the case. But Clare has to stay faithful."

"Clare?"

"I hate Clarissa."

"I can see why."

"I think I like Nate better than Noah," Clare said. "Both the person and the name."

"So call me Nate." Noah shrugged. "You should do that in public, anyway. And since it's okay to fuck around if you're role-playing, if I call you Tiffany, will you help me win that bet?"

"Forget it." Clare was fighting her body's annoying impulse to help him win the bet right there and then. "I'm not a cheater."

SIXTY-EIGHT
NOAH

"If you're not going to sleep with me, maybe you'd consider working with me." Noah wasn't sure if Clare believed the whole FBI thing. She acted like she did, but then of course she would, if she wanted to make it out of the room alive. He hoped he hadn't scared her into bolting — although bolting would clearly be the smart thing to do.

Clare rested her chin in her hand. "You mean you want to collaborate to find the killer?"

"My assignment is to figure out the cheating scam." That was true.

"Mine's to find the killer," Clare said. "So I guess there's no conflict if we work together. But I have to talk to my handler to see if she even wants me to stay in the game."

"Because of me?" Noah didn't want Clare going anywhere.

"Partly. Elizabeth is sniffing close, too," Clare said.

"Tell your handler about Elizabeth. But not about me."

"Why?" Clare's eyes darted up to meet his.

"It's stupid." Noah tried to keep his voice soft, conspiratorial, devoid of any urgency. "It's law enforcement politics. The RCMP will hate the FBI if they know we're here."

Clare wrinkled her forehead. "You're not even allowed to be here. I have to tell my handler, or I'm a traitor."

"Can you give it one more day?" Noah asked.

"Why should I?"

"It's complicated." Shit. That sounded condescending.

Clare started to walk toward the door. "It's okay. I'm sure I'm not supposed to be talking to you either. We're probably better off working solo."

"We probably are," Noah said. "But look — we know about each other now, we might as well pool resources. Otherwise we're competition. It could hurt both of our games."

"Games?" Clare shot him a new glance.

"Sorry. Jobs."

Clare unfastened the deadbolt.

"Clare, wait." Noah needed to secure her as a partner, if only to guarantee her silence to her handlers. "I'm not here to hurt your case. Really. The FBI sent me to get the cheating mechanics down. So casino bosses in the States can seal up any security loopholes and make sure it can't happen on home turf."

Clare stopped. Her hand was on the door handle, but she didn't open it.

Noah said, "I'm also pretty sure that our targets are the same person. You're after the Poker Choker. I'm after the Dealer. If we work together, we can nail him that much faster, and we can both chalk it up to a win."

"Dealer?" Clare frowned.

"The ringleader of the cheating scam. He gave himself the name." Noah paused. Was he truly going to share information, or was he better to pretend to share, and learn what he could from Clare?

"So we know he has an ego."

"What do you mean?" Noah hadn't seen it that way.

"Please. The Dealer? The guy who determines what cards everyone holds? He might as well sign the notes 'God.'"

Noah nodded. "You have a point."

"Of course I have a point. Only a man wouldn't see that."

"For someone so in love with your boyfriend, you don't have a high opinion of men."

"Kevin's different." Clare's eyes took on a dreaminess that Noah would prefer they didn't.

"Fine. Kevin's different. Me and the rest of men are all assholes."

Clare tapped her fingers on the door handle. "I'm not convinced we're after the same person. The killer could be some guy like Mickey. Pissed off at the cheaters; trying to keep the game pure for professionals."

Noah snorted. "No one kills for noble reasons."

"The killer on my last case kind of did."

"Nice that you can sympathize with evil. How about a theory that would fly in the real world?"

"Like whatever brilliant thing you're about to say?" Clare snapped.

"I don't have a specific theory. But I know a cracked one when I hear it."

"Good, then," Clare said. "How about if I brainstorm — you know, keep an open mind about it all — and you can tell me why everything I say sucks. Until I say something that doesn't suck. And then we'll have our answer."

Noah couldn't tell if she was being serious or sarcastic, so he asked.

"Both," Clare said. "I mean, it would be great if you could open your mind, too. But since you're so reluctant to think anything that might be construed as stupid by a fly on the wall of your brain, keep your mind closed, and we'll use our individual talents in combination."

"You want to see something my individual talent lifted from Fiona Gallagher's hotel room?"

Clare took her hand off the door handle.

"I'll take that as a yes." Noah went to the safe, punched in his code, and retrieved several single sheets of paper. He set them on the desk, which Clare walked over to.

Clare picked up the first one. "*Do you want to save your mother's house? What's this?*"

"Keep reading. I'm pretty sure they're in order."

Clare flipped to the next page. "*Do we need to involve your techie? If you can do it without his knowing, order orange juice and coffee on your room service card. If he needs to be involved, order grapefruit juice.* What the fuck, Nate? Noah. Whatever."

"I found them in Fiona's suitcase. My guess is she ordered grapefruit juice. Keep reading."

Noah watched as Clare read one page, then another. When she'd finished with them all, she looked up and said, "What do you want to do with all this?"

"I've started already. I mimicked the style and gave Fiona a note to cancel the cheating broadcast. It stopped today."

Clare's eyes narrowed. "You could get Fiona killed."

"I have surveillance on her room. Anyone drops off a new note — or shows up with a piece of rope — the game is up." Noah didn't mention that Fiona hadn't been staying in her room, or that he had a camera on George's room, too.

Clare frowned. "You seem to have everything taken care of. What do you need me for?"

"I like you." That, and he didn't want her spilling any beans to her handler.

"Spare me," Clare said. "I was a bet so you could get in with Joe Mangan. What's your next genius plan?"

Noah didn't have a next plan. He'd hoped pausing the scam would have given him more information. So he put it on Clare: "Isn't now when you start your brainstorming?"

"No," Clare said, heading back toward the door. "Now's when I run this by my handler."

Noah grabbed her arm more forcefully than he meant to. Her bicep was small, but it felt strong — Clare had more muscle than it looked like. "Don't breathe a word about me."

"I meant about Elizabeth," Clare said. "And let go of me."

SIXTY-NINE
CLARE

Clare's grip tightened around her phone. She was nervous calling Amanda. It was what Amanda said she wanted, but Clare wasn't used to sharing brainwaves with someone so perfect and prissy.

"Hello." Amanda's voice was crisp.

"It's Clare. Um, I have a question."

"Shoot." Like Amanda had so many other operatives working undercover in the world of competitive poker, and didn't have time for what she naturally assumed would be Clare's minor issue.

"It's . . . um." Clare kicked a pebble. She looked around to make sure no one was listening. But she was alone by the river outside Noah's hotel. Safe for talking.

"Are you okay?" Amanda asked.

"Yeah. I think so. I have a problem. And I think I have a solution. But I don't know if the solution is the best course of action. And I thought maybe . . ." Clare didn't know whether to tell Amanda about Noah or not. But she knew she had to talk about Elizabeth.

"Are you downtown? Can you come to my apartment?"

"I'm still in Richmond. I could come downtown, but I kind of have to act fast."

"Okay. What's the problem?"

"I might be made." She told Amanda what Elizabeth had said at lunch.

"Do you think Elizabeth suspects you're a cop?"

"No," Clare said. "I think she thinks I'm part of this cheating ring. But regardless, I don't want my identity under scrutiny. She definitely doesn't like me. If she finds out for sure that there's no James who's a big shot in furniture importing — which I think she's pretty close to concluding — she's likely to tell the whole scene. And then — okay fine, they don't put it together that I'm a cop — but any social inroads I've made would get barricaded fast."

"So what's your solution?"

"I could sleep with Joe." She filled Amanda in on the prop bet.

"Busy day. What would sleeping with Joe accomplish, besides getting crabs?"

"It would buy time." Clare shuddered at the crabs reference. Anyway, she disagreed. Joe seemed clean enough to her. "If Elizabeth blows my cover and I've slept with her boyfriend, it makes her look like she's grasping at straws to discredit me. I might lose my inroad with Fiona — women sometimes stick together — but for some reason, I don't think Fiona cares about the nobility of friendship too much."

"But you wouldn't lose the men? Mickey Mills is your biggest asset at the moment. And you don't think Nate would disown you for sleeping with Joe?"

Now was Clare's chance if she wanted to be honest about Noah. "Nate thinks I'm mad about the prop bet. I'm sure I could go crawling back to him afterward. Mickey — I don't think it would bother him enough to stop coaching me. Don't know. I think he'd be more bothered if he thought I'd been lying about my identity."

Amanda was quiet for a moment. "I'm still trying to understand your logic. If you sleep with Joe, you're giving Elizabeth more incentive to blow your cover, not less."

"Which is why I make sure she only finds out *if* she's blown my cover. You see what I'm saying? I sleep with Joe tonight for insurance. I overheard Elizabeth say she was going to dinner with her family tonight — without Joe — and I'm not sure when I'll get this chance again. Joe obviously won't scream it from the rooftops that he fucked me, but he'll have to tell Nate in order to collect on the prop bet. So *if* Elizabeth finds something on me that she *can* share with the poker world, I can make it look like she only did it because I'd slept with her boyfriend — which I'll get a modicum of sympathy for, because I can say I only did *that* because I was angry with Nate about the prop bet. Tiffany would still have to leave the scene, but it would take longer for the fallout to happen because Elizabeth would be under scrutiny as well."

Clare could imagine Amanda's immaculate brain synapses trying to fire their way around this. Eventually, Amanda said, "In one way, it's insurance. In another way, you're giving your cover role an end date. It's like you're planting a stick of dynamite in the scene and setting it onto slow burn."

"I think the dynamite's already planted," Clare said, though it killed her to acknowledge this out loud. "I don't see Tiffany James's cover role holding up much past this leg of the tournament. To use your dynamite analogy, I see sleeping with Joe as extending the wick a bit longer."

"I'm not sure, Clare. I wish I had more time to think this over."

"I wish I had ten years to learn how to play poker. I also have a backup story ready, if this is blown open before I can bail from the scene. I can say I lied about being a trust fund brat because I didn't want to admit how I'd really made my money, through Internet porn or something."

Amanda laughed. "Try stripping. Or prostitution. If you say web porn, people will want to see footage."

"Oh yeah."

"It's risky," Amanda said. "I see your point — you don't know if you're made, and your progress so far has been excellent."

"It has?"

"Sure. Or we would have pulled you immediately for talking to Roberta McGraw."

"Right." Clare felt her posture slouch. She didn't understand how she could try so hard to be good at this job and screw up so royally so often. It was like there were ten thousand things she had to be on top of all the time, and if she let even one slip for five seconds, it would turn into some major catastrophe.

"Don't get gloomy. It's a compliment." Amanda paused. "I don't want you to feel like you have to whore yourself out for this job. I like your creative thinking, and it's great that you called me with this, but you don't need to sacrifice your body —"

"It's no sacrifice. It's a tricky situation; I think it needs a creative solution. Hell, I might even enjoy it. I just want to make sure, before I go ahead and sleep with Joe, that you agree that my logic makes sense."

"Yes," Amanda said. "I think the logic makes sense."

SEVENTY
GEORGE

George was beginning to think staking out the ice machine had been a harebrained idea at best. He and Mickey had been casually strolling the hallway all evening, using Mickey's room on the third floor as a base. They hadn't seen anyone even glance at the door of the ice room. "Maybe T-Bone didn't get the message because he was about to give the note to someone else."

"Yeah," Mickey said. "Or maybe T-Bone made the cash drop while we were knocking back beers in White Rock."

"Why don't you think T-Bone's the Dealer? Isn't that the most likely explanation?"

"No." Mickey tossed a peanut in the air and caught it in his mouth.

George hadn't told Mickey about the notes Fiona had received. The one George had seen, the note calling off the scam, had been identical in font and format to this new half-price ice machine note.

"The only game T-Bone likes is poker," Mickey said. "I think he killed Loni, and I think he's cheating. But he wouldn't be the mastermind behind this. If he had a point to make, he'd make it without all this subterfuge."

George felt his eyebrows shoot up his face. "You think the Dealer has a point to make?" It's what George had thought originally, but Fiona had convinced him that it was probably all about money.

"'Course he does." Mickey leaned back in his chair. "If it was only for money, he wouldn't create all this drama. He likes to be the smart guy — the one in control."

"You never finished telling me what makes you think T-Bone killed Loni."

Mickey tilted his chair back so far that George thought gravity would soon pull him over. "You know the morning Loni was found?" Mickey said. "As I was leaving my room for breakfast, I saw T-Bone heading toward his room — the room where Loni was later found dead. That was after eight a.m. But T-Bone says he was playing poker from seven o'clock on and never went back upstairs. Why would he lie if he has nothing to hide?"

George wondered, too. "Do you think he killed the others?"

"Who knows? It's Loni I care about. But if you were going to kill someone now, what method would you use? Choking, right? Because it would get lumped in with the serial killer. And if you have an airtight alibi for just one of those other murders, then it's not you, is it?"

George thought that made sense. If nothing else, it could make a cool twist for his fiction. Shit, he had to stop thinking fictionally.

Mickey crinkled up his forehead. "You think the note meant another hotel? T-Bone's staying at the casino, but some of the others — Nate Wilkes, Oliver Doakes — are at the Delta. Maybe there's a third-floor ice machine there that's already been established as the drop point."

"What time is it?"

"Eight thirty," Mickey said. "That's four hours we've been stalking this floor."

"Time to get some ice." George stood up and took the

now-familiar ice bucket with him. In the hall he saw Joe walking toward him with a bucket of his own.

"Caught me." Joe grinned, sheepishly holding up his bucket. "I'm stealing ice from the hotel, and I'm not even staying here. Though technically the marina is under the River Rock umbrella . . . so I guess it's not outright theft."

George didn't know what to say. He could ask why this machine, why the third floor and not the second or the fourth? But he didn't want to tip Joe off that he was suspicious. "Planning a romantic night on the boat?"

"I sure hope so. Lizzie's out, though, so maybe don't say anything if you see her." Joe pushed open the door to the ice room and started filling up his bucket. "I know you and my girlfriend are newfound best friends and all that, but no need to hurt her, right?"

George didn't know whether to hate the guy or applaud him. "Fiona?"

Joe shook his head. "Tiffany."

"But she's — isn't she dating Nate?"

"Broke up. She found about the prop bet, and she's damn mad. At Nate; not me. She sent me a text asking if I wanted to meet for a drink."

"So let me guess," George said. "You suggested your boat."

"We have everything we need there." Joe put one more scoop of ice into his bucket and moved aside to let George fill his. He didn't seem concerned about looking through the machine for any cash drop, half-price or otherwise.

"What if Elizabeth comes home?" George knew he sounded like a square.

"She has to call me to let her onto the dock. We only have one gate key between us."

George thought Joe was pushing his luck. What if a guard let her in, or if another boater was coming through the gate at the same time Elizabeth arrived? But who was he to tell another man how to keep his woman? "Have fun," George said. "And good luck, man."

SEVENTY-ONE
CLARE

"So you finally agreed to go out with me." Joe leaned back in his deck chair and folded his arms in front of him.

Clare sipped her beer. "This is not a date."

"No?" Joe said with a laugh. "What is it? A serious meeting between two industry professionals?"

"This is a revenge drink."

"Revenge. I see. Who are you upset with?" Like he didn't know the answer.

"Nate. I found out at lunch that he had a prop bet with you about sleeping with me." She decided not to tell Joe that Elizabeth knew, in case it would deter him from cheating. Clare's head was starting to spin from all these stories she had to maintain for different people, but so far she had them all straight.

Joe said, "Uh, not that I want to dissuade you from this revenge fuck in any way —"

"Revenge drink." Clare was glad Joe had made the leap, though.

"Drink. That's what I meant. But shouldn't you be mad at me equally?"

"Oh my god. Maybe technically." Clare threw her hands in the air. "But I really liked Nate. I know it hasn't even been a week, but I felt really strong chemistry. I thought he did, too. Maybe you're right — maybe you're not who I should be talking to right now."

"No, no," Joe said. "It's cool. I'm on your side. So you feel ripped off? Betrayed? Both?"

"Yeah." Clare pretended to calm down a bit. "Maybe I'm naive. I always let my heart get too involved too quickly."

"That's a good thing," Joe said. "And I think Nate actually does like you. For what it's worth."

"It's worth nothing. I can't give him another chance — that would make me *really* naive. Onwards and upwards, right?" Clare gave Joe a small hopeful smile.

Joe's eyebrows shot up. "I'll see what I can do."

Clare leaned forward. "We could really piss him off, you know?"

Joe swirled the ice around in his half-full vodka seven and downed the rest of the drink. "You want to come into the stateroom?"

Clare was surprisingly scared. She did want to go into the stateroom, but maybe not so fast. "What about Elizabeth?"

Joe smirked. "You mean that like a conscience thing, or like a what-if-she-finds-out thing?"

"Both," Clare said.

"Lizzie's out with her family. She won't be back until late."

Clare hoped this was true.

"Come on. Everyone wants a famous guy in their little black book."

Clare lit a new cigarette. "Little black book implies I'd be calling you back."

"Ouch. Famous notch on your bedpost, then?"

"Fame doesn't impress me." Clare at least had this in common with Tiffany. "Success does, though."

"What's the difference?"

"Success is earned."

"Not always."

"No," Clare said. "In fact that's — Joe, I have no idea who I can talk to about this. I was going to talk to Nate, but he turned into an asshole. Have you heard the rumors that are going around?"

Joe rattled his ice. "What rumors? If you're talking about my massive member, you'll have to come into my stateroom to see for yourself."

"You like to take risks, huh?" Clare moved her chair closer to his, trying to feign fascination. "I think it turns you on that Elizabeth could come home anytime."

"I take risks for a living. I guess it turns me on."

"But that's the rumor I heard. There's someone — some people — who might not be taking risks. They might be cheating."

"I have heard that." Joe's voice lowered. The tarp was covering the boat, but someone on the dock could easily hear through it. "But since my win rate hasn't gone down since this cheating supposedly started, I haven't paid the theory much attention. Where'd you hear it from?"

"I overheard people talking when I was in line for coffee. So I asked Mickey, and he said yeah, that rumor's been around since the tour was in Calgary. Did some guy die there?"

"Jimmy Streets," Joe said. "An old-timer. A really good player."

"I was hoping to stay on this tour for a while — at least until I got my game not sucking enough that I could go home a winner. But I think this is too much for me. I wasn't made for the dark side of life."

"Most of us aren't." Joe gave her a look of what seemed like genuine concern. "Hey, I'm sorry for always trying to get you in bed. I think you're cool. I want to know you. We can hang out and talk if that's more where your comfort zone is."

"That would be great." Clare widened her eyes to show vulnerability.

"You're not going to bail while you still have money in the game, are you?"

"No." Clare shook her head. "I'm not worried that I'm the next victim or anything. I'm not part of the cheating ring. That's what the rumors say, right? That the two are connected?"

"Yeah." Joe nodded. "That's what Lizzie thinks, anyway."

"You're not so sure?"

Joe met her gaze gently. "On this scene, stories buzz around like black flies. If one person isn't speculating about a cheating scam, someone else is. Yeah, you should be careful. But there's no point worrying about something until you see direct evidence."

"But I think —" Clare paused intentionally. She was going out on a limb here, but something was keeping her from trusting Noah fully. "I think I might *have* seen something. And — oh my god, I hate this. I don't know who to trust."

"It's okay." Joe took her hand, stroked it. "You can trust me. You're fine."

"But — what if it's nothing? I don't want to spread more rumors."

"If it's nothing, we'll forget about it."

"Yeah?"

"Of course," Joe said. "You need to get this off your chest."

"It's Nate."

"Nate?" Joe's mouth dropped open.

"I'm not saying this because I'm mad at him," Clare said. "I mean, I'm sure I am, partly. But I'm also really scared. What if he's the killer? I don't think I'd be the next victim, because I don't know anything about the scam. But what if he thinks I do? What if he comes after me?"

"He won't come after you." Joe got up and stood behind Clare, kneading her shoulders in a way that actually felt great — Clare hadn't realized how tense they'd been.

Joe's phone beeped. He picked it up and read a text. "Lizzie's staying at her parents' place overnight. We'll have the boat to ourselves if you want to stay over."

"Said the spider to the fly."

"Hey, you called me." Joe traced a finger along her neck and down under the top of her shirt. "Who's the spider? Who's the fly?"

SEVENTY-TWO
GEORGE

Fiona was out. Good for her. It wasn't like they were a couple and George had any right to know where she was.

George sipped his Scotch. He told his fingers to do what they wanted with the keyboard. Trouble was, they wanted to go nowhere. George threw on his jeans and dialed Fiona's cell again. This time she picked up.

"George?" She sounded tiny.

"Fiona? You don't sound like yourself."

"Yeah," she said. "I took your advice."

"My advice?" George pulled a rake through his brain. "What did I suggest?"

"I left. I rented a car and I got the hell out of there. Oliver can run the technical side of things. I'm sure the network can find another commentator. There's no shortage of staffers who would kill for a turn in the spotlight."

"But . . ."

"Ha ha. I guess I might even mean that literally. I got another note. The Dealer wants things back on. And — this is the fucked-up part — he seemed pissed off that I'd stopped the broadcast."

"Wasn't it him who told you to stop?"

"That's why it freaked me out. If this guy is losing it, maybe I *am* next on his list."

"Do you think he's bipolar?" George asked.

Fiona snorted. "Bipolar is manic depressive. Are you talking about split personalities?"

"I guess." George laughed, though nothing was funny. "Or maybe there are two Dealers and their agendas have diverged."

"And thanks, George. I would never have got up the balls to leave if you hadn't convinced me it was smart."

"I wanted to come, too." George picked up the red T-shirt he'd slung on the back of his chair. He thought of putting it on while he was talking, but he didn't want to pull the phone away from his ear for even a second. "I didn't mean for you to take off on your own."

"I don't want you here."

George's head felt weird. He pushed his Scotch aside.

"That sounded harsh," Fiona said. "I didn't mean it to. You've been awesome to me these past few days — these past few years, really. But I don't even want to trust you right now."

George crunched his phone between his shoulder and ear and moved to put the shirt on anyway. He needed to be dressed. He needed to take action. "Are you at the airport?"

"I'm not saying."

George opened Safari on his computer. He could at least find out where the nearest Zipcar location was. "Fiona, please. Think about it. I can write a book from anywhere. I can help keep you safe. We'll run together."

"God, that sounds so tempting."

"We'll go somewhere tropical. Somewhere they don't extradite."

"You really love me, don't you?"

George closed his eyes. "I really do."

SEVENTY-THREE
CLARE

Clare opened her hotel room door to let Noah in. He looked scruffier than usual — at three a.m., his morning facial hair was already starting to surface. "No one followed you, right?"

"Right." Noah sank into the armchair. "Our cover characters are sworn enemies. What did you tell your handler?"

"Nothing about you," Clare said. "And by the way, you owe Joe Mangan twenty grand."

Noah's jaw fell.

"Joe knows what he's doing. Got me off in record time, and now he's playing poker dressed as Snow White. Twenty grand's a bargain. You want a coffee? Something from the minibar? It's on me — actually, it's on the RCMP. To say thanks."

"Are you mad at me?" Noah unzipped his navy blue hoodie. "Did you call me here to gloat?"

"No." Clare opened the minibar and pulled out a beer. Bud, because she wasn't pretending. "I called because I have a plan. I think you were right earlier. I think we *should* work together."

"I'll have one of those, too."

Clare passed the first beer to Noah and grabbed another for herself.

"What's your idea?"

Clare still wasn't sure if she was playing this the right way. She should be running this by Amanda — including telling her she'd officially been made. In a perfect world, Amanda would then check to make sure Noah was for real, and Clare could go ahead with her collaboration.

But Amanda might not react that way. Her most likely reaction would be to pull Clare — there were too many doubts surrounding her role already. In fact, if Clare were in Amanda's place, she'd think the safest thing would be to pull her.

But the safest thing wasn't always the right thing — or the most effective. If Clare's plan *did* work, they might actually catch the Choker before the Vancouver tournament ended. A lot of people planned to leave the scene after this — there was even talk about the Canadian Classic shutting down. It would be too easy for the killer to slip out into the world to kill again. It wasn't only her own career Clare could save with this collaboration — it was the lives of future victims.

She smiled grimly. As weak as it might be, she had her justification.

"I think we should mix things up," Clare said. "I think we should deliver notes around the scene — like the one you gave Fiona, only everybody gets one — we sign them 'The Dealer,' and gauge people's reactions."

Noah cocked his head to the right. "Do you have specific notes in mind?"

"I have a rough plan." Clare nodded. "It would help if we had a better handle on who's cheating. You said you had a spreadsheet. How close are you to narrowing the field?"

SEVENTY-FOUR
GEORGE

George wandered into the high stakes poker room — bad move, no doubt — and gave the dealer five thousand dollars to change into chips. He was even glad when T-Bone sat down beside him.

T-Bone changed twenty thousand and said to George, "I never seen you play these stakes. Feeling lucky?"

George shook his head.

"So get away from the table," T-Bone said. "You're a shit player anyway."

"I don't care if I lose."

T-Bone tilted his head, peering into George's eyes. "The fuck's got you down?"

"Fiona," George said, too despondent to keep things to himself. "She panicked. She left. I don't know if I'll ever see her again."

"What do you mean, she left? Where did she go?"

George shrugged. "She won't tell me."

"It's the middle of a fucking tournament," T-Bone said. "Does she want them to freeze the fucking game again?"

"The cards can be dealt without a commentator," George said.

"Changes the fucking point. This is supposed to be television — we got names to maintain, books to promote. You should care, too — your book is newer than mine."

Before George could respond, Joe walked in. Or rather, Snow White walked in, and only Joe Mangan would wear such an outrageous costume at the poker table.

"Who wants to be my dwarf?" said Joe's voice from inside Snow White.

T-Bone groaned. "Not me."

"Is Elizabeth back from dinner?" George didn't want to be at the poker table. T-Bone was right; he'd only lose if he stayed.

Joe shook his head. "She's staying at her parents' place. I can gamble 'til dawn like when I was single." Joe rubbed his hands together. "Who wants to be my first victim?"

"Not me." George got up and took his chips with him. "Good luck, though."

"Hey, thanks," said Joe. "You said that to me earlier, in the ice room, and I got really lucky."

George rolled his eyes. "I guess you won the prop bet."

T-Bone was still disturbed. "You hear anything about Fiona bailing?" he said to Joe.

Snow White shook her head. "Like, bailing bailing? Never coming back?"

"Yeah," T-Bone said. "George here says she spooked. I wonder how that could have happened."

"Beats me." Joe pulled out his phone and typed out a message to someone. "So are we going to play some poker?"

"Fuck that." T-Bone stood up. "This Canadian scene is going to shit. First Loni gets killed, now we're not even going to be on TV anymore. I'll stay because I still have chips in the tournament, but after that I'm getting the fuck out of here. I'm going back to the States as soon as this shit game is over."

"So go sulk," Joe said. "You bailing too, George?"

"Yeah." George picked up his chips.

"From the scene, or from the table?" Joe's voice sounded like it held a smile, though it was impossible to tell behind the Snow White mask.

"I don't know," George said. "Maybe I'll go online and see if I can find Fiona."

"You think she put her location up on a website? Maybe Facebook?"

"No." George knew he probably shouldn't be saying this out loud, but his head was swimming, and he'd been drinking, and . . . "Fiona has an iPhone. I can track her anywhere in North America."

"You need her password for that."

"I know."

Joe's phone beeped. He picked it up and typed another message.

T-Bone was still standing listening. "If you find her, tell her to get her ass back here for tomorrow morning."

SEVENTY-FIVE
NOAH

Noah watched Clare stretch her legs out then curl them underneath her as she leaned into the headboard.

"Pretty close." Noah reached into his canvas shoulder bag and pulled out a clunky-looking black laptop. It actually wasn't clunky at all — it was supremely fast, with built-in satellite technology so he could be online anywhere on or near Earth without anyone's wifi being able to hack into it — but the plain casing would fool most observers.

He opened the file with players' statistics.

"I think Joe is cheating for sure," Noah said.

"Really?" Clare looked skeptical. "I thought Joe was some genius player. He even wins consistently at cash games — where there are no cameras to run scams off."

"Look at his historical win rate." Noah pointed at the graph. "Joe came onto the scene four years ago. He did well right away: in his first year he cashed in one out of four tournaments, netting him an ROI — that's return on investment in trust fund princess language — of close to 300%. But look at his win rate since Halifax. He's been in the money every tournament but one. His

ROI is up over 1000%. He might not need to cheat to be a winning player. But the stats say he almost definitely is."

"Okay," Clare said. "Who else? T-Bone?"

"T-Bone's on my maybe list," Noah said. "His win rate took a dive a few years back, when new players came on the scene. It stayed low until . . ." He pulled up T-Bone's stats and looked at them. "Yeah, okay, until Halifax."

"What's his ROI now?" Clare slid down the bed so she was lying on her back. It was just past three a.m., but Noah was nowhere near ready to sleep.

"It's up there. Maybe 500%."

"T-Bone knew what I had." A realization seemed to be hitting Clare. "That hand in Niagara Falls when I doubled through him. I think he wanted to push me off the hand — and for all I know, I probably should have folded — but he knew before the cards were flipped over that I had him beaten."

"You sure?" Noah said.

"No. I'm sure I need to sleep, though. My mind is shutting down hard."

"We don't have time to sleep. We have to solve this case." Noah was wired. Since Clare had left his room that afternoon, he'd drunk about ten gallons of coffee while staring at his computer and trying not to think about what Clare was saying to her handler.

"Okay." Clare pulled off her jeans and tossed them onto the floor. Noah must have been staring at her legs in an obvious way, because she said, "I'm not taking my clothes off to turn you on. I'm getting under the covers. Keep working if you want. I'm going to sleep."

"If you weren't planning on getting any work done tonight, why did you invite me over?"

"I didn't know I was going to crash so hard. Joe has a gorgeous cock; too bad it's circumcised." Clare yawned widely and stretched her arms behind her.

Noah walked to the window and looked down at the boats in

False Creek. "What's wrong with circumcised? I thought women preferred that."

"Maybe women who don't like cock." Clare slid out of bed and moved, bare-legged, to the coffee maker. "It might have been the beer that knocked me out. I'll try making coffee. So do you think Joe's the cheating ring's instigator, or just some guy who's been profiting?"

Noah wasn't sure. "My guess is some guy who's been profiting."

"Doesn't Joe fit the psychopath stereotype perfectly?"

"Because he's charming?" Noah snorted. "There's a little more than that to profiling a serial killer."

"Not only because he's charming," Clare said. "I felt more guilty than he did for cheating on Elizabeth. And P.S.: just because you're with the big-time American FBI doesn't mean you're smarter at profiling than your Canadian counterpart."

"Right," Noah said. "We don't even get assigned a horse."

"A horse?"

"You're a Mountie, aren't you?"

"I'm on loan."

"Oh, so you only get a pony?"

"Are you stupid?" Clare turned and stared at him. "We don't ride horses, we're not from the backwater, and the average Canadian IQ is twelve points higher than the American one."

"You're making that up."

"I'm sure it's true."

Noah laughed. "Just because you wish it was true doesn't mean you get to say it like a statistic."

"Oh." Clare poured water into the coffee maker. "Does the FBI get to tell me how to speak now?"

"Clare!" He wanted to pull off his own jeans, toss her back into bed, and see where things went from there. But he fought the urge — he had to respect her monogamous mindset — he actually, grudgingly, respected her for it.

"What?" she said.

"Nothing. Sorry I thought you got a horse with your job."

"You didn't really think that."

"I really did."

"Do you also think I grew up in an igloo?"

"No. You're from Toronto. They have buildings there — running water and such."

"I'm from Orillia. It's Tiffany who's from Toronto."

"Where's Orillia?"

"About an hour and a half north of Toronto." Clare put the coffee bag into the machine, but she didn't press On. She sat back down on the bed, instead.

"An hour and a half by horse, or by dogsled?"

"Go fuck yourself."

"I guess I'll have to." Noah closed his computer. He could see Clare was tired. He zipped his hoodie back up and steeled himself for the cold night ahead. He didn't plan on sleeping.

FRIDAY / MARCH 25

SEVENTY-SIX
ELIZABETH

Elizabeth had aces. Which would be great if she could concentrate on poker, but her mind was somewhere else — somewhere back in her old bedroom at her parents' house, where she'd been coerced into spending the night. Her mother always wanted more. Give her a smile, she wanted a hug. Give her dinner, she wanted a goddamn sleepover. And she made Elizabeth feel like a cold, selfish bitch if she didn't oblige. Elizabeth had vaguely heard of families who enjoyed spending time together, but she was pretty sure they were all on Prozac.

She looked at her opponents. A raise and a call from players she didn't know. What was so difficult? She had aces. It was a clear re-raise, but she couldn't summon the minimal brain power required to calculate how many chips to put in.

"Call," Elizabeth said. Stupid move, but who cared? She was trying to ignore the imagined rumbling from her stomach, the tiny voice inside asking if she really knew she wanted to get rid of it. Fucking thing was only cells. Elizabeth fought the urge to punch it.

The sound of static came over the loudspeaker. It was followed by a voice: "Dealers and players, at the end of this hand, the Canadian Classic Vancouver will be on break for the rest of the day to mourn this morning's death of Fiona Gallagher. Play will resume tomorrow at one p.m."

Shock traveled fast through Elizabeth as she pictured Fiona lying dead on a hotel room floor. Bizarrely — though she and Fiona had squabbled more than they'd gotten along — Fiona's was the first death since Josie's that made Elizabeth feel a massive sense of loss. And fear — Fiona and Josie were also in their late twenties, also in the public spotlight, also in the same crowd, also . . . well, Elizabeth hoped that was all they'd had in common, but she suspected both had also slept with Joe.

The loudspeaker made it that much more surreal. She understood that players had to be looped in, but a loudspeaker? That's how you announced sports scores and school assemblies, not the murder of someone you've been working with for years.

It seemed insane to even play the hand out. Elizabeth saw Joe two tables away. He frowned and put his magic wand down (today's costume was the wand and a Merlin cap) before tapping the table to check.

She scanned the stands for George, who saw her looking and waved. It was a subdued wave — one hand opening and closing, then falling back into his lap — but of course George would be gutted. He stood up and slumped off the stands toward the exit. He looked like he had no idea where he was going.

The flop came and Elizabeth said, "All in." She was out of turn, but who cared? The other players folded and she took the tiny pot.

She stood up and walked toward Joe.

"I'm going home," Elizabeth told him. "I'm going to stay with my parents. This is crazy." Because as awful as it was at home, with her mother fretting over her lifestyle and constantly trying to feed her Hong Kong delicacies she loathed, the alternative was to stay in this emotionally vacuous scene and hold her throat out for the killer if he decided she was next.

"You sure?" Joe gripped her shoulder in a light massaging

motion. "Why don't you come for a boat ride? We can stay out as long as we like. Drop anchor, chat, whatever."

"Yeah?" Elizabeth liked the warmth of his touch. The massage felt nice, too. "No poker game?"

Joe shook his head. "You were right. I should have canceled the game when Loni died, too."

Elizabeth didn't want to go back to her parents' house. And alone with Joe on the boat — away from the casino — she'd be just as safe, if not safer. "I'd love to hang out, just you and me."

SEVENTY-SEVEN
NOAH

Noah closed his eyes and held them shut so hard his jaw hurt. He opened them and said to Clare, "I fucking got her killed."

"How can you say that?" Clare took Noah's hand. They were at Clare's hotel, sitting on her bed, getting the letters ready that they planned to deliver that day. They'd printed them on Noah's sleek travel printer, and they'd divided the notes between them for delivery.

Noah felt like his head could explode. He wished it would. "I shouldn't have taken all the letters from Fiona's suitcase. I could have taken one, from the middle of the pack, one she wouldn't have missed. I could have copied the font and format from that — I didn't need them all."

"They were evidence," Clare said. "You couldn't leave them behind."

Noah looked at Clare, trying to figure her out. Sometimes she seemed beyond brilliant, and other times it was like she'd pressed Off on her brain. "The FBI didn't send me here to gather evidence."

Clare's eyes narrowed. "I don't get it."

"No. Clearly." Noah pulled his hand from hers, and wished he hadn't.

Clare rolled over and pulled two smokes from her pack on the bedside table. "I'm going outside. Are you coming?"

Noah nodded. They rode the elevator down in silence and took the back door to the alley instead of the street. From the poker world's perspective, they were supposed to be not talking to each other.

When they were outside, Clare said, "So where were we? Right. You were calling me a moron for not knowing the detailed specs of your assignment."

Noah frowned. He didn't like this alley. The walls were too close and large garbage bins made the exit route awkward. He stepped a few feet away from Clare while they lit their cigarettes separately.

"I don't think you're a moron," he said. "I think — well, don't you feel like you're a bit over your head in this job?"

"No."

"Fuck. I do."

"Thanks a lot." Clare walked a few paces further away. She turned her back on him and faced the narrow entrance to the street.

Noah squeezed around to her other side to face her. He tried to ignore the claustrophobic feeling. "I feel like *I'm* over my head. And then I look at you, and you're so much younger. And newer. Look, what I'm saying is, okay, so my dumb actions made Fiona bolt — which is probably what got her killed."

Clare didn't say anything. But she didn't turn away again.

"I don't like that she's dead, but Fiona knew what she was playing with — or she should have. But you look like you're barely out of high school. How can I justify including you in some harebrained disinformation scheme that may or may not work? I could get killed, fine — I'm old enough; I'm trained for this. But you? I couldn't live with myself if our antics got you killed."

"First," she said, "these aren't antics; they're a strategy to do our job. Second, I do not need another fucking watchdog. Third, I am so trained — a year in the police academy and a year on the job have taught me a hell of a lot. Fourth, you're only five years older than me. Fifth, I've chosen this life. And I love it. Sixth, this so-called harebrained disinformation scheme was my idea. I'm the one including you. Not vice versa."

Noah studied her face and decided she was telling the truth: she might be scared, but Clare was exactly where she wanted to be.

"Aren't you going to say something?" Clare asked.

"I was waiting for number seven," Noah said. "That was a pretty good streak you had going."

"Seventh, fuck off," Clare said, but with a smile. "So what are you here for, if it's not to gather evidence or arrest anyone?"

"To learn how the scam is operating."

"Why?"

"I told you already. So it can't be run the same way in the States."

Clare's eyes were on fire. "You're not even planning to expose the cheating ring once you figure it out? Just use Canada as your exploration ground. Like Area Fifty-one — any human casualties are incidental to the higher cause?"

Noah kicked at a pop can on the concrete ground. He used more force than he realized, and the can went clanking loudly to almost the end of the alley. "I'll tell my boss what I learn. That's my job. But no, I don't think we'll officially break it to Canadian authorities."

"That's disgusting."

"Come on, Clare. Are you forgetting that you're Canadian authorities? The message will reach the right ears. I want to find the killer as much as you do. It might not be my assignment, but I want to see this resolved."

"Those are words. You'll get pulled as soon as the scam is solved. I'm surprised you haven't been pulled already."

"My boss wants me to stay in until the end of this leg — I think for appearances, in case they want me for more poker stuff in the States. It's the same player pool."

Clare tossed her smoked-out cigarette to the ground, and stepped on it. "I have a meeting with my handler. I'll text you when I'm done and we can meet back here in a few hours."

SEVENTY-EIGHT
GEORGE

The sky outside was gray. George had drunk too many coffees to count, and his head felt like it was closing in on itself. He'd taken a walk by the river; he'd poked at his lunch alone in the bar. Now he sat in the glow of his computer because he had no idea what to do. This project wasn't any more fictitious than *The Da Vinci Code* was literature. But maybe it would sell half as well.

He'd just deleted a page and a half of backstory detailing Willard Oppal's career as a cop — because really, who cared? Backstory was for creative writing grads. He looked at his keyboard. It was time to bring this story forward, to what was happening now.

He fished his iPod from his carry-on bag and set Michael Buble's "Hollywood" on repeat. The song could have been written for Fiona.

Mount Baker Highway, Washington State

March 2011

Fiona Gallagher. Take a look around you. No, I
don't mean at all the people staring back at you.
The world is not your fucking mirror. I mean take
a look outside yourself and get a fucking clue.

You're alone in your motel room. You should know
by now that this is about the least safe place to
be. You're on the run -- but, well, you're pretty
fucking dumb 'cause you've admitted it. You're
drinking wine -- cheap wine from a gas station,
which wouldn't meet your snob test in a cocktail
setting, but it fits this scene perfectly, and
you're into the romance of the run. The TV's on but
you're not paying attention.

You're pretty sure you're safe. Mostly because
you've suddenly turned into an idiot. There's a
knock on the door. Should you answer?

George rolled his eyes. He should have been writing bad
suspense novels, where the hero or heroine always walked into
danger that was obvious to even the most obtuse reader. But
who was he to knock genre writers? He was only a poker writer
aspiring to genre.

Your shoes are off and you silently creep toward
the peephole. You're relieved when you see who it
is. No way this guy's the Choker.

But just in case he is, you step away from the
door.

You sit in the armchair. The fabric is torn in
a couple of places, but it fits the rustic atmosphere. As you're contemplating what to do -- open

the door, phone the police, or do nothing -- your
cell phone rings. It's the person at the door.

You click to answer.

"Fiona? I can hear you're inside. If you don't want
to let me in, no problem."

You say nothing.

"I'm here for you. No one should have to run alone.
I'll sit in my car. Take your time. I know why
you're scared."

You click Off on your phone. You sit in your chair
for some time before you open the door and bring
your killer into your room.

SEVENTY-NINE
CLARE

"We're being shut out." Amanda fingered through a rack of dresses at Holt Renfrew. "The FBI isn't letting us anywhere near that Washington motel room."

"That's not fair." Clare pulled a T-shirt from a different rack and pretended not to be shocked by the price. "Fiona's death is part of our investigation. Why wouldn't they pool information?"

"Maybe they don't trust our professionalism."

Clare glowered. "Is that a dig? I thought we'd moved past that stupid phone call I made to Roberta."

"Nope; wasn't personal. Cute shirt. Why'd you put it back?"

"Because it's $400." Then Clare ventured, "I have an in with the FBI."

Amanda narrowed her eyes toward Clare. "You *what*?"

Clare took a deep breath. She was probably saying goodbye to her cover role. Still, to *not* say it was worse. "It's Nate. I should have said something earlier. But things have been so intense — with Elizabeth and Joe yesterday, and Fiona's death this morning."

"Nate's FBI?"

Clare nodded. "He told me yesterday afternoon."

"He *told* you?" Amanda shook her head. Her hand fell from the rack of dresses she'd been flicking through. "Why would you believe him?"

Clare tried to cop a casual smile. "It was a comedy of errors. He let it slip that he knew my real name, and I guess he saw that he'd spooked me, so he told me who he really is: an FBI agent named Noah Walker."

"Clare, you have the capacity to astound me constantly."

"Thanks."

"It's not a compliment."

"Oh. Right."

"*Maybe* Nate's story is true. But maybe not. What if he's mob? What if you're made?"

Clare turned away and looked at a wall full of folded jeans. "I thought this was a good thing."

"I know." Amanda moved beside Clare and pulled some Sevens from the shelf. "That's kind of the whole problem."

"Is there any way we can find out?" Clare asked. "If Noah *is* FBI, things are fine, right?"

"Fine? No, I'd say not. Your cover might be compromised and you've been handling yourself like an eight-year-old playing spy games in her grandparents' farmhouse."

Clare shook her head as Amanda held the jeans in front of her. "Too generic. If you're going to spend $250 on jeans, they should look like they cost it."

Amanda gave her a small smile as if she was pleased Clare was learning. She folded the Sevens and replaced them on the shelf.

"So you don't want me collaborating with Noah, even if it gives me access to FBI information?"

Amanda curved her mouth into a frown.

"I have a point, right?" Clare said. "I may have stumbled, however stupidly, into something very useful."

"We'll talk about your future once we've confirmed your new friend's identity."

"What about in the meantime?"

Amanda began walking toward the exit. "My first job is to protect you. My official advice has to be for you to return to Toronto and stay with friends where you're unlikely to be found."

"But . . ."

"But that would end this case for you," Amanda confirmed. "They'd debrief you and send someone in to take your place."

"Even if Noah's legit? I'm sure people leave all the time for family emergencies."

"Not when they still have chips in the game," Amanda said. Apparently she suddenly knew something about poker.

"I think I could pull it off." Clare wasn't trying to seem arrogant, but she felt so close to solving this case. To go home now would be awful.

"I'm telling you it's not an option. The RCMP would sub in a new undercover and hand someone their ass in Washington."

"Especially given my screw-ups, you mean."

Amanda nodded.

"Okay, so as my handler you advise me to bail on the case. Since you don't seem to be making that an absolute call, what's your other idea?"

"You could lay low, show up for the game — make an excuse to get out of your coaching session with Mickey and your date with Nate; *definitely* don't spend time with Nate — and stay the night at my apartment. It'll take us a day or two at most to find out who this guy is — it's ridiculous that it even takes that long, but you get my drift about the FBI and their cooperative nature."

Clare smiled slightly.

"Would you like some time to think about this?"

Clare shook her head. "I'll take Option Two."

"Of course you will." Amanda pushed open the door and they walked into the sunny street.

EIGHTY
ELIZABETH

Elizabeth threw her purse onto the bed. Joe was making drinks upstairs on deck; she could hear him clinking glasses and slamming cupboard doors.

She peeled off the blouse she'd been wearing for the tournament. She found a clean shirt — black and low-cut for an evening alone with Joe. When she glanced back at her bed, she saw an envelope half-in and half-out of her purse. She didn't remember putting it there. It was sealed, but the outside was blank. She opened it:

Are you my Dealer?

Elizabeth smiled. Joe must have slipped it into her purse in the casino. Some kind of game he wanted to play; an evening of mystery sex with Elizabeth in control. Mild nausea aside, she could go for that.

She jogged up the short staircase. "So you want me to deal for us tonight?"

Joe looked at her oddly. "What are you talking about? We canceled the card game. Here. I made you a Long Island."

"I don't want booze." She waved the page. "I found your note. Sounds fun."

"What note?" Joe took the sheet from Elizabeth's hand and peered at it closely. "Where did you find this?"

"In my purse. Where you left it."

"Liz — I —" Joe took a large gulp of his own drink before setting down his glass. "I didn't leave you that note."

"What are you talking about?" Elizabeth's laughed, wondering if playing innocent was part of Joe's game. "You're saying someone else stuck this note into my purse and I never noticed? I guess I should go find someone else who wants mystery sex with me. Who do you think that could be?"

"I don't know. Maybe your new best friend George. You just found the note now?"

"Yup." Elizabeth was pretty sure Joe was messing with her. "So if you didn't leave it, who did?"

"I have no idea." Joe set his drink down and embraced her in a warm, flirtatious hug. "But let's forget about it and get the hell out of here."

"I'm pregnant." The words were out before Elizabeth even knew she planned to say them.

"You are?" Joe pulled away so he could look at her, but he took both of her hands in his. A smile crinkled the corners of his eyes. "Wait — are you messing with me because you think I gave you that note?"

Elizabeth shook her head. She sank into a deck chair.

Joe didn't let go of her hands. "How long have you known?"

"A few days. Don't worry, I'm not keeping it."

"I don't understand. Is it — shit, please tell me it's mine."

"It's yours." She squeezed his left hand. "But Joe, we both know you don't want it."

"I'll admit I never thought I wanted kids. But hearing you say this . . ." Joe stared at Elizabeth, uncharacteristically grasping for words. "It's like . . . something's alive in me."

"Something's definitely alive in me. Let's get out on the water and drop anchor somewhere less industrial. I'll be able to think more clearly if we're looking at something other than a casino."

"It might rain." Joe turned the key in the ignition.

"We have the tarp. And there's the entire cabin."

"Yeah, true. Tell me more about this baby."

"It's not a baby, it's a fetus." Elizabeth stared out the windshield as Joe left the dock and eased the boat into the river.

"Let's get married," Joe said. "We'll bring the baby town to town. We'll be great together."

"Sure," Elizabeth said. "Until something distracts you."

Joe shook his head. "No more distractions." He looked over at her. His grin was from ear to ear. And it was dorky — not his famous grin; his real one. "We're having a baby. Shit, I have to put this on Twitter."

"No! It's too early." Elizabeth took Joe's phone from his hand and stuck it in her back pocket. "It's only six weeks. Something could still go wrong."

"Nothing's going wrong. Give me my phone back. If not Twitter, then at least Facebook. Not my fan page; just my profile only friends can see."

"We're not telling friends." Elizabeth didn't mention that George already knew. "I don't even know if I'm keeping it."

"Please stop saying that." Joe's expression grew dark. "I've never wanted anything this much."

Right, Elizabeth thought. Like a kid in a toy store who sees something bright and shiny. Sure, he wanted it on impact. But when he got the toy home, he would have already forgotten what had been so exciting about it.

EIGHTY-ONE
CLARE

"This is fun, right?" Amanda said from the open kitchen of her condo. "I haven't had a sleepover since high school."

Clare rolled her eyes. Maybe she hadn't been direct enough about not wanting to be there. "I'd rather be with Noah."

"Not with Kevin?"

Clare shot a quick glance at Amanda, who was mixing some weird fruity wine drink.

"You might not believe me, but I like this assignment. I'd rather be working than lounging over vacation cocktails."

"Have some sangria." Amanda pushed a glass across the counter to where Clare was sitting on an über-modern stool that looked like it belonged in a lobby bar in Berlin. "Nothing's going to be decided tonight."

"That's the problem." Clare sniffed the drink. She didn't love wine, but this smelled good, more like juice. "Noah's continuing to work without me. Our plan involves both of us. I'm supposed to have his back."

"He may not be who he says he is."

"I trust him."

"What if you're wrong?"

Clare sipped the drink. It was okay; good, even. "If I'm wrong, you're right: I *should* pack it in and go home. Because it will mean that my instincts are shot." Clare's Tiffany phone beeped. "This is him."

"A text?" Amanda pulled some vegetables from the fridge and started chopping.

Clare nodded. "He's at my hotel. He wants to know where I am. What do I say?"

"Say you're busy with your handler."

Clare texted back and asked Amanda, "When will we know?"

"Hopefully by morning. Not before then; the east coast has shut down for the day and no one out here will confirm anything without consent from head office."

"Law enforcement runs on office hours?"

"No one considers this an emergency," Amanda said.

"I hope the FBI's lack of urgency doesn't cost their agent his life." Clare's phone beeped again. "Noah wants to know when I'll be free."

Amanda frowned. "Ignore it."

"He'll call."

"Ignore that too."

Clare got up from her stool and stood by the floor-to-ceiling window. She could see her hotel from here, though Amanda's condo was too high up to distinguish Noah from any other random person standing outside it.

"I think you're wrong," Clare said. "I think this is unfair to him, to keep him waiting without telling him why."

"Unfair is if the FBI sent an operative onto our turf without letting us know."

"It's not Noah's fault his agency sucks." Clare moved slowly back to the bar, and took her seat again on the trendy-looking stool that was way more comfortable than it looked. She texted *I'm sorry* to Noah — hopefully if there was any fallout on his end he'd know she hadn't meant him any harm. "I guess let's have a sangria party."

EIGHTY-TWO
NOAH

Noah looked at his phone dumbly as he walked away from Clare's hotel to grab the SkyTrain back to the casino. Clare was busy with her handler, fine. But why wouldn't she say when she thought she'd be free?

His phone rang in his hand, startling him. Bert.

"What is it?" Noah said.

"No wonder you don't have an office job. Your telephone manners don't exist."

"Good evening, Mr. Bertoli. This is Noah Walker. How may I help you?"

"Nah, stick with what you know. That second way sounds forced. I got a call about you."

"From who?"

"Head office. RCMP wants to know if we have an operative in the Canadian Classic."

"Shit. What are we telling them?"

"We're telling them the office is closed. They asked for you by name."

"Nate or Noah?"

"Both."

Noah said nothing.

"I guess you have no idea how they might have figured out your identity."

Noah kicked at a candy bar wrapper that someone had left on the sidewalk. Its flimsiness annoyed him as the wrapper lifted slightly from the ground and settled an inch from its starting point. "What are you going to do? Deny, deny, deny, like fucking usual?"

"Yup. We're planning to leak that you're with the mob. You've been cheating at cards; that's considered a crime here. You'll probably have to do some jail time."

"That's so unfair."

"It's what we *should* do." Bert grunted. "But the powers above might level with the pleasant Canadians. It'll cost us, though. We might have to let them in on the Gallagher motel room crime scene as a peace offering."

"That murder is part of their investigation. You should let them in anyway."

"Going native? I think I can guess how they got your name."

Noah fumbled for a cigarette and managed to get one in his mouth and light it with one hand.

"You want to confirm or deny?" Bert said. "Not like it's going to make it any worse on you. You'll be lucky if you get another plum assignment after this one. If you're not, you know, arrested and thrown in a Canadian prison for your mob ties."

"Fine. I told Clare. But she was supposed to keep quiet. We even have a plan to work together."

"I guess the broad was playing you. What did I tell you about letting your heart get involved?"

Noah pressed his phone's Off button as violently as he could. The horrible part was that whatever happened to him wouldn't be unfair: this mess was down to Noah's own stupidity.

Fucking Clare, and her fucking boyfriend at home.

EIGHTY-THREE
GEORGE

George watched the sun as it slipped down toward the horizon. He zipped up his fleece; the night was turning cold.

An animal moved through the water in front of him. It was swimming too fast and too straight for a seal. His first guess was a beaver, though all he could see was a furry dark head. In less than a minute, the creature was gone.

He'd lied to the police. They asked him if he'd left the hotel the night before. If he'd rented a car and crossed the border. Did they know he was lying when he'd said no to all three? Not that a Zipcar really counted as a rental. But he'd given his own ID at the border. Stupid, stupid, stupid. Now it was only a matter of time.

George adjusted his seating position on the large rock. The mountains were beautiful from Richmond — not big and overpowering, like they could appear from the city, but muted, like the backdrop of a movie set. George wouldn't want to live here; he needed a place more bustling with culture and energy. But for a stop along the way, this Vancouver suburb with its casino and fishing village ranked among his favorites.

Five people were dead. But it hadn't mattered to George until Fiona.

Of course he and Fiona hadn't been getting back together. George wasn't blind to the fact that she'd been using him as a security blanket when she'd felt herself losing control. He should have been angry about it, but no such luck. He'd never felt himself pulled to a woman like that before, and he hoped like fuck he never would again. He'd rather die single, or in some pleasant, banal marriage where at least there could be no heartbreak.

Even jail would be better.

George got up off his rock and walked back toward the bus stop. On the gravel path, two young girls, maybe eight years old, were trying to control their two small dogs. One girl spoke seriously to her dog and pulled severely on the leash before cracking up with laughter. The other joined spontaneously in the laughter, and soon they were in hysterics.

George would ordinarily have found the scene endearing. Tonight, he pictured Fiona at that age. And Josie Carter. So these girls with their dogs — full of life at the moment — should turn nine, and then twelve, only to die before they were thirty? Why bother?

The girls giggled and continued on the path away from George.

SATURDAY / MARCH 26

EIGHTY-FOUR
CLARE

Clare loved morning. She loved the smell of coffee before she'd had her first cup, and she loved the way the first sip tasted as caffeine dripped pleasingly into her veins. She especially loved morning when she was outside, the chilly air brushing her skin and making her feel alive.

She gazed over the water at the North Shore mountains and the Howe Sound beyond. It reminded her of a grade-school panorama — layers of mountain and water from big and up close to tiny and far away. Several fishing boats were out already, dropping their traps or lines for whatever they hoped to catch.

"It's the mountains." Noah's voice startled her from behind. "The water's nice, but mountains give you energy. They make you feel like you can do anything."

"I'm not supposed to see you."

"I worked that out." Noah glanced down at his Rollerblades. "Paid a kid five hundred bucks for these, and they're not even my size."

"Cabs are cheaper."

"Thanks. Mine dropped me on the other side of the park. When I realized it was the wrong entrance, the driver didn't have time to take me to the right one because he had a pick-up at the Westin Bayshore."

"Asshole. I hope you didn't tip."

Noah laughed. "It's not the driver's fault I gave him crap directions. Anyway, what's so clandestine that you only have until seven a.m. exactly?"

Clare glanced around in case the RCMP guys had followed. She was pretty sure she and Noah were alone, but since she'd never been in the spy business, she recognized that she might not know what to look for. "My handler told me I have to stop working with you."

"I figured you weren't washing your hair when you bailed on last night. Why did you tell her about me?"

"You already knew?" Clare was surprised.

"Yeah, and I'm in a load of shit for it."

"Sorry."

Noah pulled his cigarette pack from the front pocket of his fleece. Although she had her own smokes with her, Clare accepted a Marlboro. She wanted the raw, nasty edge of the American cigarette.

Noah sat on the bench beside Clare, took the coffee from her hand, and took a long sip before setting it on the seat between them.

Clare liked that Noah liked his coffee black, that they could share a cup and both enjoy it. Kevin drank his with cream and sugar, which Clare had never understood.

"See, we're meant to be together." Noah leaned back, stretched his non-smoking arm so it rested behind Clare, his hand lightly touching her shoulder.

Clare wondered if it was cheating on Kevin to let Noah leave his hand there. It sure felt like it. "If this was destiny we would have met when I was single."

"You can be single anytime you want to be. Ditch your boyfriend and move to New York."

Clare blew a couple of smoke rings. "I suppose you moving to Toronto isn't in the cards."

Noah smirked. "You suppose right."

"Is that like the Antarctic Pole to you?"

"More like Siberia. But that's not it. What if I could get you a job working with me?"

"Because the FBI loves recruiting inexperienced Canadian girls."

"They like recruiting assets. I told my boss about our plan — the notes, and the disinformation havoc we want to create. He's not being particularly nice to me right now — something about some Canadian operative spilling that she knows my real identity — but he likes the plan. I told him it was yours."

Clare wished Noah would move his arm, because it continued to send a warm electric current through her body. "That's why I called you here. I want to continue our plan with the notes whether Amanda okays it or not. I might not be able to make all the drops I was planning to, but I'll pull as much weight as I can."

"Don't worry," Noah said. "I'll run the notes around until you're allowed to breathe on your own. You just dictate what you think the notes should say. I'm used to being a woman's lackey."

"And you should move your arm; it's annoying me there."

Noah put his cigarette to his lips, inhaled, and blew the smoke out slowly. He didn't move his arm. "I got one of those notes this morning."

"You —" Shit. Of course. Because the real Dealer was still out there. "What did it say?"

Noah pulled a crumpled page from his pocket.

Stop stirring shit around.

Clare stared at the note. It didn't make sense. If Noah had been made, why would he get warned instead of killed?

Was he fucking with her? Noah could have written the note

as easily as received it. Amanda was right. She had to get the hell away from this guy until they knew who he was.

Clare took Noah's arm from around her shoulder, intending to get up and walk away, but instead she kept his hand and held it. Because she wanted to? She told herself that no, she kept his hand because she didn't want to tip him off to her suspicion. There were joggers out, and some other early risers. But Noah on Rollerblades would be able to chase Clare down easily if she tried to run. Unless she headed for the bushes . . . but that was verging on ridiculous. Better just to stay here and leave slowly.

"So tell me about your real father," Noah said.

"What do you mean?"

"You've been idolizing this fake one — Tiffany's father. What's your real dad like?"

"He's fine. He's a mechanic."

"Are you close?"

"We used to be." Clare didn't want to talk about her depressing real family. "What about yours?"

Noah snorted. "He tried to create me in his image. He failed."

Clare's phone beeped. She turned the screen away so Noah couldn't read it.

Amanda: Where r u? Thought u went 4 smokes but u'r gone 2 long.

Clare: Clearing my head. Walking on seawall. Surprised goons didn't follow me.

Amanda: Probably did. Come back. Have new info.

Clare: What new info?

Amanda: Not in a text.

Clare stood up. "Thanks for the revelation. Sorry your dad's a jerk. I have to go."

"Clare, whatever they tell you —"

"I have to go."

"They might lie. The FBI might tell the RCMP that I'm not who I say I am."

Clare walked away as quickly as she could without breaking into a run.

EIGHTY-FIVE
ELIZABETH

"You know what having a kid would mean?" Elizabeth poured cream into Joe's coffee and stirred it. Joe was driving *Last Tango* home to the casino. They'd spent the night anchored up Indian Arm, a secluded saltwater fjord surrounded by dense forest and sheer granite cliffs, and Joe's only message on Twitter had been to tell the world he was "chilling with Liz & offline until morning." Elizabeth loved that about Vancouver — how close you could be to the city, and how far away you could feel. If her family ever left, she would move home in a heartbeat.

"Sure I know," Joe said. "This baby will mean a whole new world of endorsement opportunities. Gerber ads, Huggies commercials . . . hell, if the kid's cute, he can be on TV with me."

"Oh my god." Elizabeth set the coffee on the dash in front of Joe. Some splashed from the cup as they went through a wave.

"Kidding." Joe put his hand on the coffee as he braced for the next small wave. "But seriously, this kid's going to be awesome. Cute, funny, smart — and if he takes after you, he'll also be responsible."

"What I meant was, do you know what having a baby is going

to mean in our lives? We'll have to work less — maybe enter less tournaments."

"Nah," Joe said. "That's the trouble with parents today. Their world is all diapers and child-protecting their houses. I think that's why kids are growing up entitled. Their parents' world revolves around them, so they think the real world should, too." Joe waved at a seal. "Those things are adorable. If we ever live by the water, we should have a pet seal."

"Sure. We'll have a seal. It can babysit our kid while we're off playing poker."

Joe laughed. "We could hire someone to come with us on the road."

Of course. A nanny. A.k.a. Joe's portable concubine. Elizabeth shook her head. "My parents offered to take care of the baby when we're traveling."

"Yeah? You want to stop in Richmond before and after every tournament?"

"Good point. How about a male nanny?"

"The kid's going to have enough male influences from the poker community. I think a woman is the way to go."

Joe turned the boat into the Burrard Inlet, bringing the city and its industry back into view.

"An old woman, then," Elizabeth said. "A grandmotherly type."

Joe grinned. "Fine. So will you marry me and have this kid?"

Elizabeth stared at the water. The rising sun behind them, the North Shore mountains to their right, Stanley Park becoming larger ahead of them . . . even the giant pile of sulfur that was normally a yellow eyesore in the inlet managed to look beautiful in the early morning sun. "Yeah," she said.

Joe turned sharply to look at her. "Did you just say yes?"

Elizabeth felt her throat constrict. She didn't think she could speak, so she nodded.

Joe let out a shout and gunned the engine hard. When he'd brought the speed back down, he said, "I thought you'd leave me if I ever asked you to marry me."

"You did?" Elizabeth said. "Why?"

"Women like you don't want forever with guys like me."

Elizabeth studied Joe. His eyes were on the water and his sunglasses hid their expression. "Sometimes," she said, "you have no idea what you want until it's there."

EIGHTY-SIX
CLARE

Amanda poured Clare a new cup of coffee. "You're good."

"You mean . . ." Clare tried not to get her hopes up.

"Noah Walker checks out."

"He's FBI?"

"Yes. We're obviously not pleased that they launched their own investigation in our territory without first attempting to gain our cooperation . . ."

"Will they share their Washington motel info with us?"

Amanda gave her short, sharp laugh. "They don't feel badly about being caught, if that's what you're asking. No, they won't change their position on the motel room murder scene."

"That's so unfair." Clare decided not to correct Amanda's grammar from "badly" to "bad."

"Welcome to dealing with the United States of America. You want really unfair, try dealing with Iran."

Clare smiled.

"At any rate, we've resolved that issue. You're sharing information on the ground level with Noah Walker."

On the ground level. Leave it to Amanda to find a way to be condescending. Clare wished she *had* corrected her grammar.

"I guess I'd better get back to my low-level work, then. Seeing as it's the only thing that's actually accomplishing anything."

"Really, Clare? After everything, you're still the pouting princess?"

Clare lifted her head to face Amanda. "Me? What are you talking about?"

"I fought for you to keep your job after you gave up classified information to Roberta McGraw *and* to Kevin Findlay on an unsecured phone line. Instead of pulling you from the case when you started pooling information with a suspect who claimed to be law enforcement, I went behind the scenes — possibly creating conflict with U.S. law enforcement — to find his true identity, again so you could stay in place. How could you possibly think I don't value your contribution?"

Again, with the word "contribution." Or maybe Clare was being overly sensitive. "Thanks, Amanda."

"For what?" Amanda looked surprised.

"Cloutier would have had me pulled at Roberta." Clare pushed away her nearly untouched coffee. "Your gourmet coffee's actually pretty good, but you understand if I don't stick around and drink the second cup, right?"

"No pancake breakfast to finish off our sleepover?" Amanda looked almost disappointed.

"Have you ever eaten a pancake in your life?"

Amanda grinned, nearly blinding Clare with the whiteness of her teeth. "Only when I've had one sangria too many the night before."

"Another time." Clare picked up her phone to send Noah a text. "I need to get back in this game."

"The game doesn't start until the afternoon." Amanda glanced at her watch. "It's not even eight thirty."

"Yeah," Clare said. "I'm talking about my metagame."

"Is that a poker term?" Amanda frowned.

"It's the game above the game. It's where you create illusions in order to trick people into making mistakes."

EIGHTY-SEVEN
GEORGE

George felt like he'd been drinking the same cup of watery coffee since the beginning of the Canadian Classic Poker Tour.

He could turn on his computer, but why? He'd already written everything he had to say.

His plane for Las Vegas was leaving that night; he'd go back to his crummy apartment and regroup. If he couldn't buy his writer's cabin in New England, maybe he could rent one for a year.

That actually sounded good. George booted up his computer to look at cabin rentals. Anywhere except a city, and nowhere that a poker tour was stopping by. Fiona was dead — he couldn't change that. But he could avenge her murder the only way he knew how: through fiction.

George entered his password — "darkroast" — and opened Safari. As he was contemplating what search term to type, he heard a shuffling sound at his door.

He looked over and saw an envelope at the base of the door. Blank on the outside and sealed. He pried it open.

Stop stirring shit around yourself.

George grabbed his room card and ran down the hallway to the stairwell, where he thought he'd just witnessed the door closing. He shouted, "Who are you?" as loud as he could. But all he heard was a click as a door shut on another floor.

EIGHTY-EIGHT
CLARE

Clare gazed out at the boats of False Creek. They were familiar to her now. She said a silent hello to *Polar Ice*, one of the smaller yachts that she couldn't see making the journey to either pole. The boat must have been named after the vodka.

She checked the time on her phone. Clare wondered if it should worry her that she didn't gag on the hot pink color anymore. She hoped when she got home she didn't start accidentally adding pink clothes to her real wardrobe.

Noah wasn't due for another twenty minutes. She punched in the numbers to call Roberta. She'd make damn sure not to say anything classified.

"How's that Virago?" Clare asked when Roberta picked up.

"The more I fix, the more it breaks," Roberta said. "The electrics are fine, and now the carb's like new. Damn thing just won't start."

"The starter motor?"

"That would be logical. Except I've pulled the thing apart and it's perfect. I think I stared at the insides of that starter for half a day, trying to find a flaw that isn't there."

Clare took a sip from her water bottle. "I hope you're billing by the hour."

"I'm not counting hours I waste due to my own vacant brain. Anyway, Lance was in and out of the shop, so a lot of that time was spent trying to help him find a caterer. He's pulling out his hair with wedding plans."

"Why is he looking for a caterer in Toronto? Isn't the reception in the legion hall back home?"

"Shauna's being fussy. One of her friends just got married and hired a fancy caterer from Lake Joe. Lance can't afford anything that pricey, but Shauna wants him to scour Toronto for something she can pass off as upscale."

Clare rolled her eyes at the information about Roberta's soon-to-be daughter-in-law. If she wanted to seem upscale, Shauna should stop wearing spandex to the grocery store. "Everyone wants to fool someone. So why doesn't Lance leave the planning to Slutty Shauna?"

"Because he's a modern man who believes household duties should be shared."

"Since when?" When Clare had dated Lance, he'd been as manly as they'd come. And by manly, she meant someone who belched to indicate he was ready for his woman to bring him a new beer. "Don't tell me Shauna's got him tuning into his softer side."

"I think it's nice," Roberta said. "So are you coming to the wedding? Lance says you still haven't responded to his Save the Date card."

"I'll be undercover in Helsinki."

"They plan that far ahead?"

"I was speaking wishfully."

"Clare!" Roberta was laughing, but she sounded disappointed. "I thought you and Lance were friends now."

"On the surface. But . . . is it weird that part of me still wants us to be together?"

"It's not weird," Roberta said. "You two played together since you were twelve and fourteen."

"Yeah," Clare said. "Maybe that's all it is."

"Anyhow, don't you have too many men?"

"No." Clare kicked a stone off the path she was walking on. "I'm done with the guy here. I'm waiting to go home to Kevin."

"Don't sound so excited."

Clare's gaze wandered back to the boats. "I don't know what's wrong with me."

"You're in your twenties. You're figuring out what you want. Why does something have to be wrong with you?"

"What if I can't fall in love?"

"Of course you can fall in love. You're waiting for the right guy. It isn't Lance. And maybe it isn't Kevin either."

"What if it *is* Kevin? What if I'm afraid of something that isn't letting me go that final distance? What if *that* fear is making me crave this asshole I met on the assignment?"

"Then I repeat what I said before: you're in your twenties."

"Roberta, that's dumb. I can't go through life excusing every character flaw I have by saying it's a function of my age."

"Why not? When I look in the mirror and an Italian Riviera body doesn't stare back at me, I don't whinge and complain — I say hell, Roberta, for forty-three you look damn good."

Clare grinned.

Then she heard Roberta draw in a breath. "Clare, your dad's in the hospital."

"Again?"

"This time it's serious."

"It was serious before," Clare said. "He needs a lung trans-plant."

"They don't think he's going to make it home."

Clare lit a smoke. "Did you hear that from a doctor, or from my mother when she was halfway into her nightly vodka bottle?"

"Both."

"You saw my dad in the hospital?" Clare took a deep drag and held smoke in as if it was a joint.

"He's off the transplant list."

"What? How did that happen?" Clare didn't know how that made her feel.

"They know he smoked in January. He's telling everyone you gave him a cigarette."

"I did," Clare said.

"You what?"

"Don't treat me like I'm Satan. I was smoking. I told him that if he was too, he could smoke in front of me. It's the lying I hate more than anything."

"Clare you can't — when you're dealing with an addict — it's not —"

"Can you not lecture me?" Clare felt her throat constrict. "I get it. I made a dumb mistake. When he dies it's going to be my fault."

"That's not even a little bit true."

"Of course it's true. I'm a murderer." Clare gazed out at *Polar Ice*, bobbing on the water. "Like those people I'm supposed to catch and put in jail. Bitter irony, huh?"

"He's not dead yet. You can still make your peace."

"What peace? I can say, 'Sorry I tempted you with tobacco,' and he can say, 'Oh, that's okay,' and I can say, 'Thanks for blaming me, by the way,' and he can say . . .'" Clare couldn't finish the thought. She felt a tear roll down her cheek.

"When are you coming home?" Roberta asked.

"Depends when the case is solved. A few days, ideally."

"He'll hang on until then."

"How do you even know that?"

"It's how things work."

Clare wiped her tear away. Thankfully no more had followed. "So what's the next step with the Virago?"

"I'm going to stare at it some more. Then attack the electric start."

"Totally thought it would turn out to be the main fuse."

"Totally?"

"My cover character talks like a Richmond Hill girl. What about a starter solenoid?"

"Yeah," Roberta said. "This is why I hate motorcycles. They're supposed to be so simple, but they never are."

EIGHTY-NINE
NOAH

Noah watched Clare on the phone as he walked toward her. She looked upset. He slowed his pace; he'd let her be alone. He watched her wipe her cheek, smile slightly, and hang up. He gave her half a minute more and made his approach.

He sat on the bench beside her. "You ready for an exciting day?"

"Yup." She spoke enthusiastically, but it sounded forced.

"We should stick together as much as possible," Noah said. "We can tell everyone we made up; no one will care."

"Okay."

Noah took her hand. "You sure you're cool with this?"

"I'm fine. I'm a professional. Let's do this."

"My handler made a good point," Noah said. "Why don't you suggest to your handler that the Canadian cops search bags and jackets as players arrive at the game? Then we don't have to risk our covers breaking into rooms to find out who else has phones and computers that are set up to receive the cheating signal."

Clare wrinkled a corner of her mouth while appearing to think. "We're pretty sure we know who's cheating — Joe and

T-Bone and maybe George. If we raid people's bags, we might confirm that information. But we also might tip people off that they should be a lot more careful. Searching bags looks like what it is — cop interest."

"True," Noah said. "It just might be the safest way to go."

"To find the cheaters, yeah. But not to find the killer. Or is it back to you don't care? You have your case solved, and if you can get some more free information before you get the hell out of here, so much the better?"

Noah didn't blame Clare for mistrusting him. "I can't arrest someone in Canada, but you can."

"So why are you even here now? You could be kicking back in comfort while the game finishes playing itself out."

"Are you kidding?" Noah was sitting inches from Clare, but it felt like she was a lot farther away. He remembered seeing her upset on the phone, and softened. "I want to catch this killer."

Clare frowned.

Noah continued, "Another question Bert had: have you seen reports about personal effects found in the victims' rooms?"

Clare rolled her eyes. "Like phones that just happened to be set up to receive secret encrypted transmissions? I think the killer would have taken that kind of evidence with him."

"Really?" Noah said. "What if the killer doesn't know about the technology?"

"Oh." Clare's eyes opened wider. "Sorry. My brain is mush today. You mean what if the killer isn't the Dealer?"

Noah nodded. "Mickey's angry. There must be others — maybe Elizabeth — who feel the same way."

"So does that make Joe and T-Bone, and maybe George, potential killers? Or potential victims?"

"Right. That's one question. Another is: if Oliver's running the scam, which we now know he must be, because Fiona was dead and the hole card feed was still coming through, and someone else is murdering people, is there even a connection between the murders and the cheating?"

"How could there not be?" Clare said. "They started at the exact same time."

"I agree — my first guess is they're linked. But we have to keep an open mind."

Clare shook her head. "It's time to close our minds, rule things out. All this open-mindedness and my dead grandma could be the killer from her grave."

Noah laughed.

"If you saw my grandma you wouldn't think that was funny."

"That's not why I'm laughing. I just realized that for all our two agencies' fighting, none of us have looked at the most obvious clue."

"What clue?"

"Whoever killed Fiona had to get across the border. We can get rental car records and border crossing IDs."

"We have all that." Clare looked at him liked he'd missed the short bus that morning. "I mean, you and I don't, but the RCMP is already looking into border crossing records. Anyway, when you cross the border with the intent to kill someone, I'm pretty sure you use a fake name."

"Maybe." Noah shrugged. "But it won't be a fake photo."

Clare narrowed her eyes with interest. "What are you suggesting?"

"Facial recognition software," Noah said. "We'll give them photos of Joe, Elizabeth, T-Bone, Mickey, Oliver, George . . . I'm sure we'll have an answer by tomorrow."

Clare frowned. "So should we kill our plan with the notes?"

Noah shook his head. "Because what if the killer found another way across?"

NINETY
ELIZABETH

"Is someone else on the boat?" Joe said suddenly.

Elizabeth stopped what she was doing and listened. "I don't hear anything."

"Shh." Joe put a finger to his lips. There was a soft thud, like a cupboard being closed. "Did you hear that?"

"I did," Elizabeth said, in a voice just above a whisper. "But we're on a boat. The sound could be anything. Maybe a buoy slapping against the dock."

"Maybe," Joe said.

Elizabeth heard a zipper. "That sounds like the canvas being opened."

"Or zipped back up."

"It might be another boat's canvas." But Elizabeth was scared. "Should we go upstairs?"

"I'll go." He glanced at her bare, still mostly flat stomach. "I don't want you in danger."

"I'm coming with you." Elizabeth pictured Joe going into the galley alone and a gloved killer waiting for him with a piece of rope. "I'll dial 911 and be ready to press Send."

"Thanks, Scout." Joe gave a mock salute.

"You're welcome." Elizabeth slipped on shoes and a shirt. She didn't want to waste time putting jeans on.

"You're coming like that?" Joe looked amused.

"Who cares what an intruder sees?"

"Okay. Let's go." Joe opened the stateroom door softly and looked both ways down the hall before turning toward the stairs. Elizabeth followed as silently as she could.

At the top of the stairs, Joe turned quickly to face the dock side of the boat. He motioned Liz to follow him up, and they both looked around at an apparently empty main level. The galley was intact, the deck was empty, the canvas was closed, and the poker table was as they'd left it.

After a careful search of every stateroom, they determined that there was no one else on board.

"What about the zipper?" Elizabeth said. "You heard it too, right?"

Joe nodded.

"You think someone was looking for something, and they left when they heard us downstairs?"

"Possible."

"What would they have taken?" Elizabeth said. "Do you have your computer and phone?"

"They're in our stateroom. You have yours?"

Her laptop was on the galley table, where she'd left it. She checked her purse and found her phone. "What else could they have wanted?"

"Maybe to leave us this." Joe fingered a piece of paper that had been fixed to the fridge with an Ace magnet.

Elizabeth's stomach felt weak. "You think someone left that here?"

"Wasn't here before, was it?" Joe pulled the note from the fridge. "It looks like the other note you got. The one about mystery sex. Same font, same kind of paper, I'm pretty sure."

"What does it say? Let me see it."

Joe shook his head. "It doesn't make any sense."

He didn't look like he planned to pass Elizabeth the page, so she took it.

```
Tiffany James is your Dealer. Instructions will
follow. Follow the instructions.
```

"I knew it!" Elizabeth stomped her foot in what would probably be a comical gesture under lighter circumstances.

"What did you know?" Joe looked at her oddly.

"Tiffany. She's not a little trust fund princess. I knew she had an angle."

"What do you think her angle is?" Joe asked.

"I don't know. I just knew something wasn't right."

"How?"

"Her father doesn't own any furniture importing company in the English-speaking world. I even checked China, just in case. But no."

Joe took a Coke can from the fridge. "So what does this note mean?"

"I don't know. But I know it's real. I know it means something." Elizabeth's nausea was getting worse. She sat down.

"Are you okay?"

"I'm fine." She was glad she hadn't eaten breakfast. "It's a big chance to take, breaking onto our boat just to leave a one-line note. The Choker wouldn't do that. My guess is someone's trying to warn us that we're in danger."

Joe laughed. "Okay, Liz. I'm glad to hear your take on how the criminal mind works."

Elizabeth took a Sun Chip from the bag on the counter, and immediately recognized it as a mistake. She chewed it anyway, and swallowed. Hopefully it would stay down. "I'm the one who figured out Tiffany."

"Clearly someone else did, too, if they're warning us. But this

doesn't look like a warning note to me. It looks more like a statement of power. As in, Tiffany's going to give us some orders now.
Or someone pretending they're Tiffany."

Elizabeth wondered if whoever had left the note was outside
listening to them. She decided they probably weren't — it would
be dumb to hang around on the dock once the message had been
delivered.

"Hey," Joe said. "I looked up those bags. You know they're not
biodegradable anymore?"

"What are you talking about?" Elizabeth picked up the Sun
Chip pack and looked at the back. "Yes, they are. That's what this
little symbol means right here."

"That's just the Canadian bags," Joe said. "In the States, the
eco-friendly bags were too loud and crinkly for the average consumer. So Frito Lay went back using to the old kind."

"That sucks." Elizabeth felt herself getting angry. The poison,
which had been gone for almost a day, started to creep back
in. She stood up and threw the nearly full bag in the garbage.
"That's, like, knowing you can do the right thing, and choosing
not to. I'm never eating another fucking Sun Chip again in my
life, Canadian *or* American."

"Wow," Joe said. "I can see you have a strong sense of justice."

NINETY-ONE
CLARE

Clare slunk down the hallway, which was ridiculous because if someone saw her slinking it would make her look even more suspicious. She straightened up and walked like a normal person. She came to George's room, slipped a new note under his door, and hurried for the stairwell.

She practically leapt down the two flights of stairs to Mickey's room. She hoped the killer wasn't Mickey, but you couldn't run an investigation based on who you'd like to see in jail. She slipped his note under his door and rushed toward the stairs once more.

The next room was T-Bone's, one level down. This filled Clare with dread, because despite her bravado, she was scared of the man. Even in his seventies, he looked like he could squish her with his muscles. So when Clare left the stairwell and saw him swaggering away down the hallway, she hurried back inside and held her breath.

She looked at the envelope in her hand and tucked it inside her jeans. She counted to a hundred and figured that T-Bone must be either inside his room or in the elevator on the way to somewhere. She heard a door open somewhere above her in the stairwell.

She pushed into the hallway once more. Thankfully T-Bone was nowhere to be seen. But she didn't know what to do. Her escape route was blocked — she couldn't go back into the stairwell, because someone was in it, and she couldn't afford the time to wait for the elevator. But she didn't want to give up on the plan — what if T-Bone was the killer, and this was the note that solved everything?

She saw T-Bone's room, across from the elevators. She pressed the Down button and waited for the elevator to arrive. When it came — thank god — there was no one in it. Clare slipped the note under the door, ran into the elevator, pressed G, and stood away from T-Bone's peephole's sightline.

When the elevator dropped her in the lobby, Clare was drenched in sweat, but her breathing had returned to normal. Not trusting herself to say anything to anyone, she made a beeline for the cab line and headed to Noah's nearby hotel.

He'd given her a room card. She let herself in and called him.

"I'm three seconds away," he said, before opening his door. He ended the call and eyed Clare up and down. "You look fucking terrible."

"I have makeup with me. How did your end of the note drop go?"

"Good, I think." Noah lit a smoke. "The boat was fucking hard."

"Hard as in difficult?"

"Hard as in stressful. They were having sex in a stateroom. Sorry if you thought what you had with Joe was special."

Clare felt stupid for even beginning to stress about her own close encounter. "Thanks for taking the hard part."

"It's all the hard part. And Oliver's room was a piece of cake. I saw him leaving the lobby before I even went upstairs."

"Is there anyone we've forgotten?" Clare asked.

"The only other two are dead."

NINETY-TWO
GEORGE

George watched the girl who wasn't Fiona setting up her microphone. This was the best the network could do on short notice? She was short, frumpy, and if she had any personality, it was well-hidden inside her cheap navy pantsuit. George normally liked women in glasses, but this girl wore hers with chunky frames and zero intelligence.

Today's game would be short. There were twenty players left and they'd stop when it was down to ten. The final ten would play for the grand prize the following morning. They could have played it all out today, but some organizing genius had opted for the late start. George wondered if the delay was to keep people around so the cops could do their work before the suspects dispersed.

The notes George had received were bothering him. The first one about stirring the shit around, okay. George had known he was playing with fire, stalking the ice machine, writing the "novel." He'd even included a couple of suspicions on his blog, which in retrospect had probably not been wise.

But the second note was plain strange: *Introducing Nate Wilkes as your Dealer.* Did that mean that Nate, or someone else, was bringing the Dealer's identity into the open? Or was Nate being introduced as the new Dealer on the scene? That would add up, with Fiona receiving the apparently contradictory notes. Would someone else — the "old" Dealer — soon be showing up dead? Or were they already dead? Jesus, maybe Fiona had been lying to him — it wouldn't be the first time. Maybe Fiona had been the Dealer all along. Or maybe whoever had broken into Fiona's room had taken the notes so they could replicate them. Was the original Dealer even still alive?

George had all the pieces — he knew he did — but they weren't coming together.

"George Bigelow?"

He heard the voice, but when he spun around, he couldn't find the source.

"Are you George Bigelow?" The young uniformed cop was trying to move into George's line of sight, and eventually the two connected.

"Yes." George felt dizzier than he should have from turning around a couple of times.

"I need to ask you some questions," the officer said, moving slightly to one side as if he expected George to accompany him.

"I . . ." George faltered. "I spoke with someone yesterday."

"This regards new information. Would you come into the interview room?"

George followed the young cop into a conference room the police had commandeered from the casino. Another — larger, older — cop was seated behind a desk. Inspector Smyth. The same man had interviewed George the previous day. A third officer stood against the wall.

George sat in the seat he was offered.

Smyth asked if he could tape the interview.

George said fine.

"Maybe there's something you forgot to tell us yesterday."

George thought for a few seconds. They probably had him, but why should he give it away? "What did I forget?"

Smyth slammed his fist on the desk. "You forgot that you borrowed a fucking Supercar, or, what the fuck is it really called?" He consulted his notes. "Zipcar, drove across the border, murdered your ex-girlfriend, and drove home in time for breakfast."

"That isn't true."

"Which part isn't true? You didn't have breakfast? She wasn't technically your girlfriend?"

"I didn't kill Fiona."

"So what happened? You found her dead and didn't say anything?"

George knew his story was going to sound lame. Whoever said the truth was supposed to set you free was living in a naive wonderland. "I borrowed a Zipcar."

Smyth waited.

"I drove across the border."

No expression.

"I went to a diner in Bellingham."

"Let me guess," the cop said. "You paid cash."

"All I had was coffee."

Smyth shrugged.

"I bought cigarettes."

"Also cash?"

George nodded. It was the first time he'd smoked in ages, and he felt like a failure for caving, but cigarettes were his quickest comfort when life was overwhelming.

"Please answer verbally so the recording includes your response."

"Yes," George said. "I paid cash for the cigarettes."

"So you bought coffee, you bought cigarettes. What next?"

George took a deep breath. "I drove up the Mount Baker highway."

"Why Mount Baker?"

"Fiona was there. She was scared. I wanted to protect her."

"Did she tell you she was there? Did she ask you to join her?"

"No. That's why I didn't knock on her door."

The cop shook his head, like now he'd heard them all.

"I sat in the parking lot. I didn't know what room she was in. I had her cell number, so I could have called to find out. She would have let me in. If she was still alive when I was there." George looked at Inspector Smyth. "Was she still alive then?"

"She was alive when you arrived," the cop said. "That's how murder works. When you left, because you killed her, she was dead."

"I didn't kill Fiona."

"Okay," Smyth said. "So let's humor you and say your story checks out. We'll pretend it's not in either the give-me-a-fucking-break or the does-this-guy-think-my-asshole-is-my-brain category. Did you see anything when you were sitting in the parking lot? Any other human activity?"

"Yes." George suddenly remembered the hitchhiker. This was going to sound even crazier, and for sure the inspector wouldn't believe it, but if the weird guy with the black hair had anything to do with Fiona's murder, maybe someone listening to the tape would use it to find the real killer. He told Smyth what he'd seen.

"Right," Smyth said, in the exact tone George would have predicted. "You just remembered. This white guy with dreadlocks walks onto the motel grounds, dials a number on a cell phone, knocks on a door, enters the room of a person you can't see, leaves five to ten minutes later, and thumbs his way, in the middle of the night, back down the highway. You know the hitchhiking part because . . ."

"I passed him as I left. He had his thumb in the road."

"Did you pick him up?"

"No. Obviously." George wished he hadn't added the "obviously."

The cop nodded. "You understand we're going to arrest you?"

George shrugged. Of course he understood. Nothing really mattered anyway, with Fiona dead.

But he felt fire in his veins when he thought of Fiona's killer going free. He remembered what Mickey had seen in the hallway the morning Loni died.

"Can you get security camera footage from the casino?" George said to the inspector.

"Probably."

"Check the hallway outside T-Bone Jones' room the morning his girlfriend was killed. He claims he was downstairs playing poker all morning, but a friend thinks he saw T-Bone going back to his own room."

Inspector Smyth said nothing.

"I understand," George said. "Arrest me. Fine. But I have more information. About a cheating ring that might be linked to the murders. I'll share it with you. I want the real killer found."

"Okay, buddy." The big cop nodded to two younger officers, who had been in the room but silent during the interview. They came forward now. The one who had led Geoge into the interview room put him in handcuffs while the other read him his rights.

"Do I really need handcuffs?" George said. "I told you I'll go willingly."

Inspector Smyth nodded to the young officer, who seemed to understand this as the signal to uncuff George.

"Okay," Smyth said. "Before we take you in, tell me what you know about this cheating ring."

"Can I negotiate?" George asked. Maybe not the strongest way to lead into the discussion, but he knew he had something valuable.

"What for?"

"The information I give you. I want something in exchange."

Smyth shook his head very slightly. "I don't think so. What do you want?"

"I want to keep my computer in jail. Or the holding cell, or whatever you call the place you're going to keep me. And I want a room to myself."

The inspector leaned forward, rested his chin in his hand, seemed to contemplate the request. "I'll see what I can do."

"Okay," George said. "Based on your success securing those things, I'll see what kind of information I have."

"Are you fucking kidding? You have to share what you know. If you don't, you're impeding an investigation."

George shrugged. Fiona was gone, his freedom was going. "I don't have anything more to lose."

NINETY-THREE
CLARE

Clare knocked on Mickey's door. He'd had an hour to process the note she'd left him.

"I know we don't have lessons scheduled," Clare said when he opened the door.

"You gotta leave this scene, kid. It's getting too dangerous for all of us."

"I know." Clare hoped her look was innocent.

"Look, I know you're not involved. You can't be — you came on the scene too late. But don't tell me you're blind to the fucking dead bodies that keep popping up everywhere."

"I'm not blind," Clare said. "I'm scared."

Mickey's eyes scanned the hallway. "Come in if you want. We got time for some peanuts."

Clare sat at the table while Mickey grabbed two Cokes from the minibar.

"You gotta get on a plane," Mickey said. "Like outta here, tonight."

Clare shook her head. "I still have chips in the game. Are you leaving?"

"I can handle myself one more night. And then fucking right

I'm leaving," Mickey handed her a Coke but continued to pace around the room. "I can't believe I stayed so long, thinking I was immune to his rope. Things are back on with your boyfriend, huh?"

"Nate? He's not my boyfriend. But yeah, we're talking."

"You shouldn't fucking trust him," Mickey said, ticking a finger in Clare's direction.

"Why not?"

"Just take my word for it and sleep alone tonight."

The note Clare had left Mickey had been the same as the one she'd left George: *Introducing Nate Wilkes as your Dealer.* So naturally Mickey would be suspicious.

"You think you can do that? Sleep alone for one night?"

Clare looked up at Mickey. "Don't you think I'm safer sleeping with someone than alone?"

"That theory only works if you're not sleeping with a killer."

"There are hundreds of people milling around this scene," Clare said. "Why Nate?"

"Just take my fucking word for it."

Clare wrinkled her mouth, trying to look puzzled. "It's your word that he's the killer?" She looked up quickly, as if she was finally putting it together. "Are you a cop? Nate said there are probably a lot of cops on the scene, with all the murders that have been happening."

Mickey grinned. "No, kid. I'm not a cop. I'm someone who's concerned for your safety. Here, have some peanuts." He unscrewed the cap like he was a Chinese businessman offering her tea from the top shelf.

Clare thanked him, and it was only as she was chewing that she remembered what her parents had told her when she was five and she'd first walked to school on her own: never take food from strangers.

NINETY-FOUR
NOAH

"I want to talk about Clare," Noah said to Bert on the phone. "I think we should make her a job offer."

"You're joking."

Noah looked out his window at the Fraser River. He missed the Hudson. Hell, he even missed the East River. But the thought of going back to New York without Clare made him feel bizarrely bereft.

"In the middle of one of the biggest potential goat fucks I've ever seen from an operative, you want me to take your hiring advice?"

"She's good," Noah said. "We went with her plan and we're waiting for players' reactions. I think it's going to work."

"George Bigelow has already been arrested."

That didn't work for Noah. He waited a beat before asking, "Why?"

"The usual reason: authorities think he's the killer. He crossed the border the night Fiona Gallagher died."

"Shit," Noah said. "He used his real name and everything?"

"Apparently."

"Hm." Noah's mind was racing. "Don't you think a killer who's been murdering successfully for this long would know enough to not use their real identity at the border?"

"People screw up all the time," Bert said. "Some more than others, but criminals are human. Most times we're lucky enough to be working with a dumbass who fucks up near the beginning of their enterprise. With the smart ones, it's a waiting game. They're going to do something stupid eventually. In this case, the bad move was crossing the border with a real name. Anyway, it's not our case. Your job here is done; just play this game out and come home."

Noah grinned. "You just told me I'd goat-fucked this up. Now you're saying mission accomplished?"

"Your fuck-up is your leaky mouth. Case success aside, that's a problem for me, Walker."

"That's fair," Noah said. "But here's the thing: the killer isn't George Bigelow."

There was a pause on Bert's end of the line. "How can you know that?"

"I don't. Not for sure. But this game has taught me to think in odds, and I'd lay six to one it's not Bigelow."

Bert sighed. But he didn't shut Noah up.

Noah took in a breath and continued. "Someone else may have taken a trip across the border that night. I was in the high stakes room for a bit. Joe was at the poker table all night — well actually, he fucked Clare, then dressed up as Snow White and played cards for the rest of the night. But T-Bone left the same time George did. He seemed particularly interested in Fiona's departure."

Bert stayed quiet.

Noah said, "Clare and I have another idea. Use facial recognition software — we'll send you our primary suspects — to see if someone crossed under a false name." Noah picked a T-shirt up off the floor. He was about to fold it and put it into a drawer when he remembered he'd be leaving the next day. He folded it and put it into his suitcase, instead.

"It's 'we' now, huh?"

"She's new," Noah said. "You could get her cheap, which I know appeals to you."

"You're hot for the girl and you want to negotiate a crap deal for her?"

"I want it to work."

"Why? So she'll move to New York?"

"It isn't like that. She has a boyfriend she's crazy about. There's nothing romantic between us."

"But you want there to be."

"Bert, will you listen to me for five seconds? We've been working together — we're damn close to solving this case. You know how hard it is for me to work with anyone. But her mind — it meshes with mine. I think we'd make an amazing undercover team."

"Undercovers don't work in teams."

"They sometimes do."

"If we made her an offer, it would be as a solo act. If we team you up on an assignment, fine. But she has to be able to stand on her own. How old did that report say she is?"

"Twenty-three."

"She's a fucking child. She's breakable. Buy her a sundae."

Noah groaned. "We're all breakable. We can ease her in slowly." He pulled jeans from the floor and folded them for his suitcase as well.

"What's special about her? Other than the fact you want inside her?"

"She's got it. That's all. She can read people, she can put on the face she needs — she's convincingly playing a spoiled debutante when she'd rather be taking apart cars. She kicks my ass at chess, which is more than I can say for you, that time we were holed up in Omaha with nothing to do."

"I hate games."

"Come on, Bert. You read the report on her, as much as you claim not to remember it. You know she's not your run-of-the-mill Canadian twenty-something."

Bert was quiet.

"Is that a yes?"

"I read the report. I'll talk to some people on this end."

"Fantastic."

"No one's being offered anything until this case is solved. That goes for you and your continued employment, too."

"What, now you care about finding the murderer?" Noah was confused.

Bert sighed. "I've been in touch with your little friend's handler. You're both being pulled at the end of tomorrow, solved or unsolved. We've agreed to let you work together until then."

"Good." Nice to have permission after the fact. "Does that mean you like our plan?"

Bert snorted. "Just find the fucking killer."

"You don't think it's Bigelow either?"

"I don't have an official opinion. But until the cheating scam has been wrapped up, I don't think we can know if we have our man."

"What does Clare's handler say? Is there an official Canadian opinion?"

"The official Canadian opinion is that their man is in jail, naturally. But Clare's handler is also keeping an open mind." Bert said they'd talk later and hung up.

There was a knock on Noah's door. He looked out the peephole and saw a familiar face. He froze.

No way was he letting this person into the room with him. Noah grabbed his phone, wallet, and room card, and in one strong movement brushed breezily past his visitor into the hallway.

"Just heading out," Noah said on his way to the elevator. "Feel free to come along."

NINETY-FIVE
ELIZABETH

Elizabeth watched a gull circling over one spot in the river. It wasn't squawking; it was too intent on its prey. George was in jail. Elizabeth should visit him, probably.

She was walking with her brother. Joe was in the poker room playing a few rounds before the game.

Elizabeth said, "I shouldn't marry him, should I?"

Peter frowned. "What does your gut say?"

"It says no. But my heart says yes. I never knew they were two separate entities until today."

"You thought your stomach pumped blood around your veins?"

"I don't know."

"What do those chemicals think?"

"They've been quiet." It was true. Except for the Sun Chip incident, since she'd told Joe about the pregnancy, her internal poison had eased into a pleasingly sublime feeling, as if she'd taken melatonin and could fall asleep anytime. Even the Tiffany thing didn't pack the same punch it had a few days before.

"Then congratulations." Peter was sweet; of course he was going to take the positive perspective. "Go with it. There's always divorce if things don't work out. But — don't take this wrong — I think you should stay home for a while. With Mom and Dad."

"Why? I'm here with Joe. I'm safe."

"There's a killer on the scene."

"George Bigelow was arrested. The scene is safe again. And come on — Mom and Dad's house? I'd rather be strangled than suffocated."

Peter cracked a grim smile. "You're welcome on my couch."

"That's nice of you," Elizabeth said. "But we'd get along for three days, then we'd be in each other's space."

"Your plan is to leave tomorrow, right?"

Elizabeth nodded. "We're going to Maui. Staying in a hotel for a few days, maybe rent a house for a month, figure out something more permanent for when the baby is born. It was Joe's suggestion. We're taking a break from poker. At least I am. Joe will no doubt find a lucrative side game somewhere."

"Why not just come home for tonight?"

Elizabeth shook her head.

"Just stay close to Joe, or someone you trust, until you leave."

"George is in jail," Elizabeth said again. "Why don't you think he's the killer?"

Peter frowned. "It's weird, right? I should think that, since the cops do, and what do I know about anyone in your world? Nothing. But I feel this funny instinct. Like you're not safe. You have to admit — that's the one thing Mom is good for."

"What?"

"She taught us how to listen to our instincts."

NINETY-SIX
CLARE

Clare perched on the edge of Noah's desk chair. She watched the third-floor ice machine at the River Rock Casino a few blocks away. Noah had rigged a tiny Internet camera so they could watch the room in real time.

It was a bit like watching a Russian film, only there was more at stake, so that kept things interesting. Kind of. The ice machine hadn't moved in three hours.

Clare's phone rang — relief from the tedium. The relief was short-lived, though: the caller was Amanda.

"Can this wait?" Clare asked. "I'm in the middle of something important."

Amanda spoke quickly. "Can you talk? Are you alone?"

"I'm alone for a few minutes. I'm expecting Noah back anytime." Clare kept her eye on the computer as she waited for Amanda to berate her for whatever she'd done wrong this time.

"I'll be brief. You know that George Bigelow was arrested."

"Yeah."

"He gave his arresting officers a statement that discredits the alibi of Terrence Jones."

"Who's Terrence Jones?" A light flickered on the ice machine camera.

"Jones is a poker player. I'm surprised you haven't encountered him. He's been in both of the tournaments you've played, and he was dating Loni Mills when she was killed."

"Ah, Terrence." Clare raised her eyebrows. "The rest of the world calls him T-Bone."

"Good. You know him. So Bigelow's statement . . . let me find it here . . . right . . . he has Mickey Mills spotting Jones in the hallway outside Loni's room about an hour before she was found — dead — by housekeeping."

Clare frowned. "Wasn't it T-Bone's room, too? He may have gone there legitimately."

"Jones's official statement has him playing poker all morning. He's adamant that he never left the casino floor once he started playing poker at seven a.m. If he's innocent, why lie?"

"Fear?" Clare said. "And why are we taking George's word about Mickey's word? Could T-Bone be telling the truth?"

"Security cameras don't think so. River Rock's footage has a man who matches Jones's description leaving the room at six forty-five a.m., returning to the room at eight fifteen a.m., and leaving again at eight thirty. No one else entered or left the room until housekeeping found the body at ten thirty."

"Do we know housekeeping was the real deal?" Clare had seen all the Tarantino movies. "Someone could have dressed up like a cleaner and stolen someone's cart."

"Housekeeping was real. We have the statement from the poor woman who found Loni."

"So are they bringing him in? Sounds like T-Bone was caught as red-handed as you can get him."

"The RCMP is confident."

"But you're not."

"I'm not sure," Amanda said. "It's the same black cowboy hat, the same gray ponytail. It probably is Terrence Jones in both cases. There's just something in the walk . . . the man returning to the room looks more sprightly than the man who left it in the morning."

Clare thought for a moment. "Maybe he had a heavier heart in the morning. He knew he had a problem — maybe Loni found out he was cheating — but he didn't know what to do, didn't want to kill her. Then later, once he realizes murder is his only option, his step is lighter. He knows what he has to do."

Amanda laughed. "That actually makes a strange kind of sense."

"Can you get the footage analyzed by a professional? I'm sure there are computers that could tell you if it's the same guy."

"I've sent off a copy. The results won't be back for a few days."

"They won't work faster for a murder case?"

Amanda laughed bitterly. "I'm not running the case, and the superintendent doesn't think it's important enough to ask for priority."

"How can this not be important enough?" Clare asked.

"It might contradict the truth as they'd like to see it. I don't know."

Clare chewed on her lower lip. "Are they going to arrest T-Bone?"

"Either that or bring him in for questioning."

"Before or after the final table tomorrow morning?" Clare saw another flicker in the ice room. Someone should change that bulb.

"Possibly during. The inspector says now, but the superintendent wants it on camera."

"That's weird. You'd think that to make it that far up in the police ranks, you wouldn't be about showboating anymore."

"You'd think," Amanda said. "But this call is being monitored, so let's not insult our colleagues."

Clare rolled her eyes. "What do you want from me?"

"I'd like you to look at the footage from the hotel hallway," Amanda said. "You've been living with these men. I'd like you to tell me if you think it's T-Bone in both instances."

"Okay," Clare said. "Like I said, I'm in the middle of something important right now, but I can come by your apartment later on."

"I'd like your opinion sooner. I'll email you the video file."

"Why? No matter what I think, they'll still arrest T-Bone. Or bring him in, or whatever."

"Of course they will. But it will help me understand what risk you're still in. They've pulled a lot of your security back since George Bigelow was arrested, which in my mind was a mistake."

"You don't think George is the killer either?" Clare saw a shadow move on the ice machine camera, but it was too small to be significant.

"I don't know. I just know that while you're on that scene, you need protection, and I'm not comfortable allowing security to pull all their men just because one suspect — soon to be two — has been removed."

Clare hung up the phone and was reaching for her smokes when she saw a shadow on the screen. The ice room door was opening. She felt her muscles tense as she watched to see who came in.

"Aargh," she said out loud when she saw it was just some fat guy filling up his ice bucket. She grabbed her smokes and lit one while the man bent over to collect his bucket, exposing his crack. She looked away and inhaled the nicotine, a familiar comfort coursing through her veins. It made her less annoyed with Amanda and the fat man.

She wondered if the plan would work. Noah was confident, but Clare worried that the Dealer was too smart to fall into their amateur trap. Or was it amateur? Clare reminded herself that someone, somewhere had confidence in her professionalism. Maybe she needed to have the same confidence in herself.

A few minutes later, the ice room door opened again.

Clare's heart sank.

She knew she wasn't supposed to care, but she liked Mickey.

She didn't want him to be guilty. She didn't want him to be the one coming into the ice room.

He looked angry. He opened the ice machine door so hard that it slammed shut again. He opened it a second time, marginally more gently. He took the scoop and rummaged around inside. He frowned when he found nothing. He pulled a sheet of paper from his pocket and wedged it into the handle of the machine.

He shook his head, appeared to mutter something, and left.

Clare sent Noah a text.

Check machine.

When she didn't get an answer — and when ten minutes had gone by and Noah hadn't entered the ice machine room like he should have if he'd gotten the text — Clare became worried. Had Noah dropped his phone? Had someone intercepted her message?

She tried phoning. No answer.

"Shit," Clare said out loud. She wondered if their bait had worked too well. Had the real Dealer found Noah, taken his phone, intercepted Clare's text? "Fuck," she said, also out loud. Whoever had Noah's phone now knew that Clare — Tiffany — was in on this disinformation scam.

There was a knock at the door. Clare swore again, this time in her head. She threw the bolt on the door before looking out the peephole. No one was there.

She stood at the door for a full minute before deciding not to open it. She checked the peephole three more times before deciding she must have imagined the knock. She went back to the computer. On the screen, she saw someone pull the note Mickey had left in the ice machine. The someone wasn't Noah.

The someone wore a black cowboy hat with a gray ponytail sticking out from the back. The angle of the camera was odd;

T-Bone looked shorter and slimmer than he did in real life. Maybe Amanda was right.

Clare texted Noah again.

u ok?

NINETY-SEVEN
GEORGE

George wasn't sure how long he'd be staying here, in the oddly expansive concrete cell, and he didn't care. It wasn't a cabin by the lake, but at the moment he preferred it to the generic hotel rooms he'd been living in for the past ten years. He had his computer and a room of his own. It was pretty much a writer's dream.

He stared at the screen. He still had the feeling from earlier, that he had the pieces to figure out who the killer was, but didn't know how they fit. He started typing.

```
Mickey
Joe
T-Bone
Oliver
Elizabeth
Nate
```

He contemplated adding Tiffany's name, but shook his head. He also contemplated Fiona's name, and added it.

Mickey -- Pretty sure you're not the Dealer.
Playing fair is too important to you. Important
enough that you'd kill to keep the game honest? I
don't know.

Joe -- Too good a player to cheat, unless you
thought it was some really fun game and there was
more in it for you than money. Capable of murder?
Doubt it. Best guess: you might be playing along,
you might even be the Dealer, but you are not the
Choker.

T-Bone -- Lousy fucking asshole, but again, too
good a player to cheat. Your win rate went down
when all those newcomers came on the scene, but I
don't think it dipped below positive. The Dealer
role doesn't suit you. The Choker I could see.

Oliver -- No doubt cheating. Pulling strings?
Maybe. The unempowered often seek power in weird
ways. Murdering? Again, maybe. Dark and angry.
Ax to grind with world.

Elizabeth -- Good player, no recent spike in win
rate. Angry -- chemicals -- possible brain imbal-
ance -- pregnancy doesn't really explain that
away. Unless the pregnancy is unhealthy . . .
maybe toxins in your system. Still, probably not a
killer; probably not a cheater.

Nate -- New to the scene and starts winning right
away. High candidate for cheating, Dealer, etc.
Right body type for Mount Baker hitchhiker (could
be wearing dreadlock wig). Murderer? Sure, if
people get in your way.

Fiona -- Not a fucking clue.

George looked over his page a few times. The more he looked, the clearer the answer became: it was Nate.

George had to get the message to Tiffany, who could well be spending the night with Nate. They hadn't given George internet access — though he'd wanted it to maintain his blog, George knew when not to push his luck. But maybe if he asked a guard, they'd let him make a phone call.

"Excuse me!" George heard his voice scratch as he shouted for a guard. He hadn't spoken aloud for several hours.

A guard at the end of the corridor turned and walked toward him. "What do you want?"

"Could I make a phone call? You have my cell phone somewhere. Or I can use the pay phone if I can have my credit card for a few minutes."

The guard snorted. "Don't ask for much, do you?"

"I'm sorry," George said. "I know you're making these concessions for me already. I . . ."

"I'll be right back."

George sat on the bench in his cell and waited. What would he say to Tiffany if he reached her? *Excuse me, I'm in jail for a murder that I think your boyfriend committed?* He almost laughed out loud.

A few minutes later, the guard returned and unlocked George's cell door. "You can use the pay phone, but you'll have to call collect. Come with me."

George followed the guard down the concrete hall. He dialed Mickey and waited for him to accept the charges.

"Georgie!" Mickey sounded happy to hear from him. "They let you out? Thank god. What a fuck-up. How'd you finally convince the fuzz to listen to reason?"

"I'm still in jail. That's why I'm calling collect. But listen, Mickey, I'm pretty sure the Dealer's Nate. And he's a good bet for the Choker, too. Is Tiffany still hanging out with him? Someone should warn her."

"I tried," Mickey said. "I got a note. Did you get one, too? It said *Introducing Nate Wilkes as your Dealer.* I wondered if it was from you at first, but then I heard you got arrested."

"I got the same note; but that's not what tipped the scales. Look, Mickey, I know it's Nate. You think Tiffany will accept a collect call from me?"

"Sure. She's a good kid."

"Can you give me her number?"

Mickey took a minute or so to retrieve the information from his phone. "And hang on tight in there. I'm doing what I can to find the real killer before they lock you away somewhere worse than a holding cell."

"Thanks." George hung up and dialed Tiffany's number.

NINETY-EIGHT
CLARE

Clare's phone rang on the desk, and she jumped. She looked at the call display but didn't recognize the number. Could the caller be the same person who'd just knocked on the door?

No sense ignoring it; if they were still outside, they'd heard the ring.

"Hello?"

"You have a collect call from George Bigelow. You can press one now to accept the charges."

Clare pressed one now. "Hello?"

"Tiffany. It's George Bigelow. I know we don't know each other well. But I've just spoken with Mickey, and —"

"Are you out of jail?"

"No. I have five minutes for this call. Mickey said he tried to warn you about Nate. That he thinks Nate's the Dealer."

"Yeah," Clare said. "I don't know who to trust."

"Mickey's right."

"Is that why you're calling me?"

"You should spend tonight alone."

"Mickey said the same thing. But why?"

"I saw someone outside Fiona's motel. Maybe the dreadlocks were a wig. He was Nate's size and shape. He —"

"A lot of guys are that size," Clare said. "Joe's that size. Oliver's around the same height. Hell, Elizabeth's tall — stick a costume on her and who knows what she'd look like? Why aren't you accusing them?"

"Are you with Nate now?"

"No."

"Can you sleep alone?"

"Of course I can. But like I said to Mickey, I think I'm safer sleeping with someone than alone."

George was silent.

"I appreciate the call. I'm sure you had a hassle to get through to me from jail. And for what it's worth, I think you're innocent."

"You do? Why?"

"Because you're calling me? I don't know," Clare said. "You sound innocent."

"Thanks."

Clare heard Noah's card in the door. At least she hoped it was Noah's. Should she keep George on the phone, to be safe?

Noah walked through the door. He had a piece of paper in his hand. "Any idea who left this outside?"

Clare stared. She said to George, "I should go. Nate just got back."

"Back?"

"I'm in his room." Why had she just given up free information? George was still a suspect. Dumb, dumb, dumb.

"Make up an excuse," George said. "You have no reason to trust me, but I'm telling you: go back to your hotel. Or another hotel, where he doesn't know you'll be. Just get the hell out of there."

"Thanks," Clare said. "And, um, sorry about your predicament." She clicked her phone off and said to Nate, "My handler."

Noah repeated his question. "Did you see who left this note?"

"I heard a knock about an hour ago. I didn't open the door."

"Good move," Noah said. "I think it was the Choker."

"Why?"

He handed Clare the page.

```
Nice camera in the ice room. I guess an amateur
cop is used to dealing with an amateur killer. No
such luck this time, bozo -- or bozette.
                            -- The Real Dealer
```

Clare set down the page. "Bozette?"

"I guess it's the female equivalent of bozo."

"Right. Got it. But why would he let on he's onto us?"

Noah shrugged. "Either our plan threw him off and he's making mistakes, or he has delusions of his own grandeur and he thinks we'll never catch him."

"Delusions of grandeur . . ." Clare scanned her mind for the notes she'd taken in the police academy class about pathology. "Is that psychopathology? Manic depression? Paranoia? I forget."

"It goes with a lot of mental illnesses. Fuck, I had a shrink tell me I was a megalomaniac when I was seventeen." He sank into a chair and stared straight ahead, as if back in time at a memory.

"You did?" Clare prompted.

"Yeah. Then he found out my IQ and he changed his diagnosis."

"What's your IQ?" Clare wouldn't know what the number meant.

"IQ's a load of crap."

"So yours is low."

"No." He broke his trance to look sharply at Clare.

"Then why won't you tell me?" She tried to laugh as she asked him.

Noah wiped his palms on his jeans, leaving sweat stains. "Because it's a crack science. I tell you mine, you tell me yours, and one of us feels inferior for no fucking reason."

Clare grinned, though inside she was wondering why Noah

was acting like he was due for a refresher in the loony bin. "I have no idea what my IQ is. Or what they mean."

"Good. Then we can get along." Noah relaxed his arms and stared straight ahead again.

"So, um, tell me about your shrink. What was his new diagnosis after he found out how smart you are?" Clare was wondering if she should take George and Mickey's advice. What did she really know about Noah? Even if he *was* FBI, an agent could go rogue.

Noah rolled his eyes, but it was like he was rolling them at someone far away. "So this shrink — let's call him Dr. Asshole — spends a winter full of weekly sessions telling me I'm unrealistically high on myself. Then one day he asks me my IQ. I tell him. Then out of nowhere, the guy starts in on some diatribe about how it doesn't matter how smart someone is, it's what you do with it that counts, and I have a fucking responsibility to use my mind and not waste it like some lazy self-absorbed fool."

Noah paused, but Clare didn't think he wanted a reaction from her, so she stayed quiet.

"And at the end of the meeting, Dr. Fuckhead — sorry, that was Dr. Asshole, right? — says he doesn't think he's the right person to help me going forward. Which is fucking wonderful when you're seventeen and down on yourself and you find out even your shrink doesn't like you." He looked up at Clare.

Clare didn't know what to say. "That must have been awful."

"Sorry to go down Pathetic Memory Lane," Noah said, appearing to snap back into the real world. "But long story short, this megalomaniac killer could have any number of illnesses. I'm homing in on psychopath, because I'm guessing the guy has no conscience."

"Do most killers have consciences?" Clare asked. "Hey, there's someone else in the ice room."

They sat by Noah's computer and watched Elizabeth go into the small room. She filled a bucket with ice, and left.

"What do you think she's doing?" Clare asked.

"Getting ice for the boat?"

"Why this room, though? Why not the second floor or fourth floor? You think she's looking for Mickey's note?"

"Mickey?"

Clare hesitated, then filled Noah in on what she'd seen.

They watched Elizabeth leave the room. She hadn't left anything behind.

Clare's phone beeped. It was an email from Amanda — the footage Clare had agreed to look at. She didn't know if she could trust Noah to watch it with her. What if the guy on tape was Noah, disguised as T-Bone in a ponytail and hat? Clare would recognize his movements in a second, but could she hide her recognition from him?

Shit, but her laptop was back at the hotel, and the screen on her phone would be too small — she couldn't home in and enlarge the parts she wanted a closer look at.

She looked at Noah and decided she had to trust him. "I have footage from the Fallsview security cameras. Mind if I forward it so we can open it on your laptop?"

NINETY-NINE
NOAH

"It's T-Bone, right?" Clare squinted at the grainy image on the screen.

"Duh," Noah said. "You know anyone else who wears a black cowboy hat and gray ponytail?"

"We can only see him from behind. You sure it's him, or is someone wearing his hat?"

"And his ponytail?"

Clare shrugged. "That's what Amanda wants me to look at."

"Shit," Noah said. "That's it, isn't it?"

"I think so."

"Any idea who might be in the disguise?"

Clare laughed, but she seemed to be hiding another emotion behind that. Fear? "I have to spell it out? Come on."

"Oh my god. Arrogant much? What makes you so sure your theory is right?"

"Because," Clare said. "You have Snow White playing poker all night, right?"

"Sure," Noah said. "That's Joe and his costumes."

"Is it?" Clare said. "Or are we assuming it was Joe inside the costume?"

"Didn't you two leave the boat together after he fucked your brains out so skilfully?"

"Yeah," Clare said. "And he was dressed as Snow White. I was cracking up the whole time he was putting on the costume — I didn't think he was actually going to wear it to the poker table."

"But he did," Noah said. "So that rules him out as the killer. We also don't have him crossing the border by land, and we don't have his boat leaving the dock."

"There are other ways to get to the States."

"But George was actually *in* the States. At the right time. At Fiona's motel room. That's open and shut in my books."

"Good thing no one's reading your books," Clare said. "Don't tell me you want to be a writer like George."

"Please. Like anyone would care what I have to say. So I'm still not following you. You're saying it's not George. You think it's Joe, and he had someone swap costumes with him? You think it's T-Bone, and he had someone dress up like him to walk around the River Rock catching him from behind in the security cameras as an alibi?"

Clare laughed. "Come on. It's so obvious."

"Elizabeth? Shit — she was away all night when Fiona got killed. Supposedly at her parents' place, but no one even thought to check her alibi. Joe was sleeping with Fiona — Elizabeth was pregnant — it makes sense Elizabeth would want Fiona dead."

Clare rolled her eyes.

"What are we missing?" Noah said. "Just proof?"

"I think we can get proof from the cab cameras. On either side of the border."

"Do cabs even have cameras in Canada or in backwater Washington State?"

"You are such a snob. The world outside New York City has access to technology, too." Clare spun away from Noah's computer to face him. "Anyway, what do you care about proof, or all this leading to an arrest? You're only here to learn the tricks of the hole card scam."

Noah decided to wait before telling Clare that her job offer with the FBI was confirmed, pending successful completion of this case and a ludicrously invasive background check. He still wasn't even sure he wanted to extend the offer. If Clare came, she'd no doubt move to New York with her beloved boyfriend. He said, "So how do you propose your man — or woman — crossed the border?"

"You still don't know who I mean?" Clare looked like she was having fun. "All right, while you've been gone and scaring the hell out of me, I've been browsing the web for border crossing loopholes."

"And let me guess: you found one." Noah looped a finger in the air.

"Yup. I think our killer took a cab to Tsawassen — there's a squash club they could have been dropped off at which would look normal enough, even late at night."

"You won't even give me a gender?"

Clare grinned. "It's going to feel so obvious when you figure it out. Anyway, they can walk across the border there to Point Roberts — it's this little part of the U.S. that's only attached to Canada, so the border isn't heavily guarded. From there, our person could have stolen a boat, driven it to Bellingham or Blaine, and grabbed a cab up the mountain to Fiona's motel room."

Noah laughed now. "That's even more ludicrous than just wearing a disguise and renting a car to drive across. Or driving a boat all the way from the casino. So *Last Tango* was in the dock all night. What about all the other boats? Could someone have 'borrowed' one from the River Rock marina?"

"Not unless they checked in with the U.S. Coast Guard when they crossed," Clare said. "Security's tighter with boats than it is with cars — failure to check in would result in a military ambush. Anyway, you want to check the cab cameras before their footage is erased? I think they only have to keep it for twenty four hours, so we're already pushing our luck. And your rental car/disguise theory isn't bad either. Except the facial recognition scan should have caught that."

Noah tapped a finger against his lip as he considered this. "A fake chin or nose might throw off the facial scan. You can buy stuff like that in any drugstore."

"Shit," Clare said. "You're right. We might have to slog through footage manually. But you know who the killer is now, right?"

Noah nodded as he watched the ice machine footage one more time. "I'm starting to think so."

"Kind of scary, isn't it?"

Clare took his hand. "Are you okay?"

"Of course I'm okay. What are you talking about?" Noah snatched his hand back. He felt bad for the abruptness of the motion, but he didn't want her holding it and making him feel things he couldn't act on.

"Sorry." Clare's voice held justified annoyance. "What's wrong with you?"

In the absence of a ready lie, Noah opted for honesty. "I'm going to miss you. I want to solve this case — of course I do. But when it's over, so are we."

"We can stay in touch. At least we know each other's real names."

"I'm not going to stay in touch with you, Clare. I might be perverse, but I don't enjoy torturing myself."

"What's that supposed to mean?"

"It means I like you. But whatever. You have a boyfriend. I'm not going to pretend to be your friend until lo and behold, a wedding invitation arrives in the mail, and I have to decide: do I go and smile and silently curse the guy who gets to keep you forever, or do I rip the invitation into little shreds and spend the next several weeks with a bottle of vodka?"

"I've never seen you drink vodka."

"Jesus, you can miss the point."

"I'm not missing the point," Clare said quietly. "I'm trying to push those same thoughts out of my own head. I like you, too."

"No you don't. You made it clear that you were dating me for the case."

"Just because Tiffany was dating you doesn't mean Clare wasn't having fun."

"Jesus."

"What?"

"Stop separating your two selves like that. And don't talk about yourself in the third person. It's irritating as hell."

Clare laughed. "Noah, I want to jump on you and pin you to the bed and fuck you until this stupid case solves itself on its own."

"Easy to say when you're not fucking going to."

"Yes, it's easy to say. And it would be even easier to do. But I won't cheat on Kevin."

"So break up with him."

Clare shook her head. "Not from here."

"What if I could get you a job in New York?"

"You've said that before. It's such a long shot."

"It would be," Noah said. "Except that I've spoken with my handler, and he looked into your career history . . ."

"My one case."

"He was impressed. He says if we crack this thing together, he'll consider making you an offer."

"What does that mean?"

"Since we're about to crack the case, I'm pretty sure it means you're in. After a ridiculously complex and invasive security check, that is."

Clare cocked her head and met Noah's eye for a few seconds before saying, "So do you think we'd be able to slog through border footage ourselves? We've been living with these guys; I think we'd spot a fake chin on the right face before some clerk at the border office could."

"Sounds good." Noah wondered why Clare had given him zero response on the New York move. Was she even considering it? "And if that doesn't pan out, we can go with your cab camera idea."

"I think we should do both. So how do we get these files from the border? Should we go through my side or yours?"

Noah thought about it. "Mine, I think. I'll call my boss and get him to meet us at the border. He'll clear us for access to their computers and sort out any other red tape we need help with." Noah could probably have Bert courier the image files to the hotel, but he wanted Bert to see Clare's intensity firsthand, to watch her mind at work, so he'd know she would be a good hire. "You wearing that?"

Clare looked down at her tight hot pink T-shirt and very ripped jeans. Together they'd cost more than Clare's treasured motorcycle jacket back home. "Why not?"

"It's, you know, not very professional."

Clare laughed. "It's the definition of professional. I'm undercover, remember?"

SUNDAY / MARCH 27

ONE HUNDRED
ELIZABETH

Elizabeth looked at the chips stacked in front of her. The game of poker seemed as significant as the pimple she felt forming on her forehead. Whoever said pregnancy was good for your complexion was lying through their teeth.

The young reporter who had replaced Fiona moved through the room like she was terrified of knocking something over. She conducted interviews apologetically, as if she thought she was bothering the players. Elizabeth surprised herself by actually missing Fiona.

Elizabeth looked at the other players. It was a good final table: Mickey, Joe, Tiffany, Nate, T-Bone, herself, and four unknowns. Elizabeth ranked herself third in terms of raw skill, after Mickey and Joe. T-Bone might have been better once, but his recent track record made him a clear fourth. But poker was full of surprises. With all the books and online coaching sites available to any Joe Schmoe, any of those four unknowns could be a genius waiting to spring his first public trap. Hell, even Tiffany could luck out and win.

And then the room turned silent. Elizabeth looked up to see two uniformed policemen approaching the table. She couldn't tell if it felt like slow motion or superspeed as they asked Joe to stand up, handcuffed him, and told him he was being arrested for the murders of Josie Carter, Jimmy Streets, Willard Oppal, and Loni Mills. All the Choker victims except Fiona. One cop explained that the only reason he wasn't being arrested for Fiona's murder was because it wasn't RCMP jurisdiction. Like that mattered.

Of course Joe was the Dealer. Elizabeth had known it all along, and yet she hadn't. How he always made the final table, but never came first. Of course he wouldn't come first — why attract the attention? Consistently coming in third or seventh paid well enough to meet Joe's needs. And knowing it was consistent would address that whole security thing.

Elizabeth looked at Joe, who was staring vacantly through her and everyone else at the table. He was still wearing the furry ears and dog nose he'd had on before he'd been handcuffed, and he said nothing as Elizabeth reached forward and took both off for him. He neither confirmed nor denied the charges as he listened to the cops and allowed them to lead him away.

Elizabeth picked up her purse and left Joe's costume remains on the table. Nate and Tiffany both reached for the props simultaneously. She found that odd, but didn't have the energy to care.

She followed the cops as they led Joe outside. She had tears on her face, but she couldn't feel them falling. She watched as Joe's head was pushed down into the police car, and stared as he was driven away.

She felt blood. She'd been cramping all morning, but she'd ignored it. She looked down; her beige pants were covered with red. She got into a taxi and asked the driver to take her to Richmond Hospital.

"Which entrance?" said the driver.

"Emergency. I'm in the middle of a fucking miscarriage."

ONE HUNDRED AND ONE
NOAH

Noah sat stiffly in Clare's armchair while she packed. "Joe's not going to confess," he said.

"No kidding." Clare frowned at a pink sweater while she made a couple of unsuccessful attempts at folding it. "But Oliver will testify about being Snow White. George will testify about Fiona saying she received all the notes. And we'll hopefully get some hotel surveillance footage of Joe dropping off those notes to Fiona's rooms in different cities along the tour. I'm surprised Joe didn't kill Oliver right afterwards."

"He was probably next to die." Noah fingered his cigarette pack. He should quit smoking soon. He was too old for the shit, and there were too many places you couldn't light up. Like in this fucking Canadian hotel room. "But Joe wasn't impulsive about any of the murders. He would have planned Oliver's death for a time he'd get away with — maybe later in the afternoon — maybe once the tournament was over, so Oliver could keep up his end of the hole card scam."

Clare got the sweater in line and placed it in the suitcase. "You don't think he was ready to call it quits on the scam? I think he never meant to kill anyone, just the scam got out of hand and he felt he had to get rid of people for his own protection."

Noah shrugged. "I have no idea what makes a guy like that tick. It's scary how few tells he had. Everyone else was freaking out when we sent them their fake Dealer notes. Joe was the only guy who had an even reaction. He walked around like the same old guy, relaxed and cocky and like he owned the world. Not like his life was suddenly in danger."

"Duh," Clare said. "Why do you think it was so obvious that it was Joe?"

"*That's* how you put it together? Because he didn't react to his note?"

"Sure. That's what I thought we were looking for in the first place — the one person who reacted differently from the rest." Clare looked at Noah. "What were you looking for?"

Noah didn't know the answer, so he asked another question. "You think Oliver knew it was Joe asking him to dress up as Snow White?"

"I don't know." Clare tilted her head to one side. "I'm sure it was done with notes, or texts from a blocked number. Joe probably hid the costume in a bathroom and told Oliver when to put it on, then Joe made his exit from the same bathroom in his own clothes. Anyone watching sees Snow White Joe going in, Snow White Oliver coming out. In costume, they'd look damn near identical. No one thinks to question seeing regular Oliver going in and regular Joe coming out; they both belong to the scene."

Noah watched her quick, lithe movements. When he'd met Clare as Tiffany, he'd seen her as too skinny. Now he thought her small size suited her; it matched her speedy mind and temper.

"But," Clare said, "Oliver was no idiot. Who else would be playing dress-up, other than Joe? And people at the table would have called him Joe, naturally. So even if the exchange was anonymous, he must have known who he was impersonating. If Joe hadn't have been arrested this morning, my guess is Oliver would have been dead by the end of today."

Noah leaned forward in the chair. "Have you thought about Bert's offer?"

Clare fastened one suitcase and set it on the floor. She still had one on the bed. "Yeah."

"Um . . . have you made a decision?"

"Mm hmm."

Noah's insides were screaming. "Will you tell me what it is?"

Clare nodded. "I want to go to New York."

ONE HUNDRED AND TWO
GEORGE

George walked out of the police station where he'd spent the past twenty-four hours. They hadn't told him much; just that he was no longer under arrest, but he'd have to advise Canadian authorities of his travel plans and make himself available for questioning. Since he was American, he was allowed to return to the States without issue.

But George wondered if his New England writing cabin could as easily be here in B.C. The Sunshine Coast was isolated enough. The Gulf Islands were, too. New England was where he'd grown up; it could foster his old snobbery, make him write less freely, edit himself more harshly. And the story kind of belonged here, in the Pacific Northwest where Fiona had died.

He came to a coffee shop advertising wireless access and went inside.

The strong odor of coffee beans made him feel at home. He ordered a large dark roast and flipped on his computer.

He typed *rental cabins British Columbia* into Google.

TORONTO

ONE HUNDRED AND THREE
CLARE

"I'm moving to New York." Clare was wrapped around Kevin. She held on a little longer than she knew she should. His body felt warm and strong as he returned her embrace. She wondered if she was making a huge mistake.

"For how long?" Kevin's voice was even, but Clare felt his muscles tense.

"For . . . a while. I guess. Until I move somewhere else."

"I don't understand." Kevin eased himself out of her grasp. "Are you being sent on a permanent assignment?"

Clare shook her head. "I'm moving."

His eyebrows lowered. "You mean it's your choice?"

"The FBI offered me a job. I'm currently being scrutinized by their crazy security check, but assuming they don't find out anything horrible about me, I'm going to take it."

"Wow." Kevin exhaled and stared at the ceiling. "Congratulations."

"I'm sorry, Kevin. I really liked you. It isn't —"

"Liked me?" Kevin rolled back onto his side and met her eyes. "We can make this work long distance."

"It's across a border. We've only been together for six months."

Clare didn't want to tell him about Noah. She needed an out, in case she realized in a day or two that she was making a mistake.

"I could move, too," Kevin said. "All I have is business cards. I can throw those out and start my company in New York."

"What about the synergy with your dad?" Clare said. "Findlay and Son and all that . . . and you don't have a green card."

"Do you need one if you start your own business? Anyway, I can get that figured out."

"I think anything to do with construction is run by the mob in New York. You'd have to pay them off. It might not be worth your time."

"Clare!" Kevin laughed, but he looked confused.

Clare looked at the sheets, messy from their recent sex.

"You're not telling me everything."

Clare didn't answer.

"Have you met someone?"

Clare chewed her lower lip.

"I guess I should have known."

"Why should you have known?" Clare frowned.

Kevin shook his head. "It's who you are."

"A cheater?" That wasn't fair.

"If the shoe fits."

"It doesn't fit." Clare scrambled out of bed and began to collect her clothes from the floor. She found her cigarettes and lit one. "I've never been anything but honest with you. Except when I've had to lie for work."

"Really? Why did you sleep with me just now if you came over here to break up with me?"

"Because I couldn't say it."

"If you'd wanted break-up sex, I would have obliged. It's just nice when both parties know when it's happening."

"I didn't want break-up sex. I've been awake for too many hours and my brain isn't functioning normally. I woke up in Vancouver and sent a guy to jail this morning. It's kind of surreal being here with you now. Breaking up."

"So you wanted relationship sex because it's more comforting after a long work day? How was it for you? I hope I could keep you awake."

"Sex is always good between us."

"You mean was."

"Yeah. I guess I mean was."

"Jesus, Clare." Kevin's eyes went wide. His anger seemed to leave all at once.

"I'm sorry." Clare slid one leg through a lacy pair of underwear, then the other. Two weeks ago it would have been shapeless cotton, and definitely not a thong. She wondered briefly if Noah would have even liked the other Clare.

The real one?

No, the old one.

MONDAY / MARCH 28

ONE HUNDRED AND FOUR
CLARE

"New York City." Roberta looked blankly at the carburetor needle in her hand. "You excited?"

"No."

"Why are you going?"

"Fine, so I'm a bit excited." Clare took a sip of beer. It felt good to be openly drinking Bud again.

"Have you seen your parents yet?"

"I talked to my mom this morning. My dad's off the transplant list, like you said, and they're pretty sure he's going to die soon. Am I being cold by moving so far from home?"

Roberta shook her head. A bunch of red hair came loose from its ponytail, and Clare thought she saw some gray in it for the first time. "Visit him. Tell him you love him. But go to New York. You're living your life."

"I do love him. That's the stupid part. But every time I go up there, they both try to make me feel guilty."

Roberta's eyebrows lowered. "They're unhappy. They don't know how to be the people you want them to be."

"So it's my job to smile and make them think everything's okay?"

"No. It's your job to look after yourself. Because they won't. And unfortunately, taking care of yourself includes sometimes visiting them."

Clare breathed deeply. "What if I hate New York?"

"What if the moon turns blue? The FBI making you sign up for life?"

"No." Clare felt herself smile.

"What if you love New York? Will we ever see you again?"

"Of course. I'll be home for Dad's funeral soon. God, that sounded terrible."

"But true," Roberta said. "How's your mom?"

Clare wanted a cigarette, but there was, for obvious reasons, no smoking inside the shop. "I think she might be . . . you know . . . ready . . . for my dad to die."

"She'll never be ready."

"She's calling the disease by its name finally."

"Emphysema? What was she calling it before?"

"Breathing trouble." Clare rolled her eyes. "But I think you're right. About seeing them for my sake. I have the weekend free. I'll go up before I head south."

"Can Noah go with you?"

Clare shook her head. "He's going back to New York tomorrow. And it's too soon to introduce him to my family."

"You're moving cities for a guy, and it's too soon for him to know where you come from?" Roberta picked up a new-looking motorcycle battery from her workbench.

"He knows exactly where I come from. He was fascinated, actually — he made me describe the trailer park in detail until he said he felt like he could walk around it. It's the depression I don't want him exposed to. Maybe if I had a normal family I'd consider it."

"Who has a normal family?" Roberta snorted. She opened the battery casing on the Virago and attached the battery to the bike.

"We've been dating for two weeks. One of which I thought his name was Nate."

"But you're moving to New York because of him."

"I'm moving for the job. Toronto can't even make my transfer to undercover official, and the FBI is handing me my dream job on a platter. I thought you said it wasn't the battery."

"It wasn't," Roberta said. "The old battery was weak, so it needed a new one. But that's incidental. We're about to find out if you were right about it being a starter solenoid."

"You haven't tested it?"

"I thought we could do that together." Roberta turned the key. The light came on, and she grinned. "You want to press the start button?"

Clare walked over to the bike and pressed the electric start. The bike coughed a bit the first go, so Clare pressed it again. Success.

"I'm going to miss you." Roberta's eyes were glassy. She turned the bike off.

"You can visit," Clare said. "It's only an eight-hour drive."

"If you drive like a maniac."

"Which you do."

Roberta grinned. "Maybe you'll see Shauna and Lance on the weekend when you're home."

"Maybe the moon will turn blue."

ONE HUNDRED AND FIVE
ELIZABETH

"Hey, can I ask you something?" Elizabeth spoke into the phone, though Joe was only a few feet away.

"Shoot." Joe wouldn't meet her eye.

"Um . . . this may seem really shallow. With everything you're going through. But . . . well . . . have you ever cheated on me?"

Joe looked up at her. Maybe he'd been expecting a tougher question. Through the plastic his eyes said less than ever. "Yes."

"With who? Josie? Fiona?"

Joe nodded.

"Tiffany?"

Joe twisted his mouth into a grim smile. "Yes."

"I guess that shouldn't bother me." Elizabeth frowned. "Did you like killing people?"

"I didn't kill anyone."

Same old fucking Joe. "Right."

Joe smiled.

"So can we play What If?" Elizabeth said.

"Yeah. I like that game."

"You like all games."

Joe shrugged.

"What if you killed someone?" Elizabeth said. "Do you think you would have liked it?"

"That's hard to imagine, since I've never wanted to kill anyone. But okay, let's suppose, for the sake of the game, that I did want someone dead enough to kill them." Joe tilted his head to one side. His dark roots were starting to show — for some reason, combined with his blond dye and frosted tips, it made him look more cheeseball to Elizabeth than the guys in *Jersey Shore*. He probably wouldn't be treated to a hair stylist in jail. "Yeah. I might have liked it."

Elizabeth forced herself to keep looking at him. "What might you have liked?"

"It might feel really powerful." Joe made a wringing motion with his hands. "One minute, life. One minute, death. All because of me."

Elizabeth felt her arms begin to tremble. "Would you have — hypothetically — killed these people for no reason? Or would you have needed a motive?"

"Um . . . that's a bit of a stretch, now. First you ask me to imagine I'm a murderer. Now you want me to imagine a motive?"

Elizabeth nodded, clenching her teeth inside closed lips.

"It would depend on who I killed, wouldn't it?"

"Josie Carter."

Joe pursed his lips and stared at the wall behind Elizabeth. "Josie talked a lot, didn't she? I don't remember her too well. But I guess that might annoy me."

"Talked a lot in general?"

"Yeah, and specifically. You said she wanted you to cheat at cards."

Elizabeth's fists tightened. "Do you think the killer is also the Dealer?"

Joe laughed. "Of course the killer is the Dealer. Why else would the people who blew the system end up dead?"

"Um . . . the system?"

Joe rolled his eyes. "This is common knowledge, Lizzie.

Personally, I think George is the man we should be after. I don't understand why they let him out of jail. I know they think they have this evidence on me, but there's more on him."

Elizabeth gnawed on her lower lip. The pain felt good. "So Josie talked too much. Why did Jimmy Streets have to die?"

"You forgot to say What If. Someone listening might mistake this for a confession."

It was like playing a game with a four-year-old. "What if you killed Jimmy Streets? Why would you have done that?"

"Well, I — like I said, I really think it's George, but *if* it was me — I think Jimmy was sniffing too close around the scam's mechanics. Jimmy wouldn't have cheated — he was good at the game — but if his best friend T-Bone Jones was in on the action, Jimmy might have smelled a rat. He might have been close to finding the rat and holding it up for public scrutiny."

Elizabeth's toes curled at the thought of a dead rat being held up by its tail. "And Willard Oppal?"

"Oppal?" Joe snorted. "God, anyone would have killed Oppal. Who needs another cop on the scene?"

"Loni Mills?"

"Freeloading. Loni was — you know, allegedly — cheating for free on the back of her boyfriend. *And* talking. Maybe if I was a killer, I'd find a way to kill her twice."

Elizabeth didn't laugh along with Joe. "And Fiona? What if?"

"Fiona bolted. I'm sure the Dealer didn't like that. It was his game; not hers. She should have let the Dealer keep control of the cards."

Elizabeth wondered why Joe's tone had changed so suddenly. Had he actually felt an emotion when killing Fiona? Or maybe it was simpler. "Wasn't it her murder that got you caught?"

"Some cabs in B.C. and in Washington State have images of someone they think was me in their cameras. But that guy had long black dreads, and as you can see I have short hair with blond tips, so I'm not really sure what's made them make that connection." Joe shrugged. "Is it because we both have a scar on our cheek? The scar could be makeup. There's way more evidence on George. Plus I was home at the casino playing poker. I was Snow White that night. It even says so on Twitter."

"Snow White was Oliver for most of the night. Come on, Joe. No one's convinced."

"Come on, Liz," Joe said. "No one's convicted."

"Okay, Joe. One more What If. What if you were the Dealer? Why would you have cheated when you're so damn good at the game?"

"Ah," Joe said. "Finally, an interesting question."

Elizabeth waited.

"Poker has no guarantees. You can play like God and still get beaten."

"So?" Elizabeth watched Joe's face change, somehow, from the cold killer of a moment ago into the man she could picture herself crawling into bed with.

"You know how I grew up. I had nothing."

"That's why I don't understand your materialism as an adult. You know you can survive on nothing. What do you care if you have a boat and a mansion?"

"I never want to depend on anyone again."

Elizabeth didn't comment on the irony of that, with a life in jail the most likely scenario ahead of Joe.

"*If* I was the Dealer, it would have nothing to do with materialism, and everything to do with never having to ask anyone for anything ever again."

"But you had enough for that already. If you'd invested —"

"I have enough to invest and live a quiet, simple life. But that's not me. I plan to soar, Lizzie. You'll soar with me — when you stop believing I'm guilty, anyway. Look, this game is done. I'm not the killer. I'm not the Dealer. Just get me a fucking lawyer — a good one — so I can get out of this place."

"I thought you had some super-fancy lawyer flying in from the States."

"He's not here yet. I want out."

"Are other people even real to you?"

Joe looked blank.

"If you think of someone else being in pain, do you feel any-thing?"

Joe shrugged. "Should I?"

Elizabeth shook her head, trying to clear it.

"Seriously, Liz. Should I feel something? Because I'm pretty sure people are just making that crap up, when they say, 'I feel your pain.'"

"What about the baby?"

"I felt that." Joe went quiet.

"Thank god something can wipe that stupid grin off your face."

"I mean I really felt it. I thought it was a new beginning."

"You would have been bored of the baby as soon as it kept you awake all night crying. Hell, you might have killed it if it really pissed you off."

"Elizabeth, stop it." Joe was getting angry, something she couldn't remember ever having seen. "That baby could have cried for twelve years. It was my chance to change — it's already changed me — don't you see?"

"No."

Joe shrugged. "Not like it matters now. You've already killed it."

"Have fun in jail, Joe."

ONE HUNDRED AND SIX
CLARE

"What do you have? Aces?" Clare couldn't beat aces. She couldn't even beat a bluff.

"Yeah," Noah said. "Plus the ace on the board makes three."

"You'll show me, right? If I fold?" They were playing strip poker in Clare's bedroom. Nobody cared who won.

"I'll show you anything you want." Noah spread his palms in front of him.

Clare frowned. "Except inside your brain."

"It's gross in there. All that gray matter, and blood vessels snaking through it."

"Fine." Clare looked at her fingernails. The polish was chipped in a few places. She hadn't decided whether to reapply it or let it fade away. "I'll settle for the outside of you."

"I'll show you *all* of that."

"You already have." Clare folded her cards and let her eyes rest on the uneven hardwood floor that was scattered with clothes and suitcases. She would miss this apartment. "I'm just not sure it's enough."

"Can it be enough for now?"

"Yeah," Clare said. "It can be enough for now."

"You know when I first met you?" Noah picked up his hole cards and looked at Clare over their rim.

Clare nodded. The lights from the restaurant sign across the street flickered off, darkening the window.

"Bert told me not to fall for you. He told me I should be prepared to see you as my enemy."

"Why?" Clare laughed, though a shiver moved through her fairly quickly.

"Because everyone you meet is supposed to be a potential criminal. It's what I hate about this job. You sure you want it?"

"Of course I want this job." Clare shoved the rest of her chips into the middle of her messy futon. "I'm all in."

ACKNOWLEDGMENTS

This was a fun book to write. I had help from a lot of cool places:

My husband, Keith Whybrow, pushes me to follow my dream and pulls me back to reality when I'm following that dream too intensely. He helped with the mechanics of the cheating scam in this book, and he's the guy who dared me to put real money on a poker game years ago when I was too chicken.

My sister, Erin Kawalecki, pores over each and every word of my manuscripts, sometimes multiple versions, making change suggestions on a word level and on a big picture level. Several of the zinger lines are hers. I feel like she's my secret writing weapon.

My friend, Scott Hicks, much prefers to read short literary stories or anything by Alice Munro. Still, he reads my pages-in-progress and offers really helpful commentary. Things like, "This character is boring. Get rid of him or make him more exciting." And "Have you ever noticed that all your lines of dialogue have the same structure? It's annoying as hell. You need to change that."

My friend, Christine Cheng, is another master of brutal honesty. "No, no, no," she says when something doesn't work. She's equally amazing at suggesting ways to change what she doesn't like, and her advice helped me around several hurdles with this book.

My cousin, Chloe Dirksen, put a smile on my face with her quirky enjoyment of the characters and her awesome ability to show me specific lines and areas that didn't work for her. She reads like a writer — the helpful kind!

My cousin, Christie Nash, showed me a lot of places that left her wanting more. She helped me see what areas and characters needed clarification and expansion. And she read the MS on her honeymoon — that's huge family devotion.

My aunt, Shelley Peterson — a published YA writer whose books I highly recommend — helps me a lot with the emotional side of Clare. She's a master at highlighting when a reaction isn't logical, or when I'm not writing true to a character. She's also great with plot logistics.

My mom, Dona Matthews, read this manuscript the fastest out of anyone. Her constant emails over the course of two days telling me she was tired because she couldn't put the book down the night before — or here she was, reading in the garden with a Scotch when she should be cooking dinner — were incredibly encouraging in that early maybe-this-whole-novel-sucks-and-I-should-throw-it-out stage.

On the intel front: my friends Deb Ferguson and Lorna Boyle gave me expert tips about how to cross the B.C./Washington border undetected, as well as a geography lesson about Mount Baker.

Emily Schultz is the best editor I could imagine. She gave several specific suggestions (my favorite is the line about "goat fucks") and she taught me how to breathe life into a scene with visuals. She's an excellent writer in her own right as well.

Sally Harding and her colleagues at the Cooke Agency are editorial geniuses. They helped me restructure the story to challenge Clare and make her show her stuff. They also give extremely wise industry advice. With them on my side, I feel armed to navigate this tricky writing business with confidence.

My friend Dave Scott is my poker mentor. He gave me a reading list of poker books when I started playing for real money, which turned the game into the hobby that spawned this novel.

The cover artists, Scott and Sarah Barrie from Cyanotype, designed this kick-ass cover and have shared lots of other art clips that adorn my website and brand the series. Great people to work with, too.

Finally, the people who put this all together: ECW Press is a match made in publisher heaven for me. They indulge my weird promotional ideas, they loop me into each stage of the production process, and they make me feel cool by association. These people are: Jack David, Sarah Dunn, David Caron, Crissy Boylan, Erin Creasey, Jen Knoch, Troy Cunningham, Simon Ware, and copyeditor Cat London.